With Bells on his Toes

Sacher Torte

Local Legend Publishing UK

Sacher Torte © Copyright 2009

A Record of this Publication is available
from the British Library

ISBN 978-1-907203-10-7

Local Legend Publishing
Park Issa
St Martin's Road
Gobowen, Shropshire
SY11 3NP, UK
www.local-legend.co.uk

Cover Design by Titanium Design
www.titaniumdesign.co.uk

Cover illustration courtesy of
Steven F. Cooke, Chartered Designer - all rights reserved.
Email: cookehq@gmail.com

Dedication and Acknowledgement

To my old badger, so many thanks. Love you, forever.

Also my heartfelt gratitude goes to Beth Roberts at Local Legend Publishing for leading me up a very steep learning curve. The story writing is but a small part of the finished work. Without her help and faith, I could not have done it.

About the Author

Following a career in teaching, Sacher writes from her home in Mallorca where she lives with her designer husband, the illustrator of this book cover. She has three adult sons; one an internet developer, another, an A.A. man, and the youngest, a plumber. She considers herself very fortunate to have an artistic director, a computer consultant, a car mechanic and a central heating repair man, all catered for within her immediate family.

Table of Contents

One

What a horrible, long, fraught, cold, unpleasant day! Leonie Jones was entirely disgruntled as she trudged home late from her work at the Fairview Country Club Hotel, down the long and winding hill, in the dark, to the village, gone eleven at night in the freezing depths of winter. Her duties for the day were not yet finished. She had a detour still to make which would delay her arrival home even further; an errand to be made on behalf of Mr. Ross; asked of her as a favour.

Leonie Jones was not a happy bunny! Nothing had gone right. Her first training day as a hotel receptionist, under the guidance of her employers, which had been made possible only because the hotel had yet to open for the Christmas season, had been a disaster from start to finish.

Most irritating had been her proximity to Mr. Ross, joint owner with his mother, who seemed to have a 'thing' about her; a man old enough, in fact, to be her father. He had continually hovered over her, standing too close, eyes adoring, blushing like a sixteen year old, even. His mouth trembling with the need to ask her something which, thank God, he hadn't! Her life would have been made a misery had he blurted out whatever it was he had wanted to say.

What was it with this kind of man, Leonie wondered, when they constantly harassed young women such as herself, while showing no interest in those of their own generation, having declined the responsibility of marriage and family much earlier on in their lives? It was not only uncomfortable but embarrassing. From now on, it would be almost impossible to get away from him, trapped as she had become, via her promotion, between the reception desk and his office, with few opportunities for the avoidance of his unwanted attentions when, in the past, she had always managed to hide behind Chef.

The question also had to be asked, tiredly, with an uncomprehending shake of her hooded head, as she trudged the deserted pavements of a village where most of its residents had more sense than to be anywhere but warmly tucked up in bed...what had possessed her to think that the change would be beneficial? She had, so far, found nothing to like about the job, she thought, as she looked down at her feet travelling along the glistening blur caused by the ice crystals covering the pavements, in order to ground her hopes for the next day.

Why had she ever agreed to take the job of receptionist in the first place? It had not turned out to be the glamorous post her predecessor, Belinda, had seemed to make it. An eleven hour shift, in fact, without a proper break, while she had tried her best to make friends with an unfriendly computer, take calls, place bookings, charge deposits for those booking late for the Christmas break, make up invoices, learn how to bring up staff details and print off information; all this seemingly beyond her, even before she had the clientele to pester her to death. There were two days still to go before the hotel opened its doors for its Christmas guests; fully booked, too, the place was geared up and ready to take off like a well oiled jet plane. Say what one wanted of Mrs. Fairbrother, her employer and the mother of Mr. Ross, but she certainly knew how to roll out the red carpet to encourage her guests to come back to the Fairview Country Club Hotel, time and time again, year after year.

Yet, on this, Leonie's first day front of house, as Mr. Ross liked to refer to her position, adjacent to a wide front door with its plate glass screening, the counter framed by tubs of palm plants and all about her a lobby comfortably appointed with blue and beige sofas around small, elegant coffee tables, Leonie had felt abandoned. She had openly resented the way that the unfortunate problem, caused by the wrongdoing of another member of the hotel staff, had robbed her of the help she had needed to make her first day feel successful. She could hardly believe it when suddenly she was left on her own with the telephones ringing, staff wanting information, potential clients requiring brochures to be sent out, and nagged by another million and one other things, most of which she had been unable to fathom.

The words she had used earlier, when telephoning her mother to explain that she would be very late home, had been, "I've been dropped in it, Mum. I want to go back to the kitchens and Chef, who appreciates me." Though she had not given in to the urge to blubber into tears or to go into a long deluge of explanations which others might overhear.

It had just been the most horrible day of her entire life; she considered morosely, the challenges rolling over her, one after the other. She had even found herself having to use some of her own initiative, a situation which would never have been allowed by Chef in the hotel kitchen where she had previously been comfortably bovine amongst the broccoli and green beans. She had never been expected to think much beyond organising pots and pans while getting Chef the right ingredients for his recipes. Sometimes, when he was a bit too drunk, she had got on with the cooking herself but she had seen him do it all so often that it came as second nature after nine years in the kitchens. Now she was truly out of her comfort zone when she had been left alone, mid morning, with all the trouble brewing with Bluithe Harcourt and Mr. Ross and his mother simply disappearing into the lift, leaving her alone to get on with it. Cannon, Head

Waiter, was behind it all, of course. She had seen him whispering in Mrs. Fairbrother's ear and the resultant, furious look on her face when Mrs. F. had digested his information. But it simply had not been fair to leave her to muddle through without guidance on her first day, centre stage, with everyone watching her and making comments about her proximity to Mr. Ross, with wryly spoken jibes disguised as small gems of advice. Such as the one made by Cannon, who had told her that a virgin such as herself might find an older man like Mr. Ross to be her best teacher if only she would let him. How her cheeks had flamed! How dare he speak to her like that?

What Leonie had come to learn, already, was that she had accepted a position where unfair blame would be accorded on a regular basis, so much being gauged from the reaction of the staff when she had had to tell them that their Christmas duty rotas were not ready because some kind of emergency had called the management upstairs. Also, when a supplier had phoned to check up on an order and arrange a delivery time, she had had to tell them to phone back later in the day, only to be told, angrily, that if the Fairview Hotel wanted a half stone of carrots, ten turnips...not swede...a crate of sprouts, a Mediterranean selection box, and assorted fruits baskets for the dining room breakfast bar, etcetera, etcetera...in time for Christmas, she might have to go and get them herself because there was snow on the way. She had said to deliver them, right or wrong, because she had been unable to ascertain if the order was correct due to Chef not answering the kitchen phone, most probably because he was still in a drunken sulk, with her having been stolen right out from under his nose.

There had been no one about, either, to take the telephone call from the hired entertainer who had asked if he could come a day ahead of schedule. To learn the lie of the land, he said. More likely to get an extra day's board and lodgings free of charge. Name of Slick Lick Johnson. He had sounded nice on the phone, as most people do, so she had allowed herself to be persuaded and given her permission. One of those Manchester accents with flat vowels curled up teasingly at the edges; very showbiz, she had thought. She'd said yes, but then he hadn't turned up at the time he said he would so the hotel doors had been locked and barred against him. A staff dinner wasted. Not even a telephone call to say if he'd still be on his way. She had not told Mr. Ross because she had forgotten about it, truth be told. Something else she would have to come to grips with was making notes as she went along, so that at least she'd pass on the messages right if she could understand them properly in the first place. If she tried to learn by her mistakes, kept her nose clean and repeated things for confirmation, and stayed out of Mr. Ross's way, maybe the job could only get better. It was her only hope of coping.

Her mood improved, somewhat, as she came to the streets where she would have to decide her way, making a right turn, but only until she remembered that she would have to deal on a daily basis with Mrs. Fairbrother, as well as Mr. Ross. It wasn't fair that some people could inflict themselves on others in double doses, like extra strong medicine, and get away with it. Leonie had found herself silently agreeing with the other staff, who had spent the later part of the day muttering under their mingling breaths, that the old bag had deserved every name she'd been called by Bluithe Harcourt in the course of him earning the letter she had in her hand now; his P45 to be exact. His address was clearly printed by Mr. Ross on the envelope; 12, Hillview Crescent, to be delivered on her way home. One of the council houses on the back fringes of the village, he had explained, when she had pretended the address to be unfamiliar, because of the lateness of the hour, even though she knew exactly where it was because she used to play with the girl who lived in the same street and had walked with her to the village school every day.

Had to be there, didn't it? It couldn't be closer to the centre of the village where she lived. Her toes had already turned numb in the thin-soled shoes she was wearing over thick black tights, but hardly sufficient to keep out the perishing cold. It was a bit of a cheek of Mr. Ross asking her to deliver it as if she passed this way to and from work, every day, when it was a full five minutes out of her way. But he had apologised and explained that he had a prior appointment and already he was late. Even if having a tryst at eleven at night did seem to Leonie to be a trifle unusual. Some day she'd get the hang of this self-assertiveness which women were advised in magazines to adopt before they ended up becoming doormats. The trouble was that every time she tried it she ended up blushing bright orange to the roots of her fair, frizzy hair. It was a damned nuisance, that, and finding herself unable to extract herself from situations without becoming aggressive in her manner or running away. Head down further, now, she made her way to Hillview Crescent, feeling trapped already. Just how long she could keep her temper without snapping, was anyone's guess.

Leonie Jones was head down and deep in a sulk as she 'stromped' along…short for 'stomping in a strop' as her dad liked to tease her when her mood turned sour, usually when she was tired or overtaxed. Cold, too; hands in mittens sunk in pockets, elbows jutting, head down, the plastic bag with the almost burnt mince pies…'a bit too dark for Cannon to serve at table', Chef had said…swinging from one arm. A present for her mum, Gloria, who never turned her nose up at food because she was 'gravely, morbidly obese' as her doctor liked to refer to her. Leonie tried not to be embarrassed by her mother's size but it was one reason why she had never felt able to take friends home and boyfriends in particular. What she needed was a friend to talk to, other than her mother. She had no really close friends these days, not since most of them had married and had babies, the most childish and demanding always seeming to be the husband, himself.

What a bitch she was turning into! "Now don't be mean to your best friend," she told herself, thinking of her loving mum, as she huddled into her clothing to try to ward off the penetrating cold. She was frowning fiercely, her expression bringing her chin up in dimpled fashion and causing her eyes to squash together more closely. Usually a pleasant face, now it became pleated at the sides of her turned-up nose, nostrils flared, eyes glinting like pale rhinestones in the gloom under the street light. The least gracious feature of this expression, not all that often seen, truth be told, was a flat top lip and a puckered bottom; what her mother called her dummy face. Stromping through the darkness, too, as she turned right again, two roads on, heading towards where the woodland started, instead of making down the hill, to the square itself, across it and homeward. Her slim, petit figure huddled into the folds of her only winter coat, with a decision made that should she meet with anyone she knew she wouldn't stop to talk to them. The usual conversation being the now total agoraphobia of her mother, which had been the initial cause of her becoming so obese in the first place. Poor mum, who relied on her in the evenings to keep house and cook for them both; her dad preferring to eat at the pub or the pie shop, even when she was forever urging Leonie to go out, make friends, have a bit of fun. At least such was the excuse Leonie had given Mr. Ross when he had offered her a staff cubicle in the hotel staff accommodation quarters, which she had refused because she hadn't liked the look in his eye. Maybe he had no lady friends, these days, but it was well known that Mr. Ross was a womaniser with a past because the staff gossiped about him, even yet. Apparently, he had got Lizzie Jubb pregnant and then refused to marry her, a shocking thing to do as far as Leonie was concerned, even if the tale was as old as she was herself. And he was always following her about so that even his own mother had noticed. As long as Mrs. Fairbrother realised that Leonie had never done anything to attract him in the first place. That would put the cat amongst the pigeons if Mrs. Fairbrother thought that Leonie was out for a rich husband, him soon to be in his bath chair and in need of pushing around, with all the prospect of being a rich, young widow once he was six feet under the ground. Not that Leonie could ever be attracted by wealth alone. She was still waiting for her knight in shining armour, who would come riding over Barns Hill on his white charger, ready to sweep her up into his arms.

If only that could happen soon. Then she wouldn't need to work at that horrible place, day after day. Yet more complaints about her new job sprang to mind as she stromped along, envelope in hand, along the frosty pavements, thinking how she could now no longer find comfort in the close relationships she used to have with other members of staff. It was like being stranded on a desert island when they no longer seemed to have time to stop for a chat; looking at her as if she had become a stranger to them; a different creature, even, simply by exchanging a red overall for her dull, baggy, receptionist's clothing. It had been very evident during the emergency whole staff meeting, called that very afternoon, because Mrs Fairbrother had mislaid one of her very important, little, black notebooks, or such was the first point on her agenda as soon as they were all assembled in the freezing cold ballroom, waiting for a lecture of some kind. One of the same types of notebooks in which she kept her peevish, staff observations, to discuss with Mr. Ross later. Or wrote in as she did her morning inspections, white glove to the wainscoting and a face like an angry wasp if she found anything out of place. Only this one, she had said, was full of important names and addresses. There would be a reward for anyone finding it and returning it promptly. The information it contained would be needed over the next few days. As if they were each to blame for her losing it in the first place, as they had stood grouped before her, she and Mr. Ross, the only ones sitting.

It had been made obvious to Leonie just how separated she had become just by looking at the staff groupings. The under staff wearing the red and gold braided overalls with the projectile bullet logo and T.F.C.H. embroidered in gold on their tabards had stood in one group. Leonie, in her baggy, cheap black suit with a white shirt and new, grey and black taffeta cravat, had been instructed to join the other where Chef, Cannon, the Head of Housekeeping had been directed to stand, mid-way between Mr. Ross and his mother and the red brigade as Mrs. F. referred to the lesser paid staff ranking, exactly like the diagram she had seen Mr. Ross draw once of the hotel line management system; the layers of work force never overlapping.

They had all expected that the misplaced notebook was the only reason that the meeting had been called when the bombshell was dropped, by Mrs. Fairbrother herself, about Bluithe Harcourt's dismissal. First any of them had heard of it, though it would soon become a topic of conversation for several days to come.

The icy silence that fell in the ballroom might have been spread with a butchering knife as everyone stilled to quietness to listen, so affording Mrs. Fairbrother, their employer cum benefactor, the respect that she insisted was hers. She had narrowed her green eyes and spoke defiantly while wrapping her plump, diamond-flashing, scarlet-nailed fingers about the red flannel of her business suit, a flounced blouse of expensive, genuine, French silk beneath, all of which emphasised her barrel-shaped figure. She had had her white hair newly done that very morning in the Health and Beauty salon within the Spa section, next to the new Jacuzzi pool. It remained uncoloured; as creamy white as her blouse, but smoothly swept up to be held by one of her vast array of combs which came in all shapes and sizes. This one glittered with diamante, the effect being an arrogant tribute to her advancing years while denying any senility. No rocking chair, yet, for Alicia Fairbrother. She still worked long hours and had the reigns of the Fairview Country Club Hotel tightly held in her strong and very capable hands. So tightly held that it was well-known that even her son had a job getting a word in sideways.

Leonie could feel the thrills of weakness enter her stomach just by recalling the situation which had confronted them all that very afternoon in the ballroom, as she walked along the back streets of Barns to deliver the result of it. Mrs. Fairbrother had put the fear of God into them all, when really it had been Bluithe Harcourt who was the sole culprit, with tactics she practised every day to keep the horses under control. It was her habit to let her cold, green, frog eyes travel over all in her company before speaking, nodding with little jerks of her head as if accounting the presence of each and every one of her staff on a mental abacus, before taking a very deeply drawn breath. In response, the staff, as usual prepared themselves for the rattle of her inspiration against her loose dentures which always caused her spittle to fly and a froth to form at the corners of her scarlet painted, letter box mouth. Today, however, the death rattle, as it was known, was such that no amount of stiff upper lip could hide the intensity of her anger. "You will be informed of this once only and then the matter dropped, never to be referred to again by anyone…" The pause had been deliberately intended for her message to get home before she had continued her shocking revelation. "Mr. Harcourt's employment as the Fairview Country Club Hotel decorator and handyman has been terminated, forthwith…"

If she had paused again, at this point, for an ensuing gasp, it was not forthcoming due to the very low temperature in the room diminishing all bodily functions other than those absolutely vital, her own vital signs exacerbated by the great heat her obvious anger had generated.

Instead, jaws had dropped open, eyes flickered to eyes and top teeth were gripped onto bottom lips to prevent words coming out, probably something like "…please not me, too! Not so near to Christmas with a family to feed…!" Fear thumping in everyone's chest apart from those of her and Mr. Ross, of course, both of whom seemed to think that they owned the assembled company, body and soul.

Having to make do with silence, she had carried on even more defiantly. "He has been banished. Never again will that man set foot within this hotel. He will not be allowed access to the hotel or its grounds under any circumstance. If he is seen in this vicinity, he is to be given his marching orders and then the matter reported to me, personally. You are to give him his marching orders should he even dare show his face here ever again! When the new security guard comes tomorrow, I will be advising him of the same. As well as the only other temporary person who has yet to take up his duties for the Christmas period only…some musician or other…"

Here, her son, Mr. Ross, had intervened, coughing to attract their attention as he sat short and square of shoulder at his mother's side, and smiling benignly as if disassociating himself from his mother's curt, angry words. This, while pulling on the cuffs of his smart, navy blue blazer so that the silver buttons caught the lights from the chandeliers. As immaculately dressed as ever, the knife edges of his flannels were army sharp; brown leather shoes polished to brilliance; his fair but greying moustache stretching over yellowing teeth, as if intending a moment of lightness amidst the gloom of such a shocking announcement. "Here tomorrow, I think…"

The musician! Leonie cringed! The very thing that Leonie had failed to pass on to management. He would be here today, in fact! She would have to remember to ask Chef to provide one more staff dinner which, as it turned out, had ended up in the hotel dog because he had not turned up.

"…Name of Slick Lick Johnson. Tribute act. Does a few, I gather, as well as performing songs as himself. Promises to give us all some jolly good entertainment. Liked his demo tape and photo. He'll be a boon to have when we get down to the rehearsals for the staff pantomime. Snow White. New Year's Day. Entrance tickets gone like hot cakes, already. The village needs these things to bring us all together to get the New Year off to a proper…"

"If I can finish, Ross, please. Not now," his mother interrupted, frostily, before people could start to turn away, to go back to the very jobs they were paid to do, instead of freezing to death in a room the size of a football pitch that would not be heated until the Christmas Eve Ball and, thereafter, not until the performance of the staff pantomime which most were dreading. They were already mentally shaking their heads over the prospect of a stupid, staff show with not a streak of talent present. Particularly Leonie who had been told that it would be her extra duty, as well as playing Snow White, to get suitable costumes from somewhere, without spending money. "…when, without going into quite what was said, I have something very important to say. I would warn all staff that I will not tolerate being spoken to in the way that I was spoken to earlier. I own this hotel - at least my son and I own this hotel - and anyone who gives cheek and insolence or flaunts its rules will find themselves being similarly dealt with. Their employment cut off, forthwith. Let it be known that the no smoking ban means what it says. Anyone caught drinking alcohol on duty - especially after purloining the miniatures from the mini-bars in the guest bedrooms - will have their employment terminated with immediate effect. The hotel beds are there for the comfort of the hotel guests only. Staff may not recline upon them for any reason at all and especially when there is work to be done. Neither will they…!"

"Enough, Mother, please. We should remember the Christmas spirit."

Her eyes had narrowed even further. "I will say no more upon this matter…"cold, bitter green eyes sweeping over the shivering flock, hands now thrust into pockets to keep out the bitter chill of her threats, "… other than to remind you that if I find people gossiping together about this matter, the Christmas bonus will be withdrawn. I will not tolerate tittle-tattle."

Then, quite unexpectedly, she had found herself being singled out. "Leonie, stay behind, if you would be so kind. I wish to have a word about your promotion. My son seems to have forgotten that staff appointments are usually both our concern and final decisions made only after the candidate has been interviewed."

That was when she had learnt about the qualifications she would have to gain once her trial period as a general dogsbody to everyone, not forgetting his dog, had got them over a shortfall in the Christmas staffing, since Belinda was not coming back this year. Some people have the gift of the gab, Mr. Ross being one of them. Flattering her with compliments concerning her aptitudes and diligence in order to persuade her to accept his proposition, when really all he had been was desperate to find someone idiot enough to stand in. This, while they quietly raked through the pile of leaflets from international staffing agencies for someone with an N.V.Q. in hotel management. Either that or he was taking a different tack in trying to compromise her once again. She had long learnt not to venture into lifts with him, accept invitations into his office, or to stand any closer than the requisite metre in order to listen to his instructions.

And now this! Out tramping streets at eleven o'clock at night, after starting at just gone mid-day. Walking the back streets of the village, too - something her dad would object to loudly if he knew - envelope in hand, to find Bluithe Harcourt's home, to put his P45 through the door. Streets with flimsy, drawn curtains lit by flickering television screens, blaring out a repeat of Strictly Come Dancing, and no one listening out at this time of night for things that might happen, untoward, in the street outside their windows. Hillview Crescent was poorly lit, so that finding number twelve was not as straightforward as it might seem because there was no number on the gate. The one person, other than Mr. Ross, who she would rather not bump into on any dark street, late on at night, was Bluithe Harcourt. For one thing, he would probably have been drinking with his mates in the Bald Pheasant Inn. For two, he was likely to take his angst out on her as if she was personally responsible for his sacking after working at the Fairview for twenty-six years. Not physical violence, maybe, but unpleasant words. He had a lot to say for himself did Bluithe Harcourt. Not the type to go down quietly, either. Not that he would be stupid enough to have a go at Leonie, she being the daughter of the local bobby and everyone in Barns knowing it because they lived right opposite her dad's police station, right on the market square, with what her father called 'high visibility' within a village of some five thousand people at the last census, her mother said.

For reason number three; she just didn't like the man. He had always been coming to the kitchens for his flask to be filled with proper milk coffee for free and always when they were up to their eyes in it, and getting Chef and Cannon to gamble money they could never afford; the pair of them constantly ruing one particular horse in the three-thirty called Lost Again. Either that or producing bottles from under the bib of his grubby, paint-splattered, white overalls, glances all round, winks and Chef daft enough to pass over a fiver then get blotto well before his shift was over.

Leonie found the house eventually, between number ten and number fourteen, as a deduction she felt rather proud of. The gate was stiff to open and ice lay on the path which was unsalted, with snow threatened, though she didn't expect it to be that deep because the sky was clear as yet; just a few clouds closing in from a distance. They always got the Barns weather forecast wrong, did the Met Office.

Then, when she slipped the letter through the letterbox, it was to find the door opened very abruptly, with a snatching hand, and face to face with an angry shrew; his wife, Vera, who seemed to be expecting someone else entirely. "You? I thought it might be my parcel arriving. One of them messages, is it? Bluithe said you'd been promoted over and above anyone else. He'll still be at the pub. They've got something on tonight. Something about wrapping presents for the children's party at the community centre. It's the bobby's daughter, isn't it?"

Leonie nodded. "I've brought that letter for Mr. Harcourt. The one on the oil cloth. You're walking all over it. From the hotel. Mr. Ross asked me to bring it."

It was picked up without any curiosity and relegated to an apron pocket. "I was expecting someone with my Christmas order, not you. Blue's not here. I'll pass it on when I see him...if I see him! Most like he's in the pub. It'll be a late night tonight. Don't know where he is for sure. Didn't come home for his dinner. Wasn't expecting him, anyway."

It didn't seem as if Mrs. Harcourt knew what had occurred, as yet. Leonie had done the job she had come to do. No business of hers. She wasn't about to blurt out that her husband had been sacked from his job, just before Christmas, even if his wife was about to lay out good money on presents for her family which they probably didn't need, anyway. Not that Leonie had time to say anything once the letter had been picked off the mat, Mrs. Harcourt's gabbled communications made, and then the door slammed in her face.

Taking a short cut down a dark alleyway, she was soon walking over the village square, the mince pies which had caught slightly in Chef's oven, due to the emergency staff meeting going on longer than expected, banging against her coat, crumbling probably because she could smell the sweet, spicy mincemeat and French brandy in them. Her mother would be ravenous unless her dad had managed to get home to make her something to eat, her being bedridden these days and expecting everyone to run around after her. Not that she could pop into his station to ask him. As she crossed the square she could see that the place was in darkness. He was out somewhere.

The big, blue riot van was in front of the station, though, as if he was not that far away. Not that it was used to quell disorder in a quiet place like Barns. Sometimes his specials brought it out of the butcher's garage, where it was stored all year round, simply to clean it in lieu of nothing better to do. No sign of his specials, either, all three of them, who would be required for village duties with Christmas coming in a couple of days time and a lot of merchandise flooding the place which often had suspicious origins. It was the bane of her dad's life in a place like Barns with a natural, geological facility for hiding stuff away by means of underground caves and caverns and potholes. The area was laced with them. Those that still remained open, that is. Many of the caverns had been bricked up and sealed off because they were a danger to the village children.

Not that there was a single villager to be seen out as she crossed the square by the obelisk where some of her family names were engraved along with the youthful, Barns dead, of the first and second world wars which the village mourned, collectively, on Poppy Day, each November. No one was about at all, in fact, because the weather was so bitterly cold. Only her mother, as usual, looking out for her homecoming. Where she always was, in fact; at her bedroom window, her face to the glass, spotting her, raising a hand. Leonie waved back as she rummaged in her pocket with her other hand.

Home at last! She pulled down the hood from over her frizzy, yellow hair which tumbled around her face in unusual freedom, as she found the key to the front door; a single door, next to a dimly lit shop window bearing nothing but a dried sheaf of corn, and a range of mock loaves made from salt dough and painted to look real enough. A December fly had settled and died on one, looking to all the world like an innocent raisin.

The flat was over the bakery, in fact, where she still lived with her mum and dad, though her dad was rarely home these days. It was a few doors up, on the same side of the square as the Bald Pheasant Inn which took up the whole of the corner plot. She had already noted that the curtains were closed to the bar and snug area. Something going on in there; there was a face peering out, on look out, maybe. Ask no questions!

And over the road at the bottom of the square, the last bus was just coming in. People were getting off before it made its last run back to the depot. The driver was assisting off one of her old boyfriends who was rolling drunk from the look of him. That had been a thankful escape! Christmas party time in his office, if the streamers round his neck were telling the right tale, a balloon in hand to charm the girl he'd had to marry because she would do what Leonie wouldn't. Had more respect for herself than just to give it away, like most girls did, for nothing, these days.

In fact a few people alighted the bus with him, dispersing quickly as they were embraced by the cold air. One of them, a rough looking type who stood on the pavement as the bus pulled away, looking about him as if getting to know the layout of the place. Two big shapes deposited on the pavement at his feet, one of them a guitar, the other big enough to be a body bag. She could make them out, just, and sight of the guitar reminded her of something. Her mind went back then to the call she had taken from this entertainer chap, only that morning, the same one who Mr. Ross had mentioned in the horrid, emergency staff meeting, that afternoon. If it was him. Had to be him! It could not be anyone else, could it? He would find himself a bit too late for the Fairview Country Club Hotel. If he went inside the grounds, where the front gates had been locked, Mr. Ross's dog would have him. Wasn't leashed at night when the hotel was closed and until the new security guard took over. But not her problem.

As she let herself inside, out of the cold, she thought she could hear a most peculiar sound. It sounded like children's musical bells tinkling.

Christmas was coming!

Two

He lifted his boots, first the right and then the left one, giving each one a shake to get the stiffness out of his ankles. Then he stood trying to get his bearings in the bus shelter where he yawned, stretched himself and looked about. His kit bag and guitar leant against the sides of the shelter. The bus seats had been cramped and too short for his long, thin legs to make himself comfortable on the hour long journey, when the bus had meandered through dark lanes, stopping to let its passengers alight at half a dozen places. He had had to sit with his feet flat to the cold, bus floor and because the bus was full of drunks, he had been unwilling to make a show of himself by stretching out further.

With each shake, the round, little bells on his boots made a light tinkling sound. The thin, coloured ribbons which fastened them to his laces, he was particularly pleased with, so he smiled at them as he bent to make sure that they hadn't come loose. These were new. Rainbow colours; pink, orange, yellow and blue, bought specially for his stage act; a bit like bringing your own percussion set when, as a one man band, he had to make his own music. That's what he'd come for, too. To make music, sing, help people to let down their hair and be merry. He liked to think of the bells on his boots as his gimmick. If they didn't remember him they always recalled the bells on his boots; Slick Lick Johnson's trademark.

But no time to dally, not if he was going to get a welcome pint before he made the very last stage of his journey which would be to find the hotel that had hired him for the full two weeks of the Christmas season.

The cheap watch on his wrist, viewed only after using the flickering, orange flame of his cigarette lighter, said that he was now approximately five hours later than his stated arrival time. A time made specific only by speaking with a chick on the other end of a telephone, earlier that morning, when he had phoned through to the Fairview Country Club Hotel to say that he would be coming a day early in order to do some research on stage presentation which was always beneficial to his performances, where possible. He knew he'd impressed her straight away with his commitment to his temporary job as the hotel's Christmas entertainment. It had been he who had phoned her and not the other way about, no one else to speak to being available as it turned out. Manager's out. Something along the lines of, "Mr. Fairbrother isn't available at present and Mrs. Fairbrother's out with him. Can I help?"

"You are...?"

She had said that she was the hotel receptionist. Pleasant in her manner; always a good sign of someone being happy in their work which would indicate that the Fairview Country Club Hotel would be all that he was expecting it to be; cool, real cool, and several steps up from his usual venues. She had sounded young, too, which always suited Lovick. Something in common. Old fogies were alright but you had to watch your p's and q's as his gran had taught him or get a frosty look back and no jam on your toast come the morning. He had asked her name just in case there was any comeback and there happened to be more than one receptionist, as there was bound to be from the look of the place on the brochure he had in his back pocket…a big, rambling place and posh, too, from the look of it and all that was on offer; nice rooms, silver service restaurant, spa pool and health and beauty salon, ballroom, sports and entertainment…that being provided by no other than himself! Not to mention a bar; the latter being the final satisfaction to contemplate even if he would arrive too late to sample its delights on this night in particular. He'd be lucky to get a last pint before the pub opposite closed for the evening. He was thirsty after a railway station pie that might have floated with all the salt it had in it, eaten two hours ago now, mid way through a hell of a journey, more of which would be recalled later.

The receptionist had given her name, straight into his ear, on his mobile, as Leonie Jones, in a silky-smooth voice, clear vowels but not so posh as to be off-putting for a lad who found it difficult to string sentences together away from a stage act, which allowed him to pretend that he was anyone but himself.

"I'll tell Mr. Fairbrother you'll be here early evening, shall I? Ask Chef to cater for one more staff. You are…?"

He'd given her his stage name. At first straight so that she could spell it. "Lick Johnson," an abbreviation of his real name; clever spin on words, too, as in guitar licks. And then, more memorably; "SSSSlick, Lick Johnson…Prince. Of. Soul. And. Rock. And. Roll," …ending with, "Yeah!" deep and growly in his throat, James Brown style. Never failed to amuse, especially when they got a shot of the viz in the wig, and the stage clothes, and the moves. Not to mention the music, all of it cloned. Never failed to wow them; women, that is, not men. Not that he was in favour with women, at the moment. The last one had tipped a tray of cold peas and vinegary, greasy gravy over his expensive haircut after he had reminded her of a spare tyre and offered some dietary advice. He wouldn't have minded except that he had been wearing a brand new T-shirt at the time which had Macho-Man written all over it.

Then thirteen hours later he was still on his way. He had not phoned to make an apology. Why should he? It was he who had been severely inconvenienced, not the hotel or its guests, as the latter, he had been informed, would not be there for another couple of days, yet. Opening especially for Christmas, it was, as it did every year, the brochure said. There was no real rush to get there other than to gain shelter and have a bed for the night. He had plenty of time to settle in before having to start singing for his supper for the Christmas period. He'd say sorry but only if he had to for getting someone up out of bed if there was no night porter to let him into the hotel. Explanations were not his way of smoothing over complications, either. They always made him confused and tongue-tied, feeling intrinsically, deep down, that he must be personally to blame for every wrong ever committed 'todo mondo'…one of his best friends, Quincey's, favourite expressions…on the whole twenty-five year time line of his existence, even while knowing at surface level that catastrophe was not always quite totally his fault. At least not absolutely, solely and completely his fault! His friend, Quincey, who was his accomplice in most things except anything which smacked of work, had been left behind in Manchester to make the best he could of an impoverished festive season. Quincey was usually the one who started the guilt in the first place by all his talk of wars, famines, murders, natural disasters, droughts…anything of detriment to anyone, anywhere, which always fascinated Lovick when he said it brought it home to him that there actually were people in the world worse off than himself. But Lovick knew himself to be guilty of major humanitarian lapses, at least in part, when despite being aware of these things happening in the world he did nothing about them, not even a penny in a charity box. Not that he ever had any spare pennies, but more to the point…couldn't be arsed!

So what was being late compared to international poverty, wars, famine, the economic world crisis and third world persecution? He wasn't due to start work until the day after tomorrow, anyway; contract of employment in his pocket, all signed, sealed and up to him to just get there, to this Fairview Country Club Hotel, though he couldn't say that he was delighted with its location on first introduction, even if he had been assured by his agent that he would be working in a friendly environment where all the staff pull together, gratuities were shared out equally and the workers accommodated as comfortably as the guests. "Landed on my feet for once with this one, Quince! Make no mistake about it!"

And so to all intents and purposes, he had. It was his first ever gig in a place where the employer would provide him with food and lodgings as well as thirty quid a day plus tips. Christmas remember, so he expected to be very well appreciated by an audience which was unlikely to throw things at him or boo him off the stage. As if such a successful entertainer as he would know anything about being pilloried! He'd always denied it had ever happened to him, anyway, when asked. Too disappointing and hurtful to consider even in his private moments when honesty nudged at that little dried up kernel of self esteem within himself, so fragile that anything might see it disintegrate completely, if he wasn't careful. Like the week before at the Strolling Players in Liverpool. The recollection had already been put to the bottom of his memory sack. He still had a bruised ego about the feedback from the hire and fire chap. Though what did he know; ignorant Scouse git? Something to do with a lack of originality, he'd said. Elvis impersonators being two-a-penny. Ever thought of taking up cleaning toilets as a career development, instead? He'd need to get his act polished before they'd have him back. The peevish bugger had even lobbed at Lovick's departing back, "If you can polish a turd, that is!"

But this was no time for pessimism. He'd doubled his rehearsals in front of the mirror at his lodgings and bought some better stage clothes and props. The one thing that a prospective star of stage and screen cannot afford is a shrinking ego. It was Christmas, anyway; peace and goodwill to all men and all that. An audience captive to good manners, too. He'd play them with every ounce of charm he could muster. Songs by the fireside. A simple matter of catering for the musical tastes of old duffers, he thought, for whom a bit of early Bob Dillon and Elvis was sing-along stuff these days. Throw in a few traditional carols and a rendition of White Christmas, Bing Crosby style, and he'd covered all the angles. As he had told his friend, Quincey, repeatedly, he had landed on his feet with this one for a change. He would be living in comfort for the duration as well. The Fairview Country Club Hotel was four star rated.

His lateness was all Quincey's fault, anyway. The plans had all gone wrong with a shirt that needed ironing and him, Quincey, that is, staying overnight after too much booze. His 'friend' had somehow managed to seriously offend Lovick's landlady when he'd crashed out, stark naked, on her couch. If the shirt had not needed ironing before leaving his lodgings, Lovick might already have left the scene of the crime before Quincey's blatant nakedness had rubbed his landlady up the wrong way, considering that such was all that had happened when his pal had a thing about older women; older, stout women especially; layers on layers of protective clothing. A bit like breaking into the deepest vaults of the Bank of England to make a deposit, he had explained to Lovick, once, in tones of hallowed respect, when you could have gone to the first cash machine on any High Street and done the same business. Willingness on both sides a given, of course! Quincey did have a basic level of decency even if his ethics were not always clearly represented in his actions. No harm intended, mate! None accorded!

It had been while ironing the shirt in her kitchen, Lovick's smallish, borrowed suitcase packed with his stage clothes and little else, that the landlady…whom he had borrowed the suitcase from…had told him very irately to vacate his room and find lodgings elsewhere, forthwith, cheeks aflame and her chest heaving with an indignation that caused Lovick some concern, should she fall down with a heart attack and he would have to give her the kiss of life. He did not have the same persuasions, as Quincey!

And rant! She would not have her home and her person abused in that way, ever again. Common decency had been offended, etcetera, etcetera. Finger jabbing at the window; "Out, out, out, out, out!"

Lovick had listened in silence, iron gathering heat and hissing steam in his stilled hand, his shirt creditable, even, to the same standards as a Royal Marine Commando…assuming he knew any, which he didn't. While with an open mouth and mind, all manner of conjecture ran through his vivid imagination, no descriptive explanation forthcoming. Though knowing, guilt ridden as ever, as one knows one's own brother, that whatever sin Quincey had committed it must have been bad because she had had a face like a mortified gorilla and meant every word she had said. On this occasion, she wasn't listening to a very heartfelt, "Sorry, Mrs. Butterworth," even when he tried his best to communicate a sincere apology on his friend's behalf.

Because of Quincey he was out! And what was he supposed to do with all the rest of his possessions if she expected the room cleared totally by twelve noon? Task impossible! She had taken back her suitcase after tipping his stage clothes all over the kitchen floor which, at least, was as clean as a whistle; you could eat your dinner off it. Hence the worst part of his delay in arriving at his illusive destination with the capacious kitbag; the biggest he could buy, which had needed to be ferreted out from an array of city centre shops, with unavoidable time consumption…as it was, from the nearest Army and Navy…and stuffed full to the draw string at the top. It was the only bag big enough and cheap enough to lug all his stuff.

Somewhere behind the distasteful memory of having to clear his room of all personal possessions, was a deep regret that he'd have to find somewhere else to doss when he got back to Manchester in the New Year. Quincey, having escaped already, was not in a position to offer to repair the damage he'd caused, other than to provide a very swift apology before his mobile ran out and made even swifter on account of him having to catch a punctual bus. He had, himself, recently been thrown out by his long suffering partner and had had to go back to Chorlton-Cum-Hardy and paternal prison with his tail between his legs, carrying a begging bowl and issuing pleas for forgiveness in exchange for keeping his room as an altar to decent, family living. Quincey's life, in truth, away from his mother, was a bigger mess than his own. Both of them crocked by the intolerance of others for what was nought but a bit of fun. At least that could never happen to Lovick, not now with his grandparents gone and no other family to give a toss about him, aside from the occasional phone call from a distant aunt and uncle.

Where his own parents were these days was a matter for great debate. His Aunt Vi had said Cardiff; his Uncle Stu said they'd buggered off to Spain. Not even a postal order in a Christmas card would be forthcoming from them if the latter was the case. All his formative years had been spent with his grandparents, his granddad lasting barely a few months after his arrival, leaving his gran to wonder what to do with the small boy who had arrived on her doorstep in a taxi, with an owl nightlight, two plastic bags full of clothes and a traumatised look on his face. Gran had done her best to look after him. Until she'd had enough of him, too, and chucked him out. Nine years now of dead-end jobs, a short, very salutary stint as a guest of Her Majesty's Prison Service and then living in other people's spaces as a paying guest.

He had had a bum life all round. The bum day was not yet over. He still had to locate the Fairview Country Club Hotel, in the dark and the cold, with snow threatened and loaded up with kit, at the end of a twenty-five mile journey through the Pennine Chain from Manchester Victoria Station. What he had read on the instructions from his agent, Mr. Fifteen Percent, as Barnsley had turned out to be a teeny-weeny village: Barns; no direct trains or buses and a population so small that blink while passing through the village and it would go unnoticed.

The whole journey had been a nightmare from start to... hopefully, the finish, very soon! Please! It had been a challenge just to get out of Manchester with Christmas shoppers clogging up the pavements and jostling him mercilessly, as he tried to board any form of public transport to progress his journey, with everything he owned in the cumbersome kit bag under one arm and his guitar strung over the other shoulder. These shoppers were mainly foul-mouthed, genetically modified, barge women battling for seats on overcrowded buses or elbowing him out of the way on the train just as a seat was promising to be his.

Thereafter, standing room only. A train journey from hell. Then a last bus with the late bar flies, annoying him no end while he had sat quietly wanting to do nothing but look out the bus window as the landscape got deeper and blacker and more remote from civilization, them blowing paper whistles and recounting stories they'd regret come the morning because they were still tanked up on the free booze from the Christmas office parties and he as sober as a bloody judge. Then everyone had been ejected by the bark of a surly driver at the crossroads in a village, in the middle of nowhere, which seemed to be as cheering as Death Row on first sight; little more than a few stone cottages about a square of dismal concrete, with an obelisk, a pub, butcher's shop, a post office, bakery, chemist shop, and a Star supermarket scattered around its perimeters. Lovick's eyes accounted for nothing even remotely resembling the photo on the brochure of the impressive hotel, set in its own grounds, fishing rights apparently, woods for paint balling games and a whole hillside for clay pigeon shooting. In fact, the only person he could see walking about was a slip of a girl in a duffle coat, trudging across the square looking miserable. Even she found a key from her coat pocket and let herself in from the biting cold. Bloody freezing it was. There was a distinct lack of buildings and bright lights to warm the place up.

Where had he come to? Not exactly his idea of the perfect environment; not a chippy in sight, but he'd make the best of it for the few days he'd be here because there was nothing to be gained, now, by being negative. Besides which, he had no other option whether he liked the look of the place or not. Mr. City Boy meets Country! Maybe he should bring Country into his act. He'd always liked the song 'Ring of Fire!'

The pub was an exception. It was called the Bald Pheasant Inn, advertised by a big, brightly painted bird with long tail feathers but lacking some pate plumage, portrayed on a sign hanging over the open, glass panelled, lobby doors through which a golden light shone most invitingly. The public house was right on the crossroads, opposite the square on one side and facing the bus shelter, where he had just got off the bus, on the other side of the road to where he stood, looking about with some disappointment, a sneer forming, until he realised that people actually lived here and he had better watch his attitude if he didn't want to attract trouble. At least until the drunks had teetered off to a safe distance.

God almighty! Noddy in Toy Town! The pub was actually the only aspect of all that he saw to promote his slightest interest even, as he crossed the road, noting that the curtains were drawn but its main doors still open. If he absently considered that he had never before known a pub to draw its curtains unless wishing to hide something going on inside…late night drinking or drug dealing being the usual scenario…it was an idle observation not worth another thought. He was more interested in despising the absence of other public houses, fast food establishments and a complete lack of commercial outlets other than those already noted and what looked to be a farm chandlery with a brand, spanking-new, mini tractor centre window…a child's delight! He'd take a better look tomorrow.

The only other shop he could see was a charity shop from the look of it. You could always tell from the various, unrelated, shabby clutter in the window even when he couldn't see which charity name was on the board over the glass, in the dark; Help The Bloody Aged, no doubt! The village looked as if it would be full of them.

There was also a bank he could see with a hole in the wall machine, though he had no bank account so it was no use to him, and he assumed, due to the large, high-sided wagon with 'Police' written in large, white letters on the side, parked on the opposite side of the dark square, that there must be a Police Station somewhere; a place which Lovick planned to stay well clear of, he and policemen sharing a lack of compatibility which had been developed in his teenage years and had persisted to the present day.

Otherwise, tiny, terraced cottages around and behind all four sides of the square and leading out along a lane which ran by a steepled, stone and brick church with a board which proclaimed; St. George's And All Angels, though he had to narrow his eyes to read it over the distance, next to a long, low, wooden building of the type he associated most with school playgrounds or war films; what his gran would have called a Nissen hut.

Most of the buildings he could see in the streetlight were built out of stone, his sneer freely increasing on a youthful, disparaging face, now that the drunks had staggered off home. Not the kind of cosy dwelling he might choose for himself, once his boat came in, when his idea of a desirable domicile was a newly built, double-glazed semi, with white plastic windows and a front door with a stained glass panel bearing a Tudor rose. Not to forget, of course, a lean-to garage, inside which was a brand new Porsche 911, full of petrol and ready to go.

The pub seemed to be the only cheerful place amongst all that he surveyed. His final destination mischievously hid itself away from him, for the time being, that is. He liked the name, too. Found it inspiring. He harboured a passing thought as his foot hit the matting of the threshold that maybe he should allow himself to explore a Country music phase as another string to his bow; Jim Reeves, or Carl Perkins, for example. He might even get away with Dolly if he could find the right clothes. Had the legs for it. A couple of balloons, a wig, and Bob's your uncle! He could write a song, too, Country style, about a pub with a name like that. No better reason for a bit of research.

Almost closing time, his watch informed him, as he swung himself and all his kit inside with his barometer gauging the interior weather initially as sunny with no rain expected; chatter and clinks to be heard and that warm, stale smell of sodden, beer-logged carpet which called to him of home. Only a small clientele remained; about six men, he gauged, one barman only who had the controlling attitude of landlord, arms straight against the burnish of his bar counter where he stood next to highly polished brass beer pulls. He narrowed his eyes at Lovick and then glanced about to share similar looks with his other customers as if an ill wind had just blown in.

They all stopped talking, drinking, laughing; every man-Jack of them, looking down at the bells and ribbons on his boots with total derision, as if he'd spoilt a select party with his down market appearance, though none of them looked to be much different than the ordinary man he considered himself to be. What was the matter with him? Two heads? Flying low? Time gone for last orders?

He wasn't too impressed with a first impression of the locals, either, even when they cleared a space at the bar, after turning cold shoulders and quietly walking away, to take up table space, beer glasses in hand and most of them ignoring the smoking ban in public places. All of them had looked his way, laughter stemmed, glum faced.

Even the landlord's approach had been grudging. "What can I do you for, lad?" His middle-aged face was creased with worry lines and a bold curiosity directly attributable to Lovick's entrance; his eyes looked Lovick over like a security guard. "We don't usually get strangers at this time of year in Barns. Not till Christmas."

Lovick might have taken a hint and left as quickly as he had arrived if he had seen anywhere else to quench his thirst, also to discover the information he needed concerning the whereabouts of the Fairview Country Club Hotel. "Pint of bitter, mate, ta. Nice little village you have here." There was never anything lost by being friendly to strangers.

Unfortunately, his sentiment was not returned. "Just stopped off on the way, have you? Don't usually get visitors at this time of night, either, like I say." Iterated, with deep curiosity, so that an explanation was more demanded than suggested. "You staying?"

Lovick felt pressured. "You could say that. Just got off the bus as a matter of fact. I'm on my way to the Fairview Country Club Hotel…know it?" chinking the change in his pocket as he found a couple of quid for a pint of ale.

The landlord's frown was sharp and a look of disbelief entered his eyes though he had his glance on Lovick's hand full of coins as he shuffled through them. He picked up a glass with one hand and placed his other to a pump handle. His tut was evident as was the same from the rest of the men who Lovick realised had all eyes glued to him.

"The Fairview! Oh, aye! The Fairview, you say? Not open yet, son. A few days to go. There's a room going spare here if you want one. You'll have to take it now as we'll be closing up shortly. Nowhere else does rooms in December in this neck of the woods."

"Day after tomorrow it opens, I think. I'm to be the entertainment."

The landlord glanced over the guitar and then onto the large, brown, canvas bag now propped against the counter. "What's with the kit bag, then? Magic act are you? Got a couple of lions and a set of giant mirrors in there?"

Lovick shrugged. "Singer actually. Come up from Manchester special."

There seemed to be more interest in the kit bag than it warranted. Bloody nosey lot! What did it matter what he had in the kit bag? Truth be told, mainly threadbare clothing other than his stage clothes, his music centre, sports kit and football. His snooker cue, which folded in half and was protected by a plastic case, was the only rigid item stopping the bag from sagging to the floor. Most important was his nightlight, made out of blue pot with a smiley face cut out to make him feel that he was not alone and friendless, should he wake up at four o'clock in the morning with the dark closing in. Not something he liked to be common knowledge. He had spent the whole of his life being frightened of the dark.

Suspicious behaviour wasn't in it! It was as if he had walked into the middle of something private but once having done so it had perhaps become necessary for him to be detained for a period of time, for some reason that did not become evident, though Lovick expected the cocaine to be fanned out and chopped up on the shiny tables at any time, rolled up notes at the ready. Either that or the nude dancer would come out of the closet, wiggling her fanny in a dance of the seven veils. He had always preferred the fan dance, himself. Then, while he watched the swill of a pint of strong bitter rise up the glass the landlord was holding to the pump, while levering it slowly and gently, Lovick had the suspicion that, maybe, something was going on outside which they did not want him to be aware of. Before even finishing pulling his pint, the landlord nodded to one of the men drinking at a table near the door but spoke to everyone present. "Time to close the doors, gentlemen, I think. The bar'll be open for another hour." Then to Lovick, "No need to fret, lad. We do things different here. You look like the type to enjoy a few pints."

"Is that why the curtains are closed? A lock-in?"

"Ask no questions, be told no lies. Do you want a pint or don't you?"

"Never been known to refuse."

"Glad to hear it."

A damned expensive pint too; three pounds eighty! But delivered unto him with worshipful adoration; a head on it that might have done justice to a bottle of full cream milk, coating his lips with promise. Now you're talking!

Lovick paid the landlord's price, even if with ill grace, because the taste pleased him, causing him to tip his head back and glug down the first few mouthfuls to quench his thirst. There was nothing like the flavour and sensation of that very first pint of the evening though he left the last gill to take his time with, placing his glass reverently on the table and looking at it fondly, too smooth a pint to be disrespected, a brimming jar, properly pulled from a cold cellar; homebrew if he was not mistaken, probably with a name like Gentle Hen or Butter Barrel.

A couple of fags later and a full hour had passed. He'd been encouraged to strum a tune or two by the landlord who had refused to allow his glass to remain empty though no one else was invited for last orders, gentlemen, please. Filled it and overcharged him again. No one seemed to be enjoying his playing much, either. Most looked the other way or down into their flattened bitter. Some kept glancing at him awkwardly, fingers rapping their table, as if his very presence was doing their heads in. It was as if they resented a stranger in their midst, though the landlord was being friendly enough, if a bit preoccupied. Couldn't afford another one though and told the landlord so when he reached down a fresh glass and put it to the pump once more. "Same again?"

"Sorry, mate, ta. Bit too expensive for me."

As he made a move to leave, the landlord levered him another half glass anyway, with a sullen look on his face as if to offer a free one went against the grain. "On the house, then. You can't go anywhere until you've got that down you." It was spoken like an order.

It wasn't often that Lovick looked at free beer with suspicion. But that one, he did! There was something about the quiet company, supping lightly, tapping impatiently, not much to say to each other, all dressed in dark, winter clothing which they had not even bothered to unbutton against the warmth coming from a blazing fire over in the empty snug, as if they hadn't planned on staying this long, which unnerved him. It was the strangest lock-in he'd ever got caught up in. Usually, the pints flowed as if there would be no tomorrow and the juke box would be on full blast and jiving all on its own. There'd be all kind of stuff going on, usually stuff that never went on at home. These men made him feel nervous, watching him quietly with frowns on their faces, talking little between themselves and, when they did, in whispers. One man had even gone to lean against the bolts of the closed doors and another had lifted the hem of the curtain to take a look out to the other side of the square, his whole head hidden and staying there for a half hour or more. A punishment of some kind? On the lookout? For what? His missus?

Lovick had begun to feel even more uneasy when he was asked by the landlord, "Give us another tune then. Something Christmassy," in a tone as if to refuse would not be a wise thing to do. He had obliged by giving a stilted rendition of 'In The Deep Midwinter', Elvis style, flat and tuneless because he wasn't able to concentrate, bringing forth nothing more than a few cynical smiles and not a single clap when he finished, though the chap with his head under the curtain put his thumb up and everyone nodded in unison, as if a message had been passed. The last notes died away to silence. Lovick waited for some kind of appreciation with his lip hitched on his right incisor, his whole body wrapped around the guitar, feeling utterly foolish as he propped himself against the bar once again and then set to draining his glass, his mind working to sum up his situation. He planned to get out of the place a.s.a.p., once he'd discovered which direction to take to the Fairview Hotel, only the chap leaning against the door looked to be preventing his exit and wouldn't be about to shift until a sign was given by the landlord whose authority in this place seemed to be law. The man with his head under the curtain seemed to be pivotal to this decision and that decision seemed to depend on what he saw as he looked out onto the street. Thumb raised once more, and his time-out punishment finally done with, he brought his head out from under, resumed sipping his pint with a grin on his face and a mood of relief seemed to sweep over the place. Laughter suddenly broke out much to Lovick's consternation.

The landlord clicked his tongue against his cheek, stretched laced fingers until his knuckles cracked, and then poured himself a small brandy as if in celebration. "Last orders gentlemen. I'll shut the bar in ten minutes. Time enough, I think. Want directions to the Fairview do you, lad?"

Lovick nodded, having decided to say nothing. No point! None of his concern! He doubted he'd ever be in the Bald Pheasant Inn again, anyway, as long as there was a decent bar at the hotel where he would be working.

"Straight up the hill at the crossroads. Keep on the same road to the top of the rise. Can't miss it. It's laid back, on the left hand side, before the steep climb down into the next valley. It's signed clear enough. Just stay on the main road and you'll be alright."

Something had been odd, that was for sure, as the landlord had issued a last drink to each man, excluding himself, before the bolts were drawn back and Lovick was allowed to escape with a feeling of liberation. He still felt intimidated by watchful eyes even after he'd left the establishment and made off, loaded up once more, across the bottom of the square for the road which travelled up the hill, feeling slightly inebriated due to the strength of the brew he had been given. He would not be tangling with that lot again unless he could help it and was careful to keep his head down as he turned the corner to embark on what should have been the last, shortest leg of his journey.

All he had to do was to follow the road to the top of the rise.

Three

Tiredly, Leonie let herself into her home. As she went up the narrow staircase she called out so that her mother could be sure that it was her coming in. Not that her light tread could ever be mistaken for her father's footsteps which were much heavier than hers, him being such a big man; size twelve boots, even. "Only me, Mum!"

Gloria's voice was light and melodic as she replied with an invitation for her daughter to show her face. She started talking as soon as Leonie's tread told her that she had come to the top of the stairs and that her daughter could hear her clearly, drawing her closer with the warmth of a spoken welcome, when it was impossible to go to meet her because she could no longer heave her bulk off the bed. "Come and say hello to your mum, Leonie, me darlin'. Just switched off my little telly. The repeat of Strictly was lovely. Only to think that I used to be able to dance like that at one time. Not that long ago, either."

Obediently, Leonie found her way along the carpeted corridor which adjoined all their rooms, past the open lounge door, light off, the family television off, probably having never been switched on for several days by her father when he was so rarely at home these days, even for the ten o'clock news which he liked to watch, but had to settle for listening to on the radio in his office. Leonie would be too late to put it on for the weather forecast which was always of interest when she would have a two miles walk up the hill come the morning, her shift pattern now set at eight thirty to five thirty for the duration of the hotel being open for the Christmas season.

Her own bedroom was next to the lounge and, across the hall, a bathroom next to the small kitchen though, these days, invalided as she was by her own obesity, her mother had to have the facility of her own en suite shower room and a kettle on hand for hot drinks if she wanted them. Kitchen and bathroom were only used by Leonie and, very rarely, her father. Or the very occasional guest; sometimes the doctor, sometimes the District Nurse to wash their hands, sometimes her mother's sister or one of their neighbours. Mostly though Gloria liked to converse with the world, which she had never managed to part company with entirely, by rolling towards the window side of her reinforced bed where she could be close enough even while lying down, to open the window and talk down to people passing. If she wanted anything fetching for her, she'd ask a passer by or tap on the bakery window with her long cane. Then send down her lidded, wicker basket on a rope before hauling it up for collection.

Foraging for food, for Gloria, was never usually a problem, though she was aware that her access channels, namely her small and often inadequate rope and basket, had necessitated that she acquire some better technology to assist her when there was food in the kitchen cupboards but no way of accessing it with any independence. And Christmas was coming. All the kind people who fed her compulsions changed their routines at Christmas and would no longer be available on a regular basis. Snow was on the way, too. With knowledge that her husband and daughter would be out of the house over the Christmas period due to their occupations, fear was settling in. It was alright people telling her that she should not eat compulsively and that if she had to, to stick to only certain types of food. No one understood, absolutely no one understood the desperate cravings her body could muster. Especially when she had been brooding so much lately over the prospect of Leonie's twenty-fifth birthday and the terrible, terrible calamity that might befall them all on that day. She and Gareth would be shamed. Her family could be destroyed completely and Leonie would never forgive them ever, never. They might even find themselves prosecuted, though Gareth said that it was not possible because everyone involved had been allowed written, signed copies of each other's consents, all except Lizzie's, of course, but then Lizzie's had been the least important. No crime had been committed. Gareth would never stand for that, given the law abiding man that he was; dedicated to the preservation of law and order so that people might live fairly and happily together. He was a good man though she doubted that she could say the same for Ross Fairbrother, whose promise to silence would end on Leonie's twenty-fifth birthday.

How would she cope then if the worst came to the worst without the comfort of food to sustain her? She knew exactly what Gareth would say if he saw what the postman had already delivered in the long, thin, wrapped box that had been far too big to fit in her basket, and had brought it up for her, even, after she'd pressed the button by the side of her bed to release the catch on the street door, with a curious look on his face. "What's this, then, Gloria? A set of crutches?"

But she hadn't told him. She'd keep her counsel until she was sure that the tools would work. She'd been practising already with them though she hadn't yet got the knack of opening the fridge door or the door to the cupboard where the biscuit tin was kept. The cupboard which Gareth and her daughter were using to store all the extra Christmas goodies which she thought of as extras to the hoard under her bed.

What they had not considered, but Gloria had, was how she was going to access them with no one being about over the lonely Christmas period. It had been a bombshell dropped when her sister had said that she was thinking of going for an 'all in' to Turkey, though it hadn't been booked yet as it was cheaper last minute. Gareth was never at home Christmas Day or Boxing Day, anyway, because of all the domestic violence the season caused. And with her daughter's new job, she doubted that she would be home at all at Christmas. At least when she had worked in the kitchens, she had been able to pop home between breakfast being served and the evening dinner when the Gamekeepers bar served lunchtime snacks.

Just to think about being on her own, now, in the flat, without anyone to call on unless she picked up a telephone, caused her to panic, making her mental state sometimes impossible to bear. Already, the doctor was threatening the borough hospital and enforced starvation. It was only because she had a loud scream and knew her rights that that situation had been kept at bay. Not that she wouldn't ask for asylum herself if what was threatened to happen did happen, on Leonie's twenty-fifth birthday.

God willing, she'd pass to heaven first, tears welling just to imagine it, because she would miss out on the rest of her daughter's life even if Gareth, her husband, had already deserted her, to all intents and purposes, that is. Though he always popped in several times a day so that they might pretend for the sake of the villagers.

However, he rarely came home at night, these days, because if he did, he would have to share the bed with her. Preferring instead to avail himself of the cot and a sleeping bag, stored on its side behind his station counter and near to his phones, close to the wood burning stove which warmed his downstairs office across the square, all of which could be seen, at face value, by looking directly out of her bedroom window. All the better to spy on him, maybe. She didn't trust his insistence that the only thing that took him so much away from home was his work, as he was the only policeman serving a wide, local, rural area which was not quite as law abiding as it seemed.

Gloria's jealousy was behind all of her health problems, Leonie had always supposed and Gloria had never enlightened her fully, when, in reality that was only a part of the problem. What would Leonie think of her mother when she knew that she had been lied to and deceived?

Would she be coming home then to make sure that her mother had all she needed? Keep the house clean? Share the shopping with her dad? Do all the weekly washing? She could hear her in the kitchen now despite her bedroom door being only slightly open. Her footsteps over the tiled floor, opening the fridge to deposit something. Gloria's nose twitched; mince pies with sweet pastry and laced with French brandy, straight from the oven. The kitchen which lay directly opposite her bedroom door, the door lying open despite a draught from the small, curtained window which looked out over the cottages at the rear, causing Gloria to remember the unexpected visitor she had allowed to come up only that very afternoon; the one who had brought the ham and then deposited it in the fridge in the kitchen before leaving so that it would remain wholesome. Would she know that Gloria had eaten all the cheese and spring onions which Leonie had bought for all their suppers?

Then, there she was, opening her door. Pretty as a picture; as light in colouring as she and Gareth were dark, so slim and petit, looking tired but smiling. Her daughter. She was such a good girl. It was she and Gareth who had been wicked, God help them!

"Hello, me darlin'," she said once more. "My little angel from heaven."

In fact, as soon as Leonie came to the top of the stairs she could smell cheese and spring onions which she knew had been in the lower canisters of the fridge because she had put them there the day before yesterday. Her mother must somehow have managed to avail herself of them after Leonie had telephoned to say that she would be home too late, this evening, to cook an evening meal. A quick look, while popping the mince pies into the fridge, was sufficient to see that the whole packet of cheese and a bunch of spring onions were no longer there although there was a large, plastic wrapped Christmas ham sitting on the shelf in their place. She had had a visitor. Probably a neighbour or her sister who lived in the village and was as thin as her mother was gross, but always willing to keep the family peace by coming in to cook for her. Someone had popped in to make her something to eat and bring the ham, that much was evident she thought, as she took off her coat and hung it up on the rack of pegs outside her mother's bedroom door, which had been deliberately positioned so that Gloria was always knowledgeable about her family's movements, in and out of the house.

Then, with her coat hung up with her scarf and gloves pushed down the sleeves, she opened her Mother's bedroom door to see tears in her eyes, nothing unusual in that. The doctor said it was all part of her neurosis, that and the tantrums and throwing things occasionally, hollering and screaming sometimes, though the neighbours these days took no notice.

"Hello, me darlin'. My little angel from heaven. Them naughty Fairbrothers kept you till this time? You should have phoned your dad for a lift. You know how he doesn't like you walking home in the dark."

Leonie nodded, noting that her mother's eyes were redder and puffier than usual. It was evident that she had been crying. She gave a mental shrug. "Need anything, Mum?"

Gloria swallowed her tears as her daughter entered her warm and comfortably appointed bedroom, even if the bed was more than a king size and took up most of the space. It had been made especially by a bespoke bed company once Gloria's weight had become epic. She had managed to break the back of the last one when it had collapsed under her. It was rumoured that her mother was now over thirty three stones in weight and ever growing. "I am a bit peckish."

Leonie looked at the bed for the real truth of the situation. As always, these days, her mother was within it, lying high on several pillows which allowed her a wedge shaped ramp upon which to lie without too much discomfort. She was draped in a pink parachute of a nightdress, under a thin, blue coverlet, her stomach the size of a giant physiotherapy ball which looked about to pop, her legs overlapping with flesh as defined through her bedding, little more than props, which along with her flesh-padded elbows, assisted the huge, occasional effort needed for any movement to take place.

It did not take Leonie much to deduce that her mother could not possibly be peckish. The coverlet was mounded up on the hill of her stomach with a heap of empty Belgian chocolate wrapping papers, but no sign of the chocolates themselves, a plastic cheese wrapper, empty of cheese, and the inedible stems of the spring onions on a patterned plate; all balanced upon table mountain; Gloria herself. "Just a snack to keep me going. Your dad hadn't time to get me a take-away from The Bald Pheasant before he had to dash off."

"Had a visitor, Mum?"

Gloria nodded. "Now you tell me all about it. Not gone well, hey?" She looked pale as anyone would who never got out of bed but still managed to look pretty of face with the warmth of her pleasure to see her beloved daughter, her dark hair brushed neatly and brown eyes shining lovingly. "This new job of yours had better stump up some extra cash if you'll not be coming home till this time of night. I thought it was too good to be true. Had to be a catch in it." Then, because she had already heard something of what had been going on at the Fairview Country Club Hotel and her curiosity always won out in the end, "There's been rumours flying all day. Something to do with Bluithe Harcourt being sacked from his job. A whole pot of anti-fungal wallpaper paste hitting the wall, apparently, and him making all kinds of threatening promises against the Fairbrothers. Been in and out of the station all day. He should learn to keep his mouth shut, should that Bluithe Harcourt. Know anything, our Leonie?"

Leonie's eyes stretched as she sat on the side of her mother's bed, shaking her head in wonder. How had her mother learnt already what Bluithe Harcourt's wife still had to know?

Her mother, reading Leonie's thoughts provided the answer to her unspoken question. "Someone passed up the gossip in a note in my basket...not wanting to yell it all over the street...apparently his wife, Vera, doesn't know yet."

Leonie should have known; the jungle telegraph, better and faster than British Telecom. "She will soon, I think. I've just put his P45 through their door."

Gloria was animated. Being bedridden had never stopped her from hearing and discussing all the gossip or knowing what went on. "Well? Spill it! That Mrs. Toffee Nose got rid of him is all we know. About time, if you ask me. Him not taking it all lying down, either. I saw him through the window talking to your dad at the station this afternoon and earlier this evening. Went off together about ten minutes ago something to do with Barnston Farm, I heard. Had a few from the look of him, Bluithe, not your dad. He got in your dad's police car with the specials and they went off up the hill. Your dad won't park his car down Old Barnston Lane because of the mud and getting stuck there. Not with snow forecast within the next forty eight hours. He will have wanted an element of surprise too if he was looking for something." Her head swivelled with her thoughts to peer through her own, open curtains, across the frosty, darkly lit square where she had seen Leonie approaching home, barely a few minutes ago, and the moon casting light over the shimmering rooftops. No sign yet of the snow, not a cloud in sight and the moon still bright, though they could scud in quickly enough; quick and silent. The sky was still an open cobalt filled with twinkling stars, chimneys smoking when coal fires were back in fashion, house lights up and down the street, being turned out in some. Those that remained open had their Christmas trees displayed. Lights still out in her husband's station, she noted, as they travelled back to her real place of interest.

But was something there that had not been there just a few minutes ago? Well! Well! That time of year, of course. She should have known! Everything matched her memory, never known to fail her, except for one feature. The riot van! Not there a few minutes ago, but there now, plain enough. Parked up right in front of the police station where it would attract the least attention. Appeared from nowhere. Lights off, too...if they'd ever been on...but neither her husband nor his specials were to be seen anywhere. Someone must have brought it out of the butcher's garage where it lived, largely unused, except for training exercises. It wasn't

Gareth who had put it there, either, or his specials. Of that she was certain. However, she could make a very educated guess, her eyes flicking down the street, though she was unable to see the Bald Pheasant Inn, from her bedroom window. Aloud, she said, deeply. "Well! Well!"

"What is it, Mum?"

"Nothing you need concern yourself with. Just a thought."

"I hate it when you keep secrets."

Gloria winced, she knew she would have to replace her suspicions with something else. "I'm just wondering what Bluithe was doing carrying big sticks with rags wrapped round them. Put them in the boot of your dad's car." Here she paused, her eyes rolling. "He always did get carried away with pretending to be Roy Rodgers."

"Who?" Then, "Never mind," because she'd twigged it would be one of Gloria's old cinema heroes. Cowboy films were still one of her passions. Leonie joined in with the derision. "He's never grown up. Dad neither. Still playing cowboys and Indians."

Gloria nodded. "Tell me what happened up at the Fairview to have him mad enough to get your dad involved?"

"Only if you tell me what they're saying in the village, first."

Gloria wriggled herself upwards, leaning forward as much as the vast mound of her stomach would allow so that Leonie could plump her pillows for her. "That's my good girl. I don't know what I'd do without you. She's sacked him apparently. Has she?"

Leonie nodded. "Flouted all the hotel rules."

Her mother's eyes flashed, emboldened. "Great, stupid pillock! Does he think no one knows his games? It always was one of his tricks to point a finger one way and then run the other. He's got your dad and his specials round at Barnston Farm on some pretext or other. Or at least that's where I think they've gone. Even when it's not as much Hannah Jubb as Ross Fairbrother he's after nailing."

It didn't make any sense to Leonie. There was a river and a steep and thickly wooded rise between Barnston Farm and the Fairview Country Club Hotel. Then she twigged. "Oh, I see. You told me about the caverns and potholes underground but I never thought they actually existed."

"They're there alright but bricked up long ago so that there's no access any more. There was a time when Ross and Bernard Jubb…Hannah's husband, Lizzie's dad…had a game of Robin Hood going together as it's known. Bluithe's after dragging up the past so your dad will think he knows something no one else knows. He's been saying Ross Fairbrother and Hannah are in cahoots again. Got the old cavern full of Christmas stuff to be sold off cheap. Opened the old, dry caves up again which I can't see myself. There are better storage places." Her eyes flicked across the street.

"Stolen goods?"

Gloria frowned and shook her head. "No one deals in stolen goods round here. Now, that is bad, that is. No need to. It's just stuff that hasn't had government taxes levied on it. No import tax, no V.A.T..." she sang in remembrance of a favourite television comedy theme tune.

Leonie shrugged. She had often enjoyed some good perfume from Cannon when he managed to get a suitcase full from the 'man with the van', as he referred to his sources. But it was the caves that fascinated. "You ever go in them, Mum?"

Gloria nodded. "Me and Lizzie used to play in them when we were children. Eccentric, Lizzie was, even as a child but we played together on the farm. Her dad was a good farmer and Hannah...well...it doesn't bear thinking about what she was like before Bern's accident. The poor sod died as a result of him taking a short-cut up to the hotel through the old chambers and pot holes. It was the same day that Ross Fairbrother jilted Lizzie. God bless her poor soul, too, when she's as batty as a witch's broom stick these days. Little wonder!"

"Why do you think Bluithe's making mischief?"

"Heard him myself. With my own ears. Right under my window when he came out of the bakery, at lunchtime, with a pie in his hand, saying the Fairbrothers will pay. He's due some compensation after twenty-six years of keeping the Fairview held together with wallpaper paste. More like retribution, nasty little toad that he is."

Leonie found a chocolate within the folds of her mother's coverlet which had not been eaten. Without apology, Gloria wrested it from her, unwrapped it and ate it, sucking at the sweetness with total pleasure, even as she thought about what she had seen and heard further. "Your dad's had to act on something Bluithe said, I know that much. Said as much, without saying anything, as he does, when he came home looking for some batteries for the big, police torches, just before they all got in his car and went off together. Star's all out of them apparently. Something about having to follow up on a tip-off. Has to be Bluithe Harcourt causing trouble if he went with them. Though I can't see what Hannah Jubb and Lizzie could have to do with anything. It was her husband, supposedly with Ross Fairbrother, who did all the Robin Hooding, of old, though nothing was ever proven. It all came to an end, anyway, when Bern had an accident. Got his foot caught in the old iron ladder coming out of the entrance, in the old well, on Fairbrother land..."

"It's all covered over now."

Gloria nodded, not that she'd ever been up that way since being a child.

"How do you get into them?"

"You can't. Not now. The old caves behind her cowshed had a passage under the river bed, through the rock. They were bricked up donkey's years ago." But enough of Hannah Jubb and, in particular, her daughter, Lizzie. Her laugh was brittle. "Here's us putting two and two together when it all might be a wild goose chase. Maybe she's not been paying the V.A.T. on her milk yield, like half the farmers round here."

Her mother's smile informed Leonie that she saw it all as a joke, unlike her father who took the distribution and sale of untaxed goods very seriously. Gloria's eyes twinkled brightly, too. Outside of her daughter's wellbeing and her husband's whereabouts, the only interest she had was in the local gossip. She gathered that as effectively as she did her forbidden foods.

Leonie was never much interested in her dad's police business. But she was glad to see Gloria leave her depression behind for a few moments. She told her mother as much as she knew of what had happened that day at the hotel with regard to Bluithe's sacking, knowing that her mother would never implicate her as being the one to have passed on the gossip. Too many others to come first for that accusation. It was all over the village, by now, anyway, apparently. Just Bluithe's wife being the last to know. Her mother would never go blabbing that it had been Leonie who had told her. If there were two people in the whole world that she trusted completely, they were her parents. Though they were not always kind to each other.

Finally, the conversation ended with all Leonie's complaints aired and her mother cooing sympathy and understanding; her own problems placed on the back burner. Leonie decided to skip her supper and take herself off to bed. "Nighty night, Mum. Try to get some sleep instead of staring through that window of yours for half of the night. He'll see you when he gets back. Dad does worry about you, you know."

Gloria's pleasure disappeared as her face closed in and her chins became distinctly wobbly where they lay about her neck, one on top of the other. She could not resist a jab at her husband, spoken with a hurt expression. "Your dad said not to expect him home as he won't be finished until the early hours. He'll get a few winks on his cot at the station." Then, more bitterly, the words she spoke to her daughter at least once a day without any real expectation that her daughter would listen. "He should have said when I married him that he was already married to the job. Might have thought twice if I'd have known the job comes first, second and third and me a long way behind you and the rest of the village."

Here we go again! It tugged at her heartstrings when her mother was in this mood. So Leonie went to the kitchen and loaded a tray with six slices of bread and butter, a wedge of fruit cake the size of a church door stop, six mince pies, and then boiled the kettle for a giant flask full of hot, sweet tea, spooning in extra sugar. Nothing else ever improved her mother's mood the same as food did, and plenty of it. It also warded off any family trouble that might be brewing!

Taking the loaded tray back to balance on the edge of Gloria's bed, Leonie's voice was cajoling even though she had to ignore a pang of guilt for putting yet another nail in her mother's coffin. "Here you are, Mum," she said brightly through her tiredness and the headache which had now turned her neck to a metal bar. "Can't have you feeling peckish in the night, can we? I have to be back at my desk at eight thirty tomorrow. No being late, either. She's warned me already." With the loaded tray and her mother's so-called, 'secret' box under her bed full to overflowing, and her dad out of the way so that they couldn't start rowing as they often did when her mother refused to accept his explanation of where he had been, a quiet night on the home front was promised. Even if her mother would most likely be awake and staring out of that window of hers, in the dark, till all hours of the morning. On account of her spending all day in her bed, too heavy now for her own legs to weight bear. This, despite all the doctor's warning. She did not even get herself to the en suite bathroom anymore. It was up to Leonie and her dad to empty the contents of the covered bed pans and disinfect them, on a daily basis, which Leonie did before finally excusing herself, wondering how she would cope if her mother became incontinent. The village nurse came twice a week to give Gloria a bed bath and the doctor had given Gloria sufficient warning, if she would but listen. If there was one thing her mother would detest in her dependence, Leonie guessed, it would be to lose control of her body functions. Though that was the way she was heading!

It was all very sad. But what could Leonie do? This was the same situation she had had to cope with all her life. What her mother failed to see was that she was the only one who could do anything about it, short of them locking her away and throwing away the key, in order to control her eating.

But what Leonie did not know was that Gloria could see no further than her own guilty secret. A guilt that was only ever pushed to one side by the activity of eating. And the day of reckoning was fast approaching with the advent of Leonie's birthday, soon to be. Very soon to be; just one day away.

With Bells on his Toes

Leonie had been too busy to make any plans for it.

Four

Dead of night; pitch dark; not another human being; remote house or much wished for taxi cab in sight. All about him, the earthy smell of lonely woods and a dark, meandering lane underfoot, which seemed to be taking him nowhere, in a region which Lovick Johnson's gran might have referred to as 'the back of beyond'. The Fairview Country Club Hotel! Where the hell was it?

This was definitely not the sort of place a dyed-in-the-wool, Manchester-conurbation lad was used to being in, at gone one in the morning, for he was nowhere near his destination and, in fact, hadn't a clue where he was, other than that he had walked and walked and walked, loaded up with his kit bag and guitar, getting more and more disorientated with every step he took.

This was an alien place and an alien time of night for being out and about anywhere but city club land where the nearest anyone got to a leaf was of the silk and plastic variety or one of the pages in the menu of his local Indian take-away, next door.

The real stuff was in abundance, here. Thick undergrowth and tall trees giving off different shades and shapes of blackness on both sides of the mud-slicked, pot-holed lane he was walking; the smell permeating into his clothing along with a penetrating dampness, a concentrated smell like his granddad's allotment without the tantalising shelter of his potting shed where he might once have curled up on a sack and fallen asleep.

How dumb can anyone be to be walking in this godforsaken place at this time of night, in the depths of winter? He was beginning to hear the derisive sounds of his own stupidity tinkling within the laughing bells which danced jauntily on his boots, louder than he had ever been aware of them sounding before, as he trudged along the dark lane with only his own company to consult as to his uncertain situation.

There were times when even Quincey's opinion would have been appreciated. Instead all he could hear was the clip and chink, chink, chink of his boots. The odd owl cry and fox bark coming out from the woods all around were unpleasant to his wary ears. His confidence was diminishing rapidly, eyes keened about him for clues, while a mocking woodpecker tapped warning drills deep within the hollow of his brain. The bells might be the affectation of a vain man who played court jester most days of his life from force of habit but, now, for once, he was rapidly losing all sense of humour and allowing a few serious thoughts to enter his head. They caused his contracting, beetling brows to plunge over hazel eyes dark with whirlpools of unusually deep thought. Normally, he was not much of a thinker, preferring to look no further than the shallow bottom of his beer glass for guidance in life, he and his friend, Quincey, usually sharing much the same perspective, shoulder to shoulder, propped on a barstool. One thing was for sure; Quincey would not have been in this situation. Quincey would have given up on the outskirts of Greater Manchester and found the nearest pub.

For now, Lovick Thomas Johnson, was well and truly alone. And in the dark.

So what was new? More to the point, what was he going to do about it? No one to consult but his own best judgement which he had never known to be reliable unless it involved the sure certainty that he would have a hangover the following day. Whatever decision he made was bound to be wrong. Quincey was not answering his phone due to the trouble he'd caused. No Scout Masters about here, either, as the blithe cheerfulness, which characterised his nature, rapidly disappeared down his own plug hole and a sneaking suspicion seeped into the sink of his weary brain that he ought, perhaps, to do something about this feeling he had that he might be heading in totally the wrong direction at gone the witching hour, on a bitterly cold, ink black, December night, in the middle of nowhere.

So, once again…he felt like shouting it out…where was this Fairview Country Club Hotel? He should have come across it well before now. Besides which he had certainly left the main road well behind; not a car, house, road sign or street light in sight since leaving the outskirts of the village. Fifteen minutes of a hike out of the village of Barns and still no sign of the high slate roofs and barley sugar chimneys which now lay like a snap card picture at the back of his eyes. Lost and alone. In woolly-back country, remembering the baas which had issued from the fields during the bus journey. Out in the sticks. Removed from all sensory aids for efficient orienteering such as street signs, food smells, party sounds drifting out over the night, and even someone with only half a brain might regard themselves as abysmally lost and, in a place like this, in danger of succumbing to frost bite.

So, to go back to his original question: What was new? Answer: Uninhabited country, on a steep tilt, was new to a man who had been unsuccessful in the adoption of any skills remotely connected with boy scout adventures. He had been a cub scout for a short three weeks when asked to leave on account of his gran not being able to afford the uniform or pay the weekly subs. This had been one of Lovick's greatest disappointments when he liked to 'consult' with his much adored and fondly remembered scout master, even yet. He had only ever slept in a tent in a field when there was a music festival going on around him, with a thousand other campers for company. On flat terrain, too. Not this hilly stuff! A lane that went up and down and curved this way and that in the space of a few heel clicks. Like turning a series of half circles so that there was no telling in which direction he was heading. A cobalt sky filled with stars occasionally appearing between the woven branches overhead, as close as a kitchen ceiling. He thought he had felt cold after getting off the heated bus and after coming out of the warmth of the pub, but now he was freezing, quite literally. Fresh, cold air constricting the veins in his nostrils until his nose felt as if it had been chiselled out with an ice pick, same acrid smell as the dry ice used to promote atmosphere on a theatre stage. Glistening cold, too; funny the way it can shine like diamonds when moisture begins to freeze in tarmac and the world becomes a jeweller's shop window all of its own. Something was happening in his head, too. Imagination working overtime. Fear occurred in the sudden shiver that ran all the way up his spine.

If only he could see his way, but tree-lined bends precluded the opportunity of distant views to know quite how far uphill he had walked from the village. He never had had much of a sense of direction even if his street survival instincts were second to none. His best maxim was when in doubt, carry on with a bright whistle to advertise a lack of ill intent and to put out a signal of hope that someone might hear and come to his rescue. Make as much noise as you can, his instincts said, short of proclaiming oneself a sissy. Stamp the boots so that the beribboned bells chunked even louder with the sharp clicks of his heels. Ignore the lateness of the hour, too. The dark of the country lane, the bitter cold of December high up on the Pennine fells. The rapid breath that was chuffing into the tunnels of his icy cold nostrils as he gripped more tightly onto the only friend in his company he might trust, himself included; his guitar!

Even the kit bag complained to him of his lack of he-man strength when he had always been weedy and thin with muscles more reminiscent of knots in cotton. "A long, thin, streak of nothin'," his gran had used to describe him. "Can't knock the skin off a rice puddin'!"

Eat ten at a time, though, especially now, Lovick thought. Bloody hungry! As well as frightened that he would never reach his destination alive, though it could not be that far from where he was now. His eyes were growing into saucers; the mischief of his hob-goblin thoughts. He pushed his fear of the night dark to the back of his mind and kept his immediate predicament to the front. Just about!

So where was this hotel? The Fairview? Had the landlord at that pub in the village sent him the wrong way quite deliberately because there had been something queer going on there? He had been a witness, of sorts, even if he couldn't think to what. His mind kept dwelling back on it.

And once he did get there, assuming that there was such a place as the Fairview Country Club Hotel, would he find himself turned away because he had failed to present himself at the appointed time despite the fact that none of the problems he had hit, to make him late, had been of his own making. If one discounted two and a half pints of strong ale to bolster him up for the last leg of his journey, which no one had forced him to drink. Or had they? He was not quite certain!

Then he saw the first of the flickering lights. Vague at first, tiny specks, and with a peculiar, flickering quality about them. They seemed to be moving about through the trees ahead. Lights meant people. Onwards, was the only way to go, into the black hollow before him.

And he was frightened of the dark!

***

A shadowy figure had followed Lovick up from the village to make sure that he was who he said he was and his destination was kosher. The man kept close to the houses, following behind and taking care not to be noticed, dipping in and out of any dark place, once the village was behind him, so shielding himself from view until the village lights were well behind them and the pavement lamps were well spaced out.

He watched as Lovick took the bend onto Old Barnston Lane, keeping to the same pavement, instead of crossing over to the road bridge and carrying on up the hill, which would have taken him directly to the Fairview Country Club Hotel. He was not following the clear directions he had been given as the road was even sign posted to the Fairview Country Club Hotel. It was clearly posted. The man could not have missed it.

Two deep nods of his head were sufficient to confirm to himself that he had seen enough. Time to report that the stranger was heading in the direction of Barnston Farm, which he did by use of a walkie-talkie; a child's toy to communicate a serious message.

Lovick Johnson would have to be watched. A stranger in their midst! Tonight of all nights. The snow forecast was forcing them all to take risks. 'The Boss' reportedly was not pleased with Bluithe Harcourt going off on his own tangent, even if Gareth Jones needed to be distracted. But Barnston Farm was all too close to one of their major storage places, other than the room over the police station in the village. Playing a two handed game when really he was after putting Gareth Jones onto Ross Fairbrother as punishment for his sacking.

All too close for comfort. Still, as long as he was out of the village for the next couple of hours it would be time enough. The specials would make sure of that. Bluithe would think of something if he had to. One man on the side of law and order was no match for the four who were not.

So who was he, this stranger? Come unexpectedly into their midst tonight of all nights? Now heading directly towards Barnston Farm with a bag big enough to carry an arsenal from the look of it. Too cold for camping in the woods, he thought, as he felt the icy cold even through his sheepskin gloves. Clouds were drawing over the moon, now, like an upside down table cloth being pulled overhead. Snow clouds bringing with them a mauve cast to the night, not a breath of wind but the smell of the burning torches coming to his nose. Whose daft idea was that?

He saw the first flakes beginning to show against the black of the tarmac roads. It was sticking to the glistening frost as a car passed him by on its journey up the hill, headlights picking him out. Ross Fairbrother, if he was not mistaken.

Nothing to be done, now, though. Too late. Bluithe Harcourt would have to use his wily brain to think of something if Plan A was interrupted. All they needed was a couple more hours this night for what needed to be shifted. Then one more night's grace to get the rest of the stuff moved on. God willing, of course, taxes being manmade!

Five

Fifteen minutes out of the village and the beer was pressing within Lovick's extended bladder, making it impossible to walk a step further without relief. The place he chose was by the wayside, on the moonlit, shiny, prickly leaves of a holly bush growing to the side of the narrowing lane; tarmac suddenly ended, freezing mud ruts underfoot. His mind was unable to decide whether he should turn back or press onwards with the same stubborn resolution that often proved disastrous yet impossible to curb. With suitable care being taken, of course, for his most prized possession, while the steam from his flow rose to his nose with an unusual sweetness to remind him that the drink had probably been the main cause for his disorientation. The landlord's last words as he had unbolted the door to allow Lovick out into the night were; "If you get stuck, lad, come back. Doss down in the old stables out back and come to see me first thing in the morning. Same price as a room, mind. Forty quid with a cooked breakfast. Whatever you do don't stray off the main road. You don't know who's about in the woods at this time."

He was even more tired, now, with thoughts of even an old stable sounding pretty good. The kit bag felt like a giant roll of heavy carpet under his weary arm. His guitar had become as cumbersome and the strap was cutting deeply into his shoulder after almost a full day toting it about.

Now he was altogether certain that he had come the wrong way. He could hear a raging torrent of water flowing somewhere close by and realised that the road bridge he could recall seeing ahead of him when he'd followed on round the bend, probably spanned a noisy, turbulent river which most probably lay dead ahead. He should, perhaps, have crossed over instead of following the bend.

"You didn't listen, did you, lad?" he could almost hear the landlord saying. "Can't recall directions? Pea-brained, are you?" Much like his old Headmaster had used to take the mickey when he was a lad. "Lost your way, have you, Johnson? Science room is that way. Though what's the point? You probably think that the Periodic Table is where the girls go to sit when they're menstruating!" Finger jabbing to a room behind Lovick's head. "Can't even consult a timetable with a room guide when it's all written down for you."

Then he could see lights between the trees, again; lights moving like fireflies do in the dark, on a warm summer night. If only it were summer and not the middle of a freezing winter. They were twinkling at him like bright, friendly, winking eyes, just a few dots of them and, seemingly, not too distant. He could smell paraffin, too. Sure of it. He used to have to trim his granddad's paraffin lamps in his shed when he went down there with his special magazines where gran couldn't see what he was reading, just a few short months before he died. Lovick could smell burning rag, too, as if what he was seeing were torches of fire moving through the trees ahead of him; real flames, like the ones he used to try to make as a boy by wrapping rags round a stick and soaking the lot in paraffin before setting it alight with matches. On the one occasion he'd used a different inflammatory agent…lighter fuel…it had puffed up in flame unexpectedly and he'd set fire to his own hair and singed his eyebrows.

The flickering lights, combined with the bitter cold and dark, reminded him, too, of a parade of moving torches up on the snowy mountains in Austria when he had gone winter skiing with his class from school; same effect when moving through a dark forest; flickering, weaving a warm yellow light, in and out. He'd got lost there, too. Got lost everywhere. Saved only because he had been drawn compulsively to bright lights like a moth unable to control its attractions. He had always been insatiably curious. He needed to know what the dancing lights were about; what the smell of paraffin and burning rags was for, even though he would be better to turn and go back in the direction he should have taken in the first place. Lights meant people too and especially as they moved about, through the trees. Mesmerising; all kinds of light attracted him. Candle flames; bright torches, stage lights, spotlights. Couldn't resist them; anything to prevent darkness and oblivion drew him moth-like towards them. He'd follow them anywhere, particularly spotlights on a stage.

This was yet another performance gone badly wrong like so many before…time wasted, home too late, in trouble again. His gran waiting up with a sour look on her face. You can't say sorry to the business end of a sweeping brush when it's being wielded by someone intent on bashing your brains in. Had enough of you, Lovick Johnson. Out, out, out, out, out!

All thoughts to ignore, tiredness was making him morbid, as he continued to relieve himself on a holly bush which should be jolly grateful for the improved micro climate he was making. However, there was something about this lane that was giving him extra creeps as the passage of two and a half pints of strong brew finally slowed to a few drips and he could shake himself off and fasten himself in.

Picking up his gear, he set on his way again, the kit bag now gripped in front of him to redistribute the strain. He was also using it as a shield to a growing fear he realised as a creeping, icy spider under his skin. He was not alone. Something was watching him! He could feel eyes upon him. Or was it that imagination of his? Soft lad exposed to his own stupidity again. It was as well he was in the lurid, pitch dark, he thought, as he made to walk on, his population of spiders increasing with every step he made.

He had not only seen the dancing lights but he was hearing things. It was hard to resist the urge to light a fag to calm his nerves.

Then, low and behold, as he walked around yet another bend on the lane, the trees ended abruptly and the sky became an expanse of white cloud closing in above his head. The smell of paraffin and burning rag was cloying the air strongly and a commotion was going on somewhere.

He found himself by a stone wall, in a place where he could see a large head of something moving on the other side and making a match with the sounds he had just heard. Sure of it when he heard the repeated rustlings and shuffling probably amidst the same stiff, frosty grass as was growing in the ditches.

Startled into alertness, he looked carefully around through narrowed eyes which settled most unexpectedly on the head of the old, grey donkey that had come poking over the wall; one shiny, weary eye turned his way like a big glass marble, hairy ears twitching, displaying a set of piano-key teeth as it shuddered its bad breath at him, inviting explanation of his presence. A shivered bray.

Relief flooded through him. "A donkey! Gets more like Christmas every minute."

Then he looked to where it stood in relation to buildings because a donkey meant that there was probably an inhabited dwelling close by. Sounds of people, too. Probably the torch bearers. Where'd the lights gone? Where were the voices coming from which he could hear as rips of cries in the cold sheet of air which was wrapped all about him.

He moved on, the donkey following on the other side of the dry stone wall, its head poking over. Sort of calling out to him softly as it scratched its chin along the top of the rough stones and spoke to him in its hee-haw voice of things that interest donkeys.

He saw the house like a silhouette, side on. It was in darkness except for a dull yellow light coming from the rear. That smell of burning rag again, but stronger here of petrol or was it as he had at first thought; the thick, sweetish smell of paraffin. Some kind of acrid substance registering even before he saw a smouldering bundle with an orange tip slowly being extinguished by the frozen melt water in a shallow puddle. Dropped by accident? All mixed up with animal smells. Live ones. Cow and pig poo, though it was many a year since he'd visited the cows and pigs on an urban farm with his gran, in his childhood. Some smells, though, are unforgettable, and farm manure was one of them.

The lights and the smells he had been aware of must have come from here. A rambling, shambling place with an open yard, just barely visible, on the other side of a five barred gate. The hulks of sheds on the far side were animated with darkly hidden, moving shadows, the cows themselves, milling before the wide open door to the sheds. A vague light created a dull, flickering illumination. They were pushing and barging at each other as if in desperation to get inside out of the perishing cold but hadn't the sense to realise that single file was necessary.

Then Lovick realised that the scene was not lit by artificial light but from burning torches being held high by three men wearing dark, protective clothing. This, while two others moved between the cows as if they had become trapped by the restless herd and were having to fight their way out. Lovick thought it an ungodly hour to have to start the milking!

The men had yet to see him, allowing Lovick time to make a quick inspection and gain some knowledge of the lie of the land, so to speak, before timidly approaching them to ask if he might beg shelter for the night. The one thing he did not want to do was startle them. Then again, he was quickly suspecting that this place was nowhere suitable for a fussy lad to lay his head down for the night.

What his eyes and nose told him was not the best of news to a man who was looking for wholesome food and clean accommodation, somewhere out of this perishing cold. Farm and farmhouse not up to much from the look of it. Not been shovelled up for years if the smell that reached his nose was anything to go by. Looked to be near derelict or, if lived in, a near ruin; sheds leaning, a side garden full of brambles, dried, winter stalks and lumpy hummocks of frozen sod; a green keepers nightmare. Even the donkey was complaining. Lovick gave it words to describe his own sense of disappointment. "Hey, mate, get me out of here!"

What a dump! Some of the panes of glass in the house, nearest to the lane, looked to be broken. A once proud stone farmhouse gone to rack and ruin from the look of it. It had been built side on to the lane, facing the yard, with one of those round stained glass windows in a metal frame, high up in its gable end, where the donkey couldn't get for the piece of corrugated tin propped in its way. A light shone from there also. The round attic window was winking at him with a light from within, on a tilt, open, at right angles, to catch what looked like a bird's feather drifting down from the sky. The first of the snow. At first one flake, then two, then four, then eight perfectly symmetrical crystals and before he could count further they were falling in their millions onto the brittle ruts in the lane and the cold, hard flags of the farmyard, and upon the cows and the men who seemed to be struggling to get out of the herd of milling beasts so not to be trampled to death in their haste to get within the sheds.

And on himself! He put out his tongue to catch one and realised that he was starving hungry, cold as death and might soon be, in reality, unless he could find some shelter for the night. He'd murder for a hot drink and a slice of toast. Anything to end the horror of his journey. Charity was what he needed, now. This ramshackle farm seemed to be the only place where he could find it.

Nothing else for it! He walked, bells jingling softly, to where the five barred gate stood closed across the entrance to his salvation. 'Barnston Farm. Keep Out' the notice on the gate said. The night sky seemed to have lightened to a purplish-grey as the snow began to thicken but visibility, long distance, was severely diminished. He could no longer make out the men and the cows and the burning torches, even if he could still smell the beasts and hear the din; a commotion going on which prevented any of the men from seeing him.

He shivered deeply in double ripples, rubbed his hands together and stamped his feet to advertise his presence. No one seemed to notice him. They were far too busy with the cow problem. It was as if the temperature had plummeted even further at this particular spot, away from the trees, wrapping him in icy plumes of cold air. A stone water trough, next to the gate, which he opened by unlooping a band of frayed rope from a post, had the sheen of frosted glass on the water within it. It was already layered with a thin film of cotton wool. Keep Out? No one would leave a dog out on a night like this even if they did leave out a donkey. Cows insisting on their own shelter from the sound of them, while the men shouted at each other as if they were afraid for their own safety and in a state of panic.

Lovick was thinking life and death, himself in that moment, as his beetling eyebrows caught the thick snowflakes like trawl nets making his forehead grow numb and his nose feel even number. Already, the melted snowflakes were running through his thick sideburns and down into his collar. The icy crystals were sticking to the unshaven whiskers on his shivering chin and blotting his jacket to form a crust of white shoulder padding, the same as it had done so very quickly to the bars on the gate, the window sills and the mucky flags under his feet. Soon he would be indistinguishable from a snowman. No hat, scarf or gloves in his kit bag, either. Nothing warmer than the shirt which had caused all his problems in the first place, a crew neck sweater and a reefer jacket over his denim jeans. A few more shirts and T-shirts and more jeans rolled up in his kit bag because they were soiled and in need of washing. Unlike Quincey, Lovick drew the line at wearing unwashed kecks. Nothing fit for the Arctic, though. Nothing wind or waterproof and the clinging cold was enough to freeze the bones of a polar bear. He was Commando, too, underneath. A lack of forethought and planning in a place like this. Bum as cold as an iceberg.

Not that he fancied asking if he could take shelter in a place like this. Even his own low standards of domestic comforts were better than the pig-sty of a house his eyes roamed for any sign that his first impressions were mistaken.

So how about a lift being available, instead? From the look of the place, not much chance of help in that direction. He would have begged one had there been any sign of a roadworthy vehicle on the premises other than the severely battered tractor which was parked up by a low wall next to a tangled heap of old farm implements, melded together with rust and old leaves from the look of it. The tractor didn't look as if it was in working order. Just a home for the randy hens which suddenly came squawking down onto the muck-ridden path right in front of him, adding to the cacophony that was going on still in the farmyard. They fluttered useless wings and then went skittering across the snow to the shelter of an open barn stacked low with winter hay. He would not admit, even to himself, that they had scared him. The whole place looked like a slum to him. The whole place scared him.

An old bike with a wobbly front wheel and flat tyres leant against a wall. Tempting! Had he not learnt a serious lesson in the course of a misspent youth. Fingerprints had done for him last time. He would get nowhere with the kit bag weighing him down, also. Reason enough! He sure as hell wasn't abandoning it.

There was still that feeling of being watched, surreptitiously, and not just by a donkey or the men who still had to see him; to ask him why he was wandering in the snowy wilderness at this time of night. They had appeared again, the trapped ones having extricated themselves, and none of them going where Lovick would have gone in their situation; into the sheds. They were forming a group now in the middle of the flagged yard where they pushed the cows away with firm hands and huddled in deep conversation, one man with an angry voice shouting louder than the rest. "There's a way in there to the caverns that's not bricked up. I know there is. Why else is she as mad as a wasp when all we wanted to do was take a look."

Lovick became aware that one of the men had seen him. "Over there, Bluithe. There's someone watching all this mayhem. We'll leave and come back in the daylight."

"And let her and Ross Fairbrother get away with it? He makes money hand over fist as it is. There's no way to get his cargo out but through the farm buildings and up the lane. Back of the cowsheds if I remember right. I say we wait it out."

"We're being watched, Bluithe. No point in making things worse." This from the man who took a torch, now, from one of the others and held it high, so allowing Lovick to make out the silhouette of a big man in a wide, padded jacket and ski cap, the type with a peak and ear flaps that fastened under his bold chin. Lovick couldn't see any other features but he was sure in his view of a tall, masculine silhouette, broad shouldered and barrel chested, wiping something off the front of his jacket which caused him to mew in disgust.

The man he seemed to be addressing directly in hot argument snatched a torch as well from one of others; men who stood listening but seemed not to be involved in the argument that was raging between the big man and the one in the red, woolly hat, a cigarette clamped tightly within his mouth. Lovick saw him exhale, remove the butt from his lips and cast it over his shoulder as if unconcerned where it landed. Lovick could only hope that he hadn't lobbed it where methane gas might lurk, though the snow would soon extinguish it.

Then all the shapes were absorbed amidst the hulks of moving cows as the men disappeared into the curtain of thickly falling snow. Lovick had no real idea which way they went other than that they were not coming in his direction. Wherever they had gone, despite having seen him, they were paying him no heed. He would have to find them, beg for shelter if he had to. A space in the cowshed would do. If there was no one else inside the house that was.

He had his hand on the gate still as he saw her. Standing in a glass lean-to; a sort of porch which was glazed much like a greenhouse, her face impressed with age and fear as she keened her hands against the falling snow, looking out. She had seen him before he had seen her, he thought.

When her head swivelled away to somewhere behind him, he turned to see that the men had gone to stand behind him. They were climbing over a low stone wall onto the lane he had just come from, talking in loud voices muffled by the falling sheet of snow, arguing hotly between themselves. The same five men with three torches held high between them, the fourth torch of flame, for some reason, the one he had already seen abandoned to a puddle in the lane, remaining uncollected as it continued to smoke and smoulder, the smoke drifting low with the density of the snow, mingling grey on white, obscuring his vision.

Lovick could barely see them through a smoke and the snow but their voices drifted to him, muffled but angry still. The same two men who had been arguing by the cowsheds continued to hold a heated conversation, the other three mere audience, venturing nothing to the argument other than to make urges for them all to go elsewhere, in agreement with the big man, out of favour with the man who argued to stay.

Then he heard one of the men say. "Who the hell is that?" and knew he had been spotted again.

Another replied. "Let's get out of here."

The big man said. "Can't recognise him. No one's called here for years except me. Someone Lizzie knows, maybe."

"Unless she sent for him. Look at the bag. Shotgun in it, maybe."

The sooner Lovick got behind a closed door, the better! He didn't like to be the subject of their conversation, not by men who brandished burning sticks and who falsely accused him of carrying a weapon. No one carried a burning stick without bad intention. Better to take a risk on the old woman he could see rather than the men. Lovick turned his attention back towards her. Swinging his kitbag before him, he made a more hurried path the few short yards to her door.

Her eyes came back upon him with a snap as he ventured closer; eyes as big as sun bleached gobstoppers in a corner shop window, fear in her expression, he thought. He wasn't used to people being frightened of him. Or maybe it wasn't him that she was frightened of. Maybe it was the men who were now walking off up the lane, disappearing into the trees, vanishing through the falling curtain of snow. Whoever they were, they had no cars parked close by on the lane or Lovick would have seen them. Something didn't feel right, though the cows had quietened, only a few clattering hooves over the icy flags of the yard, wandering, slipping this way and that, as if they hadn't sense enough to find a way into the sheds unless directed. Their backs were caked in white, but the woman was not heeding them. She was too intent on staring at Lovick, frightened of him even, just as she had seemed to be frightened of the men who had now gone away. Or seemed to have gone away. There was neither sight nor sound of them, just whiteness, all around.

Upset was what he sensed, too. Disorder was more than suggested in the dereliction of the buildings which looked worse as he walked the path, in her direction, raising a hand to denote that he had seen her. The woman still keened her head to look at him, on the other side of a glass door, her old face solemnly watching.

Lovick being Lovick, he made for a jaunty walk, holding the kit bag out in front of him, a bit like the travelling salesman. Not exactly the right time of day for selling anything, though the kit bag was big enough to hold a full range of ladies clothing. All the time sensing that he was once again interrupting something of a serious nature. More than once he'd walked between mates in the middle of a quarrel and got his face punched in. There was that same sense of aggravation in the air even though the men seemed to have gone away.

All except one! She raised a row of cockle shell knuckles to rap out a warning of ill intention. Her face, stretching wide, before Lovick turned to see one of the figures on the lane again; the one with the red woolly hat. He was no longer brandishing a burning torch. Empty handed he bent to pick up the near dead torch from the frozen puddle on the lane. Standing, he positioned his limbs then crouched low, his left leg coming up in front of his bent shape and then thrusting forward like a baseball player wanting to deliver his missile as far and as hard as he could. Something top heavy came tumbling through the air, a glow reigniting to flame before the missile hit the corner of the gable wall with a splash of sparks, just missing him, before clattering into an upturned, zinc bucket with a resounding din.

God Almighty! It had landed close enough to cause Lovick to alter his jaunt to a panicked dash for safety, dragging his kit bag through the snow, his guitar banging hard against his back as he ran for any shelter he could find. Slipping and sliding on an icy path, in a final dash to her door. The voice came clearly through the thickly falling snow in tones of threat. "We'll be watching you, Hannah Jubb. You and Ross Fairbrother."

He was called on his way, angrily, by the big deep voice which came through the trees. All the men calling him loudly, then, one after the other. "Leave it, Bluithe. Leave it. This way."

Shivering now with teeth chattering uncontrollably, he made his appeal. "Let me in before I freeze to death, please, lady. I'm lost."

Still she dawdled. Age evident in the strands of white hair poking down under a raggy head scarf, the old woman called out loud enough for her words to travel through the glass. "Don't go! I's thinking!" her lips pressed in a wavy line against the smear of her breath on the dirty glass. "Wait. I'll open the door fer yer."

As if he would go! Shivers coming now, one after the other. Hurry up, lady! Another look to the lane and it was still empty; the men finally gone. Not caring of anything now but his need to get within. But if he thought that she was merely some old, feeble, unprotected woman it was because his own panic was uppermost. He was unaware of the object she let fall from her grip. He heard it; hard and heavy as it clattered within the porch. She had discarded the heavy shotgun along with her doubts and started to unfasten the door, drawing back bolts and turning keys in locks. Not one bolt but three. Not one lock but two, the place seemingly a fortress of defences. Her hands shook like last year's autumn leaves about to disintegrate leaving only fragile old bones. She opened up to him, just one thin chain between him and some shelter from the ice and snow. For all the world looking like a destitute town vagrant. A brown gabardine coat covering her like a cloak. Slack, muck caked boots on her feet. Around her head, the raggy scarf fastened like a pirate's head gear with its knot at the back. Trails of plaited, matted, white, rat's tails came from beneath it. The face that she allowed him to look at had eyes as wild as a feral cat's, nose and chin nearly meeting in a half moon of withered flesh. Her eyes glinting suspicion still and narrowed as she took a good look at the guitar and the kit bag he had hauled with him, his inadequate clothing covered in snow; the thickly falling snow, the bells on his boots which tinkled as he stamped numb toes, the need on his face showing. They stood looking at each other through the crack in her door for another few moments before she made the final decision to remove the chain.

For another moment she hesitated still, looked over the yard, back at him, beyond him, her chin working up and down as if she had not a tooth in her head to stop her gums gnashing together. Her mouth moved in and out, the skin dimpling, pleating, papery thin, as white as the silver skin of an onion under the streaks of dirt from the window glass where she had lain her face.

She waited for him to speak, explain himself again, looking at him deeply, almost malevolently, promoting yet another wave of fear as a rush of cold spiders brought a premonition that he should take care. She had piercingly, pale blue eyes which she directly at him, unblinking.

His teeth were now chattering with shock as much as cold, making it hard to get the words out coherently. "P...please, lady. I'm on my way to the F...Fairview Hotel. Took a wrong turn. I'll pay you for a night's bed and breakfast if you'll let me shelter here."

"You not with them, then? Don't recognise you. They didn't either."

"It's bloody cold out here. I gather they weren't friendly."

Her sneer was a grisly snore. "Meaning me and my Lizzie harm they were. Letting the cows out...spilling the feed...pouring the milk all over the shed floor from the churns. No one here but me and Lizzie, see. Women on their own see. Think it's easy to bully women on their own. Wrong! Not me!"

"Were they trespassing?" Silly question but the gnat brain had shrunk smaller with the deepening cold. Two more degrees and he'd be catatonic.

Thinking deeply as she looked at him with hooded eyes, brows low, weighing him up, suspicious still. What she saw caused a sneer to pass over her lips. She straightened herself up but still had him stand on her doorstep. "You got one of them phones that don't need a wire?"

Lovick nodded, fighting to control his chattering teeth. He did if it had enough charge and money in it. Nodded again.

Her chin went up in a manner that said that she was testing him. "Call the police."

"What?"

"Call them on it. Seen folk using them in the village. Standing talking to themselves like idiots. Nine, nine, nine. They'll put you through to Gareth Jones, local policeman. Tell him that they've been at it again at Hannah Jubb's farm…Barnston Farm, off the Old Barnston Road for your information, if you be truly lost. They been here before. Bluithe Harcourt without asking…looking in my sheds. Not known I've been watching." Then reiterating, making it clear what his message must be; her words, not his. "Let the cows out again. Not the first time he's done it, neither. Emptied the milk churns. Spilled feed out of the silo. Had burning torches, too, this time. You saw. Might have set fire to the barn with that fag of his. Locked myself in and watched, I did. Had they come near the house and me and my Lizzie I'd have shot 'em dead." Her eyes turned down to the shotgun lying on the floor. "Me taken then. Then what my Lizzie do?"

He found his mobile from his pocket, pressed the buttons with stiff, thin fingers so cold that he couldn't feel the depression of the number nine, three times. He put it to his singing ear and then waited. One ring and part of another later, he found himself talking to the emergency operator, fumbling for the words to make a coherent explanation. "Er…It's like this. I'm at this farm and someone seems to have been worrying the old woman who …"

Before he could explain she had snatched it from him, disconnecting the call as she pressed her grubby hand all over the keyboard and stared at it as if it was a magic wand, the cure for all her ailments. "Maybe I'll get one of these new-fangled things. No wires to cut. I believe you. Get in." Hardly a welcome. "I'll need help anyway to get the cows back in the sheds and lock up the sties. No getting a pig out of a sty on a night like this. More sense than cows."

Lovick saw her pull the door wide. He put out his hand to take back his phone; it had cost him an arm and a leg. State of the art technology, took photographs and short clips of video. Needed it for his stage work but would have been better off without it. He got too many calls from Quincey sitting lonely in some pub or other, wanting company; no will power, either.

Once it was safe back in his coat pocket and tucked well down he thought about what she had said, his hazel eyes musing, brow deep and his teeth chattering together still. He was thinking that if what she said was true, they might come back again. He was no hero. Cowards didn't come more yellow than him. He was in a state of confusion. "If you were being harassed why didn't you let me finish the call?"

"No point. They are police, except one of them. They won't come again in this weather. We'll be snowed in by morning."

Confused with cold, Lovick's thoughts lay entirely with his own survival. "Can I stay, lady, ta very much?"

"Cows need putting back in the sheds." Then when his face showed his consternation, she relented. "I'll do that. You can fix a brew and something to eat."

"What about this Lizzie?"

"Why you asking about my daughter? Her's upstairs. Sleep through anything, does Lizzie." Then she laughed, harshly. "Wouldn't have been able to help any roads. Can't get out her room, see. Locked in."

She opened the door that would lead them into the house.

Lovick followed her over the threshold. At least he wouldn't freeze to death.

Six

Her mother was sleeping in after the fuss and upset of last night.

The stranger was still sleeping, also. He had hardly made a move all night as he had snored and grunted in his bed; dead to the world. Outside, it looked as if no one would be going far because of the depth of snow, so they might as well stay in their beds; nothing to get up for.

Not so Lizzie! She had already piled up her greying, mid-brown hair; the hair grips rough with rust as they slid into the greasy waves and held the long, untidy tresses where her shaking hands put them. She had already rubbed cold water against the thin, lined features of a once pretty face, now gone dark and long and lined about pale, pebble-shaped eyes as luminous as a lantern glass. The rag she had used had smelled of mildew, but no mind; habit was habit, her nose unperceptive to its acrid stench. She had pinned up the rip in her soiled, once-pink under slip in a gesture of acknowledgement to the rip itself. No bra was needed for the two sagging poached eggs beneath.

There never had been even a peck of fat on her. In the months since summer she had lost the thin membrane of subcutaneous fat that had until that time made her appear reasonably, physically healthy. Her eyes had since become rimmed with brown smudges, her neck a crepe bandage over the hollows of her poking clavicles, ribs to play a tune on, legs little more than the thick-kneed bones of a skeleton, making her feet look oversized for the tiny, tiny bird she had become in middle age.

Not eating properly was the trouble. Her stomach had stopped calling. Hannah scolded her about it. And the state of her finger nails which were chewed down to the quick, her hands continually cold and shaking, not always with weather but, usually, caused by the judders which could come upon her without expectation. Not enough medication, Hannah said. It was as if she was living over her own underground station, trembling with the trains of her deeply disturbing, angry thoughts. Miss Carnage rattling her cage, again. Ignore her, Lizzie. It's Miss Happy's day, today. Push her down, keep her down, and push her away. Got to get dressed anyway. The snow's calling.

Today was one of the coldest that Lizzie had ever known. The tap had been slow but worked eventually to provide the trickle of water which had travelled long and hard through frozen pipes underground before coming into the house; icy cold from its stony journey, pipes not yet frozen up, though. At least Hannah hadn't had to lug the river water in, as yet, in a slopping pail, thin legs drenched as it swilled under the laces of those old, cracked boots of hers. Cold work that was, on a bitter December day, in a place where the wind could cut you in two and make a white-out blizzard with weather like this.

What could one expect in a farm house as old and past its best as Barnston Farm was, these days? Her mother could only do her best which was never enough. It was where Jubbs' had lived for a century or more, farming the land as well as holding livestock, the latter of which was all that her mother, Hannah, could manage in her old age. And they in the village would have it that the Jubbs were savages instead of two land woman subsisting alone, no men to help them, no extra hands taken on when Hannah would not have anyone near them, eking out a meagre living, one of them ill and one of them old and in need of a restful retirement. Poor souls, Lizzie thought of herself and her mother.

To the uninitiated, the dark attic room might have looked no more organized or cared for than the strewn clutter of old lumber and ragged furnishings, all piled together, suggested. To Lizzie, this room was where her spirit was happiest because she had incorporated the bits and pieces into its careful arrangements and placed them, each, like a shield of defence about the heaped nest of ragged, buttonless coats littering the floor, which was where she slept, her head on a sack filled with chicken feathers. Everything she valued within that cluttered space was reminiscent of the day when her chosen life had been lost but, which Lizzie was sure in her heart of all hearts, would come again, soon, as long as she was patient.

These items were arranged about her as she stood drying her face now on the first thing that came to hand which happened to be her own under slip, just a pair of someone else's summer shorts beneath, which Hannah had bought from the charity shop, with streaks of yellow and brown upon the crotch and smelling of fish, now, but of no consequence to Lizzie.

The objects which surrounded her were her sacred possessions though one might not regard them as anything more than the same clutter which characterised the rest of the house where her mother banged about below, never above stairs, drunk or sober, getting on with all the work that had to be done. Last night's work was disturbed just as she had settled in her chair after draining a newly slaughtered piglet of its blood, soon to be hung in the curing shed for bacon.

Still thought of her belly did Hannah but Lizzie, these days had no interest in food or all the things her mother did. The kitchen was always cold, too. Rarely a fire these days when her mother warmed herself on gin-laced tea in that armchair of hers, usually fell asleep there and still there at morning light when the cows would be in need of milking once more.

It was better to stay up in her loft where the drafts were less and she could stay out of the way of Hannah's temper when they both had to share the same space. Here, in her private attic lair, Lizzie could do exactly as she pleased, be who she wanted, think what she wanted, imagine the day when all the accoutrements to her long held dreams, these stored objects so preciously preserved, along with her expectations, in her attic, would be used to furnish a happy ending to the horror story of a life of twisted reflections and cruel illusions. It would happen. It would. One day it would have to or know that all her painful life since Ross had been for no purpose.

It had been Hannah who had moved the tea chests and furniture up to the attic, in a fit of angry tears, all those years ago, shouting out in her rage; "The less I see of all this stuff the better. Too many cruel memories attached. Not to mention the money wasted. I should write out a bill to the Fairbrothers, I should, for the cost of one wedding, the loss of one husband, a mentally unstable daughter made even more deranged, and a grandchild to be born without a father. I never want to set eyes on these things, ever again."

Not so for Lizzie when the very same accoutrements had beckoned her to move from the bedroom she had used to have below, the same one where the stranger now slept, because she had cared to take the opposite tack. She would keep the bitter memories alive, because to banish them would banish the sweet rays of hope which still lived within her. Ross would one day realise what he should have done all those years ago and repent, she was sure. Lizzie would not relinquish that one last, fervent wish no matter how he turned his face from her. Where there is life, there is hope, she told herself. Her memories were strong, even yet, so that she could still drift back in time as if it all had happened only yesterday and find some gladness worth reliving. The memories of that day stored all about her. The wedding dress intact. The full contents of a marquee set for a wedding reception which had not occurred, along with the wedding when the groom, priest and guests had failed to turn up, lay within the large, plywood, tea chests, now stacked, one upon the other, like a solid wall at right angles and to the right of the rancid wash basin where Lizzie prepared herself to be a bride once more.

These items represented several sets of crockery, cutlery and glassware, Irish table linen, boxed, and tarnished silver salvers with matching pots and serviette rings. A dealer would have cast a surprised eye and declared it to be fine stuff in need of a good polishing. Not that Lizzie would ever polish it like her mother had used to do, once upon a time. Just as the stored furniture would remain dull of shine, pitted as it was these days with woodworm and split in places where the damp had penetrated.

Its condition made no difference to Lizzie's determination to keep it as it stood, stubborn in her conviction that one day it would serve the purpose for which it had been selected, because her stalwart, steadfast mind said that it would. Bluithe Harcourt would not have it, either, because in Lizzie's mind, he was stealing into their byres and sties and barn, looking for things to rob and sell. Just as he had always done. Her dad had always said to her, "Stay away from Blue Harcourt. He's a bad 'un!" As if she didn't know that for herself, talking all this rot about Ross Fairbrother and her mother, as if his made up tale gave him the right to trespass. Enjoying, too, alarming them when he came at dead of night under one of those flaming torches, pulling on a cigarette, casting the butts anywhere. Not the first time he'd thrown missiles at the house, like last night, risking the house setting alight, everything in it ready to go up like a tinder box. Cows and pigs and hens burnt up in their sheds and sties and no one to care, either. Gareth Jones on his side, too, it would seem. A law for one and none for the other after Hannah had shown him all the cigarette stubs Bluithe had thrown down, coming a lot lately at dead of night, without grinding them out. All Gareth Jones could ask was if Lizzie had started smoking again. It made Hannah mad. As so many things angered Hannah, bone weary as she was.

But Lizzie used the preservation of her memories to bind her purpose and keep it strong. The crates and furniture had been stacked to form a private enclosure. An oak table had been set at right angles to the tea chests, with a set of scratched and battered Chippendale dining chairs stacked upon its broad surface. A cobwebbed carpet of fine pattern and rich colours hung from the rafters which increased the impression that Lizzie was standing within a solemn place, at her wash basin, clothes assembled for dressing, under the little round stained glass window, as if in a chapel or in a darkened, secret room, within a room.

It was only the gap under the table which provided a sort of low doorway through which she crawled upon retirement like an animal entering a burrow, on hands and knees.

The love seat, which had been specially purchased but never used for bride and groom, stood next to the chair of claret coloured velvet, scattered with bridal wear. The love seat was now bent with damp but bore her stubby candle in an empty jam jar close to the nest of coats. Lizzie was always careful never to knock it over, always recalling her mother's words after bringing it up from the kitchen, where her mother lit it for her, last thing at night.

"Got to be safe, Lizzie, got to be safe. No laying the light on your bedding while you read at night. Isn't safe."

The candle was the only light which Lizzie had when the night grew black outside and the donkey slept, though she had been musing how to bring more light to her other dark places, recalling as she did so Bluithe Harcourt's flaming torches which gave out more light than Hannah's paraffin lamps.

The rest of the lumber in the attic space had been shoved behind a screen which divided the room into the small space she preferred, under roof spas bent and twisted with the age of the house and the natural sagging of the foundations which had sunk with so many galleries and potholes running deep under the house itself and collapsing in on themselves. Every now and then, the twisted spas produced a creaking noise which Lizzie thought must be like being on a ship in the middle of an all white ocean. She could sense the weight of snow on the roof slates, too. White snow; the colour that had inspired her choice of clothing.

All lay ready for her dressing on the wide, claw footed, claret coloured velvet chair that the mice had chewed to get at the horsehair within. Lizzie stood before a small cracked mirror over a rancid basin which her father had screwed to the wall under the little, round, stained glass window high up on the gable, in this, the attic space. The broken mirror offered her a facial image that was fractured into a disjointed three part reflection where the glass in the round frame had separated from itself, as if the cracks reflected the cracks within her personality, cracks which had made Lizzie Jubb a laughing stock, with names that had been cat-called over walls and fences for as long as she could remember.

Mirrors mattered to Lizzie, greatly. These mirrors were vital to her peace of mind, as were her dressing up clothes, her props and her trays of make-up. Though Hannah would not allow her to keep all her clothes within the attic room because she was forever replenishing them with trips to the charity shop in the village and refused to tramp up with them. These days, she rarely came upstairs. So they were kept, "...in the boxes in the kitchen, Lizzie, so I knows who yer going to be today from what's been taken."

First, though, to apply her make-up. Somewhere she had kept the bit of magazine article, neatly folded, that had informed her questing mind that a bride should always apply warm tones to the skin to counteract the stark whiteness of bridal wear. Lizzie used her panstick freely, rubbing, smearing, blending, until she had an orange mask upon which to highlight her eyes with a soft mauve shadow, black liner and mascara from the thickest, blackest wand in her tray of second hand cosmetics, first one eye completed in total using the left side section of the broken glass, then the other completed in total to the right side piece of broken glass. Her lips she coated with a pearly blush using the triangle of glass at the bottom of the frame so to feel satisfied that she had shared her face with all three parts of the looking glass in exactly the same way as she communed with the image in the glass, each day.

The fractured mirror images made little difference to Lizzie's dressing; she had never known wholeness of person in the whole of her life, only counterparts, sections and segments, as she looked at portions of her one face, separately, never together until her make-up and dressing were completed, when she might turn to view the complete result. Such was part of a routine that had to be obeyed in exactly the same sequence, each day of her life, though the colours and the clothes might change in order to produce a unique persona which would transform her into quite a different type. She would only look at the whole when she was dressed in total, make-up, props, clothes, complete. No easy matter to decide what to wear with final consideration because what she had brought up from the big, battered, cardboard boxes in the kitchen below meant only one thing; sneaking away off the premises before Hannah could prevent her, annoying people, upsetting herself even more, bringing Gareth Jones back to the house again, maybe, to speak to her mother about, "That Lizzie of yours!"

Her inner counsel of the day needed a final consultation, too. Miss Happy could be split into different faces, all with different looks. One glance and Lizzie knew, because of the suggestion in the weather initially, that her choice had been satisfactorily made. She had already been down to find the ill-fitting, soiled, white, silk and lace dress, swagged with sagging bows and gathered about the sweetheart neckline which Hannah had made for her wedding day, when she had been so much plumper, so very long ago. The lace veil was dusty and grey with age and moth eaten. It draped over the claret velvet of the chair back like a shroud, with a rent of six inches which Miss Proud might have mended where the flower shapes joined. The accessories, she kept collected together in a plastic shopping bag so that they were never lost to each other amidst the shambles of her dressing up boxes where so much rummaging occurred. Lizzie could be organized when Lizzie wanted to be.

Finally, only then, when she was fully dressed, could she turn to look at her reinvention within the other, full length mirror on the adjacent wall to the wash basin, with eyes shut tight. Turn three times and tap the wall twice, hands together, pray to God for His kindness in granting her wishes. Then open them. Abracadabra!

She was, today, the bride of Ross Fairbrother, again; the same person who had stood before the hall mirror, so many years ago, storing up her reflection which was never to be forgotten. It had been summer then, not winter. Still no matter for the day had been the coldest of her life as it had turned out by the end of it, despite such a happy beginning. A day to be relived only for its joyful parts and the constant hope that the ending might change. As she so hoped it would, one day. Would change, one day. It must because she could not carry on living with the fear and desperation that a bride in a bridal gown would be jilted once again. And she would not think of Bluithe Harcourt casting jibes, coming to the farm to pry and poke about, when all she wanted to do was to find her happiness, bring it forth into the shining light, be married. The scene set, outside.

Today, God had draped a white dust sheet over all and declared a holy holiday a few days prior to the actual event. A winter wonderland had descended, causing Lizzie to be feverishly excited over and above her constant layers of dread. A world of white presented Lizzie with an opportunity that could not go wasted.

Seven

Fresh out of the shower, Leonie dried herself off with a fluffy pink towel, wrapped a dry one about her, and then put on her makeup in the warmth of a bedroom which was all pink and white furnishings; exactly the room of a daughter cherished by indulgent parents, even though she was almost all of twenty-five years of age.

Stuffed toys looked at her from every surface as she sat at her dressing table on a heart shaped stool to put on her make-up. Her work clothing for that day hung, newly washed and pressed, laundered by herself, on a hanger to the back of the shut door; paintwork lilac; her favourite colour along with lipstick pink. The room was ruffled and untidy only where she had made a disturbance in the process of arising from the snug warmth of her single bed and then by discarding a frilly, baby-doll nightdress of lilac silk and lace which had yet to be folded and placed in her dark purple, furry nightdress case.

Before she left it, the room would be exactly as she liked it again. A place for everything and everything in its place. The only thing she was not orderly about was her timekeeping, though last evening she had set her clock to give her an extra twenty minutes of get-ready time. It was the decision processes involved in getting ready that slowed Leonie down. Hair up or down? Should she go sultry or sophisticated? Better neither with Mrs. Fairbrother vetting her and Mr. Ross eying her up all the time. The grey silk crunchy was brought out instead.

Leonie was pulling her black pleated skirt up to her trim waist, blouse in place but in need of a final tidy, when her mother called out to her. Leonie froze as she listened. She had five minutes in which to be out and be on her way to work if she was to be on time and not find herself sacked. "I'll have some breakfast before you go, Leonie, darlin'. Toast. Six slices. Butter not marg. I'll not eat that crap. Bring the peanut butter and a pot of strawberry jam. I think I'll eat healthy this morning and have a banana with it. And a thermos of hot chocolate to keep me warm. It's snowing out."

Leonie was fastening the last button when the last snippet of information registered. She went quickly to the window to look out. She had forgotten all about the weather forecast. When she pulled back the curtains all she saw was the whiteout. How was she going to get there, now, on the last minute as usual, and still be on time, with so much snow about? Mrs. Fairbrother would not accept excuses when there was so much to do; guests arriving tomorrow, crackers to order, deliveries to check, the panto to sort out, costumes…

That's when she looked across the square and saw her dad getting out of his police car in front of the terraced cottage building which housed the police counter and a cell for anyone who broke the peace; the law being something else entirely.

What was her dad doing out at this time? He was wearing the big, padded, black ski jacket and a peaked woollen hat which came over his ears. Underneath would be his uniform only that was not visible except for the blue serge trousers and big, polished boots. Then Bluithe Harcourt, wearing the distinctive red bob cap, got out on the passenger side, his own blue estate car parked close by. He was shorter, squatter, but unmistakable over the short distance. Leonie recalled her mother telling her that they had gone off together the evening before, her mother guessing it was something to do with Hannah Jubb, Ross Fairbrother and the old cavern to the rear of Barnston Farm, from comments she had heard made by Blue Harcourt earlier.

Dare she beg a lift? He looked to be both too tired and too busy. She had also always been encouraged to think ahead of herself. Her tardiness annoyed her dad, no end. Maybe, it would be easier to just be late than have her dad scowl at her. He looked busy anyway and very aggravated as he would be if he had been in the company of Blue Harcourt all night.

It was hard to tell whether Bluithe had been home or not as he was always dressed in the same bib and brace overalls with one shoulder strap unfastened, unless hiding something when the bib pocket would require support. She could see the strap dangling down under what looked like his dark raincoat, a cigarette in his mouth, as usual. No work to go to either. His wife probably knew by now that he'd been fired so he perhaps wasn't eager to get off home. What he was saying to her dad was a mystery. She noted that her dad looked worn out, as he listened and a finger stabbed the air, stopping just short of her dad's barrel chest. Always too much to say for himself, had Bluithe, droning on when others realise they've said enough, pressing things when his suggestions were unwanted, making a real nuisance of himself. Leonie felt her dislike of the man smear her face, just as she noted that one of the snowmen on the square was moving. For a moment she thought she was seeing things.

Then she heard her mother's voice travel from her bedroom next door to confirm that she was not seeing things at all; two tone; "Oo-oo!" Her voice deepened and became quieter though Leonie could still hear her clearly through the cardboard-thin wall. "Close your curtains, Leonie, if they aren't already, lest she see you looking. Lizzie Jubb! Over by the obelisk, dressed in white. Been hiding herself amongst them snowmen the children built earlier. She'll think no one can see her because of her white dress and white veil. Mad as a March hare! It's the same every year at this time. Your dad should lock her up in the cell when she causes so much bother."

Leonie had no intention of hiding from Lizzie Jubb so she did not follow her biding, though Lizzie looked far too intent on watching her father talk to Bluithe than to look up to the windows where both she and her mother were watching her. Weird she looked, too, in a wedding dress and that long, lace veil. Sort of sinister, though her reputation was not one for violence as much as spiteful, naughty mischief. The kind committed by a rebellious child or someone wanting to express their anger and knew of no other way to do it but to break something that belonged to somebody else.

Leonie was appalled to note her footwear and the absence of any kind of jacket to keep the cold at bay, just the dress, under that long white veil. She must be freezing with satin slippers on her feet, no coat and only a pair of white cotton gloves to keep her warm. No matter how much she covered herself over, though, even her face, the white gloves were her trade mark. No matter her different wigs, dress styles, and attitudes, even different voices sometimes, they always knew Lizzie by her white, cotton gloves, bought mail order and delivered in sets of ten by the postman.

Tragic, it looked, too, to see her in her wedding dress and know that she had honestly and truly been jilted at the altar by Mr. Ross. Like, at the altar itself! Not the night before or during the morning but actually when she was at the church. Leonie could not even imagine how degrading and humiliating that must have been, even if she seemed to have brought the situation upon herself by attempting to force Mr. Ross to marry her, even if he had put her up the duff, so to speak. Even being pregnant, Leonie couldn't see how anyone could force someone else to marry them if they didn't wish to. Not that she knew everything about what had happened to Lizzie to carry her into the insane, middle-aged wreck that she appeared to be today, but she knew enough to hope that it never happened to her. More than anything, to be such a victim of gossip was horrifying to her and there were always people ready to carry the gossip down the years, her own mother being one of the worst culprits for carrying tales. Though on the subject of Lizzie Jubb she had been unusually mute. So Leonie had had to settle for the tales being blabbed about her place of work. Something about Lizzie Jubb suffering from some form of deluded fantasy, too, when she still truly believed that Ross Fairbrother would marry her even now, every so often reminding folk by dressing up in the same wedding finery and coming down to the village to confront them all, before engaging in a spree of vandalism and then dashing off back home in tears.

Leonie had been raised not to speak to her, even if spoken to first, as had all the children of her generation. She had not to speak to Hannah Jubb, Lizzie's mother, either. Her mother being a smelly, old crone who could still haul a carcass of pork to the butcher from the back of that red tractor of hers, no matter her being as thin as a lath and well on in age. The stink of her farm was ingrained in her clothes. Her hair went unwashed. She wore a scarf on her head that could never have been laundered in all the years she had worn it, spring, summer, autumn and winter, for as long as Leonie could remember.

But for Lizzie to come down to the village today, of all days, when the snow was thick underfoot spoke of her madness, as nothing else. Yet, there she stood looking not the slightest bit cold. Just the sight of the snow was causing Leonie to feel frozen stiff and she had yet to venture outside.

Distracted away from her time keeping, Leonie watched with a compulsion that would not have been denied, in the same way that she was attracted towards a close study of drunks, drug addicts, vagrants and prostitutes even when they caused no problems to anyone but themselves. She looked like a ghost defined in outline only against a background of snow, wearing a long, white dress with lace sleeves. That creepy veil, of course, which hid her face so that one would be unable to judge her mood.

Then she moved to stand on the obelisk steps, white against grey stone. Her dad and Blue Harcourt still had not seen her. They were further distracted, away from the presence of Lizzie Jubb, by being hailed by a whistle coming from the direction of the Bald Pheasant, one of his specials, perhaps. It was customary to have a morning debriefing meeting over breakfast after any kind of significant event. As her dad raised his hand to salute his communicant, they made off in that direction themselves.

Still Leonie remained unseen by Lizzie, her mother as well who would not have heeded her best own advice and closed her curtains but would be looking out as well.

Leonie was suddenly reminded of the time and called to her mother. "Sorry, Mum. Can't do your breakfast. I daren't be late. I'll have to go. Dad will be here soon enough. He'll get you your breakfast."

Within the other bedroom, Gloria Jones was momentarily disinterested in food for the few seconds it took to lock into a memory and become aware of the cold hand of fate on her back. Her reaction to the sight of Lizzie Jubb necessitated stemming a bad feeling which she attempted to wipe from her face with the backs of her porky hands. The feelings of guilt had never abated and never would as long as Lizzie Jubb came down to taunt her.

Gloria heard her daughter hurriedly put on her coat right outside her bedroom door, without coming in. "I'll be late. The old witch will sack me," was all she said before she dashed off down the landing and clattered down the stairs.

Gloria was shouting to her. "Your boots, love!" But it all went unheard as the door was opened and closed, the dead lock turned, and she could then be seen heading in a diagonal over the snow, her head uncovered, hurrying along the path that an early bird had scraped down to the far corner of the square. Lizzie Jubb, standing with her back to the obelisk, was watching her daughter closely as she pulled up her hood and lowered her head. Leonie was wearing nothing warmer than her ordinary Cuban heeled shoes. She would be wet through before she got round the corner, never mind all the way up the hill to the Fairview Country Club Hotel.

Then, horribly, from her vantage point, Gloria saw Lizzie bend and squat and knew exactly what she was after doing. Snowballs. Her rap on the window was short and staccato, sufficient to warn her daughter. Lizzie Jubb as well. The veiled head turned in her direction. Her head was tilted under the veil to make her look like an avenging ghost. Gloria felt the fear rattle in her throat as she closed her curtains as quickly as she could.

She spent a good half hour crying, thereafter. When she phoned her sister for a gripe and a whinge, there was no reply. So she phoned Gareth instead. Somebody would have to bring her some hot food and quick. She was saving the Christmas ham until Christmas Day, or told herself as such. The 'secret' box under her bed needed replenishing, too. Marty would be bringing her order before the morning was out but she couldn't manage that long. Who else was there to ask?

Like Leonie, she had seen her husband go across to the Bald Pheasant Inn where she suspected already his specials would be waiting for him. Not as much suspected, but knew for a fact, because she had spent the night watching them go back and forth with the riot van filled to the brim with boxes, carried out on a trolley. What a place to stock untaxed goods but over the police station, itself!

They shouldn't do it. She would not be able to bring herself to tell Gareth directly but maybe she should hint. Otherwise they would have him compromised and he would loose his job.

"Can you bring me a bin lid please? I'm starving. I've yet to eat."

Eight

The peeling hand bells were already clamouring in Lizzie's head, even if the world inside the house, and outside her round, stained glass window, was silent, telling her to make on her way for her wedding, once again. A veiled vision in silk and lace and satin slippers with a ring of artificial violets on her crown and a pair of her best white gloves to lift the delicate hem of her dress.

Couldn't go, though, without one last look on the stranger, whose coming had so unnerved her, even if he had been the saviour they had been praying for, ever since Blue Harcourt had taken to visiting the farm at night. One of several times of looking, in fact. When she had gone down for her mother to light her candle after he had retired to his room and her mother had come to unlock her door, her mother had whispered, "Stay in your room, Lizzie. The stranger's in your old bed. Not safe to lock you in when there's been fire brandished this night. Sparks fly. You would have seen them. Aimed the burning torch right at your window, he did, wanting the sparks to come in. Be a good girl, now!"

Lizzie spied down through the peep hole in the grubby floorboards, a white ghost on hands and knees, her eye to the fish eye lens so that she could see into the room below, clearly. The same way that her father had used to check on his wild and wayward daughter when he had had occasion to lock her up, too. The only way to deal with the tantrums and temper when her bewildered, undeserving parents had been driven to the very end of their tether. Lizzie could look back on herself screaming and hollering, red-faced and fighting, hammering her fists on the door; "Let me out of here. Let me out!" and enjoy even yet the power of her moment.

Through the spy hole, she invaded his privacy with a huge sense of warm satisfaction, more than just a voyeur; her eye moving slowly over him as her hand longed to do. He was there, still, as he had been all night, on his side, sleeping, totally unaware in his deep oblivion that she was watching him, where he lay, fully dressed, under the patchwork quilt Hannah had sewn for her bed when she had been an angry, sobbing child. The light was now coming through the window and the lamp had gone out.

She had been watching him, on and off, ever since her mother had told her, unable to sleep, disturbed and fretful, unsettled by the intrusion of a man in the house. Watched him, she had, as he had prepared to sleep, taking off his musical boots, first the left and then the right. She had heard the shivering bells, along with his chattering teeth, as he had removed first one and then the other; freeing those beautiful, colourful, soft, silk ribbons from their neatly tied bows and then dropping them; thump, chunk, thump, chunk, before climbing in.

Dead to the world, he had been, as soon as he'd got himself sorted. His coat to the back of the door. His kit bag close to the bed where he could put a hand to it. The guitar he had leant into the corner, strap dangling; shiny curves of smooth brown wood, with a ring of inlaid pattern around the sound hole, under the stringing. This, after he had polished it dry with a handkerchief where the snow had melted all over it. A guitar! Distracted again, Lizzie thought that she had never played a guitar, not even to strum.

She was remembering, too, that she had seen what he had done with his phone. Lizzie wanted one so desperately sometimes that it was an ache inside her. Numbers fascinated her. Telephone numbers, house numbers, patient numbers, hers was 6379/2 when she went every three months, with the District Nurse, for her appointment. Saw a doctor in a white coat who had more problems than she considered she had herself; kept rocking himself and biting the skin from about his nails, staring out the window while his tapes gathered her voice like a combine harvester; off with the fairies, hardly listened to a word she said. Told him what she had to and what he wanted to hear; that her medication was keeping her stable, not making her gums overlap her teeth, or give her more epileptic fits than she might have anyway. She had had her real teeth removed some considerable time ago.

Why would anyone want to listen to other people's phobias, neurosis, obsessions, compulsions, bad thoughts and harmful ambitions? Those others in his waiting room looking like wandering ghosts of human beings with shaking hands and dead faces, ticks and twitches the only sign of life. And their lostness! Lizzie wasn't lost all of the time and never had been. Lizzie knew, most of the time, where she had to go and what she had to do, when Hannah let her. Let the village know it, too. Load of hypocrites. Thieves and liars. Cruel hearts and thoughts inside peevish bodies and sly, devious, dishonest minds, blowing hot one minute with nasty words and blazing eyes, freezing her out the next with the backs of their heads. Smiling at her face only when they had to while raising the knife to her back.

"Selfish buggers," Hannah called them, shouting it sometimes as she stormed up and down the farmhouse kitchen, too much gin imbibed, only Lizzie to hear it. No love in their hearts, no kindness, no charity. No soul, even while going to the church to pray before God in all His goodness. No real compassion for their fellow men and women, even while poking a collection tin under everyone's noses and shaking it loud, bullying for money. Hannah knew what happened to the money they collected, she had told Lizzie often enough. The subject was one of her hobby horses, eyes glittering with accusation. Half went into their own pockets, a quarter to the fundraisers and the rest wasted...apart from a penny in the pound which went to the victims for whom the charity was intended...the rest spent on advertising and jolly promotions; cocktail parties, fine wines, trays of fancies and limousine cars to ferry them around. In the same style, in fact, which Lizzie had planned for her own wedding reception.

Not that this man was from the village. Different look, different mood, different voice. Big city boy from Manchester he had told Hannah. A musician. Got lost on his way to Ross's hotel. Ross! Her Ross and no one else's. Never had found another woman, had Ross. Not after their poorly babby boy had been born with its head to one side, all bunched up and twisted. The stranger had reminded her because he would be of an age similar to that poor deformed babby of hers and Ross Fairbrother. Had he lived, Rossiter Bernard Jubb would have been his name. Lizzie had seen him just twice. The first time had been after Hannah had told her that the baby was stillborn, bathed him and cleaned him up as much as she could, she had, wrapped his frail little body in a shawl, a little bonnet over a cornered head full of dark hair as most babies had when they're newborn, blue veined, silver eyelids closed on still orbs. Dead, not a breath. Though Lizzie had heard him sigh as some breath had escaped his deformed, little body with the force of the birth. His eyes had never opened, according to Hannah; lids stuck together, lips melded. Though her mother had done her best using the same ways as when a calf or a piglet or a lamb didn't show signs of life immediately after its birthing, Lizzie was sure of that. She had blown up its nose with a straw, she said, shook him and called to him, rubbed her rough hands over his lifeless limbs, before putting him in the old cradle, before the roaring fire, to keep warm while she brought the afterbirth away and dealt with the terrible flood of blood that had threatened Lizzie's life and made her so weak and ill for several weeks after.

Just the once, after she had slept, had she been allowed to hold him in her arms, the dead, new born son of Ross, the man she loved as she could never love another. She had let her tears fall upon his porcelain cheeks and known a sorrow so deep that it transcended all that had gone before it. The child she would have loved so much, gone to heaven, his daddy refusing to have any truck with either of them until paternity tests might be made. He had claimed to have been so drunk on their coupling that he had no memory of the baby's conception. He had not even attended his babby's funeral after the doctor had come to say that it was dead, grossly deformed, could not have survived no matter where it had been born. Gareth Jones was to get the permissions they needed to bury the tiny corpse under the apple tree in the orchard, exactly where the donkey lay down in the shade of summer and the snow of winter, over the grave of her poor, deformed son, never to be forgotten and ever to be protected by the bad tempered ass which lived there still.

The same donkey that had warned them both, last night, that the men were coming. Not just Blue Harcourt, this time, but Gareth Jones and his specials, also. Intruding, Hannah called it. Wanted to see their search warrant did Hannah. Instead he, Gareth Jones, arrogant in his local bobby manner, had merely asked Hannah's permission. Then not heard a word she shouted at him angrily when Hannah had tried to send them all packing, gin soaked, just before her bedtime, hands still stained from slaughtering the pig in the sink, when she was bone weary, milking finished, full churns all waiting to be collected, ready for her sleep. "Conveniently deaf, is thee?" Hannah had called through the still night air. "Well, two can play at that game!"

Maybe, but for the stranger, Lizzie might have done what her inner companions advised and gone down to their houses in the village to do the same, there and then, make some mischief, done some damage, to relieve the anger inside her breast. All the allies bidding her to go and make the lives of the villagers hell, as they were making hers and her mother's. Lizzie was not daft enough, though, to single anyone out when they'd all contributed, each and every one of them, not just Blue Harcourt. Also Gareth Jones and his specials. That Gloria Jones, more than others; fat, ugly cow. Great, giant, roly-poly pudding, she'd squash Lizzie and Hannah together, flat as an ironing board if she fell on them. Not seen her about ever since she'd caught Lizzie staring into her pram at her gurgly, little, blue-eyed daughter. Picked her up and whisked her inside as if Lizzie had meant the babby harm when all she'd wanted to do was smile at her, say, "Coo-ee, da-da, whose a cheeky girl?" Kept the baby in. Then kept herself in, never coming out; her and that babby of hers, until the child went to school with her dad taking her backwards and forwards by the hand, not Gloria.

Sometimes Lizzie felt sad because Gloria had been the only one of the school children to ever play with her, coming here to the farm, sometimes staying over. The rest had parents who refused to allow their sons and daughters to play with her because she had so many invisible friends, fits too, when she'd keel over and writhe, going blue at the gills, wetting herself. Only her unseen friends didn't mind any of that; friends who now lived inside her where she could commune with them, dress them up, let them be a part of her, taking them out with her sometimes, so that she could look at them singly in a shop window or in the mirror and see the person personified in the clothes she gave them. She spoke to them and they spoke back to her questioning mind, like they were real flesh, blood and bone. Who could say they were not real flesh because they were clad over her own real flesh, with minds and moods and words all of their own?

They were her guardians, in fact, because Lizzie needed looking after in more ways than just shelter, food and clothes. She was not supposed to go out on her own, the doctors said. Though what Hannah could do when Lizzie ran off up the lanes at dead of night, with her own ideas of where she could go and where she couldn't go, was something else again. Down to the village, where else?

Hannah had got mad when Gareth Jones had come to the farm on more than one occasion to complain that Lizzie had been down to the village at night, on her own, hiding in the bushes and jumping out at the drunks, with a black mask over her head. In a private chat, Lizzie had promised her that it was only Miss Mischief playing tricks. Hannah had believed her and gone back to Gareth Jones, guns blazing. "If it was my daughter, it's only her having fun."

He never caught her at it, at least not yet. She wouldn't let him bring her home in that police car of his, even if he did. Hannah wouldn't like that. Not authority, in a uniform, knocking at her door and him with proof of it. And Hannah in the state she was in!

What for, anyway? Just frightening folk? Lizzie was cleverer with the vandalism and her other, more serious, naughty tricks. Though Gareth Jones had knocked once or twice, standing on the threshold; a big man in his police clothes, with one of those batons and a pair of handcuffs dangling off his belt. The last time was just a week or so before. A close call.

"Can't take a joke!" her mother had defended. "I keep her in mostly and well you know it. She gets disturbed easily does my Lizzie. No phone. I'll do my best to keep her away from the village. Keep her in. Can't swear, mind."

"No pointing that gun at anyone, Hannah."

Her mother's scowl such that her chin and nose met over the toothless gums. "Country way is a shotgun. I keeps it to shoot vermin that comes into the house. Yer can't blame my Lizzie for everything with so many thieving, lying, cheating buggers about."

"There's been washing missing off the lines, too…"

"Her's no need to take clothes. I keeps her dressing up boxes full to the top …"

"And flower pots smashed and unpleasant things posted through letter boxes."

"Any one would think that my Lizzie was responsible for every ill in the world instead of just being hurt and afraid and abused by it…as she is, Gareth Jones. And you know it. You better than most. Ross Fairbrother got away Scott free while my Lizzie suffered. Abused, too. In that mental place. I treat my animals better. We know she were, don't we?"

"We do! We do!" thought Lizzie. Yes, he was guilty because he was the one who had fished her out of the water just as her seeking hand was about to take a grip on the floating, green beards of her saviour, only happiness in her heart and mind, ready as she had been to go with him to the land of peaceful oblivion.

"That all happened years ago, Hannah. People forget. All they know is that they see a veiled face at their window peering in on them, and who else can it be?"

"It's not often," Hannah would say. "Only when her needs more pills. Gets out of kilter. I gives her medicine regular. How can I lock her in with that Blue Harcourt prowling my farm with burning torches? He's been putting ideas into my Lizzie's mind when I've caught her collecting the sticks and the rags to do the same. Impressionable, she is."

"Keep her in at night, please, Hannah," had been all that Gareth Jones had had to say further. "If she's doing these things when people can see her they don't get frightened the same. Make sure she's in at night and just don't let her have access to matches. If she gets out you can call me and I'll bring her home before people start asking for her to be sectioned again. It's when she starts stalking folk they get the wind up them."

Sectioned! Never again. Hannah was firm. No more black wandering with the prompts of her deepest soul, Miss Carnage, at dead of night, taking her over. Lizzie liked the dark because it was only in the dark that she could converse with Miss Carnage. They could walk together, side by side, talk, share; a white glove in a black gauntlet. A forbidden relationship. Hannah had forbidden her to countenance Miss Carnage ever again. Lizzie had had to seal her up in a jar and lay away her clothes, her drawings, her friend's possessions. Never allowed out in the dark, ever again. "Never, ever, Lizzie, please," Hannah had begged of her. "Never out in the blackness of night ever again."

Her parents hadn't ever trusted her, see, and never had done on account of her 'friends' though they welcomed them as her distraction, harmless most of the time, keeping Lizzie amused and sociable as they played together, laughing and happy with a silver backed mirror and a dressing up box and the make-up trays. They had always been with her, had her 'faces', as Hannah called them. All Hannah ever need do was look at the face Lizzie had on that day to know much of what to expect. This face today; that face another. These clothes, those clothes. Should Lizzie be allowed out to go sit by the river, under the bridge; her favourite place? It all depended on the company she was keeping. Her 'friends' sometimes crowded her out getting Lizzie annoyed and in a bad temper. Sometimes shielding an escape, when Lizzie could slip away unguarded. Sometimes good and sometimes bad, sometimes happy and sometimes sad. Like the words of the song she liked to play on the wind-up gramophone, on account of the electricity having been cut off to the farm long, long ago, which had been in the donkey's stable where the donkey only went when he wanted. The same old records that belonged to her mother, played over and over when Gloria had come to the farm to play. Moved now to her secret place, the only place where she could truly be alone, radio wouldn't play there.

No T.V. these days, either, and unless her mother bought her batteries from the village for her small transistor radio which she took with her about the house, they remained totally out of touch with the rest of the world. No batteries in the Star supermarket recently, see, because of the children's Christmas toys causing a sell out. "All sold out..." Hannah had said, "...to the greedy folk."

So Lizzie couldn't listen to her radio when she wanted. People should always be allowed to do what they wanted to do. That way the world would be a happy place. Lizzie wanted so for people to be happy. To get what they hoped and dreamed for out of life and then, maybe, they wouldn't all be so nasty to deal with. Just as she wanted Ross; wanted to be with him even yet despite all that he had done to hurt her and drive her away, wanted for him to love her and tell her so. Hold her in his arms and lie with her. In a bed together. Just with Lizzie, none of the others. Her friends might then drift away because she would no longer need them to hold her firm.

Strange to think, too, that the only man she had ever seen sleeping in the whole of her life, all forty five years of it, other than this stranger, had been her dad. Not even Ross because they had never been in a bed together. Only lain the once on the grass under the apple tree in the orchard, with the donkey watching. She had seen her own poor, dead babby son sleeping though; just once more, as he went into the butter barrel and Hannah buried him deep where the donkey laid down at night, to warm him.

Looking down, thinking, "It might be my babby grown, sleeping as he is in that same room…same bed…as I did." remembering all the times that she had been flung in there and the door locked behind her. What else was there to do with a wild cat in a tantrum? Screaming and yelling and kicking and fighting. Spitting and swearing and cussing and blaspheming. Chucking all her toys, one by one, at the window. Smash! Her dad weeping and her mother in tears at the bottom of the stairs, also, "…for your own good, Lizzie. You'll have to learn yer can't have everything yer want, just because yer want it!"

"Can, too!" when she was strong in herself and her medicine wasn't making her drift away and her hands didn't shake. "Can, too!" always Lizzie's mental reply to a statement like that. Lizzie could have whatever Lizzie wanted because if Lizzie couldn't get it, Miss Naughty could. If Lizzie couldn't do it, Miss Mischief could. If Lizzie wasn't allowed in her pitiable, sorrowful madness to be happy and bonny and blithe and gay because she was Sunday's child, then Miss Happy could.

There was a face and a mood and an outfit to fit every mood in the boxes in the kitchen. Every day going there, first thing. Creeping through the house in the first light of morning. A strange, cold, quiet, white light in the house. Like being inside a shoebox wrapped in cotton wool, looking out through white candy floss windows. Hannah fast asleep in her chair. Hush, mustn't wake her, yet!

The cows weren't calling this morning to be let out of the shed, either. This morning Lizzie was happy because of the snow which had stopped falling but not gone away. Dressed to blend, all in white, her wedding day, again. Everything white. The sky white. Roofs white. The yard white. The cold white. Her breath white as it drifted up before her face. The world whitened out. She could do as she wished today because she would be as one with the snow outside the farmhouse windows which was like the world having a veil of its own; a veil they could share, a veil on the past, a clean sheet of white paper on which to write her future, her marriage to Ross. Her wedding day.

She would go wherever she wished to go, today, because of the snow, for the next hour or so, down to the church and the village, perhaps, before Hannah was even aware. No one knowing but her. Just to watch, look, pry, nothing more intended because she was happy. Out and back before her mother arose because she would then need to stay in her room all day. What with a stranger in the house!

Happy today, she felt the happiness warm in her belly, sadness behind her, back to back, dancing back and forth on youthful feet as light as thistledown, down the quietly creaking stairs, down the flagged path and through the snow draped gate, onto the lane. Dressed in silk and lace, her figure as it had always been if only Ross would look upon her to see the longing beauty that still existed, deep within. One glance, when she raised her veil and smiled at him with love in her eyes, would allow him to see that she had never relinquished her persistent wait, her love for him, and her sorrow at the death of their babby boy which she should not be blamed for. If only he would look instead of turning his back and walking away, the river of time flowing faster and wider with each passing year. Time flowing by before her eyes in green beards, one after the other. No point now of wishing that it had taken her with it, so long ago. So long ago, lifting the hands in white, cotton gloves to her face, their smoothness soft against the lace of her veil.

The occasional puffs of wind showered her with confetti from the overhanging trees as she used the bare branches of the bushes to assist her slippery journey. Then, on the flat, to know that she could dance her way up the levelling lane, swirling her skirts in the snow, donkey left behind just as he had watched her travel to her wedding long ago, in a long black car, her silent dad at her side, staring gloomily through the window. Mustn't be late, she thought, as she picked up her skirts and ran, ran, ran as if there was nothing to impede her will this time. No one would stop her this time. Ross's mother would not stop him, this time. Not this time. This time nothing would stop her from marrying the man of her dreams. He would be waiting this time. At last. At last. Happiness in her head despite the disapproval of her parents and his parents and those in the village who had called her names, spat at her, shouted out what they thought. Cruel, nasty words when all she had done was to fall in love. "Fool," her mother had said. "Don't think he'd be marrying a Jubb but for the babby in yer belly. We can still get round that. It's not too late."

Her mother's face had closed as she had said it, pleading eyes deep with the need for her daughter to cooperate, but Lizzie knowing that it was her own mental fragility her mother was fearing most. Her father long-faced in a silent sulk all through the journey, though he had hung up his farmer's garb and put on a fine suit with silk lapels and told her that all he wanted was for her to be happy. He would do his best. Little did she know that his best would be his last, also.

Her dad, her daddy! Coming after her, now, even if reluctantly, because Lizzie was stealing his best friend away for herself. She could feel his spirit all about her, despite her being the cause of his going up through the caverns and potholes to tell Ross of her heartbreak after she had thrown herself into the river to end it all, only for him to fall off the ladder, his foot catching, and drown upside down in the well. He had been the one to drown, not her!

The past was chasing her through the snow as she ran on headlong, stumbling, slipping and sliding, getting up and charging on because it was in her head now that she must not be late. Apprehension was growing sharp within her because the ending to a dream that began happily never changed.

She ran straight to the church on the outskirts of the village, skirts flying about her thin, blue mottled legs, breath juddering in her chest, to take a look. Nothing had changed, the brick and stone with a spire and the plaque that declared it to be named after St. George and All Angels, save for its coating of white powder, a hand already having been to the latched gate and a sweeping pattern of disturbance to the otherwise virgin snow, going ahead of her. The same church where she should have been married all those years ago. It was so pretty with the snowy cape over its spire and lining the battlements and the arches over the stout wooden door, either side the leaning gravestones, blackened with age.

Where were the guests? Please let them have assembled, the organist about to play, Ross standing waiting, a smile on his face. "Please! Please!" as she ran through the gate and up the path, disturbing the deep snow once more as she swirled her own pattern over the skirts that had gone before.

Her hand pressed lightly upon the latch and she saw the door give way, before her questing eyes behind the veil. Her breath was short in her throat, with hollow sounds coming to her listening ears as she entered the cold interior. She searched for a different scene than the one she was looking at. It looked just as it had on the day she had come with her parents to marry Ross Fairbrother. It was empty of congregation, flowers undelivered, no red carpet, no music, nothing but the smell of polished wood and dampness. And cold, so very cold!

Then she saw him, the vicar; the very man who should have stood before them. Supposing, that is, that he had turned up at the church, having been told by Ross's mother, to stay away. This man being the same as should have joined them together as man and wife.

Now, turning, he stared at her, looking as surprised as if seeing a ghost for a moment, teeth bucked, his black frock sweeping a hem of dry snow which he had brought in with him as he made up his altar steps, one foot on the top and the other on the bottom. Then, with realisation, his rising shoulders sunk down again onto his sunken chest and pot belly under the wide belt of his cassock, extending with an air of relief. "Lizzie

Jubb! Go away. Not again."

Lizzie's eyes keening, tears forming. "Where…the guests…my Ross…?"

He came then, towards her, like a waddling goose, fat, cruel hands clasping her tiny, thin shoulders, pushing her; pushing her out. Then, as the realization dawned that it had happened again, she heard the iron key turn in the door. She was out in the cold, once again.

Her eyes glazed with tears, her breathing coming quick and shallow. Why did it keep happening? Where was everyone? Where were they hiding? Why were the crows in the trees laughing at her still?

It was all too much, too much. She would not let them get away with it again. Tears and temper now as she stamped her feet and then ran out of the church onto the lane again, past the vicarage and the community centre, in the direction of the square and the shops where the snow was no longer virgin; snowmen populating but early children chased off to play in the park. No throwing of snowballs; villagers couldn't be doing with them when there was so much still to do to be ready for Christmas and weary already. The tall snowmen stood on guard duty, like soldiers on duty in a ring looking at each other. She was as one with their whiteness. Then sounds of tyres travelling; a soft crunch on dry snow.

Hiding, now, she saw the police car pull up on the other side of the square, next to Blue Harcourt's battered blue wagon, outside his police station where a black patch of the tarmac was showing. Gareth Jones got out of the driving seat with a long strapped bag over his shoulder and a set of binoculars, if she was not mistaken. He looked tired as if he had been out all night. Not gone home to that fat, roly-poly wife of his after causing all the upset and mayhem. Even Hannah had been disturbed by it all. Crying into her gin fortified tea, she'd been. Tired of it all. Tired, tired, tired!

No sign of his specials. Then Bluithe Harcourt got out of the passenger seat of the same vehicle; that red woolly hat pulled right down over his brows, face sour, jowls hanging, fag in his mouth, and a curl of smoke entering one eye. Why wasn't he at work? Decorator and handyman at the Fairview. Saw Ross every day; spoke to him, she might ask him to deliver a message; "Love you, Ross, love you! Marry me?"

Not him, though. Not the man whose laughter had lasted longer than the rest, following her, skitting her, calling her names. Wasn't called for. She'd get him back. Put paper up his exhaust pipe or do something to frighten that hard-faced wife of his. Hated them all, hated him the most.

Creeping now, Lizzie went to stand with her back against the stone obelisk knowing that if she walked quietly and slowly, blended in, they would not be aware. Men were never aware of what happened around them when deep in conversation with each other. Snow cold all about them, too; having to stamp their clumping feet, rub hands against arms and blow steam into each other's faces as they spoke.

Their voices carried to her ears as deep mutters. Talking of her. Bluithe saying in a thin voice, "It is there, somewhere. We could try again when the snow's gone. That stranger's not there for nothing, is he? Went into the house and didn't come out. The agent, maybe. Got to organise a clearance. No way Ross can get it out unless that way. All he has to do is to pay Hannah Jubb a backhander."

Never! No! Talking rot! But Lizzie kept quiet, listening, not wanting them to twig her. Lizzie knew the snow to be her friend, not theirs, because it let their voices travel to her ears as long as she stood, watching and listening without moving, perfectly still. The snow hid her away, she thought erroneously, her back to the grey stone, as she looked at them under the full fall of her lace veil.

Hot with her anger, now. Her feet in the little, silk slippers remained as warm as toast. She did not feel the cold even as she stood stock still and let the coursing blood in her veins, slow. She was hot as toast straight off the toasting fork, her breathing fast and coming out with vapour even under the veil as she watched them talk together. It heated the tip of her nose and then steadied to a slower rhythm as she let her senses heighten, plans form, mischief grow inside her head. Lizzie was thinking, looking, listening while wondering how she might pay them back; pay him back, pay them all back; Blue Harcourt and Gareth Jones especially, when the coast was clear.

The Bald Pheasant was directly before her, to her right hand side, further down the square. She saw the figures come to the doorway as part of her peripheral vision when she wanted to keep looking onto her prey. Someone whistled shrilly, waved, but not at her. Gareth and Bluithe lifted their hands in greeting, and then began to walk that way, following the path made by an earlier disturbance in the virgin snow, across the square, seeming not to be aware that they were being watched by her. Ignoring her. Lizzie didn't like to be ignored now that she was looking their way. Temper rising. How dare they ignore her! Miss Trouble came to her aid, now wiping the tears away. "Go get 'em, Lizzie. Go get 'em!"

If there was one thing Miss Trouble disliked it was to be ignored. It was always the same when she came down to the village in broad daylight. "Take no notice of Lizzie Jubb," they said, "Who does she think she is?" they complained. Always the same. Turned their backs and walked away. Turned away and went inside; telephoned each other. Maybe on one of those wireless, plastic things; a mobile telephone. Wanted one, Lizzie did, like Hannah did. What mischief then could be made? No locking doors and closing curtains on her, then. Miss Trouble would show them, then; mix things up, cause confusion, swap things round, get inside their heads just as they got inside hers.

Meanwhile, she might throw a stone through the policeman's window. Or put dog dirt through the bakery letter box if she looked in the right place up the alley where they all took their dogs to crap without a plastic bag to carry it home in. Couldn't get her clean white gloves dirty, yet, though.

She thought up other mischief to make that didn't entail getting her gloves dirty, her brain active and alive, her eyes drying as she sniffed the tears away, animated. She could take up a cudgel and put a dent in their cars, walk up the bonnets, stamp and jump up and down on the roofs in her white, silk shoes. Would snow in a petrol tank do harm? Or swing on gates to damage the hinges? Kick her way through their flowerbeds, pulling the winter pansies out of their pots as she went through the entire village and scattered them about or chucked the dirty roots at clean windows? What about their fancy Christmas trees, then?

Stealing the washing was one of her favourite games. No floral scented washing out on the lines to take, today, though. Not today with the snow lying undisturbed in long white chains; such a shame. Clothing she liked to take home and sniff at, run her hands over the shapes that their bodies had made, trying to recall whose lines she had pillaged the individual items from, as she did so, putting her hands inside the pockets and squeezing hard.

Snow was spoiling things now. No people about to torment other than the men going into the Bald Pheasant Inn. To do what at this time of day? Pubs had changed in the times of their openings and what they had for sale. Breakfasts even; a painted sign outside showing a full plate of eggs, bacon, sausages, good enough to smell them, with a steaming mug of coffee thrown in. All for four pounds ninety. Men went in, wiping their feet, leaving clumps of snow on the mat, rubbing their hands. Bellies calling, they would be looking elsewhere. Maybe she should go there, too, but where they couldn't see her, round the back, find the crates with the empty beer and wine bottles where they would be stacked by the old stables. Start a smashing raid. Crack, but no tinkle of satisfaction followed the imagined activity; her frustration growing. Snow was spoiling things, good and proper, because the glass might not shatter again and again, into littler and littler pieces. She so loved to hear it shatter and smash on the cobbles of his yard, to smithereens. No less than he deserved; that Marty, thieving, overcharging bugger!

It was while she was thinking of ways for some form of retribution which would satisfy her craving that she saw Leonie Jones come out of her front door. Leonie Jones, the policeman's daughter; Gareth Jones's daughter, head down, deliberately not looking her way. She had yellow hair in a frizz about her temples, brought back into a fuzzy bunch and tied with a grey band of crinkly, silky satin, ears bare to the cold, much as Lizzie's darker hair had used to be when she was younger before she went punk. Pretty enough in a plain clothed way, a little slip of a thing, light as thistledown. How could she have a mother like Gloria? How could Gloria have a daughter like her?

Lizzie felt the first rush of jealousy because Gloria Jones had everything that Lizzie had been denied; a home of her own, a husband...though Lizzie turned her nose up at the thought of Gareth Jones...just Ross...no other...and a child. Jealous of the daughter, too, because she worked at the Fairview Hotel. Not that she believed all the gossip about him fancying the little slip of a thing with the frizzy, yellow hair. Seen no proof. Ross was pure. But the girl would be catching sight of Ross each day through her work at the hotel and talking to him, maybe, as they went about their everyday business, nothing more.

Lizzie could imagine it all because she had gone there once to do the same, at one of her low points when she had been bleeding with hurt, taken by Betty, Miss Carnage's guardian, who had managed to get a job in the kitchens when Leonie was away on a Kitchen Hygiene course, but was then called back home by her angry mother even though no one sussed. Come for her, had Hannah, and dragged her away.

Other times, Lizzie had seen him since about the village or up on the ridge, at a distance only. Sometimes, though Hannah wasn't aware, she had made seeing him happen, as he went about his work, in the hotel grounds when he was always taking the hotel guests clay pigeon shooting or to do archery or just to go paint balling in the woods. It was not hard to hide somewhere where she could watch him, in a naughty but harmless way, which was one of the games she was especially good at, was hiding, because she had learnt how to keep very still.

That and to keep things from her mother. Hannah must not know even if she never went inside the hotel, itself. Hannah had been so angry with her for going there in the company of Betty and Miss Carnage, making it necessary for lies to be told, because she dare not make Hannah so angry with her again. She knew that but for Hannah, her mother, she would have been sectioned and shipped off out to a secure mental hospital once again, long before now. She dare not; dare not, ever estrange herself from her mother. What would happen if Hannah was not there to protect her, from herself, as well as others?

It did not bear thinking about. Even if Hannah had understood that it was only when her jealous feelings got out of control that Miss Carnage came about. Jealousy was one of the main reasons that allowed Miss Carnage to rise up out of her core and take over. Jealousy of those who might claim his fond looks, his rare laughter, his passionate embraces. The rest she merely despised and detested.

"Get that man out of your brain," her mother would shout when Lizzie started to be demented with jealousy. "We've never been happy since the day he came into the house. Him and your dad always going off on a run together. Going into the caverns together. They didn't fool me. Thought they did. But they didn't. First him and then you!" Another mug of gin laced tea usually sorted her out. It would not do for Hannah to lose control, entirely!

Hannah must never know, but…hush!…sometimes, she had managed to get into the grounds of the hotel by her own way in, not through the big, front gates, nor across the river by the bridge and down the steps to the big stone where Bluithe Harcourt liked to fish, then up through the trees, past the bird hide which, other than her own way, was the quickest way to get into the grounds of the Fairview Country Club Hotel. Not that it was entirely all her own secret. The ladder Lizzie had found in the shaft showed that. But once within the grounds, there were lots of trees and bushes and places to secrete herself, usually by his gun room and the outside dog kennel where he went most days, if only to feed it and train it when retrieval should have been in its instincts, great, stupid, loopy thing, always pointing at her with its nose and one paw raised, and coming her way. Nuisance, that dog of his, was. A real nuisance when it would come barking and sniffing and wanting to play, paws all over her best Miss Naughty clothes, licking the make-up off her face. Then get shouted back. Lizzie felt jealous of the dog. Ross stroked it and gave it tit-bits.

Mainly, what she knew, she knew by hiding in the telephone box outside the Star supermarket. No better place for listening to gossip, one of Miss Naughty's best tricks that, listening to gossip. All the better to make mischief with. Set dog against dog, make up something damning and then put anonymous notes through letter boxes. Listening in, and then finding a way to cause trouble. She found a lot of things out that way. They who had the blasted cheek to ignore her when they didn't know the half of all the things she got up to. If they did then they would be shivering in their beds at night, not just she and her mother. They wouldn't ignore her if they knew what she did and had done, that was for sure!

Lizzie thought some more as she saw Leonie Jones appear out of her front door. She knew that the girl had seen her, because of the way her face had mewed when she had come out of her door, slammed it shut, locked it, and deposited her house key in her pocket. Little Miss Swivel Eyes! That Leonie Jones, pushing her away with a turn of her shoulders before bringing up that hood of hers so that Lizzie couldn't look on her face, maybe make a dash and poke her hard in the ribs, stand on her toe. Just Miss Naughty not being nice and letting her feelings show. Lizzie distancing Leonie through narrowing eyes behind the veil, yet fencing the daughter of Gargantuan Gloria Jones and Mr. Nosey Plod, the village policeman, within her thoughts as someone who should bear the brunt of her own blame and accusation. Leonie, a mere representative of the group as a whole, was no more than a focus of her angst against the villagers in general, and a little, slip of a figure but with curves in the right places, as she had used to be herself in her younger days.

Lizzie's bile was rising as Leonie moved forward, to make past her, with a strutty little walk, using the snow-free path that someone had shovelled at an angle towards the bottom of the square; her way to work, never once turning her profile to look Lizzie's way; a threat not worth acknowledging, nose in the air.

Lizzie nipped quickly and lightly down the obelisk steps to where the snow was still thick and virgin. She crouched with knees poking against the lace skirt of her dress and sat, body folded on her haunches, slippered feet splayed, the snow she gathered being bunched up first into a heap, then balled up in the palms of her white gloved hands, the wet passing through but her hands within the sodden gloves as hot as branding irons before she stood up quickly.

That was when she heard the staccato taps coming from somewhere above her head; one of the first floor windows. Feeling her anger begin to smoulder and burn like one of Bluithe Harcourt's torches within her, as her head swivelled and her eyes narrowed, better to see through the crocheted flowers of her veil, up through the rip where the fabric had rent, never mended.

She found herself looking directly into the moon face of Gloria Jones, who else? Warning her daughter that Lizzie was there and wanting to look at her daughter, that was all, just look, Gloria! What harm was there, in snowballs, anyway? Lizzie cocked her head that way to let her know. "I can see, you…Fat Knickers, Hippo Arse, Pig Dug Tits!" Before Mrs. Snout Nose Barrel Belly disappeared within a sweep of closing curtains.

Walking now in front of her, was the little slip of a thing, ignoring her, again, just as they all did. Rude it was; no manners. We'll see about that!

One snowball exploded on Leonie's stiffening back. Thud. No reaction. Then two, then three. Splat, splat, splat. Leonie quickened her pace. Lizzie's did, also, gathering more snow as she went, chucking, lobbing, bowling fast pace at Leonie's back as she had started to run now gripping that handbag and brolly of hers to her chest in crossed arms, feet clattering on the icy path over the square.

Lizzie was incensed with rage. How dare she be ignored like this! Fresh hurt and rage and anger in Lizzie Jubb now, under the veil where her eyes were hidden, hands on hips, shoulder blades protruding through her dress, trotting after her, breathing hard, eyes as pale as gull's eggs, turned on their side, under the veil, shining with anger. Thought she could get away, did she? No one got away from Miss Naughty when she was riled and wanted confrontation. She could run just as fast, if not faster, she could stalk, too.

When Leonie turned up the hill, Lizzie decided to follow. She would stalk her; another of her favourite games; stalking. First find a target; walk behind, stop, start and move as they do, eyes never meeting eyes was the sinister key to the whole performance. Watch, wait, smile the patient smile, sit on walls, stand in gateways, follow quietly up paths and look through windows, right through the nets, right into their very houses, right through into their eyes and their cold, cruel hearts.

It was then that she saw the car; his car. Ross's car; a shiny, black four wheel drive vehicle coming down the hill towards the square. Her heart leapt in her breast. Had she left the church too early? Had he changed his mind and decided to marry her after all? She could see him as he slowed, knocked on the car window to beckon Leonie over the road to where he stopped and brought the car into the pavement. Leonie ran to the car quickly and bent her head to the glass.

Lizzie could taste the dust within the fabric of her veil as she stopped walking and watched him, sucking at the fingers in her mouth. She could see him through her veil and the glass of his car window, all the better to see his face as he wound it down, and spoke to the girl. "Thought I might catch you!"

Was he really speaking to her? Had he seen her and wanted Lizzie to run to get inside the vehicle with him, go with him, up to the church, vicar still within, Lizzie supposed? Ross, so handsome, so smartly dressed. A moustache, still, remembering that night in the orchard and its feel against her cheek. He had realised, at last, that there was no other way but to marry her, to repent, for Lizzie to be truly happy at last.

Then she realised that Ross was not aware of her presence. He could not see her. He was leaning the other way, holding his passenger door open for Leonie Jones and appealing to her, with his wide, blue eyes to get inside, with him.

Was that why she had been dashing? Why she had not even seemed to feel the thud of the hard, cold snowballs between her shoulder blades? Had she been hurrying to meet him? Dear God no! Not Ross! She had to know. To be sure that her trust and faith in him had not been mistaken.

Keep back, Lizzie, watch, hide, so that you can be sure that what seems to be happening before your very eyes, is not happening. Not today! Not when she was wearing her wedding dress!

He was in ignorance of her presence as she laid her veiled head on the rough stones of the corner house, seeing a very soft, adoring smile turn his lips. His voice travelled in the cold air. "Leonie. Get in. Better not to be late again. You'll be wet through, walking. I've come for you especially. I can't have my new girl tramping through the snow."

Lizzie felt the jealous pangs in her chest like stab wounds. In her belly shards of glass, and deep within her core a terrible shaking, battering and banging started to rattle at her foundations. Her jealousy made her cry out as she saw Leonie climb into the car. "Should be me! You get out o' there. Minx!" Then her eyes narrowed. "Will be me! You'll see!"

They did not hear her. If they did, she was ignored as if of no consequence as they went on their way, a U turn made. She turned on her heels and ran back up the square, throwing back her veil, teeth gritted, her eyes filled with gushing tears, her face spread as it had been that first time with an aguish that never diminished. Ross! Ross! No!

When she got back to the farm she saw that her mother must be within the byre because the door was open a crack, steam from the cows being emitted. Same place she was this time of day, most days, when the cows had to be milked by hand. That was when she felt Miss Trouble nudge her again. Needed something. Not time to cry and weep and wail and throw things at the wall, yet, Lizzie. Tell them about it. Devise an uprising. Make Ross Fairbrother marry her which he would thank her for in the light of tomorrow.

Even though her body of troops was rallying within, they would have to wait, except for Miss Mischief, whose advice was being heeded. She needed something.

Now where were the red hat and the blue coat and the plaited wig? Where else but in the boxes, in the kitchen!

Nine

The men saw Lizzie through the window at the Bald Pheasant Inn when she moved to make the snowballs; her knees poking against white silk as she bent to the ground to gather it up in her white gloved hands, her dress sodden and trailing, and her veil covering her like a wigwam. They were each making comments like, "Not her again! Loony, bloody Lizzie Jubb! Why is it always just before Christmas she's at her worst?"

It was Gareth Jones who noticed his daughter walking fast on her way to work and guessed immediately what Lizzie Jubb was up to. He saw the snowballs hit the centre of Leonie's back, one, two, three, in quick succession, covering the back of her coat in dry, powdery snow. Had Leonie made anything of it and turned about, he might have left his breakfast order and gone out to speak to Lizzie, maybe run her home to her mother. He might follow up again on Bluithe's claims, this time in a less hot-headed way, even dog tired as he was after a night in a bird hide with a pair of binoculars to his bleary eyes, looking for God knows what. Bluithe Harcourt insisted that untaxed goods would be moved tonight if not last night and it would be Ross Fairbrother and the stranger who would be doing the moving from the old caverns under the cowsheds at Barnston Farm.

As if he had not suffered enough at the hands of Hannah Jubb, last night and on several occasions throughout his twenty eight years as a village policeman, with endless complaints made against both mother and daughter by suffering villagers.

He had had enough of the Jubbs to last him a lifetime. God, the woman was a Banshee! Last night nothing had gone in the calm and sensible manner he had planned, his authority in evidence and intact, as he fulfilled his duty. He had had no other choice but to follow up on what Bluithe Harcourt was saying even if he did suspect that it was because Ross Fairbrother had sacked him and would be making trouble for Ross Fairbrother in a roundabout way. Gareth would have to have him in to answer the accusations made against him sooner or later. He should not have turned out without a warrant, of course, though he had followed up on a hunch that turned out to be wrong. However, he had felt that the strength of the information he had received would be sufficient explanation to his superiors if anything untoward occurred and his decision was questioned. Not to mention the threat to public health and safety if the caverns and potholes between Barnston Farm and the Fairview Country Club Hotel had indeed been opened again. Lives had been lost in the past through people falling down the shafts - not just Bernard Jubb's - when many of the access points were open holes in the ground. For those who went down the potholes, even when properly equipped, many had become trapped in there when the ground had become rain logged and the river poured its excess into its old courses, deep underground. It was also possible to wander the wrong way for miles because the ridge was like a rabbit warren. He knew it from the eager, boyish adventures of his own childhood when he and his fearless friends would slip down one of the many gills on a rope, with a torch, and might have been lost forever had they not had the sense to use a guide rope. Black as pitch, they were. Made even more dangerous these days since they'd channelled the river overflow system to use the underground tunnels as storm vents, to save the flood water pouring down into the village.

Not that he had found the slightest evidence to suggest that what Blue Harcourt had to say was correct. He and his specials had ended up with a small riot on their hands, much of which had been exacerbated by Blue Harcourt's presence and his hot temper. They had been arguing after Gareth had already decided to abort the mission, just as the stranger had arrived. How long he had been listening to the shenanigans going on, Gareth had no idea, but it was hardly the stuff to be proud of.

They had found nothing, either, though they had given up looking when it had taken all their energy just to stop Hannah's beasts trampling them under their panic-stricken hooves. Whipped them up to cause mayhem and disorientate them, she had, as she had gone running into the shed hell for leather, opening the bolts to their stalls, as she ran, rattling their gates to spook them and slapping their backsides to get them out. She had set off some trigger in the animals that made them make for the door and into the yard at hulking speed, pushing and shoving at each other, so that he and his men had had to fight to stay upright and not slide under on the mire, the brainless beasts trapping him until his breath was stemmed. He and Bluithe had been trapped in their midst like jam in a Swiss Roll, only the flavour wasn't as wholesome.

She had been beside herself with rage because they had entered her property and started looking about without her permission. Gareth could not see what she had to hide anyway. He had listened to Bluithe Harcourt with a pinch of salt. Made her hopping mad when they started walking towards her shed over the midden of her yard, Gareth's sense of smell was seriously offended by the stench. Then Gareth had been unable to predict her mischief even after she had her cows stampede into the yard. It had been her who had pulled the handle on the silo to put a barricade of feed across the entrance to stop them entering, and then pushed over the full churns, waiting outside the shed doors for collection by the milk wagon the following morning, though that would not have happened anyway with the snow having fallen so thickly, to make a noxious, evil slick of full cream milk mixed with cow excrement, the smell of which was sufficient to make their stomachs baulk. This had compounded their situation when they had been unable to get out of the frightened herd for several minutes.

She had run off into the house then, and locked herself in the glass lean-to with her gun in her hand ready to shoot if need be. Hannah with her shotgun poised was enough for anyone to be mindful of their own safety and keep a wide berth. Especially with that stranger arriving just at that point. They'd climbed over the wall, back onto the lane, to give him a wide berth also and keep Bluithe Harcourt out of range of her shotgun, for his own safety, even though he had wanted them all to go back into the mayhem and try again.

His specials had been out of there like a shot, though they had blamed the cows trampling, barging and butting them, as well as the noxious stains on their shiny boots, rather than sight of a wild woman with a gun in her hands as reason enough for beating a hasty retreat.

They had regrouped on the road but they were not after repeating the experience, not with an unknown stranger having walked up her path and being let in like an invited friend after he had made a call on his mobile. It was as well that Blue's throwing of the guttered torch in temper...the one that had failed to light properly in the first place...had created no damage or injuries to either the house or the stranger or Hannah and her daughter, Lizzie, whom he could only assume was within.

Hence an upset Lizzie coming down to the village this morning, even in the snow, because what had happened last night had disturbed her. She would be on one of her wrecking missions. Truth be told, he couldn't blame her. It was within human nature to give as good as one got; in the Jubb nature, anyway, both she and her mother, termagants, the pair of them.

The excitement had frayed everyone's nerves, in fact. Reason enough to leave her alone for the time being, but he had given Bluithe one last chance with his suggestion for a stake-out in the old bird hide, though he had sent the three special policemen home because he couldn't see how they could assist further. They were part-timers only, without any rights to give cautions or make arrests. Men from the village who had been trained to assist in the community policing only, do the leg work, show old ladies across the road, give directions, keep on eye out when Gareth was elsewhere on police business; things like that.

Gareth would have loved nothing better than to have retreated to his own warm station, with his wood stove lit, after leaving Barnston Farm in the early hours of the morning, his own eyes red with tiredness, once the snow had started falling. There was more expected, too. He expected to be called out to all kinds of accidents and emergencies caused by the drifts.

As it was, he and Bluithe had then spent the entire night on watch from the bird hide in the grounds of the Fairview Country Club Hotel, permission not requested from the Fairbrothers because, if they had nothing to hide, there was no reason to refuse. It had been too late, anyway, them all being abed. Though Blue had spent the night hiding himself more from any of the hotel staff who might wander in than from any chance of Hannah Jubb seeing him spying down on Barnston Farm and getting that shotgun cocked again. It was a favourite place for a good kiss and canoodle by truanting hotel staff, if he remembered correctly. Or could be when it wasn't five degrees under and snowing thick enough to freeze the devil himself.

Truth was, too, the lad had looked like a villain. He had looked to be the very type which Gareth would have invited into the station for the lad to prove that he wasn't up to any mischief. Strip searched, even, had objections been made. Wallet examined, identity checked, explanations of his presence in the village, made. Any pretext would do; those boots of his for example or the fact that he might have looked at Gareth the wrong way.

Gareth was also curious as to why he had made for Barnston Farm which no one would head to without just reason or bad intentions. People out at that time tended to be up to no good which was certainly the case in these parts. He might be a village policeman, on a soft touch as they thought at his Head Office, but he wasn't quite the P.C. Plod he was often made out to be. He knew what went on in the Bald Pheasant Inn when the curtains were drawn and the lights still on at three in the morning. One had to turn a blind eye to some things. Home brew being one of them, though the brewery that employed the landlord would think differently if they were made aware of the fact.

But he wasn't after the petty stuff. When Gareth thought of contraband he was thinking real smuggling on a scale which flooded not only Barns Village but also the nearest major cities with illicit goods. It was unfair to the honest traders who had to try to compete with major brands being on the market without import tax and V.A.T. added on.

And Bluithe Harcourt had a connection with that because Cannon at the hotel had let it slip that it had been Blue who had sold him the aftershave which Gareth had commented on. Not that Gareth had ever been able to prove it was smuggled stuff, probably brought in from the Channel ports in a transit van with hay bales of fags and enough booze to sink a battleship, but he could not find a like product in the local chemist shop.

So why had Bluithe Harcourt brought Gareth's attention so close to his home patch? Of course, the answer was easy enough to work out if the most recent events were taken into consideration. Pure and simple: revenge. He was as mad as a rabid dog at his sacking by Ross Fairbrother. Why not make his life uncomfortable; land him in the shit in any way he could, to be precise?

Even if it made no sense to Gareth because there was no liking between Ross Fairbrother and Hannah Jubb, it was his duty to make investigations when he received tip-offs like that. Of course he could have made a report to Customs and Excise, but then he'd have a major problem with Lizzie on his hands if Hannah got nabbed for running merchandise. As long as Hannah was willing to cope with her daughter, then he was happy to turn a blind eye to almost anything except the major stuff. Just the thought of Lizzie without anyone to look after her, sent a shiver up his spine. He'd been trying to offload her for years on the medical side. They were having nothing of it when they reported that her medication was keeping her stable. Who gave a toss, anyway, about the living conditions of a middle-aged woman? As poor as the quality of care she received at home was, it was better than her being left to her own devices. God forbid! Her rampages in the village were few and far between anyway. As had been mentioned already, the time approaching Christmas was always one of the worst.

Unless the stranger was a relative of theirs! A nephew, maybe! There was a distant cousin of Hannah, somewhere. Betty someone or other, who had once got a job at the Fairview and then left in the middle of the night without an explanation, not even a note to explain her whereabouts. She had eventually phoned to say that she'd gone back to live in Harrogate. Her son, maybe. She had had to leave abruptly because her mother was dying, but he had been informed only after him calling out the Fell Rescue and, thereafter, on the point of reporting her disappearance to his superiors. There would have been egg on his face if he had! There had been a big fuss made, too, about one of the larger, sharper hotel butchering knives going missing from the kitchens of the Fairview Country Hotel at about the same time because a row had ensued over its disappearance. A minor disturbance of the peace; Chef accusing Cannon and Cannon accusing Chef of some sort of inefficiency, them both implicating this Betty Somebody-Or-Other in the events leading up to it, until their disparity had broken out into a drunken fight between them which had had to be settled by a night in the cells for Chef. Gareth had put the missing knife down to a case of misadventure; Chef being Chef, and, more often than not, being as stewed as a prune with all the alcohol he drank. As far as they knew, Hannah Jubb had no other relatives, not another soul, because he had made enquiries when Lizzie sometimes proved too much to handle at home.

So who was the stranger if the relative theory had no grounds in fact? Someone sent for perhaps? Had she sent for him? Could she have sent for him as protection, as Bluithe was saying must be the only reason for her letting him into her house? Every stranger that Gareth knew to knock on her door, Hannah had chased off with that shotgun of hers, hence him knowing about it. And she wasn't as poverty stricken as the villagers assumed, as judged by the way in which she and Lizzie lived. He had gained the authority, once, to look, secretively, into her bank accounts when he had been concerned about whether they were eating enough, making them both a Social Services issue. It had come as a shock to realise that she was a long way from being destitute. She had money enough to buy in protection in any amount she wanted, in fact. Bernard Jubb had not been what one might term a 'gentleman' farmer but he was efficient and astute in farm management.

And, no matter what Hannah's complaints, he had listened to her accusations about Bluithe Harcourt trespassing in her sheds and sties and barn more than once which would have offered reason enough for two women living alone, so remotely, to hire some private help. Hannah had seemed to genuinely think that a bag of discarded cigarette butts would be evidence enough of someone invading her property, at dead of night, with suspicions that someone was trying to set fire to her farm. Though he did now have a suspicion that he ought to have taken more notice because of Bluithe's vitriolic accusations against her and Ross Fairbrother. That kit bag the lad had been carrying was big enough to hold a firearm and there had been a shape in the bag to suggest as much, as Bluithe had said.

However, steady on! He had not been thirty years a policeman altogether, and not learnt that calm surveillance beat aggressive confrontation, without evidence or a warrant, into a cocked hat. It would only be by putting in coherent reports to his superiors that he would gain proper support. He had had his nose rubbed into the mire before because he had gone off half cocked and without the proper evidence he needed to conduct an official, police enquiry.

Then there were the villagers to consider who would not broach snoops anywhere, having too much to hide of their own, as a matter of fact. The term 'country ways' embraced a lot of sharp trading in Barns. They had ways of doing business that tried to avoid the tax man at every exchange of goods for cash. Gareth had to be careful that he didn't destroy the very community he wished to protect and so had opted for a policy of community policing in its widest sense. As much as described in his tolerance of Lizzie Jubb, whose peculiarities were the bane of his life, he took it upon himself to offer her insane behaviour some tolerance. Overall, she was containable as long as she was watched.

He had been lost in his own thoughts, the subject of which could now be seen running as if being chased by the devil, past the pub window, with her veil turned back, tears streaming over a face thick with orange gunk and eyes black-rimmed like a badly painted doll.

They all seemed to be watching her now as they gathered at the bar to be given menus by Marty, the landlord, who had bags under his eyes. He had nothing of a sensitive nature to discuss, so what did it matter if he listened into their meeting. Five of them to represent a night's police work, in the Bald Pheasant for a debriefing over a good breakfast, with the landlord scratching his head at the bar and yawning not once, twice, but constantly, over and over again.

It was the landlord, who spoke for all their attentions, eyes seeming to find it hard to stay awake, but teeth barred to Lizzie Jubb as his door would be if she tried coming in for one of those Babychams she was always asking for. He had stopped selling them years ago. "It's alright. Leonie's safe. Lizzie's turned back this way? What's made her so upset, I wonder? Never seen her cry before."

One of Gareth's specials who had to be shooting off soon to open his shop, this being his busiest time of the whole year, a man by name of Tom Greaves - the local butcher - shrugged his shoulders. He laid down the menu. It wasn't his bacon and sausages Marty served. "Women cry at anything. Thought you'd have learnt that by now."

Jim Lamb, a local forester who lived near Bluithe Harcourt, shook his head. "I'll have to have a brandy, Marty, to warm me up."

He was standing next to Bluithe at the bar while sharing a whispered conversation with the landlord, leaning deep into his ear as he spoke. Gareth tried to listen in but they stopped as soon as he gave them some notice. "You lot look as if you could go to sleep propped up against each other."

Whatever comments had been passed, Bluithe Harcourt seemed to find the subject matter worthy of taking his red, woolly hat off to. This he folded roughly and pushed deep in his pocket of his mackintosh, face as haggard as the complexion on an over ripe lemon, just as his mobile rang.

It seemed to take Bluithe an inordinate amount of time to locate it in his pocket. His ring tone stopped. The others lost interest. Bluithe stopped searching.

The other man present was Ian Garstang, a young solicitor who liked getting involved in the sharp end of things. It was something of a mystery to Gareth why he gave his time to voluntary, community policing which in the most part was a dull, boring, and thankless task. Last night's excitement being an exception to a special.

Thing was, all three men looked as tired as he felt. Bluithe, to be expected, but the landlord should have got some shut-eye even if he'd had a lock-in last night. Claimed that the stranger had come into the Bald Pheasant for a drink on closing time, too.

"What did he look like?" Gareth asked.

The description matched. The stranger had to be a one-off if only from the description of his footwear.

Jim Lamb, a young man, claimed to be so tired as to ring in to his work place and be put on the sick list. "Didn't get a wink of sleep."

Now why would that be? Gareth had sent the specials home to their beds, admittedly very late, but even if they had risen early to make the debriefing meeting before they had their bread and butter work to get on with, they should not be as tired as they claimed.

"He's been sent for," Bluithe Harcourt said for the hundredth time in his reckoning.

Gareth heard the phone ring in Bluithe's pocket again while he deemed not to answer it. His wife probably wanting to know his whereabouts. Besides which, he looked to be in a sulk. The man had been sacked. Did he have a fiver in his pocket for a breakfast? Probably not, Gareth guessed, when he saw him fling down the menu he had been handed with a look of disgust on his face. Not a good prospect for any man was being out of work at Christmas!

They moved to the tables where the landlord would serve them, each taking a seat, Gareth gathering his thoughts. The others, except Bluithe and the butcher, Tom Greaves, removing coats and settling in seats, the warmth of the bar increasing tiredness but edgy. They were making Gareth feel edgy. Now what was all this about?

Gareth began to feel more uncomfortable when he saw that all five men, landlord included, were intent on watching him with an anticipation that exceeded the gravity of the situation. His instincts were aroused and especially when he knew the men well. None of them were relaxed. They were all jumpy. It was like a premonition coming from deep within his mind. Odd things here and there magnetising themselves together. Floating over his head in the ether. He found his eyes looking over the cheese board on the counter; not a piece of crumbly, tangy Lancashire, but all the fancy foreign stuff with names he could hardly pronounce. There was no reason why the pub should sell, almost exclusively, the French spirits and liquors, French cigars and wines that were now filling the shelves to the back of the bar.

One of his well tried tests to gauge when people were either telling the truth or lying was the sudden eye contact trick, so he looked down casually at the table and then quickly up again with a dark eyed glare. They almost jumped out of their skins. Each man nervously looked down or away much too quickly. There was a sudden fit of coughing amongst them which Gareth noted. Guilt! He had always been able to smell it. Like strong perspiration on men who had been sweating heavily and stunk of it. Why would anyone sweat in this weather unless having exerted themselves considerably? Ian Garstang was glistening with it. The man was sweating and Gareth thought that the heat of the bar had nothing to do with it. He was nervous. They were all nervous. What the hell was this atmosphere about? His suspicions were raised.

Gareth frowned, looking at the way they had all leaned into each other. There was an air of conspiracy about them, as if they all had the same string of a thought running through their heads, knotting them into a band. They all looked over-tired, the kind of tiredness when eyes become staring and people lose their animation, yet four of them, at least should have had a reasonable kip. His eyes glanced over their clothing. He bent down to look under the table on the pretence of picking up something he had dropped. Dried cow shit still on the upper shoes and turn-ups of his specials, turn ups still smeared with milk mixed with cow dung.

"Been home, Tom, since we parted company?"

"Er…Well…I got a few nods on the couch to the back of the shop rather than disturb the missus."

"What about you Ian? You live a good few miles out of the village. It must have hardly seemed worth going home and back."

Marty was a bit too quick to reply for him. "He slept in the stable. Ask Jenny." Jenny being his wife who was hovering in the kitchen. Even she seemed nervous. Gareth could see that she had her ear to the curtain which separated the bar from the kitchen. He'd never known her to be up at this time of the morning before. It was usually Marty who cooked him a breakfast.

"That's right," she replied without having to be asked. "Get a move on with your orders, please. I need to get a wash on."

Not a man amongst them was morning shaven. Not even the

solicitor who would be going from this meeting straight to his office. Even the landlord was wearing the same whiskers, shirt and waistcoat as he had the evening before when Gareth had been in for his curry and rice supper. Him with a wife who would nag him to death if yesterday's shirt wasn't in the wash basket before she put the first load of washing for the day into her machine. The butcher was a fresh-clothes-every-day-man, too. Just as Bluithe Harcourt never seemed to change his overalls from one month's end to the other. Something was nagging him. Then he saw that Jim Lamb had his hand bandaged up. "What happened? You were alright when I last saw you."

He shrugged, staring, unable to blink, as Gareth kept his eyes pinned on his. He seemed like a frozen rabbit caught in car headlights. He said, "A glass cut."

Just as Jenny, Marty's wife, started to make some explanation about a hot cup of coffee.

Strange! Strange! Strange! They had been up all night, too. Four trolleys lined up by the outside doors. He bent to pick up a strip of brown binding tape that had been stuck to his boot. It had French writing all over it.

He was certain that the landlord, Marty Greenwood, along with Tom Greaves, Jim Lamb and Ian Garstang had been up all night just as he and Bluithe had. There had been no need for Bluithe to accompany him to the hide but he had insisted.

Put all the clues together and a suspicion was growing in his head, and then growing even bigger; hardening like glue does when you mix the right compounds together, into a solid idea that came with a huge sense of hurt disappointment. Had he been duped? He had certainly been pointed in a direction away from the village by Bluithe Harcourt and his specials. Had he been sent off on a wild goose chase? Had the buggers been at it again? Distribution time for the Christmas rush? Every year the same. The village awash with foreign goods, mainly French, as well as some big brand names, and he never managed to trace the main supplier when, usually, he was fed confusing information and had never had time to follow it up anyway.

His face hardened as he let his mind travel over a menu he knew inside out and upside down because this was where he ate most days of his life, amongst honest friends, supposedly. Indeed, the men he worked with. Now, that was a serious state of affairs when one can't trust one's own colleagues.

Why had they stayed up, cold sober, if there was no need to? It had been Bluithe Harcourt's idea not only to go on a raid at Barnston Farm but also to use the old hide to watch out for the stranger as well as any movement of merchandise, which meant that there had been no police presence in the village from eleven o'clock the previous night to almost eight in the morning.

When he looked to the bottles lining the bar at the Bald Pheasant Inn, for additional confirmation, they all looked to be new, full to the brim and with French labels. Christmas coming! If that wasn't a give away, nothing was. The buggers had been Robin Hooding! Running! Trafficking! Call it what you will. Got him out of the way and what better ruse than to implicate Ross Fairbrother as a guilty party, as well as Hannah Jubb, who Bluithe saw as someone he could intimidate, and did...all in order to take the law enforcement out of the village for the requisite period of time needed to shift the stuff out.

Suddenly things made sense even if it didn't go down too well with a swig of thick, strong coffee; bitter indeed, when Marty filled the cups he had deposited on the table and Gareth had added just a tip of cold milk. So bitter that he had to hide his shock by a fit of coughing when he might otherwise have found himself gasping at their temerity and letting his suspicions get ahead of the proof that would be needed. Bloody cheek! Gareth's cheeks were beginning to burn and not with the heat inside the bar as he struggled out of his padded jacket and divested himself of his black, peaked cap and tried not to let his distrust show. "Christ almighty! Christ Almighty!" were the words that kept repeating themselves in his head. "I've been set up good and proper!"

"Good night's work," was what he said. "I think we might have found a villain in our midst with this lad who's turned up. Good work, lads. Good work!"

All five of them visibly relaxed and got stuck into their orders, menus studied with extreme care.

Gareth mentally got out his spiral bound notebook and sharpened his pencil to a very fine point indeed, wrote each of their names at the top of a clean page, and started to make lists. Because proving his suspicions was a different matter, him being the only man present, he considered, who had any real respect for the law which tried to ensure a level playing field for everyone. This, despite one of them practising it every day of his working life, and all of them being the first to ring him if they felt they were being treated unlawfully, themselves. A cold, hard, bitter smile stretched his lips as he read on the menu that 'pigs in blindfolds' were sausages baked in batter. How apt. He was tempted to opt for that instead of his usual fry up, but he wasn't after giving his thoughts away just yet.

Then there was his own family to consider in all of this. Leonie always smelled nice; too nice for a girl who should not be able to afford Dior or Giorgio Armani. There was always French cheese in his house, too, as well as thin slivers of earthy tasting truffles which, personally speaking, the pigs should have eaten themselves. Gloria had a thing about truffles with duck pate. It was one of her, "Oh, God, it's gorgeous!" orgasms. He sure as hell never provided her with any other kind, these days.

His own fridge at home was probably hiding merchandise that hadn't been import taxed or V.A.T. accounted. Someone had donated a very large, expensive looking wrapped ham with French writing on the packaging for their Christmas dinner, Gloria had said. He had seen it in the fridge last evening, though what had possessed him to look in the fridge was anyone's guess, when he had been on the hunt for batteries. Gareth only ever inspected the contents of his fridge at home when he had to find something to placate Gloria with when she was in one of her screaming paddies and the shoes were flying in his direction. There were bottles of wine and champagne and French liqueurs building up in his wine cupboard. Gloria always seemed to have the Christmas shopping done without putting a foot out of bed. When he'd asked her how she managed it without his or Leonie's help, she always rolled her eyes, shook her head and told him, "Mail order, how else!"

Was he being manipulated? Was he being duped? Was the whole village in on it? Even the Star shop? He had only to think back to his quest for the extra large, square batteries which were the only type his police torches would take. He had never had a problem buying them from the Star before. It had been Bluithe's idea to substitute the flaming torches which meant that they could at least go ahead and get the raid over and done with, even if the light they brought to the job was unusual. They would have been like little beacons shining in the night, so much easier to keep track of than torch beams. Making it easy for a look-out to know exactly where they were at any given time. Maybe the shop was not as out of batteries as it seemed to be. He'd be checking!

That was when he lost his appetite.

Bluithe's phone rang again. A Lone Ranger ring tone. He went to face the bar in order to conduct a private conversation which only the landlord could snoop in on. When he returned, after passing glances back and forth with Marty, who was supervising more coffee and offering out toast with miniature cartons of butter and marmalade, while his wife was already grilling bacon and frying mushrooms and tomatoes, knowing in advance of an order exactly what every man would have, his face looked slightly more animated than it had before. "Got to see a man about a dog.

My tool bag is still in the back of the car. I'll be off then." He had a wide smile on his face.

Then, as they watched Bluithe depart the pub, leaving the door wide open after him, Gareth's own phone blared out the theme to Z Cars. One look and he saw Gloria's name on the illuminated screen. That could only mean one thing.

His remaining companions were ears cocked to his conversation as Marty came rattling cutlery which, in his tired state, he seemed to have forgotten about. An explanation seemed required by his specials. "Only Gloria. Been awake all night. Watching out for me getting back to the station. She'll have my movements plotted to the minute since I arrived back and parked up. She's ravenous." Then to Marty who was rubbing up a knife on a serviette to get rid of an egg stain. "Gloria wants one of them bin lids loaded with fried breakfast, Marty, please."

"How does she know you're here?" young Ian Garstang asked, eyes flickering around his pals, a frown forming, as if something had just occurred to him that hadn't beforehand. "I thought she never left her bed, these days."

Gareth nodded. "Her bed's right under the window. Must have seen me across the square when we pulled up in front of the station. I didn't go home last night so she'll be wondering where I've been. It's her way of making sure I report in." Gareth's eyes rolled around them all. Why the interest in Gloria? He didn't inform them that when he got home, with a hot, barm cake in hand the size of a bin lid, loaded with bacon, egg, sausage, mushrooms, tomatoes she'd grab it off him and start stuffing herself even while accusing him of having spent the night with another woman. If he ever did, which he didn't, it would most probably serve her right. But that was his private concern and none of theirs; sensitive about Gloria, he was. His face said that he did not like to talk about her.

"Doesn't sleep, you say? I never knew that!" This from Marty, whose frown was deeply concerned, worried even. His next comment was insensitive in Gareth's presence. "Eats too much does Gloria. Must keep her awake having to digest all that food."

Gareth looked away, squirming. What business was it of his, anyway?

Marty wrote down the order. "Does she want one bin lid or two?"

Tom Greaves spoke on a bark of laughter. "Make it three. Gloria's best kept happy. Whatever she asks for I always double it. Women should be kept happy and in the dark if a man's going to get some peace and quiet." Then, "She's already got a big order in for some garlic sausages. Goes down a treat with a nice slice of Brie."

Was there a threat in there somewhere…a piece of advice which Gareth should heed, perhaps? Gareth's frown deepened.

The landlord agreed with Tom. Marty nodded. As soon as Gareth made himself scarce he'd pop some nice, cold roast beef in that basket of hers.

By the time Gareth was letting himself into the flat - a hot bin lid burning his hand through the waxed paper bag he was holding - he was feeling intimidated as well as potentially compromised and humiliated. Had Gloria been buying on the black market? He wouldn't put it past her. Gloria had always been able to manage her housekeeping better than any other woman he had ever known.

His problem was…should he group Gloria, his wife of twenty seven years, in his 'us' group or his 'them' group, if there was any 'us's' and, if not, merely 'I'. He was remembering the plastic wrapped, French, Christmas ham in the fridge, decorated with slices of orange, cranberries and glazed with Dijon mustard and honey. Under her bed, there had been boxes of Belgian chocolates, fancy cakes and biscuits, bottles of French sherry and packets upon packets of cashew nuts. The one thing he could be positive of was that her giant hoards of expensive, luxury foods sure as hell hadn't come from the Star!

Even his own family were disloyal to him. Gareth's mouth set in a very grim line.

Ten

Leonie was outside her comfort zone as she travelled up the hill from the village in Ross Fairbrother's car, not knowing whether to believe him when he said that his mother had sent him down to collect her. It was not like Mrs. Fairbrother to be considerate of her employees comfort, though there was a lot of preparation work to do if a hotel full of guests was to have everything it needed over Christmas.

Past experience in mind, there could be only one thing that he was after as far as Leonie was concerned so extreme caution was necessary. She left the hood of her duffle coat up after climbing up into the passenger seat with only the yellow curls over her forehead poking out, so that he could see nothing of a face which held a very wary expression; blue eyes narrow with suspicion. She also held her knees tightly together and gripped onto her handbag with a plan of action to turn it and its contents into weapons before he could as much as lean in her direction. The bag, with its short strap, might be used as a sling shot, should the need to defend herself arise. There was also a brolly with a pointed tip dangling from her wrist, which she could utilise for head battering or epee work; whichever fighting tactic proved to be the most appropriate, should he try to overwhelm her.

Her mother had told her that one of the best ways of dissuading unwanted attentions was two fingers up the nostrils and a determined thrust backwards of the offenders head, followed by use of the pepper spray which she always carried in her handbag. It not only brought tears to the eyes but created a nose bleed of the type that would take a week to stop. The nose would swell and the scabs would be very sore and painful. Telltale bruising would develop. The eyes might puff up and close altogether and the effect to the pulmonary system, overall, would prove to be very disabling. There was even a chance that pneumonia or pleurisy might ensue because of the germs which breed rampantly in the nasal passages and which could no longer be blown away on tissue paper. Thereby they would multiply freely. So bringing the assailants life to a total and complete denial of any joyful activity, justly applied. Let anyone deservedly dealt with in such a fashion, try stealing kisses which were not freely given, with a conk in such a state! That was why Leonie kept her fingernails like talons and reinforced them with pearly lacquer. She would not be giving her virginity to the likes of Mr. Ross Fairbrother and the sooner he realised it, the better.

That she was travelling in daylight on an open road, on her way to work with a considerate employer, did not affect her scathing opinion of

Mr. Ross Fairbrother's supposed licentious intentions. She paid no heed to the spreading dampness on the back of her coat or her wet feet now that she was ensconced within the woman trap of his luxurious vehicle, heater blowing, a packet of tissues on the dash should she wish to blow her pretty nose, a bar of chocolate passed over, just for her Mr. Ross had said, in case she had not had time for breakfast. She half expected a bouquet of roses and half a bottle of champagne to be reclining on the back seat of the car, and flooded with relief when all that was there was a thick, dark, soggy overcoat and a black woollen cap of the special forces type which would come down to the collar, with a cut out to expose the face. There was also a pair of very wet leather gloves, a torch and a roll of industrial sticky tape, a Stanley knife, and a pair of Wellington boots dripping with melt water, which all denoted, to Leonie, that Mr. Ross was an old fuddy-duddy who would be better off chasing widows of his own age, rather than her.

Why should the weather conditions cause her any concern, anyway? Or gratitude be felt for his kindly considerations displayed by the fact that he was risking his own health and wellbeing by coming down to the village to get her to her place of work...on an almost impassable road...driving over several inches of compacted snow because the ploughs had yet to clear it off the tarmac...up a one in five gradient with dangerous bends...on a road which, while closed in by woods to her left side, was open to the steep sides of a ravine to her right.

So what? Leonie gave it no credence. She was not about to worry that they might get into a skid and life might be over in the time it took to tumble over the edge and into the fast flowing river below. The winter rains had already caused it to come up to the top of its banks but Leonie found it all of no interest, whatsoever, other than to read in the local paper that the torrent sluice gates, controlled by a computer, her dad had said, in the little pump house they could see before the bend in the river, had had to be used twice this year alone, in order to divert flood water away from the village houses.

It was just the weather. And the weather was the weather unless it got spiteful in a really serious and ultra personal way. Nothing to be overly concerned about. Nothing to be grateful for. But everything to be suspicious about when it had led to Mr. Ross coming down to the village specifically to give her a lift and nothing else.

If Mr. Ross made small talk as he drove them both carefully back up the hill, largely to the effect that the threat of continuing snowfall was causing he and his mother horrendous worry...it could see an end to the Fairview Country Club Hotel as a viable business if the guests did not arrive due to the snow!...according to Leonie's suspicious mind, it was just another of his ploys to lure her into a false state of security where her defences might slip and she would allow his violation of her to begin. Before she knew it he would be asking her to unbutton her coat and she knew where that would lead. She had not sat in cars with boys and not learnt a thing or two. She had heard it from others, also, as far as Mr. Ross was concerned...the maid who had answered his call for room service and found him in his underpants...one of the cleaners who at the time of his advance had been bending over a half made bed in a tucking-in manoeuvre. He had insisted that all he was trying to do was swat a fly on her lower back...his habit of talking randy, to other men, in the Gamekeepers Bar when he'd had a few too many...so many bits of tittle-tattle gossip to prove her point, and all of the type Mrs. Fairbrother went spare about, if she caught her staff having a snide laugh at someone else's expense.

So Leonie was not as much listening to his words as weighing them because at any moment she expected him to start the hanky-panky business; a hand on her knee, an arm about her shoulder, his hot breath on her face.

Though, he did drone on about the boring weather. "When all this snow melts we'll be thankful, I think, for that new pump house and the sluice gates to divert any flood water. We can hear the power of the river just by putting an ear over our old well. I do so hope none of our guests want to go potholing this Christmas...considering that they can get here with all this snow. I've had to give that considerable thought. Mother and I have contingency plans. Even I don't fancy being underground when the river floods." The latter said to remind her, using the phrase 'even I', that when away from his mother he was the daredevil type, quite at odds with the Mr. Ross who paced about the hotel like a caged animal or stared out of rainy windows doing his rises and falls and heel rocks with his hands stretched behind his back. He relied on the guests who paid dearly for him to take them off on a boy's adventure through the woods, or clay pigeon shooting, to practice archery, or stupid paint-balling games...which the housekeeper blamed for ruining the hotel sheets though the paint guns were only ever available from the gun room in the summer months...to stem his boredom. It was said that he was a crack shot and a gallant horseman.

Leonie was not impressed, as other staff were, him being too decrepit to be considered a he-man. It was, to her, simply his main role of responsibility within the Fairview Country Club Hotel, like Chef was food and Cannon was service and she was the cog that seemed to make everything work smoothly; Mrs. Fairbrother was the slave driver who thrashed her back, to turn the wheel, with a halter about her neck.

Mr. Ross's sporting proficiency was why it was called a 'country club' hotel; because of the sports facilities on offer, as well as the pool and the alternative health therapies. Leonie dreamt of treating herself to a proper Indian head massage and facial for her twenty-fifth birthday, tomorrow. The thought was the only lure to her going into work, some days.

Not that everyone considered Mr. Ross to be far less important, in the running of the hotel, than his mother. Some of the staff like Chef and Cannon were impressed with what they referred to as his calm, cool affability; a man to be relied on in a crisis, they said. Nothing ever seemed to ruffle his feathers. According to them, it was his influence that had allowed the hotel to get over a very bad patch which had occurred a few years previously when the hotel was in financial difficulties. It had been he who had made the difference by taking the hotel from three star rating to four, along with Mrs. Fairbrother's investment in improved indoor facilities, making it possible for their guests to experience a wider range of outdoor activities, besides the ballroom dancing, cabaret and bingo which had always been on offer inside the hotel. She had been told that as the receptionist over the Christmas period, she should never say no to any request from a guest for a specific sporting activity. Mr. Ross had the army training and experience, not to mention the contacts, to make anything possible. From pony trekking to hand gliding to helicopter rides to grass boarding…which seemed to have taken over from the demolished dry ski run with so many resultant insurance claims that it had proved to be unprofitable…and often, if truth were spoken, involved trespass over Hannah Jubb's land …because Mr. Ross could provide both the resources and the qualifications, him being ex-special service, it was said.

Which reminded Leonie of Lizzie again, because she had just thought of her mother, Hannah, stromping about her boundaries with that shotgun in her hand, waving it threateningly at anyone who put a toe to her side of the river, and her own, very recent, minutes-ago, maltreatment by her daughter, Lizzie, chucking snowballs right at her while dressed as a bride. What a disgraceful family, the Jubbs were! Shameful in their clothes and habits; lacking in both decency and community spirit. She knew that her dad was forever seeking ways to help Lizzie by finding agencies which might put her away in a home where she might get the proper care she needed for her insanity, or whatever it was that made Lizzie Jubb behave as she did when she caused so much awful trouble. That stinking, crudely offensive mother of hers was no better, either. Her mother, not usually shy of anyone, shut her window when she was in the village, pulled her basket up, closed her curtains and didn't open them again until she had gone.

Leonie was so glad to have parents like her own…even if her mother did have 'health problems' which made Leonie shy of taking her own friends home because they, at least, might be considered within the range of 'normal' on the balance scale, which stretched from 'sub' to 'super', with the Jubbs off the measure as far as Leonie and the rest of the villagers were concerned. Most considering themselves middle-average except for the boffins who couldn't knock a nail in straight, but still thought of themselves as more valuable pins in the garb of social graces, than anyone else.

At least her parents didn't smell and their home was clean, tidy and warm. Her mother was kind and sensitive and loving. Her dad was a stalwart pillar of the community. They were, in fact, true 'Barnsonians', supposedly possessing hardy genes, coupled with an innate, practical intelligence, which was thought to be directly attributed to being Barns born and bred. Stable people, with stable values in a stable community where the populous respected each other, her dad liked to think. It had never occurred to Leonie to look on the obelisk list of war dead, to see that there were more Jubbs listed than any other name. Both her parents, despite her mother's agoraphobia, were well known and respected within the community. Her mother mainly for her knowledge of local folk lore and her keen interest in community welfare. Her father for his solid, honest belief in law and justice, maintaining what he liked to refer to as 'a level playing field, for all'.

She was thinking about all this when Ross moved his hand to check his seatbelt. Leonie placed a hand on the handle of her umbrella and set her lips tight.

Had he any idea that he was within an inch of his life? He was exuding that nervous vapour again, too. She could sense a build up in him when he started to ask her something about going with him to meet with his solicitor tomorrow…her birthday in fact…which Leonie assumed was to be an introduction and a swearing in to secrecy because she might be dealing with some rather sensitive issues raised by the hotel guests. That would be another course in hotel management she would have to take. Situations like the hotel having a thief on the staff. The suspicion had shocked everyone though they might now point the finger of accusation at Bluithe Harcourt after his sacking, him not being around to counter attack and point the finger of blame at somebody else.

Chef had been incensed to discover, just the other day, at the cold larder audit, that two of his French Christmas hams - the ones dressed with orange slices and cranberries and glazed with Dijon mustard and honey -

had gone missing. He had told Mrs. Fairbrother that they had most probably been stolen by Mr. Ross's dog, a Retriever called Max, which chased rabbits and had a penchant for eating live cat. It had been reported that it had eaten three in the time that Leonie had worked at the Fairview; one house trained and two feral, but like any dog to be seen outside of a butcher's door, it also knew where to beg in the hotel. She had often had to shoo it off when it had come into the kitchen to beg, once having to drive it off from inside the cold store itself where the very hams, vacuum sealed, two of ten, had been stored in readiness for the Christmas dinner.

Her reverie was disturbed by Mr. Ross wanting her to talk to him instead of staring out of the window.

"We're still waiting for this music chap to arrive some time today. What's his name?"

Leonie felt relieved because she might assume that he had not gone knocking everyone up, late at night, after the door had been locked. She need not own up, now, to having presumed more authority than her position merited by allowing him permission to arrive a day early. She answered blithely. "Lick Johnson. Ssssslick Lick Johnson. Prince. Of. Soul. And. Rock. And. Roll. Yeah."

Ross laughed shortly. "My idea! Let's hope the entertainment is good. Cheer us all up."

Leonie nodded.

"You'll be sleeping in, of course,"

Here we go! "My mum won't let me. My dad will pick me up and take me home if I have to work late."

"It will be long hours for us all, Leonie. I would think that your dad would have his work cut out just herding the village drunks."

Leonie shrugged. So far his behaviour had been impeccable, though he was building up to asking something; she could sense it. They were turning into the grounds of the hotel when he unexpectedly pulled up his car and turned to look at her.

"There's something I need to show you, Leonie, dearest. You'll have to know…"

Leonie waited no further. She retracted her brolly from her wrist and dug it into his chest. "Come any closer and you'll get this right in the eye."

"But all I want is to tell you…"

"I'll walk from here, Mr. Ross. Thanks for the lift."

She was out of the car before he could say anything further and running off over the snow to the front door of the hotel where Cannon and Chef and two of the temporary staff were shovelling snow.

Ross turned off the car engine and watched her go. He had made a hash of it all again. Why couldn't he just blurt it out to get it over with? He needed air.

Eleven

Gloria was tucking into a chocolate bar when Gareth got back to the flat. As soon as he opened her bedroom door he saw three other, empty, sweet packet wrappers on the bed clothes and some screwed up white paper bags. He put the waxed paper bag containing the delicious smelling grub down on her bedside table and watched as her plump hands came like grabbers to claim the package, desire on her face such as she had not offered to him since Leonie had been born, lips smacking as she exposed the largest, flat bread roll possible without it being deemed a full sized loaf, and filled to overflowing with double the amount of everything he had just eaten himself, brown, yellow and red sauces oozing out as soon as her sharp teeth made a first bite. Already her hands were running with grease, the same running round her mouth and down over her several chins as she ate with the ravenous hunger of someone who had been starved for weeks. She had so much in her mouth at once that her cheeks had doubled their size and could only just afford her the good manners of a closed mouth. He had a job translating what she said between swallows and chews and bites. "Lizzie Jubb's been in the village again. Throwing snowballs at our Leonie."

Gareth nodded, looking at her, wondering how the girl he had married had ever managed to turn herself into this eating machine which was on full power, within the bed before him. Sadly, he had to acknowledge that she was no more the slim, pretty, dark-eyed beauty in the wedding photograph by her bed; not that he would have compared all that well either, after the passage of twenty seven years, had he tilted the playing field straight. Then he realised that Gloria could read his facial expressions like the headlines in a daily newspaper. She would guess what he was thinking as her suspicious eyes raked him. She swallowed the last bite, and then sniffed hard. Her nose flared, nostrils wide, twitched once only. "I can smell French perfume."

Gareth sighed. "You can smell Marty's bin lids and my sweaty clothes because I've yet to get to bed. Slept well, have you?"

Gloria knew that she would have to snitch just enough for Gareth to act for himself. She screwed up yet another empty bag, balled it in her fist, and then made a successful aim for the waste bin in the corner of the room. "Better than you, it seems. I saw the riot van out and about in the early hours of the morning. Got someone in the cell?"

Gareth frowned. "The riot van's not been out. It's parked up in Tom Greaves's garage. You must be mistaken."

"It looked like the riot van in front of the station. Some men were going in and out with trolleys but then it became hard to see for the snow. It came down real thick in the square at around two o'clock this morning."

Gareth looked over her round figure in the rumpled bed, through the window and over the heads of the frozen snowmen populating the square to his police station. There was no riot van there now. It would be a case of Gloria seeing things or making assumptions. Like smelling perfume!

"That bacon was French if I'm not mistaken. Dijon mustard, too." Then she was looking at him, eyebrows raised, gaze level. What she was doing was agreeing with all his earlier thought. He would not ask her directly to spill all that she knew. Gloria didn't share his views regarding black market trading. He could read the message in her eyes, though. He watched them travel over to his police station. "I thought you must have been doing your paperwork upstairs. Light was on up there for most of the night. Opened it up for use again, have you?"

Gareth's mouth dropped open. What he said was, "I'm going over to the station for a nap on the z-bed. I might take it upstairs where I won't be disturbed. If I smell of anything its cow dung and bird hide."

"You do that, Gareth. If I were you I'd take the key to the upstairs rooms at the station back off Tom Greaves's wife. She wasn't doing any cleaning up there, anyway. She's been using the space, though. Storing her family Christmas presents, I think."

Gareth nodded, sourly, fully understanding the cryptic message she was relating. It was a bad state of affairs when his own wife was a better policeman than he could ever be. And that without taking a step out of bed. He turned to leave, after picking up her empty tray from the night before, cups, plates and cutlery and the rest of the empty packaging.

"And Gareth…!"

"Yes?"

"Ask Ann in the bakery to send me up a couple of pies, will you, on the way."

***

Gloria rolled her eyes as Gareth went on his way. She felt like a scab, even while knowing that she could not allow his specials or the other Robin Hooders to abuse their positions of friendship and trust, any longer. They had overstepped the mark, this time, though. Sometimes, she could not believe that her husband had so little idea of what was going on right under his nose and behind his back. Hopefully, she had set the seeds for him to do something to curtail the cheeky buggers who had become so cocky that they thought they could use the police riot van to move their stuff about and store part of it in the unused rooms over his police counter. They would have needed a warehouse to store all the black market merchandise in any one place. It had become very, very big business, these days, with some kind of pyramid structure to the gang so that one layer didn't necessarily know who was passing down their orders. Or so she'd been told by Vera Harcourt, in fact, one day when she'd had to come up after being too long lunchtime drinking in the Bald Pheasant Inn. Gloria had learnt a lot that day but it was only now, when they had gone too far and Gareth's job might be at stake if they were allowed to continue, that she would have to point Gareth in the right direction, for the family good. She would not snitch on them directly, though. She was Barns born and bred, after all. Some loyalties transcended all and could not be broken.

Rolling over and twirling round, she managed to reach for her basket, open the window sufficiently for it to pass through and then lower it down on the blue rope, the cold wrapping itself about her bare shoulders though she didn't seem to feel the cold as others did. More snow on the way, too, and blizzard conditions later, if the weather forecast was to be believed.

After a few minutes wait, she felt the tugs to tell her that her pies had been deposited in the basket. She hauled it up, knowing that the only reason that Gareth had been so amenable to her request, after he had already brought her the bin lid, was because she had given him information he would, otherwise, never have had. She could not get her hands on the hot pies quickly enough.

But what was she going to do at Christmas when there was no one about and the bakery would be shut for trading? She would not see Gareth or Leonie from one day's end to the other. Her sister was still planning on going for an all inclusive to Turkey. Then the ham in the fridge was calling out to her, "Eat me! Eat me!"

What she needed to do was to get the hang of her new fangled technology. She would have to devote less time to looking out of her window, no one dallying long enough because of the snow to gossip anyway, and spend some time on practice.

She would have that bloody ham out of the fridge, without leaving her bed, if it was the last thing she'd do!

Twelve

Ross got out of the car and walked over towards the trees which formed the woodland between the hotel grounds and Barnston Hall Farm. He could hear Max, his dog, barking over to him, sensing his presence rather than seeing him, the dog tethered to his kennel because of the snow in case he wandered away, as he often did when searching for a bitch on heat. Usually, he managed to find his way back but Ross had been concerned that the dog might be unable to scent his way back in the snow. He ignored its barks and whimpers and small worried whelps. The dog would be under his feet all day if he let it, or outside the door to the kitchens begging, or when opportunity called, simply taking what it could and sneaking off.

He had to be on his own for a few minutes to clear his head, have time enough to stop shaking. Why was it all so very hard to say? He knew what she thought. That she had misconstrued his attentions. But he never seemed able to approach her in the right way. What could he say anyway until her birthday? The single day he had to go would be an agony of waiting, harder even than the twenty-five years that had gone before.

Better to look where he was going on the springy ground under foot, its earthiness a balm to his worry as he continued downwards. It would be easy to fall and hit his head on the tree trunks. The terrain was steep, now. He began to walk sideways, placing his weight firmly back onto his heels on the lightly frosted, leaf-soft ground between the trees. When he looked forward, between the trunks directly around him, he was looking level with the snowy tops of those growing by the river bank at the bottom, by the edge of the water. It was, however, the only way he could get to the bird hide unless he walked, in a wide zigzag, on the slimy boards of the decking pathway with its rope handle. He could manage the way he was going in a dead straight line to the cedar building. If it snowed again, and in particular in blizzard, which would bring down the present layer of snow caught up in the tree branches, there would be a layer sufficient to get out the ski gear which was rarely used these days after the dry ski slope on the other side of the ridge had been dismantled. He would have to open up the gun room to get them if it stuck for long enough.

It was only when he had sight of Barnston Farm that he stopped walking, his breath as steam, his lower trousers wet and the feet within his polished brogues turning to ice. Here, he allowed the sadness inside himself to show its heavy burden. It was not something he ever showed to anyone else, not even his mother who had remained largely ignorant of his difference to other men, his troubles and the lies he had had to tell, to keep the truth hidden. It had all been part of the promise; a way out of his own, filthy mess for there was never any justification to be made of the tangled web of lies which he was soon to straighten.

He should not have come this way because just to look down on Barnston Farm, seeing its degradation, the decline of its pride and loss of respectability, was upsetting. Sometimes to see Hannah and Lizzie about the farm was sufficient to keen his desperate eyes to points and his breath catch in his throat. Yet there was never any other way of sorting out his mind sufficient for his secrets to be protected, for a short time more, at least.

Exposing his feelings had never been his strong point, even to Bern. There was nowhere else, at this moment in time, where he might come to hide them as he looked down on the place and recalled the people who had encircled him, so to form the trap which had kept him pinioned for the past twenty-five years in a place where only painful memories existed...except for Leonie, of course.

And neither should he blame her, Lizzie Jubb, even when she would haunt him every chance she could. A woman demented and unfit. Always had been and always would be. And, ironically, there she was at that very moment as if summonsed like a spectre from his own mind which had materialised before him as he gained a view of the distant roofs of Barnston Farm and the lane. So much dilapidation hidden under the snow.

He could see her; a distant figure running through the drifts, slipping and sliding, going towards the farm gate silently, on the ledge of land which allowed Barnston Farm a shallow purchase before the fields, which Hannah still owned, swept off into the far distance like a cape of white ermine fur.

She was running with her face and legs exposed, wearing that damned wedding dress and veil as if she had every right to still claim to be his bride, demanding even yet that he marry her, listening to no one, not even her own mother, when her perseveration in what could never be, made all their patience break.

Why should he feel such guilt? He had denied her nothing that she could ever have owned. They would have taken the child away from her anyway. Hannah had declared as such because she would not accept the responsibility of any child her daughter might bear; her frail, mad, unpredictable daughter and the house being as it was, these days a dilapidated, unhealthy ruin.

Then there was what he had taken away from Hannah, herself. For he had taken Bern; two manly men, meeting secretly, on a pretence of being engaged on other more manly things. It had not been easy for either of them when they met in the cavern which Bern had fashioned as their secret place, each knowing that resistance was impossible.

"You can't marry my daughter," Bern had said as they had lain together, "I can't bear to think of you together. Not her with you or you with her. I am her father. She seduced you knowingly, because I was watching. It was her birth that made her as she is after Hannah fell on the stairs. She is my responsibility, not yours."

The child should never have been conceived; the result of drunkenness and ignorance and a daughter wanting to pay her father back for things she had seen for herself and they should not have done. It was only later that Ross could accept the child as his own. He had never been able to understand how he could have lain with Lizzie when his persuasions were not as other men; her eyes, maybe, so much like Bern's. But it was his child, clearly his child that Lizzie had given birth to. One only had to look to see it, later, as she grew; fair of hair, blue-eyed, mannerisms which he had himself. Leonie was his daughter for in all her looks and mannerisms, she could not have been anyone else's.

The ring of deception had been necessary. She could not have lived there. Not at the farm where her birth mother was now entering the house, closing the door. No smoke coming out of the chimney. He had not seen smoke curling from the chimneys at the farm for many a long year. Plenty wood about so a lack of fuel was no excuse. Hannah Jubb was more than capable of wielding an axe even if she must now be quite old. Bern had said that he could never leave her because of Lizzie; the child they both loved despite her fits, her temper tantrums and bizarre ways. Maybe his death had saved them both from the shame of being found out. There had been no tolerance in Barns of difference, as there was now.

But rather that Bern were alive than dead and gone. His death no more than a tragic accident. Slipped his footing on the ladder in the well that should have brought him, not to remonstrate as Hannah would have had it, but for Ross to console him after the daughter he so loved had so very nearly drowned by throwing herself under the turbulent water of the fast flowing river. He had died hanging upside down. No one had heard him calling. That was the strangest thing of all.

He reached the hide after a few minutes walking steeply, and went in, seeing a winter robin which looked back at him from a branch of a tree with a curious eye. Ross could imagine it being the same one that had accompanied this same journey which he had made regularly from boyhood, summer and winter alike. There were memories within the hide, too. Ross's eyes glazed over as he stood hands in pockets, looking about.

He found himself sitting on the wooden bench in deliberation of the past yet at the same time noting that someone had recently been inside, crumbs of bread on the rough plank floor and muddy boot prints, slopped coffee on the surface of a wooden table. Automatically, he put the tip of a finger to it. The liquid was cold.

He spent what seemed like a short time deep in thought, maybe twenty minutes, before taking himself back the way he had come, planting his feet the reverse way through the deep holes made by his earlier descent and leaning into the slope.

Just out of the trees again, between the tree line and the driveway which led to the front doors of the large old, stone mansion house with its slated roofs and twisted, brick chimneys, he came to stand by the side of the old well, within which his friend and lover had died a slow and painful death.

Max was whimpering again as if to say, don't go there. It was a place that Ross usually avoided. The bricks were rough and cold under his hand, its memories bleak. Just inside the well was the culprit of Bernard Jubb's death: the iron ladder, there for maintenance purposes, or so he had been told when his parents had taken over the premises to run as a hotel. The ladder had once allowed a person to stand on the ledge where a rim of brick had made it possible to stand before a wooden doorway into the shafts, now bricked in. These days though, the top of the well was made safe with a piece of chicken wire which covered the circular top. The cross piece under the roof held a bucket on the end of a rope. A sign forbade anyone to attempt to use it. Or to stand on the coping stones, despite the safety netting. Or to try to attempt to climb within. Though, before such precautions had been taken, he had often done the same in order to access the caverns and potholes which ran like veins through the subterranean rock on which it stood and so disappear into the night dark to meet his lover.

Thinking deeply of Leonie, of Bern and what would take place tomorrow, he placed his elbows on the parapet of the well and leant over, hands cupped to his mouth, where he tapped his cold chin and listened, looking deeply into the water where Bern's spirit might help him to find a way to explain to Leonie that she was Bern's grandchild as well as his own daughter.

The water shimmered darkly below but held no reflection. Just sounds thrown up by the sighing hollows of the chambers beneath where the wind funnelled and sometimes made whistling sounds. He could hear them now within the roar of the river waters far below, the sound having carried up the funnel, as if the well were a trumpet by which to place ones ear to the coursing sounds. Sounds like someone whistling.

His brow darkened as he imagined Bern's voice calling, screaming and crying for help, the anguish having been absorbed into the stones and the bricks and the rock structure. Then just as suddenly he lost his concern. There could be another reason for what he was hearing. The fools were at it again.

Ross was unaware of how much time had elapsed; maybe an hour in total since he had seen Lizzie return to the house, but he hadn't been time watching. And still he had not resolved his problem. How to tell her what he had determined that she should know for Bern's sake as well as his own.

Ross's mobile rang just as he was getting back into his car. He looked at the screen information even as he raised a hand to his mother who passed him from behind in her dark B.M.W. coming back from the village, perhaps. He walked towards where he had parked his own black, four wheel drive vehicle. He saw that the phone call was from an unrecognised number. He decided to take it. He didn't always when his mood was low.

"Ross Fairbrother speaking. Fairview Hotel."

There was a pause. Then a thin, nasal voice with a Yorkshire accent strained his hearing.

"It's me, Betty Jessop, as was. Remember me? I used to work at your hotel."

Ross frowned for a moment and then gasped, surprise on his brow. He certainly did remember her. They had had the Fell Rescue Team out looking for her when she had failed to return to her room, five years ago now, and seemed to have vanished off the face of the earth. Older woman, he recalled. He certainly did remember Betty Jessop.

"Yes! Glad to hear you're healthy and hearty."

Her sniff replied to his sarcasm. "I want some work. I know I left you sudden the last time. My mother died, see. I had to go sudden. Didn't think to leave a note, that's all. If you remember I'm good at polishing silver."

He did remember. She had spit on all the cutlery if he remembered right before the final rub with a dirty rag. These days they used only stainless steel so her hygiene problem might be forgotten. Then he recalled that they might need another pair of hands in the kitchen now that Leonie had been promoted to reception. "It will be kitchen work. Washing up. That kind of thing."

"No matter. I don't mind. Some cleaning too, maybe. My marriage failed. I just want somewhere to tide me over Christmas. No sense being on my own."

"Come along some time after lunch. I'll tell reception to expect you. Betty Jessop. I have recalled your name correctly?" Then he placed her further. "A distant relation of Hannah Jubb?"

"Cousins twice removed. Family resemblance, nothing more. I don't use my married name any more."

"I'll tell Chef to expect you. Can you make it today?"

"This afternoon, yes. I'll be coming from Harrogate."

"In the snow?"

"Eager, see. Eager beaver, me."

Ross sighed. None of his concern, but he would not be picking her up from a station. He might turn out for Leonie Jones but Betty Jessop? Definitely not! He would do anything for Leonie Jones, though. Anything, if it would allow her to forgive him when she learnt the truth. She was his daughter, after all.

Thirteen

Lovick thought that he'd dreamt it. Vivid dreams were one of his bugbears. They came unbidden in cinemascope. The unpleasant ones were always to do with failure or being thwarted. Of effort unrewarded. Something important lost. He'd dreamt that he'd been swamped by an avalanche and buried in snow that was ten feet deep. He had been trying to dig his way out, only he was going down, not up; deeper and deeper, colder and colder, right down to ice at the glacier's core. Even when he opened his eyes he was seeing a framed whiteout through the cracked glass in a window which was thick with drift. He was a bit panicked still, freezing cold, his nose painful with the start of a boil the size of Vesuvius up his left nostril. When he turned over he caught it with the tip of a finger as he brought the bedcovers round him again in an attempt to get warm. Ouch! Sore as hell. It would be gone for tomorrow when his first performance was due. He always got thick, red lumps in his nose when he got run down. They'd go just as quickly after he'd rested. Lovick needed his z's.

His eyes shut again. They refused to stay open, lids stuck up with sleep and swollen with bleariness, a sore throat. He felt like he'd been smoking dope or sticking a different kind of white drift up his nose only he didn't do that shit anymore. Not since he'd apparently tried to fly and Quincey had stopped him. He had been three floors up at the time.

He felt rough and didn't quite know where he was on the planet to start with. Nothing new there. He'd spent the last nine years waking up in strange rooms with gaps in his memory. But he had caught a glimpse of the patchwork quilted cover draped over him. He'd had a brief, reassuring glance at his kit bag lying next to the hard, rough surface he was sleeping on, head on what felt like a rough hump of old sacking. His guitar was leaning into the corner next to the door. Sufficient to jog the memory. He remembered now how she'd flung open the door to this room on the first floor while holding up a paraffin lamp to the dark. Eerie that! Following her up the creaking stairs in the light from an oil lamp had been a new experience not to his liking. Like following the ether of a drifting ghost past shut doors over sagging, rotting floorboards, nothing underfoot but a ragged runner that had seen better days. He was creeping because she'd insisted he speak not a word.

"Shh! Don't wake my Lizzie whatever you do." Eyes glittering back at him.

She had looked like a warped image of a human being in the lamplight. Perhaps, due to his eyes being tired and feeling gritty in the dim light which was, thankfully, too inadequate to explain his situation fully. His imagination could be his own worst enemy as he knew only too well. He had to remind himself that she was nothing more than a bad tempered, sour old biddy who had begrudgingly given him a room for the night when it was not fit to turn a cow out with the snow settling and the cold the worst he'd ever experienced in the whole of his life. Then he had warned off trespassers just by trudging over her yard; a favour owed. Kids perhaps; naughty teenagers in hoods and peaked caps just after a bit of a laugh, not blokes like he'd at first thought. Just kids! Like he'd been once upon a time; cheeky, cocky, blowing raspberries and farting in the face of authority. You and who's army, mister? Always up to mischief. So they'd let the cows out! Then the cows had knocked over the milk churns and pulled down a lever, or whatever, to let feed out of a silo when she had said it was them. Or so she said; he'd yet to see any evidence that what she'd said had happened, had happened. There was that missile that had clattered onto the wall of the house but it hadn't been thrown at her, at himself, at anyone. A parting gesture from puberty, maybe; too many confused hormones, and nothing more. Gnat brained lads threw sticks without a thought in their heads as to where they might land. He'd regretted many an accident doing the same thing. The smouldering torch of fire safely landing in a zinc bucket, too, not anywhere near her sheds or the house, or her and her Lizzie. Just kids messing about in the woods in winter, causing her hassle and aggravation. High as kites with excitement because Christmas was near at hand. He soon convinced himself that there was nothing going on other than kids being kids. Get the local constable to sort them out. What was the name she had given him? Gareth Someone-Or-Other; local bobby. Jones! Get him to give them a rollicking. They wouldn't do it again. Not till the next time and then to someone else.

Satisfied with his own interpretations, he humped himself deeper into the sagging bed, looking for comfort where there was none. Eyes closed still. Sniffing past the boil in his blocked-up nostril. Becoming aware of the smell of the farm, dampness, earthy odours and his own morning breath. All within a morning quiet that only snow can bring. The earth was wearing a muffler of snow as his gran had used to call a scarf. "Got yer muffler on, our Lick?" When no one was watching later, he'd get out and build a snowman somewhere and go flying with him in his head. His favourite Christmas story that and the music. Always would be. That and the poem …

"It was on the eve of Christmas,
All asleep in the house,
Everything quiet,

Including the mouse ..."

Big kid, himself. Saying it in his head with good diction as he might have recited it if anyone had ever been willing to listen. If he'd ever known a happy family Christmas with his mum and dad at home, for once, with gran and his granddad and his aunts and uncles calling in. No quarrelling or too much drink, or snide remarks about the lack of cash spent on cheapskate presents. The tree not a thin, drooping, artificial arrangement of pipe cleaners and bottle brushes nailed onto a four inch off-cut of the real thing as a base for it to stand on. But a real, brushy bush, smelling of pine tree and decorated with wishes. A tree that's supposed to be symbolic of all that's dear to family life. A symbol of hope in the midst of winter. Not an old, dusty, tired, frazzled thing that's all bent and twisted. The fairy on the top wielding a bent wand with her hallo all a-cock; a bit like his gran after a few too many gin and bitter lemons and her party hat not on straight. A thin chicken instead of a fat turkey for dinner. Nothing in the crackers but old jokes and tat. Lovick, standing in short pants, looking at his gran as she passed out at the table and then up at the fairy, wondering where all the Christmas magic was. It had to be somewhere. A ball of golden glow circling the earth in Santa's sack for the good children only. Where had it gone?

Obviously, not here! No cheer here. The room stank, as did the whole house, of neglect and dereliction. Its stinky, peppery dampness had made his nose wrinkle the night before.

He had been uncharacteristically grateful, though, when she had handed the lamp over to him with its concentric arcs of yellow light, discriminating in his own favour, because he had not wished to look at anything too closely, her included. No other light was in the room other than that from a pale blanket sky showing through an undraped window which billowed white feathers out of pillows of cloud. Everything hushed outside and being represented like a negative, black against white.

Click, take a picture for posterity, his mind advised; store it away in the memory bank. Global warming and all that. Eyes opening and shutting again, both of them this time. Guitar by the door, leaning, where he had left it the night before. Turn over, hump in. All he could feel under his shoulder was stubbly hard lumps, his mind still trying to get going but, as yet, capable of recall only. He was still only up to getting into bed the night before in his processes of recall, something that had to be thoroughly done before forward thinking was at all possible. Planning was futile, until he'd orientated himself. He had to build himself up to coping with today by having a recall of yesterday, everything in order, sequenced like joined up writing. Read 'yesterday' and then turn a fresh page to 'today'. Thoughts only rarely ventured on further that that; yesterday, today, tomorrow. Why bother, otherwise? No cash in his pants to plan further.

Not that there had been a lot more to remember other than that his disappointment had been severe. An occasion when a fertile imagination could be used to advantage. With his eyes shut, he could think himself anywhere. He had done that last night, too, when she had shown him into the room and the flower patterns on the sphere of moulded glass had cast their shapes in shade and yellow light over a miserable prospect. He had held the lamp up only for a moment before setting it down, on the floor by the antique bed, to cast bowers of floral shadows over what was little more than an old ticking mattress on a wooden pallet with something in a brown sack for a pillow. At least somewhere dry to collapse onto when his knees gave way, which they had done as soon as she had closed the door on him. Somewhere to sit while taking his boots off, rub at his cold, sore feet to try to warm them, strip off his wet coat and put it to dry on the hook at the back of the door and then slope off under the quilt into oblivion, still fully dressed, socks on, flat on his back, seeking sleep before his fertile imagination got the better of him.

He had left the flame of the oil lamp burning but turned down low, fingers nipping the little, brass wheel which seemed to control the wick, just in case he had to get up before the daylight in this god-awful place. Not because he had felt afraid to be alone in the dark, though he had missed his smiley-face nightlight. No electricity in the place.

Thankfully, it had gone out without being needed during his sleep. Now it was daylight. Must be all of eight o'clock, Monday, the 21st. Too early for him to get up yet. Lovick wasn't used to rising before eleven, even when working. No point in being at the Fairview Country Club Hotel too early, either. They might find him a job to do like shovelling snow.

His mind was, however, beginning to compute matters of a future reference even as he lay in a pit of sluggish semi-wakefulness, reluctant to fully wake up. Despite having closed his eyes again with a stubborn determination not to move from where he was until warm blood was flowing through stiff limbs again. It happened the same every morning. Nothing rushed. A civilised approach to the day as his granddad had used to say after a lifetime on the dole. Then when you're up, you're up, ready to swing an axe over a shoulder and go fell trees with everyone else. Trouble being, of course, that the lumberjack bus had left for the forest hours before and would not be returning till dusk.

Wakefulness was increasing though. The left side of his brain had begun to communicate with the right side in feeble pulses, signals flickering and responding as the brain switched on, ears operative but hearing nothing, a minor smell dysfunction due to the boil in his nostril, but something to be glad of. He was now certain that he was sleeping on a hay pillow because he could feel stalks sticking through the sacking into his face.

An eye opened again for a brief instant. He was on his right side facing the window, behind him the door, not locked because it had no mechanism for the provision of privacy. Bare floor boards. No rug. No heat in the room. Bare plaster walls. Like the rest of the house which he had taken a good look at, without prying where he shouldn't, when she had gone out in the snow to see to the cows.

His skin felt frozen and goose bumped but he'd have to get up out of bed and run around or do sit-ups to do anything about it. But his eyeballs were roaming behind closed lids to show that his mind was rising from the thick mud of its sleep-state like a groggy, winter fly; gnat brain waking, serious metabolic changes were taking place. The congealed grey matter was beginning to pass messages; brain to toes, brain to calves and so on, his nudger doing what it always did first thing in the morning and standing up like a space rocket in decommission, but ready for take off. One of his tactics for waking was to channel his sex drive into the seat behind the wheel of a powerful Porsche 911 then accelerate like Schumacher through his own narrow, dark, mental passages; ignition on, handbrake off, gears sliding, the sole of one foot pumping the clutch as he throttled up to sixty in five seconds and climbing, the other on the accelerator then down to the floor, world whizzing by. Energy running and up to speed for a body take-off, the blood flowing, fresh air entering the lungs. Out into daylight, eyes opening slowly. The Porsche slowing. The engine barely ticking over but the man alert at last. He had arrived at his fully wakeful destination. He parked it up safely because he needed it every morning to get him out of bed then closed the garage door on it. Best thing he'd *never* bought, he said to himself.

He could look now through two, roaming, bloodshot, hazel eyeballs and know that he had not underestimated his emergency shelter. If anything, it looked shabbier in daylight than it had done in lamp light. The chest of drawers under the window were battered and scratched, the floor shriven with dust, the mat under his feet little more than a rag.

He wanted a wee now that his friend had settled back to normal. Then he recalled. As she had slung the quilt at him from the drawers under the window she had mumbled something about the toilet being under the bed so not to go out looking for it. If he woke Lizzie he'd know about it. "Won't be disturbed without spending the rest of the night hollering and hammering. Best hush. You don't want my Lizzie coming in here if you can avoid it. Not when she's mad."

Lovick, in recall, had imagined a five year old and then changed his mind about her. Hannah Jubbs must be seventy if she was a day. Accordingly, he altered his first estimation of the age of her daughter to a woman of about thirty, thirty five, fifty at the oldest, with the thinking part of his brain and then thought about her some more. What Hannah had described was no way for a sensible woman to behave. Recalling, too, words like 'locked in'. Had she said that? Yes, he was certain.

His wakefulness took another step towards alertness as he thought to put his boots on before setting socks to the filthy floor. He was feeling fussy concerning personal contact with the immediate environment, a bit itchy inside his clothes. He didn't mind his own dirt, didn't like anyone else's. Also, all the better to be prepared, just in case, for any eventuality. Better still; get off the premises as soon as possible. If he was sharpish, got his things together quick and left breakfast until he got to the Fairview Hotel, he might avoid coming into contact with this Lizzie. He had had enough of deranged women to last him a lifetime; his mother, his gran. His Aunty Vi had her moments according to Uncle Stu when it was 'that time of the month'. Then countless girlfriends going spare on him once they thought he'd committed, usually because he'd left a razor and some shaving foam on their bathroom shelf. All it took these days. They were talking babies if he stayed more than two nights in a row, the wedding only happening if they got put up the duff because they had forgotten to take a pill. Kids? Not if he could help it. Not room for two children in Lovick's life; himself and another, especially his own. Not counting his best pal, Quincey, of course.

Time to get the feet out, sit up and lean over, look under the drape of the quilt while he put on his boots, the ones with the bells on which made little tinkles as he stuffed his plates in, lacing up the beautiful coloured, thin silk ribbons as gently as if plaiting a baby's hair.

He leaned down to look under the bed and had to look deeper. Right under, deep under the bed. It was there alright. What his gran had used to call a jerry and his granddad a piss-pot. A kneel down job. Either that or risk it dripping through the ceiling below because his first flow of the day was like the Khyber Dam breaking. Not that it would have made much difference from brief recall. Another few drips coming through the ceiling would make little difference in a house that was more like a leaking sieve than a dwelling for humans, damp stains on the walls everywhere he had looked, holes in the walls and ceilings with the laths poking through. It was cluttered up more like a farm chandlery than a home; tools, boxes, bags of feed, carboys of paraffin, all stacked up in the hallway so that he'd had to squeeze himself through a passageway made for an elf. If she was small and thin, then this Lizzie must be even smaller and thinner. Hannah had wrapped her coat about her tight as a blanket before going through while he followed. Was it a booby trap to unwanted visitors like those of the night before, perhaps? A jutting elbow might have caused a major landslide of pig feed sacks stacked five high with carboys of paraffin rolling down from the shelves. He was thin as a lathe but had had to be ever so careful with the bulk of his kit bag.

She had carried in his guitar. "My Lizzie likes musical instruments. When she's in the mood that is." She could not resist a strum.

Lovick had snatched it back as soon as he was able. Guitar strings cost money.

Thereafter, carrying it over his shoulder, tied on by its strap and not laid down till she'd gone and the corner was handy. He didn't have a carry case. That's why he'd got it cheaper from the second hand shop.

So many thoughts sired by a jerry! Only way to be comfortable was to use it. By then he's realised that it was possible to use it like a portable urinal adjusted to his own height so that he needn't get his jeans in contact with the floor. He was still thinking about the house under his feet and how he'd never in his life been in a shambles like this before. The kitchen had been like the store room of a charity shop, though all he'd seen in box after cardboard box had been clothes; pretty things though, not like anything she'd wear that was for sure; frills and flounces, pleats and lace collars. And colours. In one open box he'd noted textured, multi-coloured fabrics tumbling out as if someone had been on an impatient rummage; fur, silk, crepe, velvet, nylon in layers you could see through, and glittery cloths in red, white and black which you could make an Elvis cape out of. Now, there was a thought! In another, hats; brimmed, veiled, feathered. There was even a wedding dress and a long, lace veil. What would she want that for? A box filled with white gloves; necessary too, he had thought because the house was almost as cold as outside. He had been tempted to avail himself of a pair and cut off the fingers. No warmer than a warehouse. A kitchen with a ceiling that went high up into a dark, vaulted roof with rafters and ropes hanging down over the big table where used plates and cups and dishes were piled high in tottering heaps.

Why? Why ropes? Had they been stored there? Had they been put there to tether something up? Then his imagination really went haywire ... Was someone to be hanged? The table moved out of the way. The miscreants of the night before, perhaps, hung, drawn and quartered with the slaughter equipment he had seen lying all over the far surface of the big kitchen table; knives, hatchets, skewers and meat hooks. His eyes travelled fearfully over to the sink, under the window, where a sill was crammed with blocks of green soap and scrubbing brushes. A dead animal carcass laid out flat. If he wasn't mistaken it had been skinned. Its innards filled the sink; coils of intestine, shiny brown liver, a heart and lungs still with the arteries intact. All slopped together and shining in lamp oil light. Yuk! On the draining board the dead, white piglet had been stretched out and stiff; cleaved down the middle and dripping its blood from exposed veins in its neck straight into a metal bucket that was a quarter full of the rich, dark red liquid. It was as if that's what she had been doing before the lads had disturbed her, then him, of course; she had been butchering a piglet.

Gross! Revolting. He'd never eat another rasher, ever again. He had never thought that piglets had eyelashes as thick as a woman's. Its position affected him to. It looked as if it had been trying to wriggle away when she had bludgeoned it and slit open its throat. There was a deep cleft on the side of its cheek, just over the shocked jut of its open lips, as if she had slashed at it live with a machete. Maybe that's what the ropes were for when the animals were big as a sheep or a calf, after she'd shot them.

Cruel thoughts ran through his head. Mr. Hypocrite whose mouth ran with saliva at the very thought of a slice of roast beef. She had come in from the cows by then and caught his expression, watched his eyes widen with horror. Understood as she reached for a kettle to hold over the bowels in the sink, turn on the tap to fill it with cold, clear, running water. "Just a pig. Got me a turkey hung for Christmas. Wrung its neck last week, plucked it and cleaned it yesterday. Nothing like fresh, black pudding with a thick slice of turkey breast and stuffing. That's what the blood's used for. Better than sausages. Tastier. Me and Lizzie will dress up and eat till we're full fit to burst. Got a bottle of port in the cupboard. Daren't share it with her. Join us lad. Big, strong lad like you should keep them bastards at bay. That Bluithe's been here before."

"Got a job. I'll be working Christmas."

"Where?"

"Fairview Country Club Hotel. I told you. That's where I'm headed. Should have been there last night." Lifting his guitar but making no further explanation.

Her eyes had darkened as she put a flashlight the size of a rolling pin back up on a shelf. "Ross Fairbrother. Fancy bloody hotel for folks ne'er done a day's work in their life. Blasting the skies with clay pigeon shot. Can't have no peace. Pigs won't breed. No better than the rest of them. Mustn't talk about him to my Lizzie, either. She was engaged to him once. That mother of his put a stop to it though. Jubb's not good enough."

Lovick had stood while she brewed up an uncomfortable silence.

When she spoke again her voice was deep. "What you think of my farmhouse? This kitchen used to seat and feed a dozen at a time. When my Bern was alive. When Lizzie was…What you think of my farmhouse, then?"

"It's very …er …big."

And cold. And inhospitable, though he daren't have said that. Should have been used as a barn, he had reckoned, looking around more, anywhere but at the corpse on the draining board or her dirty hands as she had struck a match and lit the gas under the kettle on an old butane stove, the top of which looked to be loaded with dead cockroaches.

The big, herringbone-brick fireplace had had nothing but cold, white ashes in it. If there had been a blaze there earlier to warm her and Lizzie's hands, he'd missed it. Only one chair, too, by the fireside. Not two. Where was one for the daughter, Lizzie?

Suddenly his hunger had dissipated. She had pointed to a lump of cheese on the table with green bits all over it and next to it a hive of bread which looked to be as dry as polystyrene packaging. "Butter, too. Churn it myself. Buy the bread. Milk's still in the cow. Don't mind tea black, do you?"

He would definitely not have stayed but for the weather. There were ghosts in the place. Creaks and groans and she was looking like a ghost of her own self, with a daughter who had to be locked up in a room somewhere in a rangy, cold, dark draughty house filled with grot. But at least he had slept.

What to do with the jerry which was now near brimming with his hot, foamy leakage? There was a question! Out of the window, he thought. Best place for it.

Across the room he went carrying it carefully, the liquid swilling up the froth on the last of last night's beer from the Bald Pheasant Inn. It even had a great visual similarity, his the better colour when he thought back to compare the two.

He heard the door creak open behind him, just a little before his journey's end, almost at the window. He stopped walking, turned, and looked across the bed, brows rising at what he saw. A white gloved hand appeared, small fingers moving slowly. They curled about the neck of his guitar and ever so gently lifted it off the floor and then withdrew it.

By the time he realised what had happened and found a place for the full repository on the top of the drawers, his guitar had disappeared. Then he heard a screech, a cackled laugh, the stampede of feet and a rumbling tumble of sound as the thief pounded down the stairs and through what must have been the cluttered up hallway.

He heard the front door slam before he could make the decision whether to chase blindly after or look through the window. The latter won as he deposited the jerry on the surface of the set of drawers where fresh rat droppings supported a probability that he had not spent a night in the room alone.

Good tactic. When he looked through the window, a woman in a blue wool jacket, red hat over two brown plaits, tied with red ribbons, striped red and white scarf and the same white gloves was running through the snow. She gripped onto his guitar and held it high as if she had won first prize at a fair and was showing it to all and sundry. Not another soul was to be seen, though. A knee-high romp through the deep snow, back straight and head arched backwards; a most peculiar gait. It could only be one person. Lizzie! Couldn't be anyone else.

Angrily he stamped to the door and opened it wide. "Hannah?"

No reply. The house was steeped in silence.

At least he could follow her even if he had seen footprints going off all over the place. Some tramped all over the farmyard and others gone off through the gate. Someone had made long traily-swirly patterns on the snow as if they had been dragging something over its surface, probably Hannah and her pig. The other way was the one he was sure she had gone; to the left because he could see something red and white on the snow and the footprints were deep and freshly made. Gnat brain should have waited to look in which direction she had gone. Gnat brain should not have left his precious guitar by the door. He should have brought it into his bed and slept with it like a woman.

Lovick reached for his coat.

***

He followed the footprints through the snow with a determined stride and a set look on his face. Hannah had been nowhere to be seen though the small, byre door was open across the yard, noxious smelling steam coming out with the sounds of lowing. No hens to be seen but they were chuckling somewhere amongst themselves. Pigs were settled and quiet in the sties. He could hear them grunting quietly. On the rusting tractor seat lay an egg, but no hen sitting on it.

He recalled the carcass that had been cleaved in half on her sink and its innards taken out, skinned and bled, revulsion swilling over him like a tide of acknowledgment to an unusual disdain. The house had seemed no better than it had the night before as he had hurriedly passed through it, even with daylight pouring in. It was an inside shed, not a home, and no warmer for the dawn of a new day either; a cold, snowy, new day, no fire in the hearth. How did she live in it? How did they live in it? Mother and daughter together living in a hovel not fit for human habitation. He would have been warmer with the cows in the byre than he had been in the house. And now he was tramping through six inches of powdery, virgin snow chasing after a woman who should know better. What the hell was she up to? His guitar for Christ's sake! His livelihood! What could she hope to gain by running off with it? He would have let her have a bit of a strum if she had asked, if not a proper go. It was not a plaything. Serious this. Theft. If she damaged it he'd have her mother pay for it. It was his work tool so if she made it unplayable he'd lose his work at the Fairview Hotel. If she scratched it he would have to have it French polished to take the scratches away. Where the hell had she gone off to with it?

It was only the snow which allowed him to follow. Her footprints were big gouges and smudges in the pristine, powdery layer. The world had turned white about him. It had layered on the gate overnight and stuck to his fingers as he went through it; cold, wet, icy, crystals melting to droplets of water on his skin. Stopped falling, at least, so that his upper clothing might stay dry. He could see where her hand had swept away the snow with her white glove as she had opened it and run through, leaving it open behind her, because she was making off with something that was not hers. Then he found her red and white striped scarf on the lane were she must have dropped it in her hurry to get away. He picked it up and stuffed it in the pocket of his coat then walked on. He would have wet boots in no time.

The snow had silenced the bells. He trudged after her soundlessly with a face carved out of ice. Her running off with his guitar had put the kybosh on good expectations and caused him to glower. Put him in a bad mood at the start of the day. If a day started bad it would get worse. That was always the way of things. A sour temper taints the sweet milk of life, or something like that. One of his gran's sayings. Too bloody true.

At the gate he turned left and looked at the tracery of the fine branches of leafless trees at the start of a dark wood. That's the way the footsteps went. The sound of fast moving water as well. Cold, cold, cold to his core. Would he ever get warm again?

Lovick quickened his pace. He turned up his collar. If it snowed again, he'd need two tennis racquets to make any progress at all. If a wind came up, it would blow it into high banks at the side of the lane, drifts several feet high, covering everything in its path that stood still. They were cut off now. No cars could get down here in this weather, he thought.

By hook or by crook, snow or no snow, he'd be off out of here as soon as he could, thinking of a cheery fire and a warm bed at the Fairview Hotel. Get this place behind him good and proper. Once he had his guitar back again!

Once under the trees he could hear the river running with a raging roar, making a thunderous noise, enveloping him in its sound. Then there it was before him no more than a hundred yards or so from the farmhouse. White water scouring over grey stones, high up its banks and swilling over tree roots on the other side, spitting at him as he looked which way to go and it roiled round and around dark, grey rocks.

Dratted girl! Her footprints turned right in the virgin snow. Not even bird prints to make any other patterns than her own and his as he followed along the river bank. A red brick bridge was before him. And there it was. His guitar; propped up on the brickwork, under the arch.

Relief flooded him as he went to pick it up and examine it. No damage that he could see. Not even a broken string. The plectrum still where he kept it pushed under a loose fret. Try it to be sure. The sound melded with the noise of the river but seemed all right.

Where was she? Where was the naughty minx who had run off with his guitar? No snow under the bridge. No footprints to say where she had gone from here. She was probably watching him, laughing at him from a hiding place. Best get back. What a waste of energy. What a stupid thing to do.

So back he went the way he had come. He didn't see Lizzie but he did see Hannah. She was coming out of the barn with a bucket of eggs. Lovick picked up the one on the tractor seat and took it over, placed it with the warm ones; some brown, some white. He had never seen a white egg before. Her face was both inquisitive and apologetic. "Saw her go off with it. Naughty girl. Too old to run after her these days."

"She left it under the bridge. Why did she take it?"

Hannah shook her head, shrugged. "Does things like that. Objects smell of people. My Lizzie gets vibes from people's things. Gone back up to her room. Likes to give folk the run around, I think. Does things like that. I keeps her locked in as much as I can. Can't keep her locked in all the time though."

"Is she ill?"

Hannah scowled, blue eyes glittering at him and her mouth pursing tight. "There's nought the matter with my Lizzie but disappointment and a broken heart. It's others think there is. Nought the matter with me either that a life of ease wouldn't cure."

Lovick was chastened. "What do I owe you for the bed?"

She shook her head. "Comes to something when you can't help

out a stranger. Invitation's still open by the way for Christmas dinner. Breakfast, too, if you want it. Nice to have company for a change."

Lovick wanted to make a clear no-thank-you but nodded instead, feeling sorry. "I'm sorry. I have to dash. If I'm free I'll maybe call in over Christmas but it's not likely. I'm at the Fairview to work. I'll be helping wait on tables and then eating with the staff as well as providing some entertainment in the evening. A fourteen hour shift."

"Better get off then." Her head lowered; shoulders down. Now she looked upset.

Lovick cussed her in his head. His gran had used to make him feel bad like this.

He steeled himself. "I'll get my bag and be off." Then he felt mean. "I'll pop down if I can."

She nodded, raised a glad eye. "Nice that. I'll say farewell here. Got to catch the donkey so I's can bring him in. Can't feed when there's snow in the ground. Ice on his trough. He'll have to go in the stable with a bucket of oats."

Lucky donkey!

They parted company then. Lovick went through the house wondering where Lizzie had gone. He looked for signs of her as he went up the stairs. He saw her hat and coat on a peg behind the front door with the white gloves poking out of the pockets. Her wet, snowy footprints carried on up the stairs. He followed them, shouting as he went. "Lizzie? I got it back undamaged. Lucky you!"

He listened. No answer. All he wanted to do was chastise her a bit. Tell her that what she had done was silly. Which was her room? The wet footprints went on along the corridor. To his own door, in fact. Lovick cringed expecting to see her inside. When he thrust it open the contents of his kit bag were all over the floor.

***

It was gone eleven in the morning when Lick and Leonie finally met. He walked into the hotel reception with wet boots, bells jingling, with a damp coat and a miserable expression. His kit bag had been so hurriedly repacked after the contents had been scattered all over the dirty floor in the room he had slept in at Barnston Farm that not all had fitted back in it. Some items he had crammed in pockets. He had not even done an inventory to see if anything was missing. He was simply glad to be out of there with his guitar intact, even when his belly was under the impression that his throat had been cut. He was so bloody hungry!

Then his eyes settled on a little angel; a real, little cracker of a girl with bright yellow hair tied back from her face in a bouncy, frizzy ball at the back of her head. The angel from the top of his best imaginary Christmas tree! Or at least what he could see of her. When she smiled at him, something joyful leapt in his chest. Bells rang, and not the toy ones on his boots, either. Big bells like they have on churches, pealing out. Ding bloody dong!

Leonie for her part heard bird song and felt a ripple of something soft and very precious pass from her head, down through every pore of her flesh to the very tips of her toes. It made her voice all soft and brought a coy look to her face. "You must be Lick Johnson."

"And you must be Leonie Jones." The fact that she wore a name badge was not relevant. She liked the way he said it.

Together they said it as one person. "Ssssslick Lick Johnson… Prince. Of. Soul. And. Rock. And. Roll, Yeah!"

Then they smiled at each other.

Fourteen

Gareth had the mystery of the riot van to solve. The best place to begin his enquiry was in the nerve centre of the village; the Bald Pheasant Inn.

The landlord, Marty, keened a worried face at Gareth the moment he asked his question.

"Who was driving my riot van last night?"

"What riot van?"

"The one I keep in Tom Greaves's garage next to his butcher's shop. What else? There's only one!"

"What about the van?"

"It was seen parked in front of the station. I've been in to have a look at it. There's water round the tyres as if it's been out in the snow."

"Nah! Someone's seeing things. The riot van's a big box vehicle. Sure that Greavsey hasn't just backed it out to get at his fridges?"

Gareth frowned. "He wouldn't park it in front of the station. That's what I was told. It was parked up in front of the station in the early hours of the morning."

"Who said that?"

"Gloria. Couldn't sleep. Said she'd seen the riot van parked outside the station in the early hours of the morning."

Drat bloody Gloria! Quick thinking was required. Marty had his hand on a bottle of French cognac even as he lied. He poured one for Gareth and passed it over only to have it refused. "Come to think of it there was a van parked there. Or more a lorry. Came off the motorway because of the snow. Driver came in here, asked for the way to Quinton down the back roads. Bought a cheese sandwich, had a flask filled with coffee and a half pint of lemonade to quench his thirst. Then went on his way."

"Oh! That so! What time was this?"

Marty saw a good reason to get vicious. Gareth was usually an amenable sort. Even though he was lying through his teeth he took offence at not being believed. Two can play at that game. He could be shirty, too. And nasty. Gareth had a deep sensitivity about the size of his wife. "Gloria started on the liqueurs, has she? As well as suffering hallucinations from the mountain of food additives she imbibes. Does that, you know, does eating more than is good for you. Could be mad cow disease. Arteries in the brain hardening because they're blocked up with toxins the body can't get rid of. It all starts with talking gobbledegook and making untrue suggestions. Riot van, indeed."

Gareth found this disturbing as he did any mention of Gloria's weight problem. But he had a nose for a liar and Marty was lying that was for sure. He had the distinct feeling that Marty was deliberately trying to change the subject by using a personal reference to get Gareth's attention away from the professional nature of his questioning.

Then again, Gareth knew Gloria. She might have imagined that she could smell French perfume about his person but one thing that Gloria was not, was a victim of bad eyesight. Gloria was also as sober as a bloody judge. Food was her problem not booze.

Maybe if she'd gone on the gin instead of the burgers their lives would have taken a different tack. His response to Marty was to frown and let him know that all he was prepared to do was to give the benefit of the doubt.

"I'll be checking up on it on a daily basis from now on to make sure that it goes nowhere unless to a riot." Then he turned on his heel and left, feeling eyes upon him, knowing that the whole conversation had been listened to by every man-jack in the crowded pub.

He then went to the Star supermarket, walking straight to where the batteries were shelved. The girl was stacking them high with what looked to be a new delivery but which Gareth thought more likely to have been stockpiled, in every conceivable size. The price on each section of shelving seemed to have risen dramatically. Aware of him towering over her, her eyes recognising the boots and the fact that the law was bearing down on her, she stood up quickly. "I don't set the prices," she muttered. "She does."

Gareth turned to look on the gloating face of the shop manageress. "If you want any, you'd better buy now."

"Where have these come from? You didn't have any last night!"

Her mouth mewed, her head cocked to one side. "Marty suggested it. Shortages are good for business, apparently."

Gareth was barged out of the way by a gaggle of pensioners, all eager for double A's.

"I don't bloody believe it!"

Her chin raised. "There's no law against it!"

"Maybe not, but there is an agency can black ball you better than anything I can do. It's called Trading Standards. If you don't want a twenty-four hour supermarket opening up here, I suggest you hike the prices down and try providing this community with what it needs, instead of what best lines your pocket." Then he growled deeply and left the shop.

***

Marty watched Gareth leave the pub before picking up the shot of brandy and gulping it down. The drinkers began to whisper amongst themselves and then their attention was caught by someone appearing in the village that they had not seen in over five years; Betty Jessop. Her presence caused some diversion which gave Marty a respite from the tension he was feeling. It was all Gloria's fault!

**

Outside, Gareth turned his collar up against a fresh fall of snow as he crossed over the square to his office. As he walked, he let his eyes stray to Gloria's bedroom window. He saw that it was steamed up with condensation so that she probably could not see him even if she was looking out. It was also slightly ajar and a thin line of blue rope ran from the gap, down over the stone front of the building to the handle of a basket which was ledged on the snow covered pavement. It was then that he saw Ann Kaye from the bakery come out and place some bulky, white, paper bags in the basket. She gave two tugs before quickly entering her shop again to be out of the cold. Slowly he saw the basket start to rise as it was winched upwards. A bin lid and two steak and onion pies, apparently, were not enough!

Was it any wonder that Gloria was getting bigger and bigger despite being confined to her bed? The district nurse had warned him, too, that unless she lost weight, her life was threatened. Her heart could not cope with humping about mounds of fat even when her movement only extended to turning over in bed. All the signs were pointing to an imminent heart attack. That was the last thing he wanted. The thing was, was that in some ways he still needed her. As did their daughter. He would have liked to take back the hurtful words he had spoken when she was fifteen stone lighter and could at least waddle about on fat little legs. Instead she had gone into a deep sulk and taken increasingly to her bed as if her agoraphobia was not enough of a problem to their family as a whole. From that point she had begun to consume twice as much as she had done before and only spoke to him to ask to bring her more savouries as well as an abundance of sweets, chocolate bars and bottles of fizzy coke. It was like she had a death wish; a way to commit suicide for which he would be entirely responsible. She was silently laying all the blame on him.

Gareth was seriously worried. It was no longer a matter of wanting a slim wife as it had been when he had first started to pass comment. He wanted a live one. But what to do about it? How do you turn about a situation that you feel that you are responsible for in the first place? Gloria had always been sensitive to criticism. Then there was the guilt. A guilt he shared in equal measure. And a fear, too, that what they had done all those years ago, as a salve to their grief, would backfire on them. He had known that it was likely to happen sooner or later. Like any kind of thief, they would, sooner or later, be found out. Only Gloria had been unable to forget about it as he was able to do through the demands of his work. Idle minds and all that. Too much time to brood and worry. Their guilty secret coming out!

He'd had a word, too, with the police psychologist about the causes of obesity in middle-aged women; on the quiet, of course, not saying who he was referring to when the psychologist did not know Gloria in person. He had said that obsessive eating could be linked to a reluctance to indulge in the intimate relationship between man and wife. That had been a problem ever since the shock of their dead baby had come home to roost. A baby born quickly in the dead of night before help could be got to save the scrawny, deformed, little mite. It had been born dead, anyway. The cord about its neck. Gloria alone and unable to move from her bed as the dead tissue that should have been their child lay between her legs. That had been the same, bitterly cold December night that he had gone out to Barnston Farm to be met by Hannah Jubb at her gate with a newborn baby girl in her arms. He had been calling there every evening after Bern had died to make sure that they were alright.

"Here yer are then. It's come. What yer've been waiting for all these months. Take that to him up there at the Fairview and get him to sort it out. My Lizzie's in there bleeding to death if you must know. Not that any o' you lot could give a toss."

She had refused to allow him in or to allow him to call a midwife or the doctor with any immediacy though that had to be done once the problem of what to do with a healthy, new born baby girl, had been solved. Instead he had brought the baby home with him for want of knowing what else to do with it, short of making a forty mile round trip to the nearest hospital, only to learn the devastating news of what had happened with his own child while he had been accepting Lizzie Jubb's daughter into his care.

What had happened had simply come to be. No one else knowing but the parties directly involved in the transaction which had followed and in their distraught state, had seemed simple common sense. He could recall to this day how Gloria had been beside herself with grief and despair with her dead child stillborn between her legs. While he had removed his dead, deformed son from their bed she had taken the baby girl and immediately adopted her as her own, holding her fast in her arms as if this had been the baby she had given birth to. Gareth had been unable to prise them apart after she had taken the newborn infant straight to her breast to suckle before even the afterbirth of her son had come away. Their Leonie; a daughter not a son, as expected. A mistake on the scan. Their guilty little secret! The secret they shared with Hannah Jubb, if not Lizzie who seemed to truly be of the opinion that she had given birth to a deformed boy child that had been dead on arrival into this cold, callous world.

She said things to that effect sometimes when she stood in the square, having managed to escape the house and her mother. Dressed up in silly clothes with a face full of make-up. Shouting about her dead baby and Ross Fairbrother and the blame she had for the villagers who had shown them no support. Anger honing every word when such was her mood to be verbal and accusing. They had no right to laugh at her. Or mock. Or talk about her and her mother in hurtful ways. Her dad would still have been alive, she accused, had they accepted their invitations and turned up at the church to offer their support. Even if Ross had failed to attend the shotgun wedding they could have turned up to support her mother and father. She blamed them all, but Bluithe Harcourt in particular. He was one of Lizzie's main targets when she was angry. Even before she accused him of trespassing onto their property at night, she blamed him especially for the mockery he had passed her way, laughing at her openly, cat-calling her as she pointed the finger of blame. "Glad I didn't marry you. Can't even grow a healthy babby, Lizzie Jubb. Get back where you come from and stop pestering decent folk."

Gloria had taken those words to heart as if they had been directed at her. "Can't even grow a healthy babby!"

There had been no going back then. Once the deed had been done it had been impossible to reverse it. They had swapped a live little girl for a dead baby boy and then let Hannah get on with looking after Lizzie. He had made the proposal to Hannah in all good faith and she had accepted it because she had no choice to do anything else. It had seemed a way out of the mire for them all, Ross Fairbrother included.

So Hannah had buried his and Gloria's deformed son under an apple tree in the orchard in a butter barrel, because she would not have another Jubb buried in the churchyard after what had happened there just a few months earlier. This, after a doctor had pronounced that the baby had been dead at birth and foul play not an issue. "Lizzie thinks this is her babby, see. Have to respect her wishes in the matter. Won't have a Christian burial. It'll go in the orchard with the donkey."

Ross Fairbrother had agreed to everything, too. Gareth had made sure of that, even if no one else knew, because while he would be furtive he would not be unlawful, while knowing that Ross couldn't do anything else but agree. Could he? His mother had refused to countenance the child, even to speak about it. Ross had been an army man in those days without a home of his own for the child to be reared in. It was that or leave his daughter to be neglected by her frail mother who had been daft enough before the human mess that had been so tragically made, and positively deranged since being brought out of the river and carted off to the nearest mental institution. Had his daughter stayed at Barnston Farm to be raised by her grandmother, she would have been reared no different to any of the other farm animals; fed and watered and kept in a play pen while Hannah did all the work of the farm. She would not have been able to trust her daughter to look after a baby because Lizzie needed looking after herself. The situation had been tragic.

So, all parties involved had been in agreement, and a discreet solicitor acquired, though Mrs. Fairbrother knew nothing about the babies being swapped at birth. Gareth's proposal had got rid of the problem for Ross Fairbrother. It was done for everyone's good. Gareth remembered that it had snowed the night of Leonie's birth, too. Now it was snowing again. Her birthday on the twenty second of December. She would be twenty-five years old. His precious Leonie! What will she have to say when she knows the lies that have been told to her? That Gloria was not her birth mother. That the mad woman who only that morning had harassed her with snowballs had been her birth mother? That she, in fact, was as much a Jubb as she was a Fairbrother, genetically speaking. Leonie was proud.

Would things have been different for Lizzie had she known the truth? Could she have become better after seeping into her madness had she known that her child had lived? It seemed to get worse with each passing year. He and Gloria had never been able to bring themselves to tell her the truth because they had loved her from the start as they would have loved their dead, deformed little mite, had he lived. But the truth had been erased and the deception so smoothly conceived and abetted and believed that they had actually believed it themselves, even when Gloria had begun to be petrified about seeing the Jubbs down in the village and more importantly, them seeing Leonie who had grown to look more like the product of her birth parents, with each passing year.

They had both suffered in silence, not even sharing their guilt, never talking about it, never acknowledging it, until it had become a canker within their marriage. That was the truth of it. That was the root of Gloria's agoraphobia and her eating disorder. They had spent Leonie's lifetime in guilty fear that she might discover the truth, forgetting from choice the agreement they had made with Ross Fairbrother's solicitor. On Leonie's twenty-fifth birthday, she would be informed of the truth. She would be legally acknowledged as Ross Fairbrother's child and heir, also as Bernard Jubb's grandchild, though why that should matter so much to Ross was anyone's guess.

Gareth was unlocking the door to his police station office, after calling in at the Star, when he saw a woman he recognised waiting on the corner, her clothes clad in snow. Someone he had not seen in the village for quite a few years. "Well, well. Betty Jessop!" he murmured aloud. Come back to tell him that she was alive and well, no doubt. No buses running. He wondered whether he should go and tell her that if she was waiting for the Quinton bus, she was wasting her time. He could also remonstrate with her a bit about all the trouble she had caused the last time. Under the normal scheme of things he might have done so because prior warnings were one of his best tactics when it came to cutting down on his workload. He could also have had a word about her cousin, Hannah, and her niece, Lizzie. Something was going to have to be done about them, that was for sure. Any support he could get from the family, thin on the ground as they were, was all to the better. Not now, though. Maybe after Christmas, if she was still around.

Still he pondered as he saw her bring a bulky envelope out of her pocket and walk towards the pillar box outside the post office. It probably would be going nowhere until the snow stopped and the post could be processed because the roads were closing up. She had stuffed it into the overfull box before he had opened his door. Would it be worth having a word now? Not that she seemed to see him despite her pebble-thick glasses and the way she was looking about herself, even waving to folk she probably didn't know from the surprised look on their faces. Also, he had to prepare himself to cope with the more peculiar characters he came across frequently in his line of work because of the need to be clear in what he had to say well before he said it. They tended, otherwise, to erupt with misunderstanding like a bottle of pop that had been shaken up directly before opening. Queer looking bird, too, though many of the old ladies of the village dressed in much the same way. What Gloria called 'charity shop'. She had a peculiar walk, too, like the leaning tower of Pizza and was carrying an old battered suitcase with string wrapped about the handle, as well as a handbag big enough to sleep in. Then back she walked to the crossing where she made no attempt to press the button, as if making her mind up which way she had to go. Gareth liked to think that she had come to spend Christmas with her cousins. There were far too many old folk in Barns spent Christmas on their own, though they seemed to be the type to think that invites were always up to others.

He soon lost interest under the weight of all his other concerns, gritting his teeth to all thought of what would happen should Ross Fairbrother carry through on the documents signed by all involved on the work of the night of the twenty second of December, twenty-five years ago. Legal documents, in fact, which were held by Ross's solicitor to be followed up on at Ross's discretion alone. Hopefully, like himself and Gloria and Hannah Jubb, it was a thing of the past and would remain so. He was not about to start panicking like Gloria; not until he had reason to, anyway. God alone knew that despite many an opportunity, the matter had never been broached between them since it had occurred. A sluice gate had descended. Gareth could only hope that common decency would prevail, for it seemed indecent to him for anyone to deliberately pull the rug from beneath his family. Gloria would not be able to stand it. Leonie would never speak to them ever again. Lizzie would have to know, too. Dear God! His blood ran cold just to think about what she would do; commit murder most likely. No, Ross would not do it. He was not a bad man, even if in some ways he seemed to be a cold man. Gareth knew though that still waters run deep. So many thoughts running through his own head, as he searched pockets which were reluctant to give up the secret of where he had placed the door keys. Placing his mind squarely back on his job, he had his fingers crossed even as he turned to the better light and began to pat his clothing, looking about, thinking now of how Gloria had been right.

He had already been upstairs to the rooms above the ground floor when he contained his work to the downstairs, as a preference to spending his life running up and down stairs. Even if the street door wasn't open, people knocked on the downstairs window, rather than use his preferred communication route for non-urgent communications; the notebook and pencil kept within the 'snitch-box' on the wall outside his door. A quick look in told him that the box was empty though, mostly, what the box contained was a mere postscript to his more urgent work; e.g. cat lost, a bollard knocked over, a dog knocked down…that kind of thing…as he rummaged, still, to find his keys in all his several pockets.

He found them, eventually, in the lower inside pocket of his padded jacket and then let himself in, having been out of his office for maybe no more than fifteen minutes, with his call on Marty and his visit to the Star overriding everything as preferable to the rest of his dismal preoccupations.

Betty Jessop was by now totally forgotten about and his personal problems rammed back into the mental filing cabinet where he hoped they would remain, the drawer locked and the key turned, so allowing his tired brain free scope to brood on the way the community he protected with such vigour, was failing to support him.

The large space he entered was as cold as his thoughts. In effect, the large knocked-through room, with a single cell; most commonly used as a bed for the night for legless drunks - Chef and Cannon being the most frequent occupants - taking up the whole of the wall opposite the main front door, was the welcome space of a man who loved his work. The only other room being the added-on bathroom which took up a good portion of the original yard area.

This was where he surreptitiously lived because he and Gloria had their pride, still, even if their marriage was an unhappy affair. Apart from popping in to see if Gloria had need of anything, these days, he had little call to even venture across the square to the flat where she and Leonie lived, other than to see his daughter, though he still helped with their shopping and did his own laundry there. Occasionally, watching a big match on the lounge telly when he didn't have a portable within the office; no point as there was never time to watch one, anyway.

He even had a locker of clean uniform, polish, sewing kits and everything else he needed to operate as the only village law enforcement, in the small downstairs bathroom, where he also kept his shaving stuff. Unlike his specials, he had managed to find the time and opportunity to shower, shave and change his clothing without being off duty for a single moment. He was always on duty, didn't even own a civvies-suit, so he never had to think what to wear. Uniform only, which he topped with whatever waterproof and headwear he had in his wardrobe most suitable to the weather. He rarely wore his helmet and certainly not in snow. Everyone in the village knew him anyway.

As he had told Gloria he would, he had earlier taken his cot and sleeping bag up the uncarpeted stairs and let himself into the front room to sleep, after eventually finding his own key to the unused upstairs rooms, from a drawer in his office, the key not having been used for years.

Within his disappointed mind, was a last ray of hope that he had totally misconstrued his wife's very cryptic communication and got hold of the wrong end of the stick. Even as he went, however, he was noticing new damage to the wooden staircase; not much, just a few fresh splinters, but sufficient to tell him that heavy things had been carted up or down, probably down and very recently.

After unlocking both doors, which had locks for security reasons only - it had been known for someone to once attempt a break-in at his station in order to try to retrieve evidence of guilt - what he had found were two newly swept, bare floor boarded rooms, totally empty, as they should be, under bare light bulbs, with newspaper taped up at the windows. He might have tutted and rolled his eyes over the square to Gloria but that proposed gesture had been before he saw the stain on the floor boards in the corner of the front room. He did not even need to crouch to realise that whoever had wielded the brush had not mopped up properly and had missed a few shards of broken, green glass in what was otherwise a thorough sweeping.

His mind had, immediately, gone back to Jim Lamb's bandaged hand. The stain could have been made by either spilled wine or blood, the former of which he could smell as it lingered, wet, between the grooves where it had not been removed. Either fluid was damning, because Jim Lamb could not possibly have had any reason to come up to this room and especially when he was a happily married man devoted to his children. His specials did not have keys to his knowledge, only Tom Greaves's wife who was his office cleaner. Tom Greaves being the local butcher, and one of his volunteer specials, who accepted rent in exchange for Gareth storing the riot van in his tall garage, where otherwise all he had were his freezers.

Not that a cut hand, alone, could be regarded as admissible evidence of Jim Lamb having cut himself in that particular room while removing contraband merchandise, but to Gareth it sealed his suspicions. His specials were infiltrators. He had been seriously manipulated, not only by Bluithe Harcourt but by them also, in order to get him out of the way for their merchandise to be shifted. They had probably been carrying out the same scam for years. Last year it could have been when one of their houses got broken into, another a car accident involving Ian Garstang, way out on the motorway that had required Gareth to be out of the village. They would have been directing him away from the village whenever they wanted to move stuff about. What better storage place, too, than the last place anyone would look; the police station itself. Gareth's anger had hardened. His face had set with an iron determination to find the buggers out. Maybe he was P.C. Plod, after all, but he'd be damned if he would allow it to continue. Thereafter, sleep had been impossible. He would have to have it out face to face with Marty because he had already seen where some of the stuff had landed. He didn't want his specials spooked for the time being, anyway. Let them all think that the only person he was onto was the landlord of the Bald Pheasant Inn.

What to do about the others who he might suspect of involvement, too? Gareth decided not to follow up on Gloria's suggestion about asking Tom Greaves's wife for the only other key to his upstairs rooms; rooms that he had never looked inside for many a long year. He had even forgotten there were upstairs rooms as he went about his business, operating happily and successfully from the ground floor only. But not in future! From now on, he would be moving his bed up here. That would put an end to one of their storage facilities, at least, which, Gareth assumed, would be only one of several.

What he should do, he knew, was to bring in the investigation team based in Manchester whose job it was to wipe the floor with bent coppers, especially specials, but this lot, he was after nailing himself. With nine inch screws, too, and a lump hammer to drive the lesson home to all and sundry. He would nail the whole cat and bloody caboodle of them; the whole ring, then let a judge throw the book at them. If he called in outsiders the gang involved in making him look like an ass-hole, specials included, would simply stand back and laugh at him, probably while they raised a glass of French champagne and smoked a smuggled Havana, blowing smoke rings in his face while they watched all the proceedings from the sidelines. Because that's all that it was to them; a game! A profitable game!

Whatever had been stored up there was probably now long gone, also. Or if not altogether out of Barns it would be gracing domestic cocktail cabinets or wrapped up under Christmas trees in red and green paper. What still had to be distributed would be stored elsewhere. Anywhere. Private garages, spare bedrooms, private cellars. He doubted it'd be in the old caves of Barnston Farm, though he had no doubt that Bluithe Harcourt was a runner of black market goods because of Cannon's aftershave. He would have had him in like a shot but on what evidence? None! And there lay the problem.

He was putting his kettle to boil and stoking his woodstove to get a bit of warmth back into his bones, when his phone rang. It was, of all people, Vera Harcourt.

"Well, where is he then? I've managed to find out that he was with you last night. Marty said you were to have breakfast at the Bald Pheasant when he got a phone call and up and went somewhere. Know where he is, do you?"

"Why are you ringing me, Vera? He isn't in the cell if that's what you're asking."

"He'll be in the bloody hospital when I get my hands on him. I've opened this letter from the Fairview with his P45 in it. He's been sacked!"

"Take it up with a tribunal if he thinks it was unfair dismissal. Why are you phoning me?"

"Because I can't find the bugger. I've been hunting him down ever since I opened this bloody letter. He isn't answering his mobile. If he's with another woman, I'll kill him, God help me. Thing is, I haven't seen him since first thing yesterday morning. Don't particularly want to, either. Thing is, though, he hasn't been home for his injection. Not just his dinner and another two packs of fags from his multi-pack and him no money on him. If he doesn't have his injection, he's in serious trouble. He could end up in a coma."

Gareth sighed heavily. When he looked out of the window, it looked as if someone had covered the glass with rice pudding. "I'll do what I can, Vera, but if I were you I'd get on the telephone to all his cronies."

"Already have. You better take this seriously, Mr. Jones. Very seriously. I'll be suing if you do nothing and he ends up dead. Where'll I get my money from then? You'd be out like a shot if it was one of them Fairbrothers went missing. Because he's only a painter and decorator...or was! If he's not back in this bloody house to face the music by half past five, I'll be on the phone to the Chief Constable, myself."

Gareth closed his eyes, wearily. He didn't doubt her for one moment. Then he frowned. Maybe he could kill two birds with one stone.

The daylight had become an eerie grey colour by mid afternoon, with a light wind which whipped the tops off the drifts like clouds of icing sugar and formed a light blizzard. Even as yet more flakes drifted down from the heavens, to be blown against the door and glass windows of every house on his side of the square. He had to pull his hat down and fold up his collar against the bitter, ice shriven wind. First he would go to Barnston Farm and then up to the Fairview, if he got no joy there. Not that he thought that Bluithe was doing anything more than hide from his wife. He might even have popped into the doctors for his injection if it was vital that he have this injection she was talking about, though it was the first Gareth had heard of Blue having a serious medical problem.

However, he knew that while he went about his other business, it wouldn't go amiss asking if people knew of his whereabouts. The things one had to do to avoid having accusations of inefficiency levelled against a man with too much work to do!

Bluithe Harcourt was causing him problems, once again!

Fifteen

Betty Jessop arrived within the village despite there being no buses running, local taxis only, and no sign that she might have got through from the nearest train station by accepting a lift on a snow plough.

She arrived wearing an old fashioned, brown, woollen bonnet over dull brown hair which had been swept back from her sunken cheeks into a bun at the nape of her neck. Her wet coat was grey herringbone fastened from neck to knee over green rubber overshoes. She had a navy blue, cardboard suitcase with a string wrapped handle and a capacious handbag which she gripped onto by hands covered in black woollen gloves.

As if wanting to be seen and for people to recognise her, she stood at the crossroads in the village, waving to people who passed, though she knew that they would not recognise her, or probably wouldn't, having been so long since she was last in the village. Cold as it was, wind whipping at her in bitter, frozen lashes of driving snow, she stood without pressing the pedestrian crossing button, as the traffic lights stayed on green because there was no traffic about.

She just stood there, waiting, wondering whether she could already expect a visit from the police, knowing, too, that he must have watched her post the bulky letter with the green ink writing on the front. She had had a few errands to run, see, before she got on with the last leg of her journey. The post office being on the same side of the road as the Quinton bus stop, gave her reason to bring the envelope out of her handbag even with Gareth Jones watching.

She had already decided to send it public post. Stamp or no stamp, it would be delivered because it was addressed to 'Gareth Jones and The Law, The Police Station, Barns Village'. Short of putting it into his mailbox, herself, the public post would be the only way to have the bulky envelope delivered without risk of it being connected to her. She was not conducting her own business anyway, but Miss Naughty's…a very naughty, Miss Naughty, in fact. So naughty that even Betty had to tut to herself. This was one of the naughtiest things she had ever done, in fact. One of them chance opportunities which she delighted to take maximum advantage of, having just happened to be at the right place, at the right time and to know that while she was away from the farm, Bluithe Harcourt would not be snooping round. He'd had a bit of an accident, you see. All his own fault, but Hannah would think that what he was suffering presently was only fair justice if she knew. And all the work he had done for them, considering, when there was so much preparation to be made, what with a wedding to cater for and furniture to shift. Lizzie could never have managed without him though it had taken a shotgun to get him to crack on with it. Fortunately, he'd had most of the work sorted before his nasty fall. What Lizzie had not been able to understand was his insistence that the shock could kill a man in his state of health. "I haven't had my injection!" Then fell asleep. It looked as if his leg was broken.

After Betty had posted her letter and made her presence known, though there weren't that many people about, she crossed the road using the same path that Lovick had taken after getting off the bus the night before, head bent against the silent fall of yet more snow. She was looking for a telephone after having disposed of Lovick's mobile and the other one, too, which had come into Lizzie's possession purely by chance. When she peered into the snug of the public inn through the steamy window, no public phone was in evidence, so she crossed over the square to the front of the Star supermarket because she knew that that particular telephone box had numerous taxi business cards stuck onto the glass information panels.

Betty made a call for a taxi to take her on the last part of her journey, comfortable in the knowledge that her presence in the village had been registered by people who would forget her as quickly as they noted her. Might as well get any curiosity out of the way, now, this afternoon and evening, before midnight when she might respectably retire to her room at the Fairview, with them having designated her to the shadows. She was quite well aware that her sudden disappearance the last time had caused more of a kafuffle than she had planned for, though she had noted after speaking with Ross…how difficult to not throw herself on his mercy and plead, that had been!…that some people might want to ask her a few questions, come looking for her as her notoriety had spread. Who would have thought they would have had the Fell Rescue out looking for her, the last time? He'd seen her, too, Gareth Jones. He'd been no more than ten minutes in his station, probably time enough for a cuppa. That's what they did, bobbies; trawled round their village shops drinking cuppa after cuppa. That and the harassing of decent, law abiding citizens while they let the villains go. Hadn't hailed her, better things to do, which was all to the good. Even though he'd had plenty of time to decide whether he was going to let the matter of her sudden disappearance drop, following her mother dying, or pursue it further. That mattered only in as much as it could cause a delay to her final purpose.

What she wanted was for any interest in her presence to be got out of the way. Lots of people had seen her. Let them look, talk, comment, the more the merrier, Betty thought, even if it meant standing out in the snow because come tomorrow they would have no interest. Then forget about her. Also, if she was suddenly no longer here, they would not be calling out the Fell Rescue, again, that much was for sure. People tended to display habitual behaviours.

After she had made her call, and while waiting for the taxi to arrive to pick her up, she went into the Star and bought several batteries of the type to fit a transistor radio and a large, old fashioned, portable tape player.

**

Some of the hardened, lunchtime drinkers at the Bald Pheasant Inn had noticed her and made her a subject of their conversation. "Look what the cat's dragged in?" being about the level of comment.

Being snowed in, laid off and trapped had certain advantages to some people. Marty was doing good business; coining it in. Those drinking in the Bald Pheasant Inn were making the most of it. It was mid afternoon and, as far as they were concerned, Christmas had started two days early. They had seen no other vehicles but snow ploughs and four wheel drives with chains on the wheels since it had begun to snow again in the mid afternoon.

Ian Garstang saw her first. He was offering his opinion over the crowded bar in the snug, pint glass in hand, holding forth on a number of opinions, with the usual group of his cronies who were crowded together like skittles. One of the topics of conversation had been concerned with the true identity of Lovick Johnson. It had travelled around the village like wild fire that there had been a visitor, stayed the night, at Barnston Farm. Never to be known in all the years that Hannah had been working the farm alone. He was looking out of the window as he spoke. "He sounds as batty as Lizzie, don't you think? Bells on his toes! Speaking of Jubbs...who's that over there? By the traffic lights. That's the woman we were all out looking for when she went missing a few years ago. Why's she back, I wonder?"

Interest was rife. They regarded her as another visiting stranger though they knew her on sight, despite it being a good five years since she had last set foot in the village because her sudden disappearance had meant that one of the staff at the Fairview, who was a creditable artist, had drawn a picture of her to flash about. That's when the Jubb resemblance had first been noted. "How's she got here? No buses running."

They watched her stand and look about with her thick glasses becoming snow covered. Her coat was encrusted with a saddle of snow over her thin shoulders as if she had done some walking in the open since it had started to come down again. She even waved at them through the pub window before posting a letter and coming back to the crossroads to look about again.

"If she's waiting for a bus she'll still be standing there Boxing Day."

"She's probably on her way to see her relatives."

"There's still a few taxis running."

"Not safe for cars, out." another commented. "Some four wheel drives, maybe. Like Gareth's yonder. Close call, was that, just now. We all heard what he said, Marty. You'll be glad he's going somewhere. He's just getting into that police car of his. Where's he off to, I wonder?"

Marty hung his head and looked the other way. The discussion he had just had with Gareth was causing him some personal discomfort. He had managed to get him off the scent, he thought, with a feeling of relief; though he had a suspicion that it might be short-lived. However, now was not the time to discuss it with other Robin Hooders. Not with the general public crowding his bar and him being run off his feet, his wife too with all the dinners. He didn't like the fact that the attention of all his regular patrons was still with their local bobby who, only fifteen or so minutes ago, had walked out of the front door of his hostelry and across the snowy square to make straight into the Star, no doubt to buy some batteries for his police torches, all the better to be prepared, this time. He had rumbled the riot van ruse and they knew it!

For a moment they all watched Gareth Jones stand on the pavement on the other side of the square, searching through his pockets for his keys to his car. A big man in ski cap and padded jacket. His boots were clogging up with compacted snow. He looked shot at and little wonder after being up all last night. Others within the bar at the Bald Pheasant Inn had been up all night also, engaged as they had been in the business of shifting what Gareth Jones would be better not to know about. They had been warned not to underestimate their village bobby, though, by 'The Boss'. That had been the message passed on by Marty, using his own terminology; "Not as green as he's cabbage looking is our Mr. Plod. Not by a long chalk!"

He was obviously going somewhere, despite the heavily falling snow. One night to go. Bluithe should have got the stuff boxed and ready for the last run, if it was possible to shift it. It all depended on what 'The Boss' said. Then the telephone rang. When he answered it using the handset on the wall behind him, it was Vera, Bluithe's wife. As it was, he did know where Bluithe was but he would have to go along with it. He was probably staying well out of Vera's way, nursing a bottle of something very warming. Where Marty thought him to be was well provisioned even if he got stuck in there or, as he suspected, preferred to stay there. It would be as well, anyway, van coming. It would have to be a hired transit, this time. Best for Bluithe to stick with it. The last person he wanted spoiling things was Vera Blabbermouth Harcourt!

"I'm to ask you all again…has anyone seen Blue Harcourt. Own up if you have because Vera's got Gareth Jones out looking for him."

All he received back was blank stares. Ian Lamb was nursing a very sore looking cut hand which nevertheless hadn't stopped him from holding a small rum and blackcurrant. "No idea!" He didn't either.

Marty shrugged. Then into the phone. "Seeing a man about a dog…Get your own coat on and go looking for him if you're that bothered, Vera…What?…No!…He needs a what?…An infection?" Marty put the receiver back with a shake of his head. "She says she hopes he gets the clap if he's shacked up with another woman!"

Ian Garstang tittered. He had no intention of worrying about Blue Harcourt. He was not going to worry about anything more than making sure the turkey was big enough for the family Christmas dinner, his drinks cabinet was crowded with bottles and his children had enough presents under the tree. Neither was he going to worry about Gareth Jones doing too much snooping. Even if he did it would be too late. At least it would be after the last of the merchandise was shifted. He would have nothing to do with that as he had to be on duty again, come the morning, as a voluntary policeman. Anyway, they played out much the same pantomime year after year. Gareth was entirely predictable. He would probably be going to sit in the library where he could write his report up in comfort, with a change of scenery. Meticulous in that, he was. He was set in his ways of conducting his business no matter how tired he might feel. After writing his notes up there, where the librarian often made him a cup of tea, he'd come back to the office to empty his mailbox and see to post and then answer the tape machine messages. Lastly he'd look at his emails, by which system he would prioritise his work into a manageable schedule. Anyone local, wanting him when he was out, had to leave a message using the handset which was linked to another tape machine. Any emergencies had to be dealt with by phoning 999 and then wait for someone to come up from Quinton, if Gareth wasn't on the job. There was a box on the wall for lost property and written messages using the paper and pencil within and prevented from being stolen by a long piece of string. He was on the job twenty four hours a day. "Does the man ever sleep?"

As he wiped down his bar between servings of brimming pints, Marty switched the conversation deliberately back to Betty Jessop's mysterious arrival by nodding to her as she peered in at his snug room window, then crossed the road to enter the telephone box to make a call, he assumed. "Name of Betty Jessop, if I recall. Had a gin off me and left without paying last time she was here. I never forget that kind of treatment. How's she got here? No buses running in this weather. No trains, either." Then he scowled, reverting to sarcasm as he always did when under threat. "Maybe she's floated down from the clouds under her umbrella like Mary Poppins." He was obviously still hot under the collar after the subject of the riot van had cropped up.

Ian Garstang joined in with the Mary Poppins theme, as he watched Betty Jessop cross over to the other side of the square. "She's probably fast-roped down from one of them helicopters. No bloody peace, is there?" he remarked because there had been choppers inspecting the villages and homesteads for those who threatened to be buried under drifts and in need of help, since the crack of dawn that morning. That meant that nothing could move in daylight if they had cameras up there without being recorded on the footage that could be checked several times over. They were all waiting on orders from 'The Boss', anyway. Nothing went anywhere without a direct order from 'God'. When she went from the phone box into the Star supermarket, he forgot about Betty Jessop, entirely.

He sunk the last of his pint before heading back to his office. The senior partner in his law firm had asked him to go down to the cellar below their offices and look up an archive reference which had been stored there for twenty-five years. Fairbrother business. They did a lot of Fairbrother business at his firm which was only ever handled by the senior partners. The packet was to be on the senior partner's desk for first thing tomorrow morning when an important meeting was to take place. Ross involved this time and not the mother. God, what a stuffy old bird, she was! Ian enjoyed his job as a barrister for the prosecution of thieves and highwaymen. It took one, to know one, so to speak.

***

Meanwhile, over the rooftops and smoking chimneys, the choppers from the Meteorological Office circled the snowbound landscape taking details of traffic accidents and snowdrifts in order to send reports back down in radio waves to Radio Lancashire and Radio Yorkshire which then broadcast them out right around the world to anyone who was interested.

Practically every home in the village of Barns listened to their local radio station because it had become important to know how deeply they were being snowed in. The weather reports were coming thick and fast in between Christmas messages and renditions of Slade's 'Merry Christmas' song. They broke the silences within the sitting rooms of Barns as the villagers bunkered in for a prolonged spell of bad weather in front of blazing fires with the spicy smell of home baked mince pies adding to the pleasure. There was even a cheerful expectation in the way people greeted each other. They talked about the coming of a Christmas when the landscape would be decorated with snow. Someone would win the bet with Ladbrokes if it lasted on a few days.

Schools had been closed for days already. The kids were out building snowmen and whizzing down hills on tea trays, having the time of their lives, all over the place. It had been hurriedly planned by the Barns Residents Association Committee, run by the vicar, for a competition to be arranged using the snow as the craft material from which they might fashion igloos and snow houses on the village square. The best family-made snowman would earn its makers a skiing holiday in Austria, all expenses paid for two adults and two children. The Residents Committee were already running raffles and organizing fund raising events to pay for it within the Bald Pheasant Inn and the Community Hall which was a square, prefabricated building next to the church, selling numbered stubs in different colours through Greaves's Butcher's shop and the local Star supermarket, the Church Manse, the Post Office Counters and some of the other parade of small, bespoke shops. All of which were as well stocked as the Bald Pheasant Inn despite the snow having closed the arterial roads, in and out. No one was about to starve, though the villagers might not get all their post.

It was near as damn it to the national holiday, anyway, with the preparations having been made weeks ago for a time which tended to meld the villagers together within a season usually preceded with quarrelsome discontent. It was the generous spirit of the festive season which ensured that no one was forgotten, other than Hannah and Lizzie Jubb, both of whom would go spare if anyone put as much as a foot through their gate. They would wheel the rest of the old and the ailing down to the community centre on Christmas Eve and give them a present and a free turkey dinner. Peace and goodwill and the spirit of Christmas allowing old grievances to disappear for the twelve days of Christmas, even if the bickering and backbiting always began again in the New Year.

Peace and good will to all men.

The only blot on the village economy seemed to be the effect that the snow might have on the Fairview Country Club Hotel which would have a ripple effect on those from the village who worked there, if the hotel had to close due to the bad weather.

Not that the Fairbrothers took a bit of something like snow lying down! As could be expected of Ross Fairbrother, his talent for crisis planning was paying off. It was rumoured that he had been in email contact with some of his old army pals and had arranged for their Christmas guests to be airlifted in by helicopter when it seemed that the snow might last into the weekend and beyond. Just his kind of mission, though he still had a lugubrious face, staff noted, as he spent a good few hours of the Monday morning planning the logistics of a major, military operation which entailed a chopper landing at the small craft section of Manchester and Leeds/Bradford airports, the pilots dressed as Father Christmases, in order to make the pretence of whisking stranded guests off to Greenland. Followed by the landing, it was rumoured, on the helipad where Mrs. Fairbrother was having another giant Christmas tree erected, which was where the children's playground had once been but had been got rid of when Mrs. Fairbrother had reviewed the Health and Safety policies of the hotel. The guests were now to be welcomed by a candlelit choir made up of staff and led by this new musician chap, Lick Johnson, who Ross had taken on for the duration of the holiday and, so far, promised to be good. The staff had already heard him practising and decided that he would be able to lead carols as well as do Elvis and Bob Dillon impersonations. He told a few jokes, too, to make them laugh. The no-hope-talent had actually turned out to be quite good. An immediate hit with all and sundry except for Chef and Cannon, and Mrs. Fairbrother who had yet to be introduced to him. He had arrived while she was out shopping. She always lunched in her own apartment up in the rafters and then napped for the afternoon. That pleasure was yet to come. They all said how much they would love to be a fly on the wall when that happened! Bells on his toes, apparently! That would not go down well with Mrs. Fairbrother who liked all the attention to be on her.

Otherwise, all the staff in their red and gold uniforms and Father Christmas hats had been pleased to meet him, shake hands and offer to help if he needed anything. The cubicle room in the basement he was given was not as expected but the company pleased Lovick who, above all else, liked to be liked. Within a few hours he was all settled in and regretting nothing. He even had a new girlfriend in the pipeline and one, moreover, with whom he had become instantly smitten and it seemed that his interest was returned.

Leonie Jones; his very own Christmas fairy!

He had already forgotten about Hannah and Lizzie Jubb as if it had been nothing but a bad dream.

Sixteen

Cannon and Chef shared a secret resentment against Leonie Jones which had begun with her unexpected promotion to front of house staff. Hitherto, she had just been a kitchen girl who took orders. They saw Lovick Johnson for what they thought he was; a jack-the-lad, here today, gone tomorrow type, who would love her and leave her at the drop of a hat. Unlike the other staff who Lovick had managed to impress as a hale fellow well met…his mating prowess aside…they couldn't see what all the fuss was about. Elvis impersonations? Bells on his boots? Vain as a peacock. Always looking at himself in the mirror and rearranging those shiny, dark curls of his, before smoothing down his bushy eyebrows with an index finger covered in spit. Strutted, too, with a habit of constantly shrugging his shoulders as if to ensure that his clothes hung off his lean length in exactly the way he wanted them to.

Leonie Jones had yet to take her eyes off him. He had yet to take his eyes or his hands off her despite them having only just met. Within a half hour of first meeting they had been seen availing themselves of burgers and sucking deeply through crushed straws, from glass, Coke bottles, while sitting very close together in a corner seat in the Gamekeeper's Bar, never for a moment having taken their eyes off each other.

Cannon, who had served them, suspected that it would take Lick Johnson less than a day to do what had not been achieved already, if speculation was right; the deflowering of Leonie Jones, local virgin, by all accounts. He and Chef had begun a private bet that entailed being aware of what went on between the young ones. It may be the depths of winter but, by God, the sap was rising in the musician's branches and Leonie was giving out a mating call like a spring bird.

Suddenly, she had changed her mind about taking one of the staff cubicles down in the basement where she could sleep between long shifts without going home to her Mum. She had been to see Mr. Ross already, to arrange it, though she would have to remind him of the allocation of a cubicle room. He was so forgetful, these days, distracted by his own thoughts which staff could only guess at, and seeming to have been taken aback by Leonie's request. Momentarily, his eyes had narrowed and a cunning expression had darkened his moustachioed face. He had practically tripped over himself in agreeing to her wishes, his hand excitedly smoothing back his fair hair so destroying what had hitherto been a perfect parting. He had begun to witter and twitter like an idiot and blush to the roots of the hairs growing out of his middle-aged ears. He only had to be in her presence to lose an ability to speak coherently.

The staff were agog. Talk about watch this space! Tongues were wagging in dark corners and broom cupboards all over the place. Eyes were rolling in Mr. Ross's and Leonie's and Lick Johnson's direction. Usurper that he was because there was no misconstruing her choice between an old fart and a young pip-squeak, they said…while Leonie and Lick Johnson had eyes only for each other.

Mr. Ross would definitely have his nose put out of joint, by now. The staff had already taken note of the favouritism in his treatment of her and, in particular, a promotion that others did not feel that she deserved. Of course, he had to be delirious if he thought he even stood a chance with Leonie when a young, very virile looking, handsome lad like Lick Johnson had come on the scene. If lust was ever in evidence between two young people, they were witnessing it between their new receptionist and the strolling minstrel. It had been commented on that fate had plucked her out of the kitchens where she might otherwise have stayed like Cinders before her introduction to the Prince. Of. Soul. And. Rock. And. Roll. Yeah!

And talk about technique as well as timing! Lick Johnson hadn't been in the hotel above a few hours, first staff rehearsal over, he the Prince to her Snow White, and his conquest of Leonie had already been declared to have passed through the first stages of undeniable, sexual attraction. As far as Cannon and Chef were concerned it was an association which could lead nowhere but to a done and dusted outcome, upon which they might bet. She would either slap his face or let him have his wicked way, within the period of his stay. They would draw straws for the sweepstake like they did for the Grand National, even if it was only a two horse race. They had only to look at his tight trousers, when he had reappeared in the foyer from getting showered and changed, to note that his equipment was stud and that she could not help but notice it either. He was wearing a pink and orange shirt with tassels and a black silk bandana to offset the tightest black jeans on his string bean legs. The bulge at crotch was big enough for Chef to wonder if the lad was wearing a cricket box. Part of his stage costume, maybe, but the bells on his boots? Cannon could not resist asking him where the rest of the Morris Dancers were. Or was he a full team all on his own.

For his part, any attention was better than none. Besides which, he was only ever embarrassed when his stage performance was questioned. He considered Morris Dancers to be manly men with bigger bells than his, even. He soaked up the attention like the showman he was, even giving an extra bit of performance with his unsymmetrical body impression of Elvis on a writhe. "Yeah! Yeah!"

He had already proved that his vanity was up to par at the first rehearsal when what was supposed to be an ad-lib performance, lasting no more than a half hour, proved to be turning into something more upmarket than any of them dared to suppose. The electricity crackling between Lick and Leonie was almost setting them on fire with Mr. Ross directing the rehearsal, too. He was, obviously, finding her lack of attention to him hard to bear when she kept ignoring his stage prompts and took notice only of Lovick. If he had had his mother's green eyes, it would have made the entertainment perfect.

Cannon saw nothing wrong in helping things along, too, if they were all to be diverted. No such thing as luck, and all that; only good management. He might slip a bit of something into Leonie's drink when she wasn't looking, given half a chance. She was tea-total. It wouldn't take much to have her swooning. Why not? If Cannon could manage it, he'd slip into her room now that she was sleeping in and look through that handbag of hers for a diary and a telltale strip of contraceptive pills. How else would they know? Even if they were already holding hands and staring deeply into each other's eyes as part of their rehearsal, a bet needed conclusive proof for it to be settled. What they got up to without an audience would probably create enough heat to steam a cabbage, but in private who would know? They might watch the condom machine in the staff gents. If he was buying on a daily basis they would have to assume that he was using them for the purpose for which they were intended.

Cannon's vindictive nature was given free reign. He would not only enjoy seeing the little, haughty bitch used and disappointed but he would also be laughing up his sleeve at Mr. Ross as well. He planned to enjoy every minute when he described in detail, to Mr. Ross, even perhaps to Mrs. Fairbrother also, what she was up to. They always listened and followed through. Look at Bluithe Harcourt. It had been Cannon who had brought suspicion on Chef over the disappearing hams, too. Though, as far as his own mischief was concerned, he had only purloined the one, not two. Just helped himself when Chef had been subdued with a hangover the size of London Bridge. Had one whipped into the back of his car and passed over the bar at the Bald Pheasant Inn when no one was looking and the money pocketed in the time it took to order a pint. Though what had happened to it after he had sold it to Marty, the landlord at the pub, he had not the faintest idea. He had had an extra ten quid in his pocket for his trouble. Where the second ham had disappeared to was a mystery yet to be solved. He had not taken the second one. Maybe the dog had eaten the other one or Chef had eaten it himself in one of his drunken states and couldn't remember. Or there had been a miscount. Worst suspicion of all; he had competition from someone else with access to the kitchen and its larders. Cannon would have to start looking out for that one. Nothing worse than a thief! Or Mrs. Fairbrother knowing. Mr. Fairbrother had decided not to worry his mother with the issue when Leonie had blurted it out after the cold larder audit; "There's two French hams missing, Mr. Ross."

Which reminded him that he had received a phone call from Marty that afternoon asking him to do a spot of investigating on his behalf concerning why the new musician had spent a night at Barnston Farm, which was a first for anyone since Hannah's husband, Bernard Jubb, had been found dead in the well. Why suddenly give a bed to a stranger when she would see the villagers freeze to death before allow them over her doorstep? A mystery, that one, which needed solving because there was a great deal of tittle-tattle going about.

***

The tale was going around which, as far as Marty was concerned, bordered on the preposterous. About the lad being Lizzie's son; the baby she had given birth to which had not died at birth, after all, but been whisked away to be adopted. It did not take much in Barns to start the gossips' tongues wagging and then make it up as they went along.

Cannon had agreed. "Maybe the new kitchen help can tell us something. She's due today, this afternoon. Betty Jessop. The one we called the Fell Rescue out for five years ago when all the time she was in Harrogate. She's a distant relative of Hannah Jubb by all accounts. Families tend to close ranks at such times. Maybe she will know what happened to the babby if it wasn't buried in the orchard after all."

Marty had made agreeing noises and told Cannon that he had already seen her in the village. They shared old gossip like a couple of old hags on a park bench as they recalled, over the phone, how it had crossed more than one person's mind that Lizzie's baby could have been spirited away to be adopted and the rumour of its death put about as a smoke screen. None of them had seen it and the local doctor who had supposedly issued a valid death certificate, had been an out and out junkie who hadn't a clue what certification he had been issuing half the time. Sick notes had rolled off his pad in quick succession. Then Ross Fairbrother would have had a strong influence on matters. The unborn baby had become an embarrassment. Marty was in agreement that Ross Fairbrother should have accepted more personal responsibility than he had. If Marty himself could be frogmarched by his own father-in-law to the church, then Ross Fairbrother should have been, also.

Only supposing this lad was Lizzie's supposedly dead son come to claim his inheritance, though. There would be a sizable inheritance to be had, too, if the farm lease got passed on along the bloodline, as was part of its legal contract. There was money at Barnston Farm despite its dereliction. Her animals all ended up at market. Say what you wanted to about Hannah Jubb, she knew how to count her pennies. No short changing her when she came down to the shops and then wandered into his tap room bringing the stench of the farm in with her. If she ordered a double measure of gin, she would have a double measure of gin and woe betide anyone who tried to give her short measure. He had found that out himself the hard way. Better to give her the bottle and let her pour her own even, though it was at Hannah's insistence that he had never served her Lizzie. "Drink makes her maudlin," was her reason, such being a rare time when he actually refused to serve anyone. The more legless they got, the more he could take off them. He was not running his pub for Alcoholics Anonymous.

Marty was mightily interested in money; his own and other people's. Somewhere would be a whole pile of money, stacked up and growing at Barnston Farm which was one reason why he suspected that Bluithe was always round there, searching. He'd got mad when his searches had proved to be unsuccessful, short of entering her house. He had told him. "And there is still another way in. A big cavern like a cathedral. An old quarry working. There's money there, somewhere. What's that daft Lizzie going to do with it?"

Lucky Lovick Johnson, indeed, if he was the long, lost grandson! There was the other side of things, too: Ross Fairbrother. He and his mother making money hand over fist!

Speculation was rife! Good for business! It was back again as an item on everyone's lips. His pub was buzzing with it. Gossip made folk thirsty and not as keen to count their change as interest took hold. Suited him nicely, too, as a distraction from the subject of Gareth Jones's riot van and the near miss of the other night when they had moved the merchandise from the disused rooms over the Police Station with the ruse of sending Gareth Jones off on a wild goose chase. What they had not considered was Gloria's sleeplessness. He would have to keep her sweet. As well as the sliced, roast beef he'd sent her already, maybe some nice French mustard and one of the hampers he had set aside to use in a draw would help to remind her that a woman of her physical proportions cannot subsist on a policeman's wage alone. That should keep her happy for the time being, at least. All they needed was another night with Gareth Jones at some distant place from where they would have to shift the stuff on a long run, tonight, snow permitting. They had to move the stash today or see it wasted because a lot of foodstuff was involved in this stash. The snow had come at altogether the wrong time, even if it would keep drivers off the road tonight. They would still have to park up a transit in a prominent position, on the river bridge at Barnston New Road, in fact, where passers by might see them on the way up to the Fairview Country Club Hotel. Then there was the matter of their order lists being mislaid. Not that they didn't have others. It was just that 'The Boss' was having kittens. She didn't like being blackmailed.

Yep! This distraction over Bluithe's whereabouts would serve them fine. Bluithe would be fine where he was for the present, set to task by 'The Boss' making up sets of Christmas hampers, all the food having been kept nice and cool because of its underground location, even if Blue had taken Gareth a bit too close for comfort, last night, when they had been after clearing the rooms above his police station.

Marty couldn't understand the fuss Vera was making. Fancy wishing her husband an infection to put him in hospital. At least that's what he thought she'd said. It also occurred to him that if Gareth was out looking for Blue, then he'd have to leave behind all his inconvenient questioning about the riot van. He'd have to leave them alone long enough to get all the merchandise to where it was going.

They had a full order book.

***

The costumes for the staff pantomime were presenting Leonie with the main headache now that she was getting to feel more organised and a little more on top of her new job in reception. Of course, with Lick being in show business, he had been the first sympathetic ear she could complain to, while he had stroked her hand, moved closer, stroked her hair; let his breath fall on her cheek. What was happening to her? The air between them was charged with magnetic ions, with electrons and atoms building by the minute. However, she was aware of being watched, mainly by Chef and Cannon, and then Mr. Ross was forever hovering, so she had to make sure that she did not allow herself to be compromised. Not that she could chase Lick away. Not when he had been kind enough to offer to help her get some panto clothes together. He said that he knew somewhere where, as a last resort only, they might save the day. First, however, they would have to look for old curtains, bedding, bathrobes, anything shiny and bright, within the hotel itself.

They scoured the hotel store rooms and linen cupboards for stage clothes with little success other than to mound up a pile of old curtains. In that time alone he'd managed to hold her hand, put his arm over her shoulder and give her a peck on the cheek. Leonie's head had begun to swim because she found him so very attractive. Drop dead gorgeous, in fact. It was the consensus of most of the female staff who had already managed to give Leonie their opinion. It had been obvious to one and all within the first few moments of meeting that they had 'tapped off' as the local saying went. Since then he had got his hand on her rump and Leonie did not mind at all it staying there.

Another drink and a burger in the bar after the costume search; two cokes and two straws, heads together, and their attachment was being consolidated in other ways. He was such a charmer, as had already been noted by everyone present in the ballroom by the time rehearsals ended. His public work on her erogenous areas had been commended by Cannon who had enjoyed watching Mr. Ross's disapproval as the rehearsal had progressed. The offending gestures had included blowing in her ear, kissing the palm of her hand with a smouldering passion and placing a proprietary hand on her shoulder which, obviously, melted like a warm emollient into her flesh. She had responded by hitching up her long, voluminous skirt at the waist to show an incredible pair of slim, shapely legs and by letting down her hair to frame an unexpectedly sexy face. From somewhere, she had produced foundation face cream and powder, lipstick, blue eye shadow and a set of false eyelashes. They had been in that capacious handbag of hers all the time. She had begun to smile a bit more than she usually did, too, and give him shy, little glances.

Cannon felt satisfied. The barriers were falling away. He could tell all the signs from his secret pursuit of Jackie Collins novels. What if he was a potential heir to a fortune? It was not always obvious. Sometimes they got people in the hotel who looked as rich as Croesus and then couldn't pay the bill. Vice verse too. He'd once had a two hundred pound tip in cash from an unwashed tramp who had taken over Eagle Suite, having being asked to pay in cash, in advance. Could he be Lizzie Jubb's son come back to claim his inheritance? Why not ask him. "You a relative of the Jubbs then are you?"

Lovick had been rubbing his guitar with a polishing rag at the time. "Nah!"

Then someone else asked him the same. "What's all this then?"

He got no answer.

It had crossed Leonie's mind, too. She had been in a position to ask him directly, once he had explained what had happened to delay his arrival, after they had kissed passionately outside the ballroom, rehearsals over, when no one was around; tongues even, his hands roving over her buttocks and pulling her against him, tight. What a man! What a talent! What a lover he would make! What a change was coming over her! Something was happening to Leonie that had never happened before. But she drew a line at going out with a Jubb. "Is it true you're related to Hannah Jubb? They're saying you could be her grandson. Lizzie's son that didn't die, after all."

"That's the third time I've been asked that same question today. The answer's no! N.O. says no! Why would anyone think that?"

Leonie shrugged. "Circumstance, that's all."

"Good God!" His raised eyebrows and enlarged orbs had then accompanied a shriek of disgust as his cheeks sucked in. "If I *was* a relative of theirs, I'd deny it. Which I am not! Stinks like one of her pigs, she does. That Lizzie's three sheets to the wind if you ask me. No, I am *not* related to Hannah Jubb!"

"That's alright then. Neither am I."

The look on her face had been one of relief. It gave Lovick the excuse he needed to move in closer if he needed any excuse. "I'm glad it's alright because I want you to be my girl, Leonie Jones. We've only just met, I know. This has never happened to me before."

"Me neither, Lick. The moment I laid eyes on you I felt I'd known you forever."

He found that his hand straying up under her blouse was not prevented from cupping a breast. Her skin felt as soft as velvet while her nipple was as hard as a rock. She had her eyes closed so he took it as permission to fondle, and did. It was only when he took her hand and placed it to feel his space rocket that she took objection but even then seemed reluctant to obey her own advice. "Best not. Not yet any way."

Lovick was vastly disappointed. Yet strangely respectful of the fact that she wanted a bit more than a swift bit of nookey and an even quicker goodbye. He had never known a woman before who had aroused feelings other than just lust. Not that he had anything against just lust. Just lust had often meant that he need not be on his own, in the dark, at dead of night, with only a blue smiley face for company. This time it felt different, though. It was Leonie herself he wanted; his Christmas Tree Fairy with a golden glow smile just for him. Was this what love was? Wanting to make someone else as happy as one wanted to be, oneself?

She obviously wanted him, too, even though she had been shy of his space rocket. Her face was cloudy with her own disappointment in having said no. Her arms stayed around his neck as she tried to explain further. "I can't just yet. It's too soon. I need to know you better. Maybe you can come down to the village to meet my parents. My dad's the local policeman."

The news had been an off-putter to Lick for about three seconds; the time it took for her to smile at him and snuggle close again. The one thing he would not be telling her was that he had a police record. Or give her dad sufficient information to run a police check on him. It was not that his intentions were even remotely dishonourable where Leonie was concerned. He really did like her. Never in his life before had he sat and talked to a girl and found himself enraptured let alone allow a girl to call the shots. But he really did like her and so had to allow her to like him before that piece of info got passed on. Attraction being one thing, trust another! Sort of build the kind of bridge which makes for people being kind to each other. They had already discovered a great deal in common just by talking over a burger and a coke. They liked the same music and food, laughed at the same jokes and though he thought her to be dressed a bit strange it was her work uniform and not the clothes he would take her out in. Then he had shown her a bit of the soft-lad side of himself; gnat brain who had never grown up and never likely to.

When he'd found out about the Snow Building Competition as the staff talked between themselves during rehearsals, he had later jokingly said to Leonie that he might enter, though it wasn't a joke. He quite fancied building a house out of snow with a resident snowman. He had the same urge to get out and play in the snow as he had had when he was five. So why not do it with the chance to win a holiday? She hadn't mocked him, either. Even said they might enter together. Now that was a girl worth knowing.

Then he'd recited his Christmas poem and told her about his dream of one day having a home of his own with a real, bushy tree, decorated with wishes. She hadn't laughed at that either. Or when he had told her of his best mate, Quincey, whom he had described to her with blunt honesty. She said she'd like to meet him because he sounded good fun. That was a first within the long line of girls he'd done little more than go to bed with. He'd stopped short, though, at phoning Quincey on his mobile and asking him to come up when the weather allowed a safe journey. Why spoil a good thing?

His decision not to mix Leonie and Quincey for the time being, at least, was one reason for not phoning. The other was that he was suddenly aware of his mobile being missing. It had been in his jacket pocket, he was sure, when he had hung his coat up behind the bedroom door at Barnston

Farm. He was sure he had not used it since phoning the police for Hannah Jubb. It could have been in his kit bag when Lizzie Jubb emptied it out all over the dirty, bedroom floor. She might even have taken it while he was asleep in the same way she had thought she could take his guitar and get away with it. There had been no lock on the door to stop her coming into his room when he had been sleeping which was the only time she could have taken it if it had been in his coat pocket.

Anyway, it was missing. All he could do was search his possessions and if still not found take a trip back to Barnston Farm to find it. He explained his absent phone to Leonie and asked her to go with him at some convenient point.

She nodded. "It probably was Lizzie took it. She does that kind of thing. Was that her scarf I saw in your overcoat pocket? I think I've seen her wearing a scarf like that before."

Lovick nodded, feeling a hypocrite. He could hardly rail against Lizzie for taking his guitar when he had run off with her scarf. "I picked it up off the snow where she'd dropped it. Just forgot about it when I found that she'd tipped my kit bag all over the floor."

"Better take it back and use that as the excuse to ask if you left your phone. It's no use to Hannah or Lizzie. They won't know how to use one. Is it a Pay As You Go?"

Lick nodded.

"No good to them, is it, once the money runs out. How much was in it?"

"A couple of quid. Not much. I could even try phoning the number to see if she answers it."

Leonie found her own from her bag and handed it over. Lovick put in his number and pressed go. The line connected. "It's ringing. At least it's not crocked."

Then a female voice answered. It sounded to Lovick like Hannah Jubb but was more likely to be her daughter. "Who that?"

"That you, Lizzie? You've got my phone."

It went dead. As expected, perhaps. Lovick handed it back to Leonie. "Lizzie, I think. Or Hannah, maybe. Hannah said she was after getting one. Maybe the only way to get it back will be to go round there. Will you come with me?"

She shook her head. "You're as well to report it lost to my dad and let him go get it for you."

Lovick considered that it was hardly worth the trouble, him being a stranger. Her dad had better things to do.

***

Betty found the number to ring for a taxi, using the public phone, from those displayed in the telephone box. She used the wait-time to shop for her batteries.

She had to wait for well over ten minutes in the cold before it turned up, though.

When it came, the driver took little notice of her until she spoke, other than to enquire of her destination. He wasn't going anywhere out of the village because as yet the snowploughs had not cleared the roads. It would be double rate for the journey. Take it or leave it.

"How much?" It was Betty's voice that people noticed first; flat, very nasal, very Yorkshire.

"A tenner."

"It's barely over a mile."

She pushed her head through his window.

He had to pull back his face. All he could see was eyes as big as speckled hen's eggs behind thick, bottle-bottom glasses though the colour was indiscernible; merely pale. Then her sallow, sunken cheeks as she sucked them in.

"Some people should be locked up and the key thrown away." She meant every word she said, literally.

"Right then. Let's call it fifteen, shall we?"

"Bah!"

"Up front."

Seventeen

Ross was in the process of assessing his new entertainer. He had already noted a flowering romance between Leonie and Lick Johnson but knew better than to say anything when Leonie would misconstrue his intentions and think that his interest in her relationships was fired by jealousy. Until tomorrow, he could not offer a paternal mantel to justify his concern for her wellbeing. What might he say, after tomorrow? Something along the lines of, "Unhand my daughter, you cad!"

Not that he would, anyway. It would be absurd. He knew the limitations that his exposure would contain. He could no more be a father figure to her as she could be a carefree daughter to him. Besides which, he considered Leonie to be a sensible, well behaved girl who would rush into nothing, anyway, so he saw no reason to worry about her in that way.

He had been surprised, though, when she had asked him for a staff cubicle; one of those they had had built some six years previously, down in the basement, which while being adequate to bodily needs were hardly salubrious. He was even considering, after tomorrow, allotting her Eagle Suite. However, it was like she was taking a step in his direction and letting her barriers down. His spirits rose before taking their usual dive. He had been so desperately looking for a lifebelt to buoy him up in the turbulent waters ahead. Ross saw her request as a supportive gesture towards his, as yet, unbroached intentions. She was growing up, perhaps; of her own age and ready to spread her own wings and become her own person, separating herself from her over-protective parents. Showing him, unwittingly, that she was mature enough, perhaps, to be able to cope with the shock of what he determined she would have to be told. For Bern's sake more than his own. He was doing it for Bern, he told himself; the only person who had ever shown him any demonstrable love. Ross thinking of himself as a lone dog with a stony existence, begging at butchers' doors for whatever emotional scraps were chucked his way. He expected nothing of her emotions other than to realise that he would lay, at her feet, all that was his. She would be crowned, too, with all that had been Bern's. His act would be the reparation, the stitches, the repair to the ripped, torn sheet of his life, of Lizzie's life, of Hannah's. He could see no reason to hold compassion for Gloria and Gareth Jones because they had held her as a precious jewel in their caring hands for twenty-five years. Now it was time to share.

The pantomime rehearsal had been a way of watching her without having to do so surreptitiously. Such opportunity was rare. He had let them, together, Leonie and Lick, get on with suggesting and directing. Lick showing a talent for slapstick humour as well as several styles of singing. Ross had stepped up only when his own part as the Wicked Witch demanded that he put aside his own embarrassment and make the pretence of an acting skill he did not possess. Between times, he stood in the background and watched as Lick tried his best to organise a dispirited staff who had had to be press-ganged into what Ross saw as a team building exercise. Then Leonie became enthused. The rest of the staff involved became enthused, also, as a chain reaction. Even Cannon and Chef found themselves smiling.

Lick Johnson seemed to enjoy nothing better than playing to an audience and had managed, by the time the first rehearsal was over, to capture the spirit of things. Even Cannon had shown willing as he played a range of minor parts. It would all come together with a few costumes and lights as a light-hearted piece of family entertainment, sufficient to amuse and bind together a New Year spirit. As a team building exercise, it was proving to be as good as an army rock climb, though he had never managed to get the staff to participate in the kinds of dare devil sports he loved.

He had watched Lick perform a rendition of 'Blue Suede Shoes' for Leonie's benefit and had found himself reasonably impressed. Especially when it came to the 'toe walk/hand droop/ hip jerk' movement while hanging a lopsided grin, very akin to an Elvis smile. As long as he could sing carols as sweetly as Elvis could sing 'Are you Lonesome Tonight' the lad would do the job which Ross had employed him to do without spending a small fortune on a renowned entertainer. Even if Ross could never predict how his mother would react, with her having a sense of propriety second to none. His pants were rather tight.

The rehearsal had, in fact, been a relief from a lot of other pressing problems for a short time, at least. If he was giving out the impression that he was a man beleaguered by worry it was not far from the mark. The most pressing, of course, of a business nature, being the snow itself. Getting the guests to the hotel in a white-out, with a blizzard presently making it impossible to walk anywhere outside the building, was no straightforward thing. While the forecast was for the snow to linger before a thaw, it was not predicted to still be falling come the morning. That would mean that while the roads would still not be open, the skyways would. Those guests coming from the west would now be taxied from Manchester Victoria Station in the city centre to the small craft section of the city airport and flown in. Those coming from the east would be ferried to Leeds/Bradford airports to arrive the same way. At least it looked now as if the hotel could open for business which had become imperative to it remaining financially viable. They simply could not afford to lose the Christmas trade.

Truthfully, if Ross had his way, the hotel would be shut down altogether, the buildings razed and the land sold off. His mother would simply not accept Ross's insistence that family run hotels were unable to compete, these days, with the international, city based chains which could provide as good a service far cheaper. The Fairview expenses, even before revenue was considered, were increased by their remoteness from cheaper suppliers. He would not sink any more of his personal wealth into what might be a dying concern, though his mother constantly begged him to make that commitment. She would not allow investors in, either. All her own personal wealth had been poured into the hotel. She had no other money but that which stood in crumbling bricks and mortar. She would not consider selling out despite her age. Or the age of the building. It had not been purpose built. The renovations had been complex just to make the layout work as a hotel. The provision of the staff cubicles in the basement, so to free up rooms for additional paying guests, had almost bankrupted them. While his mother was the person appointed to worry about profit margins, the world financial crisis had meant that they had had to slash their prices drastically just to compete. How she kept them solvent amazed him, yet somehow she did. Though affording the necessary renovations was something she brooded about in their own quarters when no one could see the worry on her brow, as she poured over columns of figures.

Staffing, despite an agreement that she would be involved in interviews of a managerial nature, were his concern, not his mother's. Which was why she had been wrong to question his decision to promote Leonie to the vacant post once Belinda, their usual Christmas receptionist, had been head-hunted, elsewhere. He had had to be steadfast in a way that she had been unable to understand, as anything more than a middle-aged man's foolish fancy, when he had defied her insistence that the appointment of Leonie to front of house should be rescinded until she had sufficient qualifications to merit the post. Though she was doing as well as he had expected. Left alone, yesterday, on her own, while they had ended up having to sack Bluithe Harcourt because of his blatant cheek…they had both known that Cannon was listening in, so making it impossible to take any other channel of action…Leonie had shown them both how well she had been able to take command of her new responsibilities. She had proved herself to be a 'coper' even if she had yet to realise it for herself. It had been a huge responsibility for her to have to act in direct representation of themselves when she had spent that morning contacting all their proposed clientele for the Christmas break, with their proposal to bring them by helicopter, the success of the venture being entirely dependent on the manner of her presentation. Leonie had emailed, faxed, texted and telephoned their booking list and so far only two couples had declined the change of travel plan. The rest had appreciated the trouble that the Fairview Country Club Hotel had gone to, to ensure that their Christmas went ahead at no extra cost to themselves. Ross had coordinated a schedule to bring ten guests at a time which was all the aircrafts would accommodate, but by midnight, Tuesday, the allotted, newly decorated rooms should be in use, fully booked. All except for Eagle Suite, of course.

One worry settled! The easiest of his troubles, even if the most time-consuming had been sorted and approved by his mother who, for once, was smiling his way. What would she be like tomorrow, he wondered, when the bomb went off? She had not been privy to what had happened all those years ago. She had had her fingers in her ears, anyway. She had even said, once she was made aware, during a very prickly Christmas Fair held at The Rectory, where she had been told, shockingly, that Lizzie's baby had been stillborn, that the demise of her grandchild had been for the best. "What else could you possibly have expected from Lizzie?"

How would she react when the truth was put before her, tomorrow?

He had felt angered by Leonie's embarrassment at the emergency staff meeting, yesterday, when she had blushed to the roots of her hair after his mother had publicly questioned her appointment, with all the staff looking at her; anger always bringing with it a rising tide of red to his head, just like Leonie's. For a moment Ross had thought that surely someone would look from himself to Leonie and realise what had become to him very obvious similarities in their gestures and mannerisms, when she shared a striking physical resemblance to both himself and her birth mother, Lizzie. She had the same petit, slim figure, though Lizzie had, lately, become emaciated by her illness. Even her fair hair and blue eyes were mirrors of his own and the soft, frizzy curls were from Lizzie. So telling that Ross found it incomprehensible that even his own perceptive and formidably intelligent mother had noticed nothing of a family likeness to her son and herself. Not even a slight resemblance to her when Leonie had the same brow and cheekbone structure.

He did hope, though, that Leonie would prove to have inherited some of his mother's canny, business acumen when he had none himself. Given time and the right nurturing process, she might rise from the shop floor of her ambition and find that she was developing the right skills, aptitudes and dedication to run the Fairview Country Club Hotel when he could never see himself taking it over. Thankfully, she had shown no signs of the illness and peculiarities which affected her birth mother, which Bern had told him had been caused through damage within the womb and was not genetic, despite Hannah's decline into eccentricity, since the death of her husband, becoming more extreme in the previous five years.

It was Leonie's birthright which Ross was determined to expose; would be exposed, tomorrow, when they would sit together before his solicitor, in the presence of his mother, and the truth would be told. It had been agreed with his attorney that he would lead the advent of Leonie Fairbrother Jubb Jones; heiress. That was why he had plucked her from her lowly school with the promise of a job before her parents could point her in another direction. That was why he had protected her within her work in the kitchen as she learnt something of the complexities of working with people like Chef and Cannon.

All good human resource management, both Chef and Head Waiter being dependants of the hotel, as his mother scathingly termed them, due to their inadequate adaptation to the demands of an ordinary life outside of the institution. He had watched her struggle to get dinners out of the kitchen even as Chef had been collapsed in a drunken stupor across his own kitchen tables. There had been nothing left for Leonie to learn about the organization and machinations of a hotel kitchen. He had now brought her front of house, into his own sphere where she was proving herself yet again to be a daughter of whom he might be justifiably proud...as long as tomorrow could go smoothly. The only dire stumbling block he could envisage being Leonie's reaction to all the lies that she had been fed.

He was standing in his office, brooding yet again, wondering if a celebratory birthday lunch might be appropriate at the local Italian...at least hoping it would...while looking out the window with the staff accommodation book in his hand. When he came out of his reverie sufficient to raise his head, he saw a taxi pull up outside the open main doors and Betty Jessop get out onto the path which that morning had been shovelled and swept and salted by Cannon and Chef, but was now several inches deep again. It had been only later that Ross realised that Leonie had been left to cope on her own again after his mother had given her the awesome task of phoning her way through the booking list, while she had gone down to the village herself. He had wished to point this out to his mother as a commendation to Leonie, when he had asked her where she had been. All that she had had to say about a total lapse within her own management dictates was that it was not always possible to do things by the book. "You do realise that I'm seventy three years old, Ross, and feeling my age. A woman of my age should not be climbing ladders…" Then her face had sagged heavily and her voice had become thin with impatience. "Never mind! Why do we have to employ people who continually cause problems? First thing after Christmas we shall have to advertise for a new painter and decorator who has all the qualities of a saint. That man…!"

Ross shrugged. If his mother had been climbing ladders, it could only be to fulfil her own stubborn insistence that it was always she who placed the fairies on top of the hotel Christmas trees. It had become hotel ritual. She would have another one to climb, too, when the men finished the erection of the one she had decided should adorn the front of the hotel to welcome the guests who will now be arriving by helicopter on a converted helipad, and come down next to it, disembarking as they did so to a singing choir. Obviously, climbing ladders was proving too much for her.

Ross had agreed with her sentiments, though. Staffing and staff problems were their biggest headache. Now, here was Betty Jessop, a staffing problem of old, walking after herself, so to speak, with that forward and to the right, leaning gait of hers. As odd-bod as ever! She hadn't seemed to change much in five years. That same thin racehorse leanness and long thin face. She even seemed to be wearing the same civvies he had last seen her in before all the staff became anonymous in their red and gold overalls. He had already left a note on Leonie's desk to inform her that she should expect another employee, hired at the last minute to cover her own removal from the kitchens, in fact.

He paid her no further heed, for the moment, as he looked to the allotment of cubicles still available. Most would remain unoccupied. They would be running on a skeleton staff for the Christmas period with as few as possible living in to minimise costs and maximise profits so that those volunteering for long hours might have an especially welcome Christmas bonus to help tide them over. Ten days from tomorrow and the hotel would be closed once more. Ross found himself daydreaming again: Would Leonie consider coming on holiday with him and his mother as they toured a few Scottish hotels to appraise the opposition? It could be presented to her, once the shock had been absorbed, as a learning experience.

Or was he wishing for things that would never happen? When he went through to the reception desk, he had to ignore the sudden frisson of fear which passed over him, because she was seated within his area, his own office being to the rear of reception, where he was determined she would remain. Though, come tomorrow, her clothes would be bespoke tailored and her hair and make-up expertly done, on a daily basis, just as his mother's was, in the beauty salons of the hotel where every service would be placed freely at her disposal. He had even planned his advice and support, within the attitudes they would all have to adopt, to rise above the gossip which would accompany what he intended to be a 'publish and be damned' approach to their true relationship. Even become remote from it, as he had learnt to do long ago when the results of his unfortunate, never intended, drunken, single coupling with Lizzie Jubb, had threatened to overwhelm him. One simply chilled oneself out, closed up the senses, and became deaf and blind until the nine day wonder passed. He would show her how to do the same, to be a Fairbrother, in fact.

He noted that Leonie had her desk cleared of all the orders he had requested, a fresh guest list printed for tomorrow, and had the staff manuals, employment forms and uniform ready for Betty Jessop and Lick Johnson. Her work was efficient. It had always been commendable. He doubted that Betty Jessop would offer the same quality of service when he noted her coming into the foyer, head down, not looking his way, not seeing him, maybe. Either that or she was embarrassed by the consequences of her sudden disappearance, the last time.

He hung back only long enough for Leonie to ask and for Betty to mumble her name before politely asking her to take a seat for a few minutes, as the staff accommodation would need to be sorted before she could be directed to the place where she would sleep.

Indeed, the woman looked exhausted from her journey. Glad to take the weight off her feet, sit, and shut her eyes, even. Ross noted that she had shut her eyes as if she planned to nap, quite openly, here in the foyer, dressed as she was, staff not clientele. He had to remind himself that the hotel was not open yet and that she would have known a horrendous journey from Harrogate. It did not occur to him to question what should have been the impossible; that being an arrival at all when all roads and routes from Harrogate were closed due to snow.

It looked to him that she had nodded off within moments of sitting in a comfortable chair in a warm foyer, her battered case and capacious handbag dripping snow all over the newly cleaned carpets, feet splayed, stockings wrinkled and that ghastly brown hood hiding her face as she dozed. Had he made a mistake in having her back to work at the hotel when further recall provided him with a catalogue of complaints from other staff members? Cannon ever being the one to drop a word in his ear, as Cannon does. But then Cannon dropped a lot of words in his ear of a telling-tales-out-of-school nature, which he and his mother tended to take with a pinch of salt. They had long ago realised that Cannon's observations were often guided by spitefulness. Another reason he had moved Leonie out the kitchens. He had already started to suggest that while it looked as if Chef had purloined the disappearing hams, it should also be considered that Leonie Jones had a very greedy mother. She had every opportunity, too. Obviously, Cannon was not in a position to appreciate that he was slowly digging his own grave and at any moment might topple into it.

One of his problems was how to get her to his solicitor's office without her being panicked into thinking that he was after her body. Words had so far failed him. Every time he approached her with an instruction to simply meet him there…when he thought that she would refuse to ride in a car with him and certainly her mother would baulk at his request to take a lowly member of staff in her own car…he got tongue tied and blushed bright orange. What he had done was scribbled a note and placed it in a sealed envelope for her attention. It simply required her to attend his solicitor's office on the following morning "…where matters will be explained to be of your very best interest." He had never been a wordsmith. What he must do was to hand it over personally, but in private. Otherwise, because it was a sealed note, if any of the other staff should see it they would be curious and rib Leonie mercilessly about it. Cannon, in particular!

"May I have a word in my office, Leonie?"

"Sorry, Mr. Ross. Whatever it is, I'm all ears, where I am. I'm just going to phone to the costumier in Leeds about the price of hiring some costumes for the pantomime for yours and Mrs. Fairbrother's consideration. Lick says that if something's worth doing, it's worth doing properly. Here he comes. He'll need to fill in his employment details and Betty, too. I see you've got the staff accommodation file under your arm. You can allot me a cubicle while you're doing one for Betty."

Foiled again!

***

Leonie was back at her desk in Reception only minutes after rehearsals were over. Her heart was still thumping and her lips throbbed as if she had been blowing through tissue paper held over a comb. She had actually let him fondle her in places…inside the cloakroom with Lick's knee on the shut door because Cannon kept following them…and in places where no man had ventured before, except maybe her dad when he had bathed her as a baby. She had been so very tempted to fondle him back, too. It was only her own naivety and thoughts of Cannon with his ear to the other side of the door, which prevented her.

The first thing she did was to telephone her mother while Mrs.

Fairbrother was having her nap and Mr. Ross was standing in his office. She could see him through the glass, staring through his outside window, as if he was on some kind of narcotic drug, which of course, he wasn't. Maybe, he had already got the message that she was being claimed by an irresistible force quite unconnected with himself, though she would resist it as long as she could; sort of draw out the aching pleasure of it.

Leonie would also have to explain to her mother that she had made the decision to ask for a staff cubicle instead of going home. It would set her mother in a panic, she knew, but what else could she do? Not when Lick wanted her to watch his rehearsals tonight and help him to learn some of the words to some Christmas carols which he had only ever mimed to before. And maybe before having a bite in the bar, together. Her ear was still tickling where he had been nibbling it. Where he had touched her flesh, she was aware of a soft, warm, peachy glow. As soon as her mother said; "All right, darlin'?" Leonie blurted out that she had met her knight on horseback and admitted that they had already shared a greater intimacy than she had ever allowed any boy she had gone out with before.

Gloria gasped. "I knew it would happen some day, darlin' but you just be careful."

"He's kissed me, Mum." Then described in great detail every kiss, every caress, every beat of her heart and how drop-dead gorgeous he was. "I don't even mind the cigarettes on his breath. It won't take me long to train him. His name's Lovick Johnson."

"Who? What did you say his name was?"

"Lovick, his name is. Lick for short. A musician, Mum. Mr. Ross's taken him on. Slick Lick Johnson is his stage name. Oh, Mum! I'm in love."

"Don't let him even as much as hold your hand without him wearing a condom. Now you promise me, darlin'…you never know where he's been before."

"Yes, I do," Leonie replied. "Barnston Farm. He slept there last night."

"Oh, him! I have heard the gossip but it's all lies."

"He isn't related to Lizzie Jubb, Mum."

"I know he isn't."

"I'd draw the line at going out with anyone who was." Leonie could not see her mother wincing and rubbing her face. "He's drop dead gorgeous, Mum. Wait till you meet him …"

A full five minutes of descriptions and be-carefuls ensued. Finally, Leonie told her mother about asking for a staff cubicle.

There was a long pause. "Yes, darlin'."

An unexpected response. She had expected hysterics. "You'll be alright, Mum?"

"Oh darlin'. I'll have to be. Your dad's only across the road if I need anything though his car's not there. Fancy trailing out in all this snow."

That was when Leonie asked her mum to ring her dad to ask him to bring her a selection of clothes from her bedroom. She specified them.

Her mother said she was making notes on the top sheet of her sticky-pad so that nothing was forgotten. "Whatever he's doing he'll drop everything for you, our little angel. Are you sure you want your baby dolls, though? Wouldn't you be better with proper pyjamas? It's snowing fit for the Arctic out there. What if the hotel burns down and you have to get out?"

"Oh, Mum!"

"Alright. But you be careful. I haven't forgotten what I used to get up to in baby dolls."

"I'm not a baby, Mum. Besides, not till I know him better. And you've met him. And Dad's met him. And the time and place is right."

"Good girl. You're a good girl, my angel. Love you so."

It was after speaking to her mother, that Betty Jessop came in out of the snow. Leonie could recall her being talked about when she had been away on a catering course. She had actually been taken on to cover for her old job in the kitchens, as a matter of fact. She was covered in flakes as big as fifty pence pieces despite having only just got out of a taxi, snow covered glasses almost obliterating her eyesight, though she approached the desk without cleaning off the snow.

Leonie had to resist putting two fingers to her nose. The perfume which hung about Betty Jessop was like the strong smell of mildew. She remembered were she had smelt the same smell before. It was the same awful, cheap scent that her gran had used to douse her handkerchiefs with. Not the best tolerated by people with more sensitive noses as the air born spores of 1946 damp cupboards came to her own. "Good afternoon. You are?"

"Betty Jessop. Kitchen staff."

"Can I ask you to take a seat for a few minutes? Here's Mr. Ross, now. He'll allocate you a staff cubicle in the basement where you will be sleeping."

"Know where to go. Been here before."

Leonie knew that Mr. Ross had already had a word with Chef and Cannon concerning her role amongst six other kitchen staff.

His voice coming from behind her, she heard him say, "May I

have a word in my office, Leonie?"

Of course he had to keep on trying, didn't he, even when she could not have made it plainer that her interests lay elsewhere? She would, from now on be doubling her efforts to avoid being alone with him. She didn't want Lick getting the wrong impression, not when the staff started gossiping about her to him. So she had to make an excuse to his request as clearly as possible. Her actual words were: "Sorry, Mr. Ross. Whatever it is, I'm all ears, where I am. I'm just going to phone the costumier in Leeds about the price of hiring some costumes for the pantomime for yours and Mrs. Fairbrother's consideration. Lick says that if something's worth doing, it's worth doing properly. Here he comes. He'll need to fill in his employment details and Betty, too. I see you've got the staff accommodation file under your arm. You can allot me a cubicle while you're doing one for Betty."

He didn't look too pleased but what else could a girl in need of a pure reputation do? And she was going to follow up on hiring costumes and props. And she did have to give Lick and Betty their staff cubicle allocation numbers and the big brown envelopes she had prepared earlier in which were the forms they would have to fill in with their employment details, with a contract of employment to explain their duties and a copy of the extensive staff rules which were on the door to the cubicles anyway.

Lick approached from the direction of the ballroom where he had been setting up his costumes and props for the entertainment at the Christmas Eve Ball. Until then, it would be songs round the fireside and maybe the odd tinkle on the piano. He would only be asked to wait on at table if they were run off their feet. His eyes were drooling all over her.

Ross sighed. He had never really understood the attraction of a woman even if he did see that Leonie was as ripe and fresh as any young woman could be. His eyes rolled. "Betty, number twelve. Mr. Johnson has already taken number five. You Leonie can have number six." The look he cast along with his words as he scribbled in his file, suggested things which Leonie resented. It would occur to her shortly that he had absentmindedly put her into an adjoining cubicle to Lick's.

"It's only because of the snow, Mr. Ross. My mum won't like me not being at home because there'll be no one to cook for her. It can't be helped. Aunty Pauline, hopefully, will keep Mum company as long as she isn't in Turkey. Dad and I will be working."

His reply was disconcerting. Leonie was never able to understand how he remembered her birthday when he hadn't a clue about his own or his mothers. He always had to consult a diary for information like that. "What about your birthday? It's your birthday tomorrow. I am

Sacher Torte

hoping…er…won't your father and mother want to make a fuss?"

Leonie shrugged. "I'll be able to dash home for some cake when the snow dies away. Mum never goes out these days."

Lick accepted his envelope and a warm, syrupy smile from her. If the management kept track of staff birthdays, he was most impressed. "Cool."

Ross looked flustered. How was he going to hand over the envelope with Lick Johnson around? He placed his gaze once more upon the sleeping form of Betty Jessop so that he could show the facial disapproval that his suspicions for Leonie's real reasons raised. "On the twenty second isn't it?" he reiterated in a fluster. "I was thinking that, maybe, we could go to the Italian…" Then realised that he was talking out of turn.

Leonie shook her head at him, saying nothing. She would not even countenance such an inappropriate date.

"Cool," Lovick smiled, thinking that he had been invited also. "Do you always have a staff do on someone's birthday? Tomorrow. How old?"

Betty Jessop's eyes flicked open and stayed open behind her pebble thick glasses though she moved not a muscle. Just listened.

Mr. Ross's gaze travelled elsewhere, hoping his blush would quickly die down if he gazed out onto the snow. At least his mother hadn't been listening, though he had a premonition of her coming in. It was going on for that time of day. What would she have to say when her eyes fell on the entertainer's riot coloured shirt and pants that looked to have been painted onto him. Not to mention the rainbow ribbons and bells on his boots.

"Twenty-five," Leonie replied, wishing that Mr. Ross would go away and leave them alone.

Lovick looked delighted and whispered very quietly. "We can have a special celebration."

Leonie nodded. "No alcohol though. I don't drink."

Cannon, hovering at the door to his restaurant, at a loose end, raised his eyebrows and smiled with some satisfaction before a chuckle escaped his lips. He'd go and have a word with Chef. No better time or place to spike a drink than on a birthday bash.

She let her eyes run over Lick's face like warm butter over a hot crumpet. "Do you think you can fill in your employment forms now? I can explain things. It's easier. Here's a pen."

Lick took it as if she had offered him her body. "Thanks." As their hands touched, it was like an electric impulse shot between them, nerves had been touched. Their eyes met and locked.

Leonie had that warm feeling again.

Mr Ross closed his file with a harsh slap. "I do have somewhere where I want to take you tomorrow, Leonie. First thing."

Betty Jessop's eyes grew narrow before closing again. She had placed the lad now. She recognised his voice and the sound of them tinkling bells on his boots. He was the same lad as the one who had saved Hannah from Bluithe Harcourt and Gareth Jones and his specials. She had kept her eyes shut as tight as possible so she hadn't seen the way that he was surreptitiously stroking the back of the minx's hand or the love signals Leonie was sending out in his direction, not to Ross, but to quite a different person.

Betty remained quite unaware when Lick, hanging over her desk, filling out his employment details could not help but take a lascivious look at Leonie's breasts which she allowed by leaning closer so that her cleavage was visible. She had left her coat off after rehearsals, removed the prudish silk cravat, taken the crunchy out of her hair and gone to town on her make-up. He had seen that she had hitched her voluminous skirt up at the waist and had a pair of very slim but shapely legs clad no longer in black tights but fifteen denier stockings. He could imagine lace stocking tops. He was pulling his wet tongue out at her in a gesture which Leonie received with a delightful shiver, when the door in the glass screen opened. Who should walk in but her dad; all six feet five of him. His smile shortened considerably. He had immediately taken the situation in. He had never ever seen Leonie so enamoured by a man before. He could tell because of her clothing and the way she was matching her own tongue to his. It had to happen sooner or later. Then he realised where he had heard them bells before and scowled even further.

He spoke first to his daughter, holding up a disruption to his police work he could have managed without. "Your case. I went straight back home when your Mum phoned to get it together."

Leonie smiled fondly at her dad. "Dad this is Lick Johnson. The entertainment."

"I can see he is. I hope I read your mother's writing correctly. What's a teddy? Aren't you a bit too old for all them stuffed toys of yours?"

His expression said that he considered Lovick to have the look of a villain. Nor did he think much of the pink and orange shirt as his eyes raked down and then up Lovick's thin frame and came back to settle on a face that was guilty of something. Gareth could tell. He could read guilt when he saw it.

Lovick nodded, straightening himself, feeling that he should be standing to attention. Only the week before he'd been chased by a policeman after taking a shortcut home from the pub over other people's garden walls. He wished now that he had worn something less attention-seeking; his most major character fault, according to Quincey, who thought low profile to be much the wiser in someone forever getting into scrapes.

"Relative of hers are you? Hannah Jubb? You are the person I saw going into her farm late last night?"

Lovick shook his head, and then nodded it. The effect was to make his head look as it was moving in circles. "No I'm not and yes I did."

"Why she invite you in?"

Lovick shrugged. "I wish she hadn't. I did ask to stay because I'd got lost and needed some shelter. That daughter of hers pinched my guitar and ran off with it. I think she stole my phone as well."

Betty Jessop maintained her sleeping position, though her hand did tap at the pocket of her grey tweed coat. She made a satisfied nod when it was empty. For a moment she had forgotten what she had done with it. The lad had helped Hannah last night so she owed him. She had taken steps to make sure he got it back.

It was Gareth's turn to shrug. "That'll be Lizzie. Guitar not damaged, I hope."

Lovick nodded his head.

Gareth and Ross nodded at each other, now. All that the others present noticed was a polite distance between them. Gareth deposited Leonie's case on the desk top for her to take over to her side of the counter.

Leonie spoke when her dad would have addressed Mr. Ross. "Where were you when Mum disturbed you? Sorry. It's just that I didn't expect the blizzard."

Her dad's eyes rolled over this Lovick Johnson. What had he had hidden in that kit bag? "Barnston Farm actually. I was just about to knock and ask Hannah if she has any idea of Bluithe Harcourt's whereabouts. If she'd seen him hanging about her farm again. He's gone to earth. Need to find him, pronto."

Ross said. "We had to let him go, yesterday."

"That's why I'm here as well as bringing Leonie her case. To ask you, as well, if you have any idea of his whereabouts. His wife's quite worried about him." His face remained blank. He had had to learn how to keep the sluice gate shut and not let the past interfere with his role as the only law enforcement in the area. He always had to come up here on police business for one reason or another. Now he had reason to turn his full attention onto the man who had the power to destroy his family completely. His face was impassive. "He's been speaking bad about you, Mr. Fairbrother. I think it might be best if we discuss what I have to say in your office."

Ross made no move to go there. He had nothing to hide even if he was recalling the sounds he had heard coming up from the well, earlier in the day, about ten o'clock that morning, he supposed, give or take ten minutes either way. It had been about the time that his mother's car had passed him on the driveway after she had been down to the village…or he assumed that that was where she had been…about ten minutes before Betty Jessop had telephoned him. He had since been able to rationalise it. He might be mistaken but he had come to think that the whistling sound had been familiar. That of a painter and decorator going about his work. There was only one man he could think of with that same tweeting whistle. He could only guess what Blue Harcourt would be doing down there.

He would say nothing, of course. He had seen the back of Bluithe Harcourt and would prefer it to stay that way. He had once been a runner, himself, with Bern. But it was more that he saw no reason to annoy the man further. He had a vindictive streak. He would have had to explain his knowledge of the underground system close to the hotel even if it had been bricked up after Bern's death. He knew it had been done thoroughly because he had paid for the work himself. However he had no wish to go into all that. What he said to Gareth was. "The man's a moral coward where that wife of his is concerned. It's my guess that he's staying out of her way until she cools down."

Ross would have turned and gone from their company but for the fact that Gareth's next question called him back.

"Why did you sack him? I've heard his version several times over. Now I'll hear yours. The man has, after all, been reported missing."

Ross nodded. "He deserved it. Mother had had enough of his bad attitude and pilfering. He was impertinent as well as dishonest. What do you mean by missing? When was he last seen?"

Leonie filled in her own bit of knowledge. "I saw him get out your car this morning, Dad, before I came to work. You went together to the Bald Pheasant."

Gareth nodded in agreement. He had to admit the word 'missing' was a bit precipitate. It was more because the man needed an injection to maintain his health. He could hardly say that. People had a right to privacy concerning their health and medication. Gareth nodded. "Thing is, he didn't go home and the weather's closing in again. His wife's concerned. His car's still parked up on the square where he left it though that's not surprising because of the snow. I've had a quick peek inside and his tool kit seems to have gone with him."

Ross looked at his watch then at anything but the assembled company. "Apart from a half hour or so when I took some air after mother asked me to go down to the village to give Leonie a lift because of the snow, I've been here all day. He hasn't been here. We lock the doors if there's no one in attendance on the desk, as was the case for part of the afternoon due to the hotel only opening tomorrow. I was at rehearsals for the staff panto. Mother is having her nap after doing some shopping in Quinton though you can ask her if she's seen him. I make it five thirty. Isn't it a little premature to register him as a missing person?"

"It wasn't a half hour, Mr. Ross," Leonie said, wanting her father to have the correct information. "You were gone a good hour hanging about in the woods somewhere. I saw you climb down and you were gone for a while. When you came up you were leaning over the well. Then I saw you on your mobile talking to someone."

They all heard Betty Jessop mumble. "Me, I thinks."

Why did he blush? Leonie must have been watching out for him and timing him. She seemed to know what he had been doing, he supposed. However, she was unable to read his mind, hence her still being here. "I wasn't particularly paying attention to time. I was simply enjoying the air. Is that all?"

Gareth replied to Ross's question. "It might be except that I want to talk to you about something related. A private matter. Something Bluithe is saying about you. All I need is for you to listen and either confirm or deny his accusations. Shall we go into your office, now?"

Ross had no choice but to oblige.

***

They watched as Mr. Ross went ahead of Leonie's dad and showed him into his office.

Eyebrows were raised all round. "He'll have gone off on one of his foreigners," Leonie advised. "He used to say he was painting somewhere in the hotel and then nip off with that tool bag of his. He was always nipping off somewhere. He did deserve to be sacked," she explained to Lovick.

They had turned back to each other and, quite forgetful of Betty Jessop, were about to share a sigh when an outraged voice rent the moment to shreds. "Betty Jessop! Well! Cheek of it! Coming here again after all the trouble you caused when you disappeared. We quite needlessly called out the Fell Rescue. Other things as well." Mrs. Fairbrother; newly coiffured. The spit had flown and had landed on her quivering chin. She had seemed more out of sorts than usual since Blue Harcourt's sacking. She twice had to suck at her dentures to hold them in place. Her eyes were popping out of stretched lids and her breast had risen in irate fashion so that she looked like a pigeon sitting on an egg.

Lovick and Leonie put space between them and looked down to the floor as Mrs. Fairbrother came round the reception counter and went to stand to the right side of Betty Jessop, whose eyes were wide and staring behind the enlarging glasses. "Said sorry to that son of yours. Mother died, see."

Betty stood up, sliding sideways into her usual eighty degree, slanted pose, head down and shoulders lowered. She was set on avoidance of what was looking like a fatal end to her hopes of having somewhere to work over Christmas. Her voice had that same flat, nasal, Yorkshire whine as when speaking to the taxi driver and Leonie. "It was a family emergency. I don't think right in a crisis. Excuse me, I'll be about my work now, if I may." She was not about to wait for her overall or anything else for that matter as she crept sideways in her rubber overshoes. "Which cubicle am I in, Miss?" she called to Leonie. "He did say."

"Number twelve, I think."

"I'll take the envelope and bring it back later when I've written on it. Hope green ball pen's okay."

Mrs. Fairbrother, open mouthed, seemed unable to make a response. Leonie and Lovick watched her go, feeling sorry for her.

Ross could not support her position because he was still in the office with Gareth. They were talking earnestly.

Mrs. Fairbrother eyed Lovick as an unknown, frowned, looked him up and down, and then groaned. Her shaking head followed after Betty Jessop as she walked over to the lift. Whatever she was thinking was too long winded to mention. She looked positively ill.

Lovick thought that her response to his appearance had been suitably dramatic. He had never been one for leaving people cold. However, she seemed to be more consumed with watching the strange gait of Betty Jessop as she loped along with her body at that strange forward and sideways eighty degree angle to the carpeted floor, case and handbag in her black gloved hand, as she went inside the open lift and turned to face them while she pressed for the basement. Staff only down there. As the door closed, Betty's face was a stiff, lugubrious mask of crossed eyes within an expression which begged forgiveness. She was now standing in the 'to attention' position. Two red patches had grown on her ivory skin, one on each cheekbone which could have been caused by the warmth indoors, no doubt, after the cold out. "I'll be reporting to Chef as soon as I'm in uniform."

"Well!" Mrs. Fairbrother looked to be at the end of her tether, which was not unusual. It took very little these days. She turned her attention to Leonie by looking over her changed appearance. Leonie winced.

Then she said with approval. "You have improved your appearance, Miss Jones. I have always considered you to be a mousy, drab, slip of nothing. I was about to speak to you upon the matter of your clothing. That would appear to be no longer necessary. However, short skirts should not be more than two inches above the knee and heels, a one inch Cuban to save the carpets. You may wear something fitted as long as you display no bosom as you are doing now. Clothing must be of white, grey and black. No jewellery, as befits a receptionist. You seem to have discarded your identity badge, I see."

Leonie immediately removed her gold locket. "It's on my coat. I won't forget it in future, Mrs. Fairbrother."

Mrs. Fairbrother raised a hooked nose and looked down it for a second opinion. "Otherwise. Well done." Her smile did not reach her eyes though her lips parted to reveal the loose dentures and froth at the corner of her mouth. "We'll make something of you, yet."

Leonie felt like curtseying but made do with a grateful look that Mrs. Fairbrother had made a veiled compliment, somewhere within all the criticism, concerning her value to the Fairview Country Club Hotel.

Lovick cancelled out his previous scowl and replaced it with a grin; the old bird wasn't that bad. It was only her manner. He extended his hand, ignoring her look of insult that staff should put themselves forward as an equal.

However, she did allow her fingers to touch the broad sweep of his palm. "Put it there, Mrs. Fairbrother. I'm Slick Lick Johnson, the entertainment. Excellent place here. Reason I'm dressed like this is for rehearsal. Pantomime is going to be great, too. I'll tone it all down for the carols."

She folded her hands over her rotund midriff. Today she was dressed in her favourite royal blue. It was a colour much favoured by royalty. As her hands came together over the bulk of her stomach, she wrung them fiercely. She might as well have taken a bowl of water and a cloth and washed them. Either that or she was simulating wringing someone's neck. "Ross's concern, not mine. His idea. We have previously allowed our guests the peace and quiet they desire by coming here. We shall see, Mr. Johnson. We shall see."

Leonie and Lovick shared glances as she moved behind the

counter and over to the closed office door where Mr. Ross and Gareth Jones were still ensconced in privacy. She was obviously loitering with intent to eavesdrop while making a pretence of looking through an old guest book where people had written comments like:-

...soup was off today. Too much sherry in the trifle...comfortable enough but I thought the weather could have been better...will come back next year as long as someone stops singing in the room next door at five thirty in the morning...

She was puffing up again, as snippets of the conversation came through.

Lovick wrinkled his nose and gave Leonie a lopsided grin. Nothing to do with them. "Want me to carry your case?"

Leonie nodded shyly. She might even let him linger at the door of her cubicle while she unpacked.

***

Ross, meanwhile, had shut his office door and had already answered Gareth's questions.

No, he was not involved in smuggling black market goods. Though he had emitted a dry laugh when he denied it. No, he had no idea why Bluithe Harcourt should think that there was merchandise hidden in the caverns and potholes underground which Bluithe had said could still be accessed either from his hotel grounds or from within the byre at Barnston Farm. The word 'ludicrous' peppered his speech. "They were bricked up over twenty-five years ago, for goodness sake."

"Bluithe seems convinced."

Ross's sigh was heartfelt. "Think what you like. You can unbrick the door in the old well if you like. Hannah won't let you on her farm voluntarily, that's for sure. Lizzie gets too upset when there's a disturbance. I hear you were there last night disturbing her."

He spent several minutes repeating and repeating the same information. Gareth Jones had an underlying anger about him that Ross had not seen before. He was usually calm and collected. However, he remained steadfastly adamant that he had not been Robin Hooding, he had no involvement with any black-market racketeering that was going on and, if Gareth so wished he would ask his mother to open her receipts to show that every item on the shelves of the Fairview Country Club Hotel had been paid for with import tax and value added tax, added.

It was at that point that the office door burst open. Mrs. Fairbrother stood imperious and proud in resemblance to an angry, fat, royal blue tarantula spider. The blouse beneath her suit was the finest, Belgian lace. She made no apology for her rude interruption. "What is that woman doing here?" she demanded of Ross. "Betty Jessop! After all the trouble she caused. She's taken the lift down as if she has every right to be here."

Ross sighed. "I hired her to take Leonie's place in the kitchen. For want of better, Mother, for the present. We have a hotel full of guests coming tomorrow, don't forget."

Mrs. Fairbrother bristled. "Well!"

She might as well have asked her son how he dare speak to her like that in front of the local policeman. "Be it on your head, Ross Fairbrother, when things start to happen. If you remember, the last time she was here, a whole cupboard full of crockery got smashed. Some of my best blouses got ruined in the wash. Telephone wires were cut and knives disappeared. One of our guests reported a madwoman wielding a knife while standing over his bed in the middle of the night…"

Ross butted in, at his own wits end after so much questioning. "Stop this, Mother, please. It proved to be a nightmare and the knives were recovered. They'd simply been put in the wrong drawers. The reason that your blouses were ruined was due to someone making a mistake with the machine temperature. You will buy silk and expensive lace which has to be washed delicately. Someone did, indeed, cut the telephone wires but that was a simple act of vandalism that occurred at the same time as a spate of other similar incidents in the village."

Gareth had finished his interview with Ross, for the time being anyway. He had something to say about this because he could recall that a guest had reported an incident with a knife wielding madwoman to him. The severed telephone wires had been blamed on a lad from the village who eventually ended up being sent to prison. "I investigated and found no cause for concern. People get hysterical sometimes and come to the wrong conclusions. My only gripe with Betty Jessop is that she disappeared without telling anyone."

"Her mother died," Ross said. "Understandable."

Eighteen

Meanwhile, the subject of their conversation had hightailed it to her cubicle below stairs, within the vast cellar space which had been converted for the use by more temporary staff. It had enabled more rooms to be given over as guest rooms above stairs. The large, dark space held no windows, it once having been a wine cellar, but was both heated and ventilated to the same standard as the guest rooms were.

Betty, tired from her journey in the cold snow had taken the lift down one floor. There was a staircase also, fitted with fire doors. The elevator was of service proportions so that large goods might be transported up and down, though when large equipment was shifted upwards it was expected to be unloaded to the rear door which connected with the kitchens and laundry rooms, the housekeeper's pantry and the staff sitting room. The interior corridors upstairs were where the permanent, long term, staff bedrooms were. Chef and Cannon had long been appointed there.

The lift was permanently lit from within so that as Betty limped wearily out of the open door she had a floodlight to orientate herself by. The area before her was dim due to both day and night staff having to be accommodated within the same area of some twenty, scantily screened cubicles all open from above and below. Pencil down lights provided just enough lights to find ones way and to find the doorways to the mainly unused cubicles. Most staff preferred home comforts even if it meant travelling at this time of year. A small cupped down-light on each open door illuminated a number. None of the doors to the partitioned cubicles were locked. Unless an occupant was within and had turned the catch, the spring-operated doors stood open. Only a few were closed. Four spaces had been given over to showers and another to a bathing area. Another to staff laundry with basic facilities. Staff had to provide their own detergents and fabric softeners.

The interiors of all the spaces were basic, too, utilitarian and as small as could be gotten away with. The cubicles were equipped with a hospital type, single bed, and the very minimum a person would need to rest between work shifts such as a tub chair and a small, folding shelf for writing letters, a washbasin hardly big enough to take both hands together, a row of brass hooks, a towel rack and a cupboard for clothes and toiletries.

A set of rules was stapled to the back of each door which laid out very clear codes of behaviour. Number one was that staff who entered the cubicles of other staff would be immediately dismissed. Number two was that staff were forbidden to borrow items belonging to other staff members. And so it went on...No singing. No radios. No laughter. No talking between cubicles at any time of day. Doors to be left open so that cleaning staff might come in and change beds. Some staff, like Lovick Johnson, glanced at their list, read the first, few words and, henceforth, would ignore it. Such staff were temporary, indeed. They had yet to be made aware that every word of the rules which governed the Fairview Country Club Hotel was meant. Betty eyed the list with the shadow of a smile. Particularly: No alcohol to be taken within the cubicle. Her facial muscles had always been incapable of making much expression but the loud jeer was in her mind, if silent. As was a blue neon light of cold satisfaction. She was here, now. She was in. Passed through the barriers like last time only this time the woman at her core would not be contained. Patience though! The situation would have to be managed. Not quite time yet to unleash the beastly crusade which had brought her here and would guide her on her path when the time was right. She must, for the time being, remain inanimate in order for the attention to her strangeness to diminish. For that was Betty Jessop; a woman who could drift as if formed of the ether, like a ghost. She could put herself into a vacuum and become almost invisible, unlike Lizzie. As long as she remained alert to her calling. For she was merely the carrier and what she carried was but a kernel inside her with the shell not yet split open. Not yet.

She quickly unpacked the contents of her case into the small locker which was already equipped with a key. This constituted a small amount of carefully folded clothing and a long, thin cardboard box tied with string. The porcelain jar she handled very, very carefully. This went on a shelf of its own. It must not be unnecessarily disturbed. Within it was something that must not be aroused for the present. Not until she had settled in and could be assured of not being watched as she went about her duties. The only lock on the outer door was an interior knob which when twisted left or right locked or opened the sprung cubicle door. The hotel took no responsibility for personal goods not locked away. The locker key had to be carried in a pocket.

Betty knew all this having worked there before. She also knew that no one could see anything other than her feet in the overshoes, once the door was closed, and that much only if the observer got down on hands and knees.

She heard Lovick and Leonie come out of the lift and whisper their way to the cubicles which were adjacent to each other and took up a whole corner space. Her own door was closed. Someone else was snoring inside a cubicle on the other side of the vast cellar space, the sound travelling like the low grunts of a sleeping boar. A chair scraped within a different cubicle across the corridor to indicate another employee of the hotel trying to rest, feet up, probably, on the sink while reading. Within the fifteen staff cubicles someone else was whistling softly in direct contravention of rule number four. No one was alone if one considered the huge space as one big, vast box separated into small compartments which, open as they were from above, could have been spied on from the low, oak wood spas which formed the ground floor of the hotel. C.C.T.V.? That would be a violation of privacy which even Mrs. Fairbrother dare not breach. Betty was assured but still listening, vetting, as she had been sent to do.

Somewhere, lovers were contravening the staff rules as Betty heard what could only be construed as the sounds of passionate kissing coming to her listening ears. A woman giggling. A man's indrawn breath. Deep breathing from them both. There was the sound of slurping and then more giggles. The minx was flirting with the singer even while encouraging Lizzie's Ross. All the more reason for Ross to be saved by being safely married to Lizzie. She would cheat on him and break his heart. No one else could ever show him faithful love like Lizzie, not even that pampered, pesky dog of his. Whispers followed on and then a zipping sound as if a case had been opened.

"Now, that's what I call underwear. Is that your teddy bear?"

"Sshhh!"

More giggles.

Betty had to remind herself that soon that little minx would be crying, not laughing. She was trying to steal Lizzie's Ross and that could not be allowed to happen. Could it?

The girl would pay!

Betty forgot about the people in the cubicles, save for the whereabouts of number six, after closing her eyes on a bitter memory that was not for sharing. It had to be clamped tightly into her mind to keep it contained.

Her face closed, momentarily, on her huge, inner tiredness; eyes, mouth, even nostrils pinched in, in grey pleats of wrinkled skin, before she remembered herself. It wasn't time yet. Keep her happy, her mind said, patience, patience! The bars on her inner cage were being rattled enough to make her hands shake. Betty needed a drink to calm her nerves.

She got on, then, with the last of her unpacking, hearing the noisy neighbours go back up in the lift. Clothes and a make-up box, of course; her darkest colours, were left out on the bed till later. Last out of her case was a bottle of gin. They didn't make Cherry B's any more. Or Babycham. She used to like Babycham in one of those wide champagne glasses with a white bow painted on it, same as was round the little fawn's neck. Not the flutes. Gin was fine drunk out of the plastic tumbler off the sink, looked just like water. If she was caught short because the flimsy glass disintegrated, she would swig it straight out of the bottle. Ice or lemon or tonic, not required.

When at last she went back up in the lift to get her uniform, she was half cut. The little fold-up desk in the staff cubicle had been useful. She had been able to sit while extracting the contents of the large envelope which Leonie had passed over. She required only the large manila envelope so she had filed the documents, themselves, in the waste bin, provided.

Lizzie's excitement had been barely containable as Betty sat at the desk and prepared her own paperwork, popped it within, and then ran a wet tongue over the bitter tasting gum on the flap and sealed it. She had written nothing on the front because this was a special envelope that had printed on it; 'Important Office Documents Within. Do not remove from office once returned with all signatures'. Someone had written her name; Betty Jessop, at the top also, in black ink so it would not be necessary to label it further. Why waste good, green ink, anyway? One never knew when one needed a green ink pen. The Star no longer sold them, only the Post Office Counters. Hannah would have to buy Lizzie a stash for posterity, same as batteries, in future, for when she would have to write out all her thank you letters and maybe inform people of a coming event, while listening to her favourite radio programmes as she did so. Ted Roblinson on BBC Radio, Lancashire.

When the doors of the lift slid back, the foyer was as quiet as a grave. No one about. Betty went on a lonely tramp to find them, though she was happy to stay out of their way. There seemed to be a lot of staff in the ballroom because that interior hall light blazed. A quick peep round a corner and she could see the wide ballroom doors folded back, next to a glorious Christmas tree. Some kind of a rehearsal going on under the blazing chandeliers, fun, jollity, a bit rowdy, Lizzie never invited.

A lot of staff in red and gold uniforms were prancing about a stage. Lick Johnson and Leonie Jones were singing and dancing about on it, above the sprung floor where Lizzie had never danced, but would soon enough. The minx's skirts were twirling high and billowing wide to show her knickers; pink silk with little lacy bits to match her stocking tops. Ross was standing watching her, looking up, seeing the lot, with a wide grin on his face. There were bottles of wine and glasses on a table and dishes of what Lizzie had always thought of as 'nibbles'. She could smell the staff dinner. It would be in the heated dishes by now, or should be, ready for the staff to go to the Staff dining room and help themselves. There would be one for her, too, but Betty wasn't hungry. Plenty of time to eat tomorrow. Everything more or less set. That pile of soft sediment which had been blocking the way, having been removed by 'the usher'. He'd kept saying that he felt a bit dizzy. Shotgun had sorted that out though. Wonderful what the sight of two loaded barrels can achieve. Everything that was needed carried over and barrowed through, before he'd tripped over his own shoe lace and been further crocked by the handle of the wheelbarrow. She had heard a snapping sound and seen the bone poking through under his overalls, blood beginning to spot the thick, white cotton but not much. Then he'd gone fast asleep. No waking him, either! Not that he should trouble them further because it had snowed again. Footprints across the yard were cancelled without Lizzie having to get a broom. She had heard Gareth Jones say that he'd gone to the farm to talk with Hannah but had been disturbed by that minx wanting a slave to pack and bring a suitcase for her. Made a slight complication but it was only one of location. No matter.

No sign of the dragon, either. That meant fun and frivolity going on. She would be lying down in a darkened room with a headache. No sign of Cannon and Chef, either. It was important to know where they, C and C, were because their bedrooms were on the interior service corridor, as long as things hadn't been swapped about from five years ago. Her plans would be scuppered should they hear a kafuffle in the night. They would have to be dealt with.

Back to the foyer, then, looking, taking it all in. Lizzie's domain this should have been as Mrs. Rossiter Fairbrother; a posh pad, the biggest in the district. While her mother-in-law, Mrs. Alicia Fairbrother, grand, dowager dame, got banished to a crumbling, windswept, moorland cottage, with a plaid shawl round her shorn head and a bitter draught chilling her legs and feet through her ragged dress. Wearing cold, rubber wellies, not warm, fur lined boots, either. No fire! There would be no time to make a fire because there would always be work to do. Betty gave her some sheep to wander after through the prickly, scratchy heather, always one missing; Ross, her son.

The main lights had been dimmed to give sufficient visibility over the reception space should there be a need to answer a ringing phone, open the main front door or cross the back of the reception area to Ross's office. The restaurant was dimly lit and quiet, tables beautifully laid with damask cloths, sparkling glassware, serviettes cascading from them in Christmas colours, and stainless steel cutlery gleaming bright. The space where they had the breakfast buffet bar was screened over but a bank of cups and saucers and a hot drinks machine, as well as plates and dishes, sat in the shadows next to it. Betty was tempted, very tempted but had to resist. She could hear Cannon and Chef laughing together in the kitchen beyond. They had already started drinking from the sound of it.

Most important, there was no one using the comfortable sofas, or the drinks bar where Betty saw another bottle of gin standing next to a set of lemons in a dish, a small knife ready to slice them into thin, little slithers. Bar all ready and set to go, lined at the back with optics; every kind of drink imaginable and shelves full of replacements, underneath. Polished glasses were hanging upside down from a slotted shelf above the beer siphons, ice boxes, nut dishes, all in readiness for tomorrow when the champagne corks would pop. Lizzie would be back here, ensconced, by then, ready for the glasses to be raised to...

Things to do before that. Betty narrowed her eyes and looked. Leonie had left her uniform ready on the reception desk for her to pick up. She put the slippy cellophane bag they were wrapped in under her arm, and might have moved on through to the office to deposit her large buff envelope, except that she saw a small pile of post on the counter. The top one had Ross's flourishing handwriting on it. He had written the minx's name; 'Leonie' and put 'Personal and Private' at the top. Betty spat on it. It was a name she disliked. She would not call a dog a soft name like Leonie. A good girl's name would have been Bernadette Hannah Elizabeth. They all had to keep Hannah happy so her name was necessary. The minx would have her comeuppance, soon enough, for stealing Ross right out from under Lizzie's nose. Lizzie would not be jilted a second time, either.

It was necessary then to go back down to her cubicle and change into her uniform. It made her feel more of the crowd, it did, when she was dressed, her brown hair coiled into a bun like wound-up sausage meat, though she could do nothing about the blank expression in her eyes other than to make sure that her glasses were on the bridge of her thin nose.

When she got back up to the kitchens she found everything much the same as she recalled. Same Chef as ever he was; the trays of iced fancies looking perfect, but himself anything but. He was well-known in the village for his drinking. It pleased Betty to see that Chef was as pickled as she was. He stood in his blue stripes and white double breasted jacket with his hat pulled down over one eye. All the better to focus while slicing roast beef with a very sharp knife. "S'you again, is it?"

"S'me, Chef. Staff meals, hey?"

Chef almost sliced his own finger as he let the blade draw through the rare flesh. "Take this through for the staff and come back."

Betty did as he asked, looking out for Cannon, who she found loading a dishwasher in the corner. She assumed he had eaten. His glance was unfriendly. "Make sure my knives don't go missing again. No crockery smashed either."

"Weren't me as did that."

"Weren't no one else and that's a fact. Too much gin, maybe? Couldn't remember walking into the shelf? Happens to me, as well, at times. Tell Chef I won't be long. Pour me a whisky."

Betty nodded, glad to know that Cannon would be joining them, soon. Let him think what he wanted. She was in. What she did when she got back to the kitchen was to make herself useful, set some cutlery on a table, find a cloth and pretend to be polishing up the shine after breathing on the metal. Chef was slowly drinking himself into a stupor.

It was a relief when Cannon showed himself still fastening the top button on his fly. "Last chance to get pickled," he said, "...before they all arrive tomorrow and we're worked like cart horses. I've taken her a tray already. I thought the problem of the snow had been solved but she's cursing it like mad."

"Shut up about her," Chef advised. "Cheers!"

Betty sat down and joined them. She had brought the loose bottle of gin from behind the bar with her.

Nineteen

It was very late in the evening, Leonie's birthday tomorrow; a panic beginning to build up in Gloria's chest which she suspected was somewhere very deep under her mountainous breasts. She was hungry in a way that caused her pain. The craving was, she considered, no different than that of a drug addict being denied his fix. If she was not to worry about what might happen tomorrow, then all she could do was obsess about food. Her box had been replenished, diminished, replenished and diminished by herself and kindly neighbours and the bakery, all through the day, but still the thought of that bloody ham in the fridge would not leave her alone. In the absence of people, what was there to fill her mind, otherwise? Gareth had been home twice, briefly, the first after her call had disturbed him while making a visit to Barnston Farm when he had had to return to pack and take Leonie's suitcase to the Fairview Hotel. He had made her a snack meal of three eggs and four rounds of toast, eating the same himself at the kitchen table. The second, after returning from there to prepare her a tray for later and see to her covered bed pans, before taking himself over the road for a nap at the station. He had allowed her the rest of the mince pies from the fridge, refilled her flask, and then taken the extra portable heater from Leonie's bedroom and carried it across the street. She had eaten them even before he had switched the downstairs lights on then off again and gone upstairs.

Gloria could see that he had now taken to using the upstairs front bedroom; a room that he had not even stepped inside for years until that morning, though he had not told her what he had discovered there. She could see the outline of his grey shape through the newspapers masking the window, through the obscuring snow, because the hanging light bulb was on and his hulking shadow had been moving about as he divested his outer garments. Eventually, the light had gone out there also. Gloria could only assume that he had finally slept. This was around seven thirty. Now it was almost midnight. He had been almost two days without sleep.

For some of the time, Gloria had switched out her own lights, drew her curtains, pulled back her nets and lay watching his upstairs window in the white-blotted dark, her hand and mouth her only moving parts as she stuffed three packets of chocolate raisins and tried to make them last. It was something she often did, was watching over Gareth, late at night, like a guard duty. Gareth looked after everyone but who looked after him? Who guarded him while the village slept? Certainly not the buggers who were making such a fool of him. Well, she would watch out, if no one else.

It had been on that second visit home that he had told her what she knew already but would not divulge unless specifically asked to. Fathers and daughters might be close but Gloria knew herself to have an advantage over her husband where their daughter was concerned. Leonie would tell her dad only what was necessary. It was the edge Gloria had over him because Leonie told her everything.

"Our Leonie looks smitten. That new musician up the hotel." His eyes had rolled. "More meat on a skeleton." Then more surly, "Looks a bit of a villain to me."

Gloria was not surprised by his comment. Gareth had detested the sight of every boyfriend Leonie had ever had.

Not that they talked for long. Gareth had other things on his mind, though he had said that he hadn't minded taking Leonie her case before the worsening weather situation made it impossible for even the snow ploughs to get out. It would be safer for her to sleep in despite the Lothario who had been hanging all over her. He had said that he had been able to kill two birds with one stone because he had a missing person enquiry to chase. He hadn't said who, but with Vera Harcourt hurrying all round the streets, knocking on doors, it was hardly a secret. The village was of the opinion that they did not blame Blue for hiding from his wife, though he hadn't been answering his phone at all and had not done so to those who said that they phoned him shortly after nine about the odd decorating job. They said that was why they had phoned him 'about a decorating job', when Gloria suspected that what they really wanted fulfilling was a shopping list of untaxed goods for which Bluithe was a runner. It was all rather worrying and especially when Vera had told her in confidence, that time when she had required a resting post after a rather wobbly exit from the Bald Pheasant Inn, that he didn't want it generally known but he was seriously diabetic, mainly because if Marty knew he would refuse to serve him ale, and secondly because a man didn't admit to illnesses. It was only women who got ill.

Not that Gareth had mentioned Bluithe's need of an injection or he would pass into a coma, most like because her husband did not share her need to pass every detail that entered her ears, passed through her brain and out of her mouth and onwards into public history, save for that of her own personal concerns. They had been speaking, though, as he had gone to make up Leonie's case from the list Gloria had given him. He had kept up a consultation because he had no idea what was meant by items described as 'thongs' and 'teddies' and 'baby dolls'. What was a 'purple body stocking' and the gold 'hipster'? But he knew where to find the smart, grey slacks with the frogged military jacket and a pair of black stilettos when she would be better to wear sensible boots.

"She's going to up the ante at work, I think. I don't think Mrs Fairbrother will approve of the shoes, though."

He had shouted through to Gloria that his Leonie always looked good in the military style, frogged jacket which would be much more presentable than the cheap, oversized business suit she had been wearing for work. "Got a good figure on her, has our Leonie."

Gloria did not feel jealous, but proud. Her Leonie was a little angel and that was a fact. Kept herself clean and her clothes nice, too. When she dressed up she could be a real little stunner. She could only hope that this Lovick Johnson deserved her.

If only things had worked out between herself and Gareth maybe she would not have gone on a death wish, never ending binge, because she had to punish him as well as herself. It was fear, see, at the back of all her eating. She so wanted him to come home and try to put his arms around her, hold her tight, stroke her hair, tell her that it would all be alright. Fat chance, being a very apt description of the fact that he rarely showed his face. If she started to talk about things that concerned her, he turned his back and left. As did Leonie but she could not expect a young woman like Leonie to understand anything about anything. Then, the way she had come to them, was an absolute no-no topic of conversation. Come home, Gareth, please. Come home, she pleaded across the big divide.

No reply forthcoming, his windows dark. There was nothing else for it. Gloria found her new technology from under her bed. The box was roughly five feet in length and a square of four inch sides in width. It did not hold a set of crutches.

***

Gareth sent Gloria a text message at roughly two in the morning, to ask her if she wanted anything. He was up and dressed after a seven hour, very deep and satisfying sleep that had admittedly only been disturbed by the landline phone ringing in his office downstairs. When he had finally roused himself to go and look at his answer machine, his mobile was ringing instead. No one less than his own Chief Inspector of Police.

"About this missing person on your patch, P.C. Jones."

Gareth rolled his eyes knowing that the reason that there might be an interest from above in Bluithe Harcourt was because there would be mileage in it. There was politics afoot because his law enforcement officers had to be seen to be working through the crisis caused by the snowdrifts instead of seeing it as an opportunity to catch up with the paperwork or enjoy a well earned rest. He had been contacted by a reporter saying that he had had a call about a missing person which would make a cracking human interest story, because the person lost in the snow was a serious diabetic. His wife was asking for a payout in exchange for allowing his newspaper exclusive rights to the story. The reporter was checking up if the story was correct before handing over a penny. Everything had to move swiftly because they would soon be going to press. Which was why he was phoning Gareth in the middle of the night.

Gareth thought he sounded half stewed which proved to be the case when his superior admitted to having imbibed overly at the Policeman's Ball though he regarded himself as offering his free time to duty. "Got to be seen to be doing our bit when half the country has come to a standstill. I've decided to make this a showcase, P.C. Jones. Human interest will be rife and we want to look our best. We have to be seen to be making every effort to find him. There's too much publicity goes to Search and Rescue when half the time it's us that calls them in the first place. I'm prepared to fund a full scale police search if this man is still missing come the morning." This from a man who quibbled if Gareth put the price of a box of corn plasters on his budget sheet.

There was no reply from his text to Gloria, so Gareth assumed that she must be asleep. Despite the snow still falling thickly, he could see that her lights were on in her room but her curtains were shut. The Bald Pheasant Inn was in darkness. His attention back with his wife, who, he knew would be missing Leonie's presence in the flat. He wondered if the peace and quiet had been a benefit to her. She had probably fallen into a doze watching that little telly of hers. At least if she was asleep she wasn't eating. He had been amazed that the festive ham in the fridge had lasted there as long as it had but then Leonie had not been home to give in to Gloria's pestering. They both gave in eventually because Gloria would start World War Three for the sake of a plate of chips and egg if it was the only way to get it.

Gareth built the fire up with additional logs in his cast iron stove, put the kettle on, and decided to get himself organised if he would have to be out at first light with a plan of action to specify the way the search would be conducted. One thing was certain, there would be no reinforcements. The only people he could call in, other than the Fell Rescue which he would call in anyway with strict warning that he would be the only one to talk to the press, were his specials. With his eyes to the rice pudding on the window, he thought it unlikely that they would be able to get more stuff moved tonight. They would be nice and fresh for helping out, each of them proficient skiers, too. Loads of ski equipment up at the hotel. He could ask Ross Fairbrother if it would be available for use by his search team. Maybe, he could make more of a friend than he had done of Ross Fairbrother. Take him into his confidence. He had actually believed him when he said that he had no idea what could possibly have happened to Blue Harcourt, though he thought that his specials might if all he was doing was hiding up somewhere away from his angry wife. Maybe if he could find opportunity to open the sluice gates, he might beg that Ross do nothing to cause hurt to his family. If Leonie was to know the truth, it would break her heart. She would never forgive them.

What he did first of all after availing himself of a large cup of coffee and a packet of Hobnobs was to open his mail from the day before, listen to all his messages, just in case Blue Harcourt had been trying to get in touch with him, and check his emails. Nothing of any great urgency, there, he went to the small, locked cupboard on the front wall right next to his locked front door to empty his 'snitch-box' which was no more than a box which was available for messages, lost property as long as it was small enough to fit inside, and a ring-bound book and a pencil for people to write with. He had looked in once earlier during the afternoon after seeing Betty Jessop in the village and deciding not to pursue what needed to be said to her for the time being; knowing now why she was back in Barns, too, after seeing her at the Fairview. He had been aware of what Mrs. Fairbrother had had to say about her being there; the box had been empty then. Now, low and behold, he extracted two mobile telephones and one letter. One of the phones he recognised because he had seen Blue Harcourt using it that morning. When he switched it on to listen to the ring tone, he heard the cry of the Lone Ranger; "Hi, ho, Tonto. Away!" It could not be anyone else's. The other he failed to recognise but it was a fancy piece of technology; took photos and short bits of video. When he opened the letter it was from one of the local villagers, a man he knew well, one of the pensioners from the Community Centre who was helping to arrange the Christmas parties, there. The letter was apologetic because he had found both phones together, while out walking his dog, in the mud, under the road bridge on Barnston New Road, on the river bank itself, early afternoon, when he had managed to get out before the blizzard started again. He had been walking his dog, noticed the phones on the path directly in front of him, picked them up while wondering if someone had thrown them over the bridge from a passing car and then decided against it because they had been laid neatly, side by side, as if finding them had been intended. He had put them in his coat pocket and then promptly had forgotten about them until after he had woken up from a long and satisfying snooze in the warmth of his living room at home. His son had trudged the distance to place both and his note in the 'snitch box'. He hoped that Gareth could find out who they belonged to.

He took them both through into his office to sit at his desk, with great interest. One of them was Blue's of that there was no doubt. The other responded to being switched on with a full battery. When he went into the personal section, he was able to find the number of the phone and write it down. Then he scrolled through the numbers to give him a clue to who it might belong to. One or two of the landline codes he recognised as Greater Manchester area codes. Then he recalled Slick Lick Johnson - stupid name - mentioning that he had misplaced his mobile, even suggesting that Lizzie had stolen it. Then he went back to the phone he definitely knew to be Blue Harcourt's. He would listen to the voice messages and text messages, of which there were several, later. Instead, he went into the register of contacts names, scrolling for what, he wasn't sure, just something to connect the two phones together. Most were names he was familiar with himself. One stood out. He stopped scrolling. This had 'Licky Lips' as its contact name. Strange.

Gareth pressed the green dial button. Lo and behold! The other phone began to vibrate with a call coming in. When he looked for the screen identity it said it was from someone who had been listed as 'Lovely Jubbly'. What? And then immediately connected it with 'Slick Lick!' So, Blue Harcourt and the lad that his daughter was so smitten with, were contacts under an alias! But why 'Lovely Jubbly'? He could only assume it was some kind of code operation name such as the type they gave to raids or the weather forecasters gave to tornadoes. One thing was for sure, they knew each other and the lad had turned up at Barnston Farm at exactly the right time. Confusing! All very confusing!

Just to make sure that the ringing phone did belong to Lick Johnson, who he was now sure was a villain, he went into that call register and rang a random number. The voice that answered was groggy with sleep. "Lick! What you phoning for at this time of night? I said sorry didn't I!"

Gareth played along with a ruse of his own. "It's not Lick. He sold me his phone because he's a bit short. Are you his mate, Derrick?"

"He doesn't have a mate called Derrick. I'm Quincey Green. I should know, I'm Lick's best mate."

Gareth disconnected the call. He slipped both phones into his uniform pocket. He'd be monitoring and noting the numbers of all calls coming to either phone. For some reason he was beginning to feel a more serious concern for Bluithe Harcourt's disappearance. He was messing with villains. Quincey Green! He'd put a call through to the police computer at head office. He'd see the kind of friends this new boyfriend of his daughter was keeping!

One thing was for sure. He would not be telling anyone else about the phones in his possession or how he had come by them. Some things were better kept quiet about in this type of case. But it would all go down in his report to the Chief Inspector just as last night's shenanigans would go down in a report to the Chief Inspector. That was one up his sleeve and would remain so.

For a moment his mind dwelled on the fact that it would soon be his daughter's twenty-fifth birthday. He'd take her into Manchester and let her choose a nice new dress for Christmas. Her cake was ordered and Gloria said she had some French champagne ready to go on ice. Then his thoughts passed, idly, on to Gloria, herself. His gaze now travelled across the square where the snow had cut down visibility so that he could barely make out the frontage of his own home. He could see her light on, still, behind the closed curtains.

He decided to let her sleep. He would have his reports typed up and emailed before he had to start phoning to get the men together for his search. Despite his superior's orders, those being those men of the Fell Rescue from down in Quinton who he felt would be remote from anything going on in Barns, his specials and Ross Fairbrother included, though he would be asking Ross a special favour if he could rope him in to help.

Before he left the office in the early hours of the morning, he had all his paperwork done and his search map sectioned out and prioritised. At least his four wheel drive should get him up the hill when it looked like most vehicles would be too iced up to go anywhere until the sun got up. The forecast promised for the snow clouds to travel on and to go pester elsewhere. He had already decided, due to the location of the equipment he would need, to start the ball rolling at the Fairview. Maybe have a coffee with his daughter, too. Gloria would have to sort her own pig trough breakfast using that basket of hers or give her sister, Pauline, a pleading telephone call. He had far more urgent things to do.

At least there was one thing he needn't worry about. Leonie would have no reason to be late for work, this morning!

***

Gloria had other aids for the 'disabled' at her finger tips that no one knew about but herself; her fold-out grabbing stick with attachments!

She had acquired it mail order after seeing it in a household gadget catalogue. "Distance no problem for what was once the unattainable," the advertisement had said. "Buy a Long Arm Bringer and walk again!"

Within her family, only she knew of its availability under her bed. They had assumed that the lightweight box they shifted for cleaning contained something of a sensitive nature, most probably crutches as the postman had erroneously supposed. It was actually an extended version of a run of the mill gadget of the type provided by an occupational therapist to assist the handicapped. The kind that would pick up a dropped item or bring a coffee cup close. Not so! What neither Leonie nor Gareth realised was that it was her sly assistant to getting what she wanted when no one would oblige. It was more than an average sized grabber when fitted onto the other telescopic parts that had come with the set and which they knew nothing about. It turned a reach of three feet into twenty plus and had different tool bits. Long enough to reach as far as the fridge in the kitchen if Gloria manoeuvred and rolled herself to the bottom, door side of her reinforced bed and set her mind to the purpose. It had come equipped with a grabber, a spike, a hook, a magnet and a mirror. She could reach high, across and through the door of her confinement once she had used the hook to open it. She could put the mirror on and look up and down the hall because sometimes she got nervous and imagined an intruder in the flat, heard noises where none existed. She could extend it further to travel into the room opposite her bedroom which just happened to be the kitchen. She could get anything she wanted out of the low level fridge without stepping a foot out of bed.

Like getting the ham! It was the ham that was on her mind as she spent several minutes achieving the desired position and then reached for the sticks which she kept next to the sealed hamper under the bed. The one she had promised her sister would still be available as an addition to their Christmas dinner together, when Gareth and Leonie would be working, as long as she wasn't in Turkey, eating turkey that was.

Mrs. Fairbrother had brought the decorated ham with her when she had made a surprise visit a couple of days ago, now. She had brought it up the stairs herself after a very concerned Gloria had released the catch on the street door, wondering why she was calling on her. As it turned out she need not have worried. Mrs. Fairbrother had no knowledge that Leonie was her granddaughter. She soon made it clear what her pompous, big hat and fur coat visit was for, when she allowed Gloria to see the ham in her carrier bag.

"For you, dear. It's too heavy for Leonie to carry on foot so I brought it myself. From the Fairview Hotel to local staff only. It's a gesture of thanks for all Leonie's hard work and for the way Gareth never declines to call when we have security concerns. There have been a few lately."

"I don't know whether Gareth will accept it, Mrs. Fairbrother. He's particular about accepting things that can be misconstrued as bribes."

"Then why tell him? I'm sure that you will enjoy every bit of the finest French ham with a mustard, honey, orange and cranberry garnish. It's decorated so prettily, too. See. What shall I do with it, dear? In the fridge?"

She had left just as quickly as she had come, shutting the door tightly behind her.

A ham in the fridge! Neither Gareth nor Leonie was partial. Unlike Gloria, they were not lovers of gammon. They rarely even noticed food unless hunger beckoned. Besides which Gareth usually ate at the Bald Pheasant Inn and Leonie at the hotel. If they didn't ask where it had come from, she wouldn't tell them. Better to eat it as soon as possible. Though she had tried to ignore its presence in the fridge for as long as she was able.

It bothered her that it should be a gift from a Fairbrother. It was the link to the secret that bothered Gloria. Maybe Mrs. Fairbrother did know and the ham was a pre-shock comforter. Even in its innocence, it had become a despised object of reference even while Gloria craved to eat it because it had come from a Fairbrother. Not that the ham knew any different. Her stomach neither. Time for the two to meet, the problem to be solved and the evidence disposed of.

She had used the stick without its extension, just the hooking tool, to open the handle on her bedroom door. Another extension and the stick reached across the narrow hallway to push open the kitchen door some more. Two more extensions with the magnet end on it and the fridge door opened. The ham was inside on the bottom shelf where Gloria had asked Mrs. Fairbrother to put it. It was approximately six inches off the floor. By retracting the stick again and putting a hook on the end of it, the same process nicely brought the ham across the kitchen floor, safe in its plastic wrapping, across the hall and into her bedroom. Gloria had a set of plates and cutlery and some nice Dijon mustard which had been sent up to her only that day with a side of roast beef Marty had had left over. It had come up in her basket wrapped in foil. The beef had been eaten but not the mustard when Gloria preferred horseradish with beef. It was in her bedside table. No need to raid the hamper though the port wine sauce was very tempting. French ham and Dijon mustard went perfect together.

By the time she was fast asleep, a half hour later, it was all inside her. All of it; a whole ham and the complete jar of Dijon mustard washed down with a bottle of coke. The used plate and cutlery had slipped off the bed to the floor which, for Gloria, was unusual. She was never slovenly unless it could not be helped. For her to sleep immediately after food was peculiar to her habits. She would usually have to spend a good hour looking out of her bedroom window following a hearty feast. The pallor of her cheeks with two little round patches of rash was unusual, too. Normally, her face had a ruddy hue all over, lips the colour of ripe cherries and her tongue a rich dark red. They had already begun to turn a majestic purple and would shortly turn navy blue. If anyone had taken her pulse they would have found it to be erratic; one moment light as a fluttering butterfly and the next as rapid and fast as the drill of a woodpecker looking for grubs in the bark of a tree. Worst of all was the quivering mound of her flesh as she breathed with a gurgling sound and the beads of sweat coming out from every pore to soak her wet from head to foot. Her parachute of a nightdress had begun to turn transparent and stuck to her skin. She had kicked the covers off herself as her temperature had soared. A hand of fat, limp fingers slipped off the bed and swung down to point at the floor where the ham wrapper was discarded. Something was not right! Was Gloria unconscious, or merely asleep? The question went unanswered. There was no one to do anything about it even if she was. Leonie was sleeping at the hotel and Gareth over at the police station, as usual. Gloria was alone. Gloria was ill.

Twenty

Bed time. The main lights in the corridor, over the aisle between the cubicles in the cellar, dimmed, yet again, by way of an automatic switch at ten thirty each evening. A few downward beams remained, sufficient for a person to watch their own shoes move over the rubber tiles on the corridor floor as they found their way to their appointed cubicle for a night's peaceful sleep. Each cubicle door had a nub of light to shine over the number upon it when the doors were closed which meant that a cubicle was occupied.

Only half the doors were shut and locked from the inside, denoting occupation. Chef and Cannon, as permanent live-in staff, had a room each on a ground floor service corridor. Betty's was shut denoting that she was within.

***

Lovick had made his adoration clear in all ways that he could. They both wanted what Leonie was intent on saving. Her red cheeks and his hard breathing had made that clear enough. Not to mention…Yep! His space rocket; fully charged and ready for take off.

It was the best she could offer. "We could put our beds together on the same wall but on opposite sides and whisper to each other."

Lovick imagined the Berlin Wall and her dad on border control. "Like pillow talk, you mean, without sharing the same pillow." He wasn't impressed but it was better than nothing. He had hidden his blue, pot, smiley faced night light inside his locker because it was a bit embarrassing. Unless you were inside to turn the lock, the door hinges were spring loaded and the doors to all the cubicles insisted on staying open wide, so showing his shabby possessions to the world. Imagine the ribbing he'd get if Cannon got wind of the fact that he had night fears, socks with holes in the toes, and still carried around with him a few, dog-eared, Rupert Bear books…sentimental reading only, of course.

Leonie had nodded, assuming a selfless respect and understanding. "What I have to give is precious, you see, Lick. I'm not giving it away to any old thief in the night. I need to know that you're as committed as I am."

Lovick thought of a prison sentence. But a prison sentence with Leonie sharing the cell was hardly Walton Jail. He'd been there, done that, got the T-shirt already!

That she placed all her misgivings in the jargon of the Law, reminded Lovick, once again, that her father was a policeman. Moreover, a policeman who was very likely to run a check on him if Lovick as much as looked at him the wrong way…or his daughter! If he had got all the vibes wrong, which his senses told him he hadn't; he might be in danger of her being the thief to his own most tender of feelings. Women never credited a man with the same vulnerability they felt was reserved only for themselves. Women always forgot that in the scheme of things, when nature set men to conquest and women to subjugation, just for the sake of ensuring the continuation of the human race, that under the hard, muscle-bound pecs might lie a tender, fragile heart, just as susceptible to abuse as theirs were. There was no safe way of approach beyond her own clearly defined boundaries, if he wanted to stay in her good books, which he did. Until he recalled some advice about women, from his granddad, when he had been a newly come lad of eight years old, to lodge with his grandparents. His granddad, chin on his spade handle, sharing a fag, kindly, in his garden shed, saucy eyed and cryptic of words, gave him the benefit of his sixty three years of experience. "Get it wrong, our Lick, and yer life's a misery. It's all about approach. My best advice is do it crafty, from the bottom up, through her feet, lad…her feet! Say things like:-

"…put your feet up, love, and I'll make you a cuppa…. Them bunions bothering you again? Come here and I'll give them a rub… You've the prettiest ankles I've ever seen… Fancy a toe curl? Afterwards I'll paint them for yer… Yer my little twinkle toes, so yer are. Shall we twinkle a bit together?"

Lovick, in his difficult listening, confusing twinkle and tinkle. Was that why he put bells on his boots, maybe, to remind him of his granddad's advice of how important feet were to successful human relationships, while at the same time protecting them with a stout pair of boots. Approaching life feet first, from the bottom up, with ribbons and bells instead of steel toe caps.

"Leonie…?"

"Yes, Lick? But if you're wanting me to slide under the screen…"

"I'd love it. But no…Do you want to see my feet?"

"Not here, in the corridor."

"No, you go one side and put your feet through the gap and I'll give yours a bit of a massage. Then you do me."

"Safe undressing!"

"Sort of. I promise. Just feet."

By the time they got into their separate beds, the mood of intimacy was developing, a bit like an imminent earthquake.

Lovick thought that to progress from feet to thigh was a sensible thing to do because, as his wardrobe existed at present, his best boxers were best kept hidden from her. Tomorrow, he could pop down to the shops for a pair of Calvin's, those with a shaped crotch to make the most of any man's assets. And take a look at that tractor, while he was at it.

But even separated, it was quite amazing the fun that could be had. Then they got on with the original pillow talk idea. The beds were light enough and on wheels, so it was just a matter of rolling the tub chair out of the way and gliding the bed to share the same portion of studding, on different sides of the same divider. Once warmly tucked up in their respective beds, they found each other through the dividing plywood wall with playful delight, both with feet all a-tingle, having swapped her stockings with the lace tops and work shoes back, she passing his footwear back to him under the ten inch divide, his boots with the soft ribbons and bells all a-jingle.

With her quilt arranged just as she liked it and pillow fluffed, Leonie, while stifling giggles like a schoolgirl, laid her hand to the wood and rubbed it to make a soft, shuffle noise. On the other side, Lovick put his open mouth to his cupped hands, head on his own hand-battered pillow, underneath his own quilt as naked as the day he was born, never worn a pair of pyjamas in his life and didn't intend to until he got carted away to the old folks home, like his granddad. Pursing his lips, he blew a circle of hot air against the wood where the vibration was guiding him.

On the other side of the divide, that was where Leonie placed an upturned glass and then her ear upon it, tapping lightly at the tumbler base. When she put her ear against it, it was as if her senses had vaporised through the knots in the wood, her mind shyly providing such a warm intimate want of him, her feet tingling from the massage, and especially when she could hear the words being whispered on his hot, steamy breath.

She could only gasp, sigh and agree with everything he suggested, at some time in the future when she was perfectly sure that Lick would live up to his promise.

Neither were aware of a pocket sized, dental mirror, a bit like a miniature submarine periscope, invading their privacy under their doors, first Leonie's and then Lovick's spaces, before a drunken voice mumbled something about getting on with it, "I've bet bloody money on it!" before stumbling away, back to the lift and up the way he had come, just a few moments earlier.

Their attentions were entirely wrapped up in the challenge of making love without actually seeing or touching each other. Her pulses were throbbing as they listened and murmured. She did as he bid and removed every stitch of her sexy nightwear; her legs folded high to contain the demanding impulses that she had never, before, known existed. She put them in a small heap by her bed so that when he got up in the morning and switched on the bedside light for his dressing, he would see them.

His space rocket was experiencing lift off on an orbit all on its own and at risk of some fuel spillage. He was practically incoherent with delirium, which was why he had remained unaware of Cannon coming to see if he could claim his bet off Chef yet and then brag about it to Betty Jessop who was matching them drink for drink, in the kitchen, upstairs. No such luck! So he would have to keep quiet. He didn't want her interfering and putting the horses off track for the final post. Lovick was, instead, risking splinters in order to tell her that she was adorable. Thing was, though….and here was what Lovick found the most amazing….he meant every word he said, first time ever. The only thing he stopped short of telling her was that he loved her.

Finally, needful of sleep, she rolled over onto her side, with her naked back warm up against the partition, fluffed up her pillow and wished Lovick a good night, a soft and tender smile on her face.

On his own side, he did the same. The warmth from their backs spread into the wood between them; almost like sharing the same bed.

Both approached the prospect of welcome sleep with a swell of happiness and, on Lovick's part, a feeling of fear that he must do nothing to upset either her or her father when the latter could so easily turn her against him. It came to Lovick then how much he might love her if she would let him. He had been lonely for too long. It would be enough just to wrap her in his arms and hold her tight for the present, keep her safe within his guardianship. He would wait for her to lust after him in return. When they did make love it would be with ceremony and respect between them. He would keep his promises this time. For Lovick Johnson, this was a first.

Leonie was exploring similar thoughts. Wanting him to be the white knight of her dreams. Did he suspect that she was still a virgin? She had never before allowed a man to touch her as she had already allowed Lick Johnson to touch her, kiss her, fondle him back…except for that! …the weaponry her mother had warned her to watch out for because once he had her pinioned upon it she would be lost. And her reputation with it. Twenty-five and still a virgin! Why feel ashamed? The only thing she did not want to happen was for Mr. Ross to get jealous of Lovick and fire him before their romance had established itself. Mrs. Fairbrother would not think twice if she thought that she had just reason.

Not that any alternative had been possible. There were other staff sleeping within the basement amidst other empty cubicles. At least Mr. Ross had placed them door to door, next to each other. The building was creepy. Lovick, her new boyfriend; her brave Lovick, was sleeping next door, ready to protect her, she was sure.

***

As they went to sleep, Betty arose from where she had been lying in readiness, on, not in, her bed where she had stumbled after making sure that Canon and Chef were demobilised and incapable of no physical responses, whatsoever. Other people had come down in the silent lift and gone to their own spaces. She was waiting for the sounds of toilets flushing, their doors closing, teeth being scrubbed and water running to diminish. All sounds that she had expected because this time she knew what she was doing. It was only when all was quiet that she rose from her bed.

She was thinking a smile because five years previously, in her aborted mission, she had been in the very same cubicle as Lovick Johnson was now. Had something with her, too, that might be useful, get the lad out of the way, in fact. Him not being involved in her purpose, though she had not been able to thank him enough for disrupting the raiders search of the cowsheds. Other than having been assured by Lizzie that his mobile would be found and returned, after what naughty Miss Naughty did, the interference designed only to get that nasty Bluithe Harcourt in trouble with his missus; no more than he deserved! No wonder that Hannah had gone shit crazy. Things to be found there but the time not yet right. Soon would be, though. Everything, so far, going according to plan. She had earlier left Chef flat out on his own preparation table within the kitchens and Cannon lolling in a chair so drunk that he could not control his vision. What he had said while trying to uphold his rolling head, was; "You's got a strong likeness to that cousin o' yours." Before falling into unconsciousness.

Betty had been confident in her nodded agreement because they would remember nothing of the conversation come the morning. "More than you think."

Both men were heading for nowhere that required sober function because they were both blind drunk and incapable even of standing up. They would not even make it to their own beds which meant that she could move about the hotel quite freely with little chance of being seen. Ross and Mrs. Fairbrother had garret rooms up in the rafters well above the hotel noise. Out of it for the time being.

Ross! Pain within to think on Ross who was chasing after the policeman's lass. Chasing after that Leonie and her young enough to be his daughter.

Lizzie could not compete, see! Youth gone, disappeared. Where'd it go to, Lizzie? What does an old bird do when a young chick starts to flutter her wings? But they'd see! They'd see that it wasn't to be. Miss Carnage would see to it that it wasn't to be as she looked at herself carefully in the mirror over the washbasin while drawing on a pair of pristine, white gloves, over which she drew another pair that the others of her self would never countenance. Black! They were black suede, heavy for the weight of hand she needed this night. She was wearing the clothes she had brought with her, specially, charity shop, of course. Different clothes trailed over the laced-up suede shoes to the ones Betty wore; a buttoned, black, velvet dressing gown with a voluminous hood folded onto her shoulders over a long black shroud which Hannah had run up on the sewing machine at Barnston Farm. She was equipped with a large torch with brand new batteries safely stowed in a capacious pocket along with a set of Allen keys and lengths of strong wire. Her hair hung about sunken cheeks that had been whitened even further with a coating of face cream mixed with flour. Her mouth was a slash of crimson lipstick, her paralysed face disobeying an order to smile because the day of reckoning had come at last. Henceforth, Betty would have outlived her purpose. However, not quite!

She had pencilled in black eyebrows and put dark grey eye shadow on her lids. Her pale eyes glittered cold with the chill of her thoughts while deep within her thin body the thaw of another personality was continuing now that the character was personified within the person who looked back at her from the mirror over the washbasin; Miss Carnage, herself.

The shell was splitting open inside Betty Jessop to reveal the kernel of a different woman. In her hand she had a butchering knife with a thick handle which she carried in a tight, thin fingered grip within the black glove. She had honed it herself on a steel poker until it was sharp enough to slice through flesh as if it was butter. On the cord of her dressing gown hung a leather sheath fashioned from the thick, cured and dried suede pelt of a pig, hand stitched with string. It was one that she had brought with her. The knife was stamped with the name of the Fairview Hotel upon the gleaming, polished blade. Betty was good at polishing knives to keep them in pristine condition. It was the same one she had stolen over five years earlier but never used it then because she had found herself in the wrong room of the hotel. Not Mrs. Fairbrother's, as expected, but the room of someone who awoke at her first, mistaken entry, had sat up in bed and screamed fit to wake the dead. Then Hannah had come and taken her back. "Bad, Lizzie. That's bad!"

Now, was to be the repeat performance based on that first practise run, with Lizzie giving her all the sensible advice she needed, such as not having let her drink too much; too much at stake, on this night of all nights, the eve of her wedding to Ross. "Put yer hood up and leave it up, Miss Carnage. If someone stops you keep going, shout something about a sarnie, it's just your nightwear, you're wearing. Use the back lift and then the fire door out to the garden. If anyone stops you keep yer back turned. Keep the knife sheathed until it's time to use it. Big place, this. You'll have a lot of coming and going before you're ready to snatch her. That minx! Sorry dog! The lure!"

The marriage of Miss Elizabeth Hannah Bernadette Jubb to Mr. Rossiter Fairbrother was to take place very shortly. Hannah would have to accept it because a marriage service legally conducted and witnessed, was binding in law. It had even been consummated, a bit precipitately, maybe, that having taken place over twenty-five years before.

There would be no jilting her, this time. Not again. Not like last time when Hannah reeled the grim reaper of justice in. No stopping things from unfolding as planned within the burning heart of Miss Carnage who could never forget or forgive. Her orders had been within the small, screw-lid pot now open on the bed; the one that Betty, her carrier, had put so carefully within the locker and refrained from opening until she was sure that the house was sleeping in darkness, quiet as the grave.

Within it was the symbol of Miss Carnage's inflamed heart with a knife drawn through it and the words; "Kill, Lizzie, kill." Her permission in writing. The same words she had brought with her five years ago but then left unfulfilled.

Hannah had no right to speak of right and wrong after what she had confessed on that last night by the fire, cup of tea in her hands laced with gin, tears on her face. It had been Hannah who had left Bern to drown when she might have saved him. She had followed him up through the caverns and chimney spaces of the potholes. But it was no use her telling Lizzie that it had been Ross he had been going to see. "Lover's they'd been. Using the big cave where the water runs under. Had a bed in there, they did. Made me feel sick, watching them."

Not that Lizzie would listen. She knew different because Ross had given her their poor, dead babby. Said what she wanted, did Hannah, but it made no difference to Lizzie. Except the refrain that Hannah had said haunted her still. "Someone help me. God someone help me. Ross, I love you. I can't hold my head up for very much longer."

Sacher Torte

Bern had sealed his own fate.

Twenty-one

"Oh, the joy of bitter memory!" Miss Carnage said with a satisfying cringe, followed by an indulgent wave to her departing guard, Betty Jessop, as she lay down inside her head and went to sleep, forever. Her redundant clothing was now folded and packed away in the blue suitcase with the string wrapped around the handle, the capacious handbag also, the gin bottle and plastic cup disposed of in the waste paper bin, wiped of all fingerprints, spectacles carefully folded and put inside a pair of black woollen gloves.

However, time was getting on; no time to happily brood, grimace, curse and plot the savage revenge which had simmered in her brain for so many years and which, at last, would be brought to fruition.

First, however, to deal with all else that might stand in her way, as she let herself out of Betty Jessop's cubicle and into the communal sleeping space. It would not matter that her door was kept open by the door springs while the building slept. No one to stop her, now, anyway, all accounted for and unlikely to wake.

"Which way that barky dog, be?" she murmured, having to think back over the years. Also over the deep snores coming from cubicle five and the quivering, trembling breaths of number six which would be sadly disturbed before the minx's sleep was out. Miss Carnage considered, in her most inconsiderate way, what would have to happen later, after she had stemmed the way of dogs to listen and bark at the slightest noise. That dog which lived in its kennel, too close for comfort, to the way she would finally go this night. The one that Lizzie didn't like because it had come wagging and sniffing when she had been hiding in the bushes, dirty paws all over her nicest frock, licking her face with a rough, raspy, wet tongue, almost giving the game away. Max, was its name. She had heard Ross call it, saw him pat it, give it tit-bits. Miss Carnage hated the pesky beast because Ross would choose to pet and fuss a mangy dog before he'd pet his Lizzie; the woman who loved him most in all the wide, wide world.

Nothing else to do but silence it. She went up in the lift then out through the back service door using Betty's swipe card to override the lock, onto the dark, silent corridors of a part of the hotel that would only become alive tomorrow, once the guests had to be fed, watered, rooms serviced, laundry washed, every desire catered for, staff running themselves stupid.

Now, she was drifting down the night-blackened corridors within her Reaper's clothing, her glittering eyes looking out to see a moon riding high in a purplish grey, cloud-puffed sky. Clouds were thinning but the snow not yet done with. A perfect setting for Lizzie's winter wedding. It would hide and obliterate Miss Carnage's presence because the snow was Lizzie's friend, promising to keep the drifts high enough and the layers growing deeper still. People inside. No one pestering.

The snow provided all the more reason to go that way down to her private, secret place. By the way down which 'she' mistakenly thought to be unknown to anyone but herself after 'she' had ordered some interior works to the cave system underground.

The gun at Bluithe's head had loosened his tongue enough to spill so many secrets. Why had he met Mrs. Fairbrother under the bridge? Where had he got the little black book from? What did he plan to gain by blackmailing her? His job back? His place guaranteed still on the smuggling ring?

The scene replayed itself in her head as one of great satisfaction. "How do you know all of this?" Bluithe had demanded. So Lizzie had told him how she had gone to the river, early afternoon, thinking what else she might use her new mobile for, before she thought to throw it in the river for Old Man Green Beard to use, when suddenly it went off in her hand, playing a tune; "One o'clock, two o'clock, three o'clock, rock...!"

She had pressed a button, and placed it to her ear, saying, "Who that?"

Silly Lizzie! A mistake but when she might have come from her hiding place to let it drop in the water, as she had planned, she was aware of a clumping on the steps right next to where she was hidden in the long, snowy grass, in a bower of snow, with her white veil over her face. Miss Mischief having played her part and been put away with a change of clothing. Betty had phoned Ross; how his voice had hummed so very pleasantly in her ear. But, back at the house, Hannah had sent her up to her room because Lizzie had had to be punished for stealing Lovick Johnson's wireless phone, even if she did covet one for herself. "It's bad to steal, Lizzie! Where is it?"

"Not telling. It's mine!"

"It's in your knickers. That lad did us a kindness. He should have it back."

Lizzie hated the way her mother knew all her best hiding places. "I'll throw it in the river first."

"Get up to your room, you bad girl!"

So Lizzie had had every opportunity to find Betty's suitcase and all that it contained, feeling angry with Hannah, as she deposited it in a convenient hiding place. The hair dye was one she had acquired from the chemist shop in the village when she had been so worried about the grey in her hair. Apply and leave on for 20 minutes. Lizzie had hated the cold water on her scalp but it wasn't Lizzie who had looked back at her in the cracked mirror, but Betty Jessop, just as expected, with that lugubrious face of hers.

Best not let Hannah see that Betty Jessop had arrived on their doorstep. Her clothes had never been kept in the dressing-up boxes. There could be only one reason for Betty being here because she never came alone, only ever as a jailer to Miss Carnage, keeping her caged and locked away. Lizzie would be locked in again and the key thrown away, fear of fire or no fear of fire. Hannah would take such drastic action if Hannah saw Betty wandering the place. While Hannah had nothing against Betty, she and Miss Carnage hated each other.

As it was, Hannah had been awash with gin and dead to the world, in her chair, her work for the morning sorted. She had got the cows milked and fed using the spilled silage, opened up the sluice gates to let the river water fill the troughs when the river was at slightly higher ground level and watched it fill every trough so that each cow might be watered. Her mother had fed the chickens and collected the eggs, seen to the pigs and stocked their troughs with plenty of water and food pellets. There was too much work for an old woman whose hair was as white as the snow outside the house. Gone terrible thin she had, Lizzie thought, as she tiptoed through the kitchen, taking exceptional care not to disturb her mother because Hannah would know immediately that she was up to trouble even if Lizzie had been hiding under her bridal veil, sneaking past her and away. The mobile was going in the river; that was where the phone was going! So there!

Then the call from the lad who Lizzie had a penchant for thinking just might be her dead son come back to haunt the village. He would know it was her. He would have Gareth Jones knocking and Hannah screaming fit enough to burst a blood vessel. So she hid in the long grass, under the snowy bower, inside her snowy veil, and had a think about what to do with it. Leave it on the muddy path, maybe, just as Miss Mischief had the guitar. There was always someone walking this way to find it and hand it in. Hannah was right. The lad had served them well. He should have his phone back.

Then, her scoop of the day! Who should come down the brick steps from the road to stand by the bridge arch, talking hotly, fingers stabbing the air, but no other than Mrs. Fat Lard Barrel Fairbrother and her arch enemy, Bluithe Harcourt. Oh yes! What was happening here? Something about her having been out looking for him, all over. Did he know his wife was having dickey-fits and baying for his blood? It was going to be in all the newspapers if he didn't get home by five thirty. Talking ten to the dozen, in her volatile anger. "You said ten o'clock when we spoke first thing. I still don't have it back in my possession. So where is it? My name and address book? You are aware are you not that if it gets into the wrong hands we are all in trouble."

"Calm down, Boss. There are other lists. It's only me when all's said and done. I got angry. I want my job back. Then I'll get on with boxing up this lot," his head thrusting to his left and a terrible, peevish light in his eyes, remembering. That's when a flying object had landed so close to Lizzie that she thought he had seen her, despite her snowy bower and her white veil. There was a big clack and Lizzie could see that what he had done was throw his tool bag down in temper. She knew it was his tool bag because it had had his red woolly hat on the top as if he was warm enough without it. Tempers flared enough for them both not to spend even a moment looking about them, making sure they were alone, or that their conversation remained private, even if they did keep their voices low.

Lizzie looked at what was in the bag as she sat as still as an ice statue. The straps were open and his tools had rearranged themselves with the jerk and then settled again. Lizzie had her eyes to the brushes and scrapers, a nice length of string on a plumb line, chalk sticks and scissors and rolls of masking tape. The scissors attracted her the most. Hannah refused to let her have scissors ever since she had cut off her own hair so that it had stuck out in sprouty patches all over her tiny skull. She would have liked to have picked them up and restyled Mrs. Fairbrother's furry hat, chopped the sleeves off her sheepskin coat, cut through the straps of her handbag, and had a look up her skirt at the kind of underwear she wore. Mrs. Fat Legs…Big Bottom…Boat Belly! Not as big as Gloria Jones, though.

Her eyes settled on two things in a side pocket which had sagged open with the weight of the tools settling, so close to her fingers that she had barely to reach a white gloved hand under her veil to pick them up, both at once, and bring them under where she could look at them; a black note book secured by two elastic bands in the shape of a cross. A mobile phone.

Another phone. That's when Miss Naughty took over. Bluithe Harcourt's wife was a nasty piece of work. Jealous, too. Lizzie thought she wouldn't like to see a sexy woman's name in her husband's phone. A green pen job was this, without having to write anything. She was getting the hang of these things. Her eyes narrowed into a sneer when she saw that Bluithe Harcourt had written his telephone number on a piece of sticky tape and stuck it to the side of his phone to save him having to commit it to memory. Lizzie still had Lovick's phone in her other hand. Deftly for one so unused, she scrolled to find the call register and pressed to store a new number, typing in the name of 'Licky Lips' and pressing save. Next, she did the same operation with Bluithe's phone, recording the number as that of 'Lovely Jubbly' and all the time laughing to herself. Wait until his wife got nosey and started looking at his phone. Naughty Miss Naughty, better than a green pen letter. The less said the better!

For the moment, Lizzie stopped still because the tool bag got kicked in anger. She had looked up through her veil to see Mrs. Fairbrother dragging him off by the arm under the bridge where their heated conversation continued with less volatility.

Having decided that the mischief was no good unless Bluithe's mobile was handed to his wife, instead of him, and knowing that she was rarely away from a blazing grate unless knocking back lagers in the Bald Pheasant Inn, she decided the best thing to be done for the naughtiness of Miss Naughty to have a chance to work, would be to leave both phones side by side, together, under the bridge out of the snow, to be collected. Someone coming to do just that, too. Lizzie could hear a whistle and a bark and a splash then a voice yelling. "Go and shake yourself off elsewhere, bad dog. I have to go straight to the Community Centre."

Lizzie had been about to pocket the notebook in its entirety, too. Then thought better of it. Both items missing would indicate a thief about. She slipped off the elastic bands which held the pages closed. When she looked at the first page, she saw that it was like a ledger with names, addresses, dates and what looked to Lizzie a bit like a shopping list. She knew that Bluithe Harcourt would not have written the entries because she had been at school with Bluithe Harcourt. He couldn't spell for toffee. Always got two out of ten for the weekly spelling test. This hand was cursive and written with a fine-nibbed pen of royal blue ink. She had seen it before. Where? On a letter that Ross's mother had written to her parents stating that they must stop their daughter from making arrangements for a wedding which would never take place. She had to follow Lizzie round cancelling the church flowers and the taxis, the choir, the bells, the red carpet. It was Mrs. Fairbrother's writing and the book, this very book, was the subject of the raging argument. Names, addresses, dates and lists of merchandise to be delivered. Lizzie had been in the caves one day when she had heard a strange scraping sound, in her private room, the one which later Bluithe would help her to furnish, with a gun pointed at his head, before, of course, he tripped and broke his leg.

Important, then. Maybe something Gareth Jones would appreciate.

Lizzie imagined her future mother-in-law wandering the wilderness, out of her way, for a good few years to come as she headed for the prison gates. Robin Hooding! Carefully, Lizzie pulled at the cotton that bound the pages. No need to take all; just enough to get Gareth Jones pointed in the right direction. She removed the loose pages that came away from the centre and slipped the elastic bands back again. To all intents and purposes the book looked to have not been tampered with.

She had slipped the black book back into the side pocket of Bluithe's tool bag and had withdrawn her hand to sit statue still again, when Bluithe came, snatched up his bag, shoved a hand in and brought the book out. He offered it over to Mrs. Fairbrother who had murmured, "Thank God!" before slipping it into her handbag and snapping closed the catch.

"So I'm to stay Robin Hooding even if I can't have my old job back. Agreed?"

Mrs. Fairbrother gave a very reluctant nod. "Get on with the crating. I don't know whether we will be able to shift the stuff in there tonight or it will have to wait for the snow to disappear."

Then what happened was a most peculiar thing. Mrs. Fairbrother, aware of the approaching dog walker, went quickly up the steps to where her car was parked. Bluithe Harcourt took a dodgy look about, went behind a bush and then seemed to have been swallowed up by the brick stanchions of the bridge itself. He could not see her because of her position on the other corner of the bridge in the snowy grass. Slowly she had extended her white gloved hand to lay both phones together neatly on the path just as the man with the dog came round the bend.

She stayed very still then until he had picked them up, looked around, and then passed on by, conscious that she would only have an hour or so until it would be time for Betty to get dressed. She might, if asked nicely, post the pages in a letter, addressed in green ink, to Gareth Jones, The Law, in person.

It was all slotting together nicely. She would run home quickly for Hannah's shotgun. She was going to find Bluithe Harcourt where he had gone to hide. What he could do was give her a very welcome hand, with the right persuasion. Lizzie knew exactly where he had disappeared to.

As for Mrs. Fairbrother, she had said, "She don't know everything she don't. Mrs. Lard Barrel. Mrs. How Dare You! Mrs. Cheat. Mrs. Not As Honest And Upright As You Seem To Be! Mrs. Big Fat Fart Knickers, who could have tea with the vicar, dine with the Mayor, raise her nose at common folk and then, get up to her own, private mischief, no better than a Jubb. Who's she to talk? She'd even stashed her own ladder to the back of the gun room. Thanks a lot! Useful was that. Something else to gloat over.

All very pleasing when the day was going right and the night was promising to go even better. The blizzard was losing some of its strength now but still had to pass as she glided past window, after window, after window in this huge place. Miss Carnage thinking that it was little wonder that 'she' had had to use the nearest entrance, so to be quickly out of sight of those who might watch and, so, had opened up an old pothole chimney and had it stepped right down to the stash cavern itself. Too many people about to see her, maybe. Cannon was forever smoking in the dark while he jacked his collar up against the cold. Chef, gut rotted, barfing up on the grass, leaving behind burnt patches where his stomach acids worked better than any weed killer, by the back fire doors which gave onto the hotel grounds. The gun room was off to the far, right side of the gardens, close to the woods.

The dog kennel was by it. Dog tied up but inside in this weather, two doggy eyes shiny in the blackness, inside. Dogs didn't like the snow. Neither Miss Carnage but a lot of things had to be sacrificed if Lizzie was to be happy. Shame, but the dog would need to be silenced before anything else. Its kennel was too close to her exit route for comfort after the deed had been done. Ross had tied it up because of the snow so it could not be enticed away with a bit of a morsel laced with poison.

Well, well! Mrs. Fairbrother, not what she seemed! Never had been. Running contraband. Up to her eyes in it. Storing it where? Where else but where others would get the blame for it because that side of the river, on the built up river bank, was Jubb land, only made available to the public by right of way.

Mrs. Fairbrother Robin Hooding! How else could she afford to strut about in them fancy silk and lace dresses of hers; Coco Channel labels and real pearls at her neck. Lizzie had seen her coming out of Gloria Jones's place, too. Or Hannah had while raking the shelves in the Star for batteries during the afternoon of the previous day. She'd seen across the square and there she was, finger to the Jones's bell, opening up and going in. What's her up to? Why go there? To ask permission for Ross to court their daughter? Betty had to stop Miss Carnage from breaking out, there and then.

First things, first! Dog had to die. Simple as that. Barked loud and long whenever she had come prowling, looking for sight of her Ross. Night security they had when the guests were here. But not tonight. No torches casting circles over the bushes tonight. Or over the board which hid the entrance hole to her way out; a straight drop down which 'she' had bridged by the use of a ladder which Lizzie would use herself, with thanks, ta very much.

What would Barns folk think of that! But a fact. Cunning one, her; Mrs. Stiff Bits, climbing a ladder! Not all she seemed, neither. Not as rich as Hannah, maybe, when her mother liked to stash her money in the bank. Had to have ways of making this fancy hotel pay its debts that had nothing to do with an accountant's profit and loss account. Ross was not involved though. He hadn't run contraband since Bern had gone. No heart for it, she supposed. But she had; that mother of his. Had to have the money to let her live in the way in which she had become accustomed: Posh!

Who should be blamed for the life of a dog? It was that minx, Leonie Jones's fault, because she was enticing Lizzie's Ross. It was Mrs. Fairbrother's fault, too, because she had held Ross back when he would have come to the church, married her, happy ever after because their babby would have lived. Shrivelled in her womb, it had, with all that had happened. Had he married her, all would have turned out right in the end. Happy ever after; Lizzie and Ross; Mr. and Mrs. Rossiter Fairbrother of the Fairview Country Club Hotel. All prevented by Mrs. Fairbrother, Senior! She, who would not let it happen in the first place. There was another who would get the comeuppance she deserved and sooner than expected now that Lizzie had gained the means to that end through her simple stroke of luck.

Lizzie liked dogs. But what Miss Carnage had to do was not what Lizzie would have wanted. Miss Carnage had only hate in her heart for Max, the retriever, whose kennel was too near to the shaft which she would use to make her escape as she had done the last time when Hannah had dragged her away from the task which would be her fate. Nothing would stop Miss Carnage this time. Not even Hannah. Plans already in the making, see, for the dead of this night when Miss Carnage might silence the barky beast; the one which might give her game away.

Even so, Lizzie, the dog lover, hoped that the dog was asleep which would let her get closer before its barks hit the air. She liked to think of it as having a doggy dream, perhaps, to cover her creeps through silent snow; chasing rabbits, paws twitching and little woofs whining into the cold, snowy night. A quick grab at its ruff and then the knife in. Silence then, no one woken. Shame that! Liked dogs, Lizzie did, because they were loyal. Such a shame that its kennel was too near to the gun room and the place she'd have to go to disappear into if Miss Carnage was to escape her mischief once again. Such a shame but all creatures face death in the end. It would just come a little bit early for some.

Time to go now. The snow would white out her footprints. Last time she had looked it was still falling deep and thick and even. The wind, too, was abetting, on this the occasion of Miss Carnage's very last outing. It was whipping up a blizzard as obscuring as a voile curtain blowing in a gale and obliterating all sights and sounds and imprints. The snow was with her in her cunning, her conspiracy, her cleverness. Miss Carnage; the Grim Reaper, was on her way, again.

***

Leonie was unsure what time it was when she was awoken by the soft calling of her name. It was too dark in her cubicle to see the dial on her watch as she raised her head to listen with sleep heavy on her lids. She sensed, though, that it was the middle of the night, still, when she heard again what had disturbed her; her name and a very quiet tap, tap, on her door.

"Leonie! Miss! You awake? S'only me."

Who was it? She could hear loud snores and grunts coming from Lovick's side of the partition so knew that it could not be him. Under her locked door, she could see a pair of suede brogues upon which was a dark, oily spillage which glistened moist in the dim light. Upon the tongues of the shoes was the fall of dark cloth of a soft, full material. A dressing gown, perhaps? The caller was someone who had slipped outdoor shoes on with night clothes.

"Leonie. Need help, love. S'only me. I's in a pickle."

She recognised the female, nasal whine which came to her ears in a low whisper. She could also smell the air bourn spores of 1946 cupboard damp and mildew wafting over her door, so knew who the faint voice belonged to.

As Leonie rose, rosy warm and naked from a very warm bed, she had to slip some clothes on before answering her door. "Wait a minute, please." She pulled yesterday's knickers off the floor and put them on (never pleasant!) then her grey slacks, a fluffy, warm jumper and the new, Cuban heeled boots which her dad had packed, despite her not asking for them.

Once respectably clad, she tucked her hair behind her ears and opened her door as quietly as she could. Leonie felt annoyed but, when all was said and done, she was the hotel receptionist. It was part of her job to assist the new staff.

Indeed, it was Betty Jessop. She was wearing a black, velvet dressing gown and had both hands clasped behind her back. Her clothing looked to be damp as if she had been out in what she stood up in. In this weather! Snow still clung to her brown hair where it hung in strings over her shoulders from a central parting. Then she began the process of arranging a voluminous hood about a very strangely made up face. She looked just like the kids in the village who dressed as Goths. Could Betty Jessop be a secret Goth? Too old, surely. It was too late for Halloween. She could have been attending a fancy dress party, though. They did things like that at Christmas in Barns. Some of the parties got a bit wild, her mother said; "If you're asked to take your door keys, don't bother going!"

She was also crying, pale eyes creased with upset, tears falling over the white grease she had applied to her cheeks. Her lips had been painted crimson. Nought queerer than folk, Leonie thought; one of her mother's sayings. Best ignore the state she was in. Been drinking gin, too, from the smell of her breath.

"What's the matter?" Leonie asked in a whisper, leaning towards her, smelling mildew, gin and bad breath, all mixed together, before stepping back.

Betty put a finger to her lips to denote that they must be quiet. She was obviously stemming the need to cry out loud. "Dog's dead, I think, in its kennel."

"What? Ross's dog, Max? Has it cut itself badly?" She was responding to what she now considered to be the sight of blood on Betty's clothing.

Betty nodded. "Shush!" a suede clad finger to her lips even while the other hand stayed where it was, behind her back, so that Leonie could not see what she was holding. "No point waking everyone, is there? Over here, Miss, to the lift. You'll have to come, see. I'll explain as we go."

"Will I need a coat?"

Betty nodded. "Best not catch a chill."

Leonie went back into her cubicle to find her duffle.

Betty continued her tale once inside the lift and rising.

"Think it's dead. I went up to make a sarnie. Looked through the window. I could hear it howling. Poor thing, I thinks. Likes dogs, me. Shouldn't be out on a night like this. Put my hood up and out I goes, into the snow. It was in its kennel, bleeding. Cut itself. Lying there panting, it is, with its tongue lolling out."

Leonie gripped her bottom lip with her top teeth. Then her tongue poked out which always denoted thoughts in process. Her brows came down. "Maybe we should wake Mr. Ross."

Betty shook her head. "Come see, first."

Leonie nodded. "Poor thing."

She went with Betty quite willingly, then.

Lovick remained deeply asleep.

Twenty-two

Lovick found himself rudely awoken in what seemed like the middle of the night by a hand shaking his shoulder. It was Ross Fairbrother who leant over him to shine a torch onto his eyes. In his other hand he had an Allen key which he must have used to let himself into the cubicle. His face was long as if he had a problem.

"Get up, Lick, please. It's after eight and coming light. Gareth Jones has just phoned to ask for volunteers to assist a search party for Bluithe Harcourt. He's still missing. There's been a development. You're the only person here without a morning duty. I volunteered you as well as myself. Today of all days!"

Bloody cheek! The unwelcome news was enough to make the Porsche 911 unnecessary. Reluctantly, Lovick got out of bed.

Ross left him to dress hurriedly. "Wear clothes for the weather. Snow's two feet deep, out there!"

Lovick had time only for bladder relief after pulling on his insufficient clothing. Lizzie Jubb's scarf, in the pocket of his coat, was a welcome find. He had already noted, when visiting the toilet, that Leonie's door was closed, as he left his own cubicle after dressing as warmly as he could. Outside her closed door was a greasy, wet patch he almost slipped on as he walked over it. The bells on his boots jangled as he righted himself. That was a near do! Water he thought from Ross's shoes. He must have been out in the snow. But Lovick was thinking about his little Christmas fairy, not Ross Fairbrother and a man he did not know who was lost in the snow. Should he slide a note under her door to tell her? Not necessary, he thought. Her dad would be able to substantiate his whereabouts as he later gripped Lovick about the shoulder, a beaming smile on his face as he declared Lovick the self-sacrificing hero of the day. Leonie would be looking on; Gareth would give him a bone-rattling pat on the back for being public spirited. His eyes would be bright with respect and a hearty laugh would accompany his cry of, "Well done, lad! Well done!" There had to be a good side to being hauled out of the sack at the crack of dawn. Leonie would be so proud of him and her dad would accept him like he was his own son from then on. Think on it! He did, even dwelled for a moment. Lovick Johnson a hero!

He determined that he would be the one to find this Bluithe Harcourt. He would give it a damned good try. Or he would if he knew what he looked like. Never met the chap in broad daylight.

So off he went without checking on Leonie, whom he assumed to be fast asleep and safe in her bed next door to his own, her door locked against him and his wish to give her a great, big kiss before he went out into the snow. She could have a bit of a lie in when all she had to do was trot upstairs to be at her work, for once. Had to be a bonus; sleeping in.

Up he went in the lift to the foyer where Gareth Jones had assembled about fifteen men and was consulting lists and maps and giving out orders. Some of the men gave him a doubtful glance and frowned at his clothing. They had 'Fell Rescue' written on the backs of thickly padded, waterproof suits. Jackets unzipped, were lined with fleece. Those with 'Community Police' written on the back of their lime green fluorescent slip-ons had padded coats and salopets. Others wore ordinary ski gear but were well wrapped up. Ross was dressed like an SAS officer. The pile of skis and sticks and boots in the corner were what worried Lovick the most.

"Can you ski, lad?"

"Course I can ski. Been to Austria, haven't I! Up on the black runs."

So he had. What he failed to mention was that what had made them 'black runs' were all the black and blue bruises he had collected after colliding with bridges, other skiers, bushes, several very large moguls and lots of fences which he had deliberately aimed himself at to stop what had seemed like a sinister hand on his back giving him perilous shoves. Half the distance down most steep inclines had been passed over in a reckless, flat-on-his-back slide; head thumping over the ruts to slow his progress; the only time in his life when his brain had worked in his favour, to put a brake to some of his more stupid escapades. He had ripped his ski suit to bits. His gran had borrowed it from a neighbour, so imagine the ructions caused when a new one had to be bought, after the event, when his gran was skint. But now was not the time for negative thoughts. Confidence was needed if a hero was to be made.

He smiled boldly when someone gave out the equipment. "Here, Lick, over here."

Lovick had to take off his boots, with their jangly bells, while sitting on a tub chair, and put them with everyone else's, in a line by the front of the public bar, so to await what he would be given.

Why were his skis longer than everyone else's? He would have preferred a snowboard like Ross had. The hard, plastic boots didn't fit him properly but he made his long, thin feet fit in them, toes scrunched up. The poles were too short. He had no gloves, no hat and no thermal underwear on. Someone mentioned that it was minus eight degrees out. Brrrr! Was he a mouse or a man?

If he might have expected to be properly kitted out for a skiing expedition in two feet of snow, he was to be disappointed. No warm clothing was on offer. He would have to go out in his reefer jacket and jeans with Lizzie Jubb's scarf about his neck, looking like a wally. Thirsty, too. Everyone else had a steaming mug in his hand. Not him. Where was his? He could smell coffee on the go but no one served him. When he looked, the jug on the hot plate on Leonie's reception desk was empty. All the cups had been used. The biscuits had been eaten, just crumbs to be had. Cannon looked mightily green about the gills as he hissed like an angry goose at Lovick's request to be served some fresh if there was any going, as the rest of the gathered heroes had been. The man was obviously unwell and stank of alcohol. Probably had a hangover worse than Quincey's. Lovick didn't mind serving himself if that was the case but then he found himself prematurely marshalled by Gareth Jones who had that look on his face again. Had him gripped by the arm like a ten year old, or a worse thought, someone he was arresting. Lovick forgot about the coffee, the biscuits, and his empty belly. Smiled. Knew he dare not whinge despite his top lip sticking to his teeth.

"My daughter alright?"

Lovick's hazel eyes widened under his beetling brows. He was aware that his hair was sticking out and his face was stubbly. He felt scruffy and must have looked disreputable. He did not know why he nodded, but he did. He had yet to see Leonie because they had kept to their own cubicles. Lovick had behaved himself. He could hardly tell her father that he had not laid a hand on her, honest. Well, he had but ...he hadn't...and then there was his reputation as a stud to consider...men being men, and all that. "Er, she's fine. It's her birthday today."

His eyes went to Ross, just as her father said through clenched teeth. "I know it is."

Lovick decided to shut up and do what he was told. Say nothing. Another of his failings; too much mouth. Why did some people always seem to know the right thing to say, while he messed up even the simplest of things? Men like Ross! As well as looking intrepid and in his element as he tidied a stack of mail on Leonie's desk, tapping the top one with his fingers crossed, he never seemed at a loss. The envelope was probably a birthday card for Leonie. They must treat all the staff well. Cool!

It was forward, towards Ross, that he was propelled roughly by Leonie's dad. Clump, clump, clump! His feet had become totally boot-locked in rigid plastic.

It was to Ross that Gareth spoke as he unhanded Lovick. "Ross, will you lead this group to search down through the woods?" He handed him a slip of paper bearing five names; Ross's at the top of the list. "Your land. You'll know it better than anyone else. Starting at the gun room and fanning out as far as the front gates of the hotel, including the well and the bird hide." He handed over also a section of ordinance survey.

Ross studied the section of map he had been given. "It takes in Barnston Farm. There may be problems."

"I have warrants," was all that Gareth said. "We'll meet up again in the village square. Because we can ski, it seems better to search down through the woods rather than walk up through them. Quicker. Maybe that hunting dog of yours can assist. This is a scarf belonging to Bluithe. It has his scent."

Ross nodded. As Gareth walked away to give his instructions to other groups, Ross turned to Lovick and spoke quietly. "Are you sure you can ski?"

Lovick nodded, stubbornly. He would do by the time he was finished even if he killed himself in the process.

So out they trooped, following Ross as he had been instructed to do after they had all put their skis on. Ross trudged in boots with his snow board under his arm. He could walk the driveway which circled round to the back of the hotel and only used his snowboard on the gradients while the rest of them travelled over the deep snow by gliding left and then right, left and then right. Lovick practised as he went, finding it all coming back to him again.

As they travelled round to the west side of the hotel…the easy bit for Lovick as it needed only the pole and side slide movement on the flat, powdery, virgin snow…Ross told them that they would spread out from the main gates and the disused well in an equally spaced line. They were to criss-cross their own section of roughly fifteen or so metres, skiing slowly, and remain silent. It was important they listen out for any instructions he might give. Or the cries of the person they were seeking. And to be able to respond to any suggestions by others that they had found something of significance.

If he blew his whistle they were to regroup by following the sound of his whistle and collect together in a group where Ross stood. Was that clear?

As mud, thought Lovick. He hadn't listened due to Lizzie's scarf being wrapped twice round his neck and over his ears. His mind was also concentrated entirely on his will not to fall over. Especially when he saw Mrs. Fairbrother open a ground floor window and call out to them, "Good luck. I'm quite sure that you'll find him alive and well somewhere." Then she hailed one of the community policemen who went to her for a private word. Mere seconds later, she had shut the window and the man rejoined the group.

"Nice lady," Lovick commented.

In reply, he received a dark scowl. "Better hurry up and do what we're told. Action Man's giving the orders." Then he skied off to join the others with Olympic style.

The three other men within their team, aside from Ross, were obviously used to skiing as they made long, sideways sweeps over the deepening snow; flakes still falling though a brightness in the sky suggested that maybe not for much longer. They were the specials; the community policemen who had taken time off their work just to help with the search. Ardent and serious men, they spoke constantly about Bluithe Harcourt as if he was a very close friend. By the time they reached their starting places, Lovick had learnt a bit about the man though he still had no idea what he looked like except for recall of a tight mouth clamped about a fag and a red woolly hat. If he was still alive that is! It did not seem likely to Lovick who had already had to suffer the perishing cold so knew what he was thinking about. His mental onus being mostly on the word 'perishing' and suffering every moment of it. How could anyone survive a night out in this weather? It didn't seem likely to him unless he'd shacked up with a woman in a love nest somewhere and then been unable to get back home because of the snow. One would have thought he would have phoned, though. Which reminded him that he was without his own phone. It could be at no other place than Barnston Farm. Probably in the clutches of that troublesome Lizzie. Maybe Hannah had taken it off her and was waiting for him to knock round so that she could give it back. What better excuse to call? "I was just skiing past while helping with the search party for Bluithe Harcourt…dastardly chap…and thought to call in! Can I have my phone back, please, and mind if I hold onto Lizzie's scarf!"

Lovick shuffled over the snow to the point where Ross directed him to with a pointing finger; by the gun room, which seemed to mark the boundary of their own particular search. His leg muscles were already aching. He heard Ross calling out. "Max! Here, Max." and saw him look about. He had the scarf in his hand which Gareth had given him so that the dog might know Bluithe's scent.

The kennel was before him but Lovick could not see a dog within. It shared a wall with what must be the gun room; more a brick shed with a metal door and big padlocks. The big chains binding all the padlocks and doors together were the size of ships' hawsers. No breaking in there. No dog in the kennel, either, or anywhere round about.

Then Lovick saw the blood.

Ross continued calling.

Should he make him aware? It looked as if the dog had had an accident if the blood inside the kennel, and the pink stain on the snow, belonged to the dog. The snow all ruffled up, too, as if people had been trampling all over by the kennel and in the direction of the wood. Something had been dragged over the snow. Probably a flat bottomed sleigh. He had seen the kids playing all over the higher slopes when he had walked up from Barnston Farm the day before.

What would his scout master do? Create a diversion or get on with the job in hand? Advice? Prioritise, Lovick! It had all had to be explained to him when Lovick had the vocabulary of the street urchin, he was. All it meant was to order tasks from the most important down to the least important and choose the most important to do first. Lovick did that. Human missing, probably dead. Dog missing and probably cut its paw. Choice? Human, of course.

Ross seemed to have given up calling for his dog anyway. He was already on his board and sliding in a slant off down a steep bit, towards the trees. He had dropped Bluithe's scarf in the snow. Too late to tell anyone now but the scarf not to be wasted. Lovick adopted the toilet position, skis in a wide, upside down V shape, poles under his arms. His first criss-cross would be in the scarf's direction. He would pick it up on his way. Wear it for warmth.

So far so good. He was controlling the speed nicely. He even managed to stop, too, when he reached the scarf. Maybe, when he reached Barnston Farm he could give Lizzie her scarf back as well as pick up his phone. Then, having lost all concentration, he wobbled slightly in a turn, which unbalanced him and sent him off with a shove of that same treacherous hand that had done for him in Austria. He saw the tree in front of a jutting out rock, directly before him and looming larger and larger, all too late. The land fell away steeply. Lovick threw his sticks up and stretched high when he should, perhaps, have tucked in, brought his knees together, and used his skies to brake.

As the world started to spin, Lovick shut his eyes and prayed.

***

It was Cannon who noted the blood on the soles of Lovick's boots, and reported it directly to Mrs. Fairbrother, because Mr. Ross had left the hotel to help with the search for Bluithe, who had still not reported in at home, or anywhere else for that matter, and whose continuing disappearance had become a serious concern. It was even on the television and radio news...the daily newspapers not having been delivered...that, surprisingly, Bluithe Harcourt was a diabetic in need of a daily injection of insulin without which he would become unconscious. It seemed more and more likely that he had collapsed in the snow. So said the policeman with gold braid, leather gloves, a stick and a big, flat hat, who had been interviewed on the telly and was saying, very smugly, that a massive police operation to find him had already been launched. Every television in the hotel was blaring and every radio switched on to hear the latest. Vera Harcourt was playing it for all she could get, crying into paper handkerchiefs in an internet video interview by web-cam, when she explained to the world how much she missed him and hoped for his safe return. Blue Harcourt was the love of her life.

Cannon's intellect and senses were still somewhat compromised by the events of the night before so that he had been stumbling about his duties with the alcohol still making his brain whirl and his feet feel as if they had to be operated by hydraulic lifts, just to put one foot in front of the other. His head was thumping near to bursting after the night he and Chef had had drinking with Betty Jessop. He recalled that she could drink even Chef under the table. And had, though, in this case, Chef had been lying full length on it, totally unconscious, or so it seemed to Cannon when he had opened his bleary eyes from where he had slept all night in Chef's armchair, arms and legs numb with pins and needles and a cold, sick horror at seeing that it had gone six thirty. Their start time should have been at six o'clock.

There was no sign of Betty Jessop, either, when she should have been there, on duty from five thirty, to tidy up all the cutlery she had left spread out over the small preparation table, rags abandoned and the polish tin left with its lid off, as if it was waiting for a continuation of the same activity which had had her sitting with them the evening before. Let alone set the staff dining tables and got on with slicing fresh fruit for the breakfast buffet. Leonie had always had most of these jobs done before leaving for home, the night before.

Maybe she'd gone on a bender, he thought painfully, as he dragged Chef like a giant, rag doll off his own table, placed him with flopping limbs on the floor, then rolled him under it. He covered him, and the table, over with the whole drape of the very big table cloth they used for weddings, funerals, and Round Table meetings.

There was no need to go looking where Mrs. Fairbrother was up to in her final, opening-day inspection after he had managed to clear the decks and hide all the evidence, before she was suddenly behind him. He heard the rasp of her indrawn breath, like a buzzing wasp close to his ear, as he was standing with a tray of rattling crockery in his trembling hands, which was why he hadn't heard her coming, and had not seen her until he turned to look down on her sour face.

This morning, hotel opening day, when she would later come down looking like the Queen at Sandringham Palace, she had come before she had been to the beauty parlour, having got up especially early because of all the fuss going on in the foyer. Cannon saw the wrinkles, folds and blackheads and enlarged pores unmasked. The hairs on her top lip and chin stood out as in need of shaving, and half a pack of Polyfiller applied over all…but even that wouldn't make her look young again…before she had them all lined up to sing bloody carols, out in the freezing cold, while the helicopters landed and spewed out their guests, Christmas lights on the outside tree and staff candles lit, staff cursing.

She had whistled as well as rasped through those loose dentures of hers, as she spoke deeply, her tetchy mood of yesterday unbroken. "Those vegetable cauldrons need a good scrubbing. The flour bin's a disgrace. This kitchen would seem to be missing Leonie already. Chef had better get on top of his staff." Eyes like a ferrets, looking all about her, then a relaxed mew which Cannon distrusted because her eyes were on Chef's table. "Well done for vetting the house table linens, ahead of use. The moths get at them." Then she noted the untidy, small prep table. "I see that Mrs. Jessop is making some effort towards cleaning the house cutlery though I do wish that she would be more orderly in the process." Then, on a parting note, "I shall ignore the smell of alcohol in here. Make sure that it isn't present on my next round of inspection. I shall be making it twice today to be doubly sure." Then, with deep suspicion, "Where's Chef?"

"A bit under. I said I'd get staff breakfast."

"And coffee for the search party. They're collecting at present in the foyer."

"Bluithe still not found, then?"

"He will be quite soon, I think. The snow last night was the worst I have experienced here." She had seemed to be very preoccupied, though, for once, her mind elsewhere even if she was making issue of writing comment in one of those little black note books of hers. She had been in a prickly mood ever since she had sacked Bluithe Harcourt. Maybe she was worrying that he had responded by doing something drastic. Cannon often felt like it himself. Blamed herself, Cannon supposed. And well she might. Twenty-six years of service cancelled. He had a record of thirty-five, himself. Both he and Chef knew that one slip up, front of house, and they would be for the waste bin, also.

However, the staff would have to shift a bit more for themselves, than usual, this morning. Cannon was seriously getting annoyed at Betty

Jessop when she should have been helping him get the staff breakfast set, especially when the kitchen would be asked to provide coffee and tea for the search party which was slowly assembling in the foyer. His only saving grace there was that Chef had stumbled off, last evening, to fill the baskets in the staff dining room with frozen croissants and bread rolls; lay out the butter which no one liked to spread cold. Most of everything else, other than cutlery and plates, and a continental array of cooked meats and cheeses...Chef could not cope with cooking bacon and eggs first thing!... they could help themselves to from the staff room fridges.

Plates and cutlery had not been set because that was the work Betty Jessop, who should have started on well before anyone else was up and the rest of the kitchen staff rolled in, if they could make it through the snow. Mr. Ross had not sent out helicopters for them!

She had left the staff cutlery scattered all over the small prep table. She seemed to have done one of her disappearing acts, again. If Cannon had stumbled down in the lift to drag her up with him, before the rest of the hotel stirred, it had not been urged by a charitable concern for her health and wellbeing, not to mention her job, but because he was the only one to be upright enough, otherwise, to get the work done. If he was suffering, she could, also.

No sign of her there, either! He had found the door to her cubicle open. It had been cleared of everything. Her locker was open and empty. Her bed seemed not to have been slept in though it had been lain on and dirty rubber marks put on the duvet. There might even have been something that looked like excrement as if her shoes had been covered with it. The smell of 1946 damp cupboards had gone altogether, though. The only thing she had left behind was a full waste paper bin and an empty gin bottle. She'd done a bunk!

"Done it again," he said to himself, noting also the two locked doors of cubicles five and six as he went back upstairs though number six looked to be wedged shut with paper, peevishness nudging between the pangs of his hangover because he hadn't had a successful outcome on his bet, yet, with Chef, which always brought on his most spiteful feelings.

When she did not turn up as the other kitchen staff turned in, he went to find Mrs. Fairbrother because Mr. Ross was too busy by then welcoming and thanking the people who he discovered were being assembled by Gareth Jones, Fell Rescue and the three Community Police which they all referred to as 'specials'. That dunce, Slick Lick Johnson, had had the temerity to ask for fresh coffee when the pots were quickly emptied. Bloody cheek of it! But Cannon's inhibited attention had been caught, anyway, when he saw Gareth Jones and Mr. Ross frostily shake hands, before Gareth drew Ross to one side for a private word which, strain as he might, Cannon could not overhear because of the steam hammer thumping in his brain.

He managed to inform Mrs. Fairbrother of Betty Jessop's bunking-off again, when she came lurking about the foyer, trying to attract Ian Garstang's attention which she finally did by hailing him. Legal business Cannon supposed when Ian Garstang worked for the firm of solicitors employed by the family. Whatever she told him had his eyes to the floor and then bouncing in his head like the balls in a pinball machine, before they shook hand on something. Most surprising! She had imparted something to him that had both surprised and pleased him, even shocked him maybe. Then he was nodding his head over and over, shaking it and muttering, "Bugger me!"

She drifted away on her rounds of inspection, once more.

It had been when Lick Johnson had asked him if there was any more coffee available that Cannon had put his tray down on Leonie's reception desk while telling the stupid lad to 'f-off', using looks without saying a word. He had put his tray down on Leonie's reception desk, seeing as he did, the cream coloured, vellum envelope with Leonie Jones's name on it and the words 'personal and private' written on it in Mr. Ross's flourishing handwriting. Enough for Cannon. If she thought that she was worth a birthday card, as she obviously was in Mr. Ross's adoring opinion, where the rest of the staff got sod-all, she would have another thing coming. That being nothing! To which end he slipped it into his pocket after a very cunning look round to ensure that no one who mattered, was watching.

Betty Jessop's employment forms were now atop of the pile. Then he smirked because there was no sign of Leonie Jones who should have been behind her counter by now, switching on her computer, opening the internal mail when it would be unlikely for the postman to get up this way, or anywhere for that matter, he thought, when Cannon looked out of the windows and realised the depth of snow. Late again! Chef had covered for her when she had been a kitchen maid, and warned Cannon not to split because he needed her, she having regularly saved his bacon along with over cooked pieces of fillet. There was no sign of her and it had already gone eight thirty. She had no excuse for being late when all she had to do was come up in the lift.

Something else to snitch on! He would collect the used coffee cups and jugs as a reason for hanging about in a place he usually had no business to be in at this time of day. Stay out of her way but be ready to note the time for passing on to Mrs. Fairbrother when Leonie did finally get in, but only after her father had gone in case Mrs. Fairbrother reacted in her usual upfront, hysterical way, berating her staff in front of others which was a tribunal complaint. He would be bound to champion his beloved daughter; spoilt little brat that she was! Cannon would then get dropped in it. He would rather not upset Gareth who sometimes let himself and Chef sleep it off in his station cell after a night of 'one-too-manys' in the Bald Pheasant Inn.

Then Mrs. Fairbrother was hovering again and flashing messages with her eyes over to Tom Greaves, the butcher, whom she hailed for another private tête-à-tête, that leaving only Jim Lamb of the specials present at the search briefing, not to be privately consulted by her.

Cannon in need of a diversion in case she approached him again…as she was wont to do when in a fuss of consternation because the gathering men were leaving empty cups everywhere…went over to the public bar to flap a white napkin as if to get rid of invisible dust. He wasn't doing another tap until they all went and he could take his own time about it.

So he hovered about the bar area watching as the first of the search party left through the front doors after Gareth Jones called out their names and allotted a team leader to each group of five men, three groups in all. Ross Fairbrother was back in his mode of army Captain. He looked as if he could defeat Bin Laden single handed.

Gareth Jones, Cannon heard, would be the one to stay at the nerve centre which, at this location of the intensive search, would be the Fairview Hotel. Cannon was managing to skive nicely as each group tripped off in clumpy boots, in turn, a forest of skis and poles on the march with them, allowing a chill wind in.

Ross's group went first, then the second and then the third. When the final man had gone he found himself staring right into the froggy green eyes of his employer who was marching across the divide, between the sofas with intent in her eyes. Had she found Chef? Maybe looked in the kitchen waste bins and realised that they had drunk most of the kitchen's stock of alcohol for the whole of the Christmas season which was allocated to cooking and not themselves, in one night's awesome binge?

His head went down on aching shoulders. Yet another head to roll? Chef having to be the sacrificial lamb, if that was the case, because he was the least capable of defending himself at that very moment.

That was when Cannon saw the parade of boots in front of the bar, all lined up like in a school changing room: big, little, brown, black, wellies and après-ski, fur lined, old and new. His eyes drew back to mid-line, where the black boots with the ribbons and bells attracted his attention. He might have lifted them and used the childish ribbons and bells to skit Slick Lick Johnson, so providing a diversion, keep talking so that she could not get a word in until his eyeballs stopped aching.

That was the precise moment when he saw what looked like dried blood on colourful, silk ribbons as they trailed against his hands. Slick Lick Johnson's boots; the boots with the bells which shivered in his shaky hands as he lifted them, just as she was bearing down on him. He looked past her for Gareth Jones, so that he could call him over. He seemed to have gone off with the last of the men to make sure that his orders were being followed properly.

Back to the boots which he turned over to look underneath. The soles were smeared with blood. It definitely was blood; red and sticky to the touch. His own hands were covered.

He was holding the boots and looking at them askance when Mrs. Fairbrother's voice came from over by the desk, where she had paused, picking up the internal post when there was no one else about to see to it. "Get reception cleared and tidy again as soon as possible, Cannon. Where's Leonie? That girl cannot be late for her duties again. No matter what Ross says, I will not have it!" She tucked the post under her arm.

Cannon's face spread into a smile of satisfaction. "I was just about to, Mrs. Fairbrother. I was just looking for Gareth Jones to show him these." He presented them for her inspection. "Lick Johnson's boots, there's blood all over the soles. What's Lick Johnson been up to that he should have blood on his boots?"

Mrs. Fairbrother was suitably diverted. Her mouth flattened into the letter box shape. He saw her cringe as if to say not again, Cannon, my head can't stand it! Cannon's tales had a habit of leading to sackings. Not today, of all days!

But then, when she saw what Cannon saw on the soles of the boots he held out to her, her thoughts ran away with her. She took the post from under her arm so as not to drop it and clutched it tightly. Her rasp of breath was unexpected, her thoughts shocking. Lovick Johnson and Leonie Jones were becoming an item. Those were his boots and not to be mistaken with anyone else's. An entertainer he might be but Mrs. Fairbrother had his measure already. A womaniser! She could tell one a mile off. Not to be trusted about innocent young girls. Not safe, either. No one knew who he was. For all any of them knew, he could be an axe murderer. She spoke the first words that came to mind, out loud, "Where *is* Leonie? Dear God! My blood's run cold!"

Cannon breathed a sigh of relief!

Twenty-three

Ross Fairbrother was not overly worried about his dog. This, despite even at a distance, being able to see that Max's tether had been undone. His mother had probably saved him from the dreadful weather by taking the dog in. Even his mother would not have insisted the dog stay outside in last night's weather. He should have brought the dog in himself; would have done but for being so distracted. Otherwise, it was his mother's insistence that the dog guard the hotel grounds, its bark being enough to raise the soundest of sleepers should intruders get in. Such was his mother's only willingness to have a dog on the hotel payroll when its food and biscuits cost the hotel money along with the inconvenience and upset of replacing the village cats which it ate, by mistake, when what it should have been doing was chasing rabbits.

Or maybe the dog had managed to escape its leash as it had done before, by chewing through it. Then, probably as now, he had followed the scent of a bitch on heat, despite the snow. The dog could be gate-sitting, shivering with cold, down in the village with one of the soft, old ladies giving him bowls of water and feeding him scraps of food while the bitch was locked indoors or taking no notice of him.

He had enough to do, anyway, in coordinating his section of the search, today of all days, so he let Bluithe's scarf fall from his hand onto the snow. The search - when as a trained army officer, he had been unable to refuse to assist - was making them late for his intended visit to his solicitor's office, with Leonie. He hoped that she had been persuaded to attend with him, to hear what she had to be told. His mother also, though she had been in such a flap that he had been unable to talk about anything to her other than the hotel reopening.

At the top of his priority list for a couple of hours, at least, had to be his special instruction from Gareth which had been accompanied by the need for a promise of dire confidentiality. Tact and stealth would be called for but then that was what Ross's army training had been about. If anyone in Barns was qualified for the mission set him by Gareth, he was. It concerned keeping a special eye on Gareth's police specials, as well as Lovick Johnson, who Gareth had yet to investigate in a professional sense, but which included Ross not letting them out of his sight, if possible. All this without giving them reason to be aware that they were being watched. While everyone else would be looking out for Bluithe Harcourt, Ross would be spying on the men in his patrol, instead.

Ross already had a good idea why, without it having had to be spelt out to him. Personally, he thought it time that the smuggling gang was rumbled. They had made a fool of the law long enough. Grown men should realise that it was a serious indiscretion that could lead to a lengthy prison sentence if caught instead of the boyish game, he used to consider it to be himself, when he and Bern had run a ring of their own. He had a rough idea who most of the members of the black market gang were, the 'specials' being only a small part of a very big team with someone who insisted on remaining incognito at the head of it. The 'fund manager' as this anonymous person was usually referred to, or 'The Boss' whose investment was always the one with least risk attached for the biggest return.

These days, Ross considered it to be a dangerous business to play about with. Not good for local business, either, in the long run. The village was flooded with cheap goods at the expense of losing the honest, local traders. He was constantly receiving phone calls himself offering French fancies at cheap prices from people further down the buying chain; people he had used himself, once upon a time, to do dishonest business. Not now. If he made the Channel crossing once every few weeks, he paid the duty on what he brought back, even though it would have been a help towards the financial condition of the hotel. His mother was the one to handle all the financial side of the hotel but he knew enough to know that there were times when they were close to ruin. There would be more than Bluithe Harcourt sacked if the worst came to the worst.

For the moment, however, his vigilance must be directed towards the men within his team who Gareth suspected of wrongdoing. Ross should let him know where they went and of anything suspicious. If Lovick Johnson went anywhere near Barnston Farm he wanted to know about it. Likewise, if his specials went in that direction, he wanted to know about it. Something about having been sent there on a wild goose chase while something else was going on in the village, at Bluithe Harcourt's insistence. He did hope, fervently, that there was no basis for Bluithe's accusation that Hannah Jubb was involved in Robin Hooding. She was Leonie's other grandmother, after all!

A wave of concern clenched his stomach. What he was doing had to be done but it was not as easy as he had thought it would be. She would already have her hand to the letter if not opened it already. He found himself gripped with fear. As he set off through the woods, guiding his snowboard between the trees with expert ease, keeping closer to his team members than he hoped they realised, he remembered the letter he had placed on the desk in reception for Leonie to find before courage could fail him.

His watch now said that it was eight forty five. She would, surely, have found it by now. The trouble was that he not at all sure, with the day having dawned, that he was doing the right thing. When he thought of Gareth and Gloria Jones, his conscience twinged.

***

So far, after picking Bluithe's scarf up from the snow, all that had happened to Lovick was a collision with a tree and a bruised ego.

If you don't succeed the first time, try, try again! This time he made sure that his body was held rigidly in the toilet position, sticks underarm, toes and skis pointed into an upside down V shape. He would just have to go with the slope while doing his best to stay upright. Fortunately the others had gone down through the trees ahead of him so that he could recover without a good ribbing from anyone but himself.

The cold was making his nose red again; the sore spot inside his nostril had come back with a vengeance. He wrapped Lizzie's scarf even higher round his face and neck in an attempt to keep out the cold and added Bluithe's to it, wondering why he was causing himself such discomfort. He had crashed into the tree just a few metres from the gun room but was swiftly on his skis again; up and running, as the slope made a drastic downturn.

In front of him a large boulder of rock protruded from the snow with a wooden board lying over the snow in front of it. It looked to have been lifted from under the snow and cleared of a thin layer of vegetation; this being the soil, moss and clumps of grass which had grown upon it.

Yet another impact was imminent. His cry was unavoidable because he could see it coming and was running out of control again. It would have made a big impact on his bony knees if he fell forward, so Lovick straightened himself up, his arms shooting into the air, the sticks going flying, his skis meeting with the edge of the board. Lovick saw the hole in the ground like a gaping mouth in front of him, too late. He was unable to avoid it. Later, he would recall a vague hope that the dog which owned the kennel so close to the hole had dug a bit of a hole in its search for a buried bone, under the snow, so that it could not be particularly deep. All that would happen then was a bit of a tumble and a chance, once more, to stand and get to grips with this skiing business. Not so! The pit, into which he plunged, skis first, seemed to be pitch black and bottomless. One moment he was part of a totally white landscape save for the trunks of silver birch and sycamore, and the next he was in the dark and falling, waiting for the jarring moment when he would come to a stop. Alice in

Wonderland came to mind. He had always felt an affinity with the characters. Now he knew why!

He had gone down through some form of hole in the ground which seemed to have no end to it. A very, very deep hole. A hole that jarred his feet and his knees, then slid him over round boulders and bounced him against sharp edges, down and down, into pitch blackness, then rolled and rolled him with his hands over his head to try to prevent it banging against anything sharp. It was within Lovick's instincts to preserve his good looks and manhood at all times so he pulled his knees up and tucked his head in, becoming aware, as he did so, of the skis coming away and the boots taking the brunt of his fall as they clattered against rocks. Then stillness.

Lovick, stunned beyond feeling, listened to his own blood coursing through his own brains and his own rapid breathing, his eyes reporting absolutely nothing but pitch blackness. The cold hit him just as his first whimper of fear emanated from him. His fear of the dark was as a night terror inside him but no one was hearing as he let a scream escape.

It was the realisation that the cold was a seepage of liquid coming through the thin denim of his cheap jeans which stemmed utter panic. When he lifted one foot and then the other, the movement was accompanied by a dunking noise. He raised and lowered his hands to splashing. He was sitting in water; cold water but not frozen water like ice or snow. He was up to his waist in it.

Fear came upon him. The dark was absolute. The quiet, which initially seemed only to be disturbed by the thud of his beating heart and the breath going into him in great gasping mouthfuls, was like a thick, impenetrable veil all about him. When the shock receded slightly, the veil lifted. He was aware, then, of other sounds as well as a big bump beginning to swell on his head and the salty taste of his own blood as it dripped onto his lips from his numb nose. He could hear an undercurrent of running water, like taped chill-out music coming from a faraway speaker in an empty restaurant. An icy cold draught of air blew over his face.

For several seconds Lovick sat in the trickling water wondering what had happened to him, feeling himself all over, finding rips and holes in his clothing, bits of him that hurt but still seemed to be in working order. He seemed not to have broken anything. He still had the clumpy, uncomfortable ski boots on his feet. His coat, he realised, had been robbed of its buttons and was hanging open. No doubt tomorrow he'd have some cracking bruises and contusions, a few cuts even, to substantiate the truth of having fallen down a shaft of some kind when he told Leonie about it. He would tell Leonie about it, wouldn't he? 'Course, he would. Things like being buried alive didn't happen to Lovick Johnson, did they? The thought was petrifying. Panic building. This was his greatest nightmare over and above any other kind. Now, he really was buried, alive, in a pit of utter, complete blackness; a blackness so deep that he realised that he had never experienced such in his life before. There had always been some light to grope towards. Here, in this dripping place, where all he could hear, at first, was an unremitting drip, drip, drip, there was absolutely none. He had become a blind man.

Then he heard his gran's voice in his head and saw her comforting face as if she actually was leaning over him. Her words were the same as when she used to advise him when he'd scream out in terror during the dark nights after his owl night light had broken. She had never failed to come to soothe him. "The thing about the dark, our Lick, is that it can be as much as a boon as it can be a nuisance. It's only your night light's gone out."

He had a lighter, somewhere. In the breast pocket of his shirt, he hoped. At least, he hoped it was in the breast pocket of his shirt and not his sodden pants. He was becoming numb from the water level down. Feeling in his shirt pocket he found the lighter. Yes! Flicked it, got a tiny, welcome flame; a baby flame but still enough to tell him where he had come to rest. He was sitting in a shallow pool of water inside a rock chamber about the size that his nan's bathroom had been. He felt like the baby of cavemen who had put him in a bath and then forgotten about him.

God in heaven! Crikey! Shit! How had he managed to get himself into a mess like this? Then he realised that over the sound of the water he could hear cows lowing. What the heck? Cows? Yes, cows! There was only one place he'd find cows around here.

***

Gloria had been deeply, deeply asleep. Her body functions, however, had not been comatose. She awoke to the daylight feeling dizzy, sweating, hyperventilating, retching and very, very loose. The evidence of the latter two symptoms of food poisoning were staining her covers, had soaked into her mattress and were horrifying her disbelieving mind. Her skin tone had changed colour to a sickly shade of lemon with black circles about her rolling, glittering eyes. Her lips were white as tape worms. All about her was brown, pink and orange with a bit of mustard yellow thrown in. Vile and horrible. The smell was revolting. She could not believe what was happening to her when her body was so out of control. Never in her life before! Never in her life before! Holy Jesus! Mother of Christ! What a mess she was in!

Then it all started again; wave after wave of it and she was unable to get out of her bed. The bathroom, just a few feet away, might as well have been across the square or even on the far surface of the moon, as far as her personal mobility was concerned. Her usual methods of maintaining basic hygiene were inappropriate and far too late. It was as if the whole of her insides had turned to liquid, the gases built, and the painful pressure increased to make for explosions of epic proportions; a reconstruction of the Big Bang as far as her innards were concerned. It was everywhere; all over her body and nightdress and the sheets.

Tears flowed but she was too ashamed to send a message down in the basket. Bluithe Harcourt would be poking fun for years if he knew. Tears of rage and temper followed. All totally ineffectual, of course. Gloria knew it. She would have to help herself.

"Now, calm down, Gloria! Calm down!" she said to herself. Screaming and crying and throwing a paddy would just make things worse. But who to ask for help? She could not tolerate even the thought of her neighbours knowing that her digestive system had finally given up and conceded defeat. She could neither send down the basket nor bang on the neighbouring wall and shout for the same reason. There was no stopping it, either. It would have to take its course. She could only hope that she had enough fluid reserves within her huge mounds of tissue to fulfil her body's intentions of getting rid of the cause of her malady in its usual way. She would have no choice but to let it run its course. If only she had stopped her compulsive eating when she had been in a condition to carry her own weight!

Lessons were to be learnt! Between repetitive bouts of helplessness, distress and a pain in her belly so big that she convinced herself that she was dying, Gloria found her mobile telephone. Her head was reeling but she managed to lift it off her noisome pillow to raise the hem of the curtain enough to see that it had become light and Gareth's patrol car was not in front of the station.

There was nothing else to do but to phone Leonie. She did it several times and got no reply. She phoned Gareth. He answered but quickly cut her off with, "Not now, Gloria. Not now!" And disconnected her call. What was she to do? She tried Leonie again and then again a few minutes later. At least ten calls later, she was beginning to suspect that something was wrong with Leonie, too. Why wasn't Leonie answering her phone? Busy, of course, working. Mrs. Fairbrother did not let staff take personal calls when at their work stations. Should she phone her sister? Pauline's reaction to vomit was to start vomiting herself. Useless!

The Community Nurse? Not at the clinic yet. The Doctor? He had long since lost all patience with her. The very thought of his po-face was anathema to her. She knew what he would say as soon as look at her: "Eating too much again, are we, Gloria? What is it this time? Half of Argentina and an Orinoco River of horseradish sauce?"

No! But certainly a big lump of French pig with too much French revenge all over it!

She tried Leonie again. Not even on voice mail. She tried sending a text which was sensitive to the fact that Leonie had a habit of reading them out loud. After two hours had elapsed, she had become seriously worried more about Leonie than herself. In that time she had rolled herself off her bed onto the floor, managed to crawl on hands and knees to the en-suite bathroom and drag herself into the shower. She knew that one litre of water was equal to a kilo in weight and by that measure worked out that she must have shed at least two stone since eating the poisoned ham. Poisoned deliberately? Her eyes became slits. She had snitched to Gareth about the riot van being parked on the square. She knew that he had followed it up, as well. French revenge, indeed!

Something galvanised; call it determination, call it desperation, but Gloria got mad. Before she had time to even work out how to make the manoeuvre, she had hauled herself up and into the shower and stripped herself off, wondering who could be responsible for the state she was in. Who had been determined enough to see her out for the count when she most often spent the night looking out of her window and watching the square? Who would not want her reporting to Gareth on just who was knocking about the streets when decent folk were abed? Cars being driven at three in the morning! Vans and lorries! Door to door callers! People staggering about with cardboard boxes they dare not be seen with in broad daylight? Who would not want her looking out? Mrs. Fairbrother had brought her the ham.

Then again, maybe it wasn't the ham. Marty had sent her the beef. Maybe it wasn't the beef. She was constantly being given foodstuffs by other people. That would stop in future! As she washed herself under a fast flowing hot shower with bubbles and lather cleansing all the folds and creases in her blubber, she found her determination rising as her wellbeing improved. She was upright also. Her feet were carrying her. If her head had yet to find its own centre of gravity after being supine for so long, it would given time and opportunity.

She, thereafter, spent some time with her head over the washbasin while she sat on the loo, phone in hand, thinking. Looking out of the window at a deserted square full of snow. It had gone ten thirty when she phoned Leonie again; her break time, usually, when she could chat over a coke and agree what she'd cook for Gloria's dinner which was usually enough for a family of five. That was something else that would change once she felt better.

This time, her call was answered. But not by Leonie. By Gareth. What was he doing answering their Leonie's phone?

"I've got bad news I'm afraid. Leonie didn't turn up at her desk for work. Her bed's been slept in but she seems to have left the hotel. Her room door was jammed up with paper to make it seem as if she was still inside. Mrs. Fairbrother phoned me when they found blood on Lovick Johnson's boots. Don't worry. They've probably put two and two together and come up with five. There'll be a simple explanation. The lad went off with Ross to search for Bluithe Harcourt but seems to have disappeared from the face of the earth. Odd that is! Let's hope our Leonie's safe and well, is all I can say."

"Oh, Gareth…!" But it wasn't really sinking in yet. Her mind refused to accept that her daughter was missing. "Maybe all they've done is find somewhere private. You know. Like we used to do."

The gurgling noise that came to her down the phone sounded as if her suggestion was a noose and was stopping him from breathing. "Let's hope that's all. I'm at the Fairview now. Don't worry, I'll find her. And him. If he's done anything to her, I'll…!"

Gloria still thought that he must be jesting. Not Leonie. This could not be happening.

"I'm coming up there. I'll get a taxi."

"I think you're forgetting that you can't fit through the door to your room, let alone walk down the stairs. You most certainly can't fit in the back of a taxi."

"Oh yes I can. I think maybe somebody did me a favour."

"You can't walk, Gloria."

Gareth obviously did not understand. She would stand and walk, even run to find her Leonie. She'd claw her way out of the house if she had to. She would do anything; chop off an arm if it meant getting out of the prison the flat had become. Better still because it entailed less blood, she would phone Gormon's Builders, get him here with a wrecking ball and demolish the house around her. Anything, before she'd be left out of the search for her daughter. Point was, too, if she'd got into the bathroom, she could get out of the house. She could get into the last street clothes in her wardrobe. She could put on a pair of shoes. She'd crawled into the bathroom on hands and knees. She'd crawl up to the Fairview Hotel, if she had to.

"Get someone to sit with you. I'll keep you informed. Maybe all they have done is found a quiet room somewhere for a bit of nookey. I can't risk that not being the case. I've sent the blood away to be analysed. Someone could just have cut a finger and he stood in it. It's outside her cubicle door, too. His footprints are in it. But so are other people's, when it took a time to notice it. Mrs. Fairbrother's and Ross's. And that sneaky bastard, Cannon."

"You say this Lovick, lad, has disappeared off the face of the earth, as well?"

Gareth was trying, now, to tone down his own concerns. "I've been in contact with Ross by phone. He should have been keeping an eye on him. Has seen neither hide nor hair of him since they set off some two hours ago. The search party's still out looking which is good if all that's happened is that our Leonie went for a walk in the woods and has had an accident."

"Oh, Gareth!"

"Don't you start, Gloria!" His voice became more determined. "The search party's still out looking for Bluithe Harcourt. I haven't called it off but now it has a duel purpose. Ross will take over from me and inform everyone that they're looking for Leonie, as well. Her duffle coat's not in her room." And then more desperately in his paternal concern, "God alone knows what's happened to her. Ross seems to think that all she's done is nip off shopping. In this weather!"

Gloria's mind was in turmoil but something was edging her towards wondering if Leonie could have seen things better not seen. Bluithe, Marty, the specials, as well as others, were all part of the smuggling ring. Leonie; daughter of the only law in these parts, would represent another threat to them if she had seen things she should not. Gareth had been diverted again, too, in a search for their daughter. Herself, perhaps, already having been warned. Her brain went into overdrive to make sense of it all. Maybe the ham had not been laced with poison to kill her, just to send her to sleep!

Gareth's voice came remotely to her ears, her brain working like a computer, making links, forming suppositions, making the suggestions of a plan. "Yep. Blue being missing can't be anything to do with Leonie not being here, though. He went missing yesterday. I'll have to go. I'll ring you later."

Gloria was still in shock and unable to believe what was happening as she switched off her phone. What she did was analyse her feelings deeply. What she found was a reservoir of fear, deep fear and not this time connected with Leonie's twenty-fifth birthday. Something was terrifying

Gloria beyond any terror that she had ever felt before. Suddenly, all the fear she had been building within herself to do with Leonie finding out her true origins, paled into insignificance. It would be a shock to her to find out but she would still be alive. She would still, surely, realise that they had been loving, devoted, caring parents to a beloved child they so desperately wished would love them back.

Gloria felt her mouth spread with the beginnings of a scream. Then narrow again. No! She'd finished with that, too. Panic, tantrums, all her attention seeking behaviours, would not help her Leonie. Her daughter needed her now. She would not fail her. Leonie was in desperate need.

She was right, too, about the clothes in her wardrobe fitting her. The illness had passed, too. She was wobbly but mobile when finally, she barged and squeezed her way down the stairs and out of the flat. She stood on the pavement, breathless with exertion, but breathing fresh air for the first time in over a year. Her face creased into a grimace of sheer determination. "I'm coming, darlin'. I'm coming." She did not know how, but she would get to the Fairview Country Club Hotel come hell or high water. Or, as on this day, through two feet of snow.

Then she saw Marty on the pavement, dressed in snow gear, outside his pub, and about to get into his van, keys in hand. He was looking at her as if seeing a ghost.

Gloria eyed him as if he had the winning lottery ticket in his pocket. What was amazing was the speed at which she moved. "You'll take me to the Fairview, please, and now, this minute. My daughter's missing."

"What?" Marty seemed to be genuine in his ignorance. "Leonie's missing? As well as Bluithe Harcourt?" He thought for only a moment. "I'd gladly run you up there, Gloria, but it's just come to me through the jungle telegraph that the road to the high fell, after Barnston Bridge, has been closed off to traffic. Police road block. The only way you'll get through is for Gareth to come and get you."

That was unexpected; the road was closed! There was no other way there? Or there was no other road directly there! But that didn't mean that the hotel was cut off entirely. Nowhere, in these parts, was inaccessible if one knew the lie of the land. When she had been a child, what lay below the surface had been a constant source of fun and adventure. This was when Gloria had a flicker of memory from a time when she had used to fancy Marty as a playmate but he refused to have anything to do with her because she was a girl. Him and Bluithe, together; they had stuck to each other like glue. Gloria had used to follow them, spy on them. She would watch their games, knew their hideaways, too. All of them!

"There's still another way, isn't there?"

His mouth fell open. There was, momentarily, a look of disbelief in his eyes. "Not as far as I know unless you're talking about climbing up through the trees in all this snow. What other way?"

"Barnston Bridge! A tunnel with the river flowing underneath. Way in behind the bridge stanchion. Just a bit of board over it. Comes out into a chamber which connects with the potholes going up the ridge from Barnston Farm."

"Nah! Closed for…"

Gloria's voice lowered to a growl. "My daughter, Marty! I'll kill for her if I have to. I'll certainly think nothing about telling tales. I have to be there for her. Understand? Have to! If that's my only way up there, I'll get there no matter the tales I have to tell!"

Marty's face collapsed into a grimace. He shook his head several times before relenting. "You tell anyone what you see there, and I'll…!"

Gloria's face hardened. She need say no more.

"Alright! I'll get a rope. You'll need some help getting up there if you can fit through the gap in the brickwork, which I doubt, because the entrance is narrow."

"Says you!" was Gloria's retort. "Maybe I know things that you don't!"

Twenty-four

Gareth had never been more ardent in his will to solve a mystery. His Leonie was missing; his beautiful daughter, Leonie!

After Mrs. Fairbrother had phoned him, he had gone back there and searched every room at the hotel. Got others to help him look into every room, quite sure that she would be found chatting to the housekeepers and room maids or making an inventory of some kind. She was still on this hunt of hers for costumes for the pantomime, too. There were lots of simple, sensible reasons why she had not turned up at her desk even if it was not like her to go off, anywhere, without telling someone. The Fairview Hotel was a massive building with a large staff coming in that very day to further get it ready for the private guests and members of the public who would be arriving later, despite the snow being thick on the ground.

Thinking ahead, he realised that he would have to put a stop to that if a thorough search of every nook and cranny failed to throw up any sign of her. If he had to, he would shut down the hotel. There was a long way to go, though, before he reached that decision, he thought. While worried, he was still refusing to heed the deepening disquiet that was building inside his belly; his guts were telling him that something was very wrong. Very, very wrong!

Bluithe Harcourt had been forgotten about, save by his own friends and family. Let the search party see to itself. Ross had been asked to take over. Gareth had asked him to keep an eye out for Leonie, too, who had not turned up for her work. Ross had seemed not to be overly concerned, even when Gareth had told him about the blood on Lovick's shoes. He had noted a few traces on his own, he told Gareth, after he had gone to wake Lovick with an instruction to join the search. He must have walked through a few drops of it on the floor of the basement staff quarters. Someone cut themselves shaving? Certainly, the lad had been sound asleep and shown no evidence of having done anything over which he needed to be afraid. "Had a job to wake him up. When I did, his eyes were full of sleep. Smelt like he'd been in his pit all night, too. A mouth full of warm sheep dung."

Gareth had seen the voice of calm reason and the need to adopt a less hysterical tone if he were to be allowed to stay with the investigation. He put his panic aside and went on professional hold. At least, while they were at it, the searchers might look out for his daughter, also. He might have stressed the word *his*. Ross said she might be excited about her birthday and had gone off to buy a new frock.

Gareth thought the suggestion nonsensical and not just because the roads were impassable. His Leonie had her head screwed on the right way. Besides she had no money for more clothes. Why would she be excited? It was only her birthday. She'd had twenty four of them already and this one should be no different. Ross's silence was followed by a quick disconnection of his phone.

What Gareth did not tell Ross, or anyone else helping with the search, was that he had been right about Lovick Johnson from the very first. The lad had form. He hadn't told Gloria, either. He'd had the information sent through to his phone. It had been in his possession since before he had allowed Ross to recruit the lad to his search party but decided not to let it influence his decision that the more help they had with the search party, the better. The lad was still a pair of eyes and ears. He had not at that point considered that he might intend his daughter physical harm, other than to try to unlock Leonie's chastity belt. Gloria had previously told him that the man who did that would have to be very, very special. Leonie had not the slightest intention of giving herself away for anything less than a wedding ring. Gareth had seen how smitten Leonie had been, though. He knew what he had put in her case; hardly the style of clothing suitable for a night in with a cup of cocoa. He just did not want her tying herself to a lad who had already been sentenced to twelve months in Walton Jail, reduced for good behaviour. Nothing since, mind, but he was a 'known' in the eyes of the Manchester police for petty, little bits of this and that. Gareth had more respect for a serious criminal than the kind of know-no-better, toe-rag type of low-life he considered Lovick to be; small time, drug-fuelled thieves and villains, in voluminous numbers, who clogged up the cleansing process of the Law like germs on a dish cloth.

However, he was soon to up Lovick's status in his own Rogue's Gallery of Serious Crime when a search of Lovick's room necessitated breaking open his locker with the multi-tools on his belt and taking a good look at what was within.

What was within…other than forty quid in a wallet without credit cards, a few cash receipts, a child's porcelain night light of the smiley-face type, and a photo of an old lady wearing a Christmas party hat with a crooked smile on her face…had been a knife; an eight inch, butchering knife with the hotel's name stamped into the razor sharp metal. It was covered in blood. The wooden handle had been sticky with fingerprints. The shock had been extreme. In his career as a policeman even in a backwater, he had seen some pretty gory things. This hit him hard in the solar plexus and threatened to knock the wind out of him. The hardest bit had been to retain his professionalism and remember that he must follow the correct procedures of investigation if his Leonie was to be found. Dead or alive, was the question! Her clothes were still in her cubicle, neatly arranged as Leonie would have them. His blood ran cold to see her handbag safely locked away in her locker. What were not there were clothes he knew her to have with her and her duffle coat. That meant that she had gone out of the hotel dressed for the weather.

Gareth assessed what could be missing from Lovick's wardrobe, too, except for those he had been wearing when Gareth had seen him go off in Ross's party to begin the search for Bluithe Harcourt. It seemed that he had brought his whole wardrobe, as well as his stage clothes, which would have taken up every inch of space in the kit bag which had been folded up and stuffed under the bed for want of anywhere else to put it. Maybe there had been a reason for him not wearing ski gear other than that he simply did not possess any, if he had a get-away in mind.

Could he have done something to Leonie, been without conscience, and then come back to enjoy a night's sleep? Some villains were without the usual strands of guilty feeling which prevent most people doing very bad things without serious self rapprochement. Or was he a good actor as well as a song and dance man? That being so, and he really had harmed Leonie, they had even given him the transport he would need to get away on; a pair of skis, boots and poles which could take someone further away and faster than anything else, in this weather. Left his bloody boots and bells behind but had more footwear in his pocket. By the time he hit lower ground and left the snow behind, he could mingle quite nicely.

All Gareth could do for the time being was to put out a description of Leonie, as well as the lad, with what they were both wearing, as registered missing persons the police needed to speak to. At least there was a recent photo of each of them in Gareth's possession. As well as the one of Lovick in his police file, taken a few years ago with a bovver-boy haircut and a sulk on his face, Gareth had a poser's portfolio of portrait photographs in the lad's phone, still not returned to him. In fact still in his Lost Property drawer at the police station. Gareth had deliberately not informed Lovick that it had been handed in at the station and was not likely to do so, either, until Gareth had had a good scroll through the great many telephone numbers in the directory; girl's names, mainly. The Manchester lot could haul this Quincey in, for a start, to find out what he knew about Lovick Johnson.

"More than a pleasure," the smoke-cracked, vindictive voice said when the call was made. There were quite a few things they wanted to talk to Quincey about, while they were at it.

The only thing that troubled Gareth was that Lovick had left his wallet behind. But then people did things like that in a crisis. He wondered about the photograph of the old lady, too. On the back someone had written; "Gran, just a week before she died. Miss you. Should have said, thanks. Love you."

Before the day was out, Gareth planned to know everything about the lad that it was possible to know, in a bid to find him. Everything! Absolutely everything in both cubicles would be analysed and finger printed for a match to the ones on his police record, already.

Other people's, too, for that matter! It was important that the whole site of the hotel was not contaminated further by more feet trampling over it than those here already. Though Gareth might suspect Lovick Johnson of - at best, kidnapping; at the worst harming his precious Leonie - and have every reason to do so, he must not be blind to other possibilities as well. While all the evidence pointed towards Lovick Johnson being the one to have done something to stop his daughter being at her work, he had too much experience to jump to conclusions.

It crossed his mind that this might be another diversion and one guaranteed to keep him out of the village, or poking his nose where he shouldn't, such as into Greavsey, the butcher's, garage to make sure that the riot van had not been out again. There were lots of other more hopeful reasons for still maintaining a glimmer of hope that it was just the smugglers up to their tricks again, though he would not have thought that anyone he suspected would be cruel enough to manufacture this one as a wild goose chase.

There were hotel staff looking at him askance, too, as if he might come upon something to incriminate them when he ordered, as he was about to, for a complete search of the possessions of everyone who had been in the hotel overnight. Cannon and Chef were looking strange this morning and in particular Cannon, who Gareth had been told had been seen ripping something up while hunched up over a sink in the kitchen. This reported to Gareth by a chambermaid with narrow eyes and a tightly drawn mouth who would be getting Cannon back for being such a tale-teller, perhaps, but that's what happens when people are under investigation. The vengeful crawled out of the woodwork. The chambermaid had watched as he had put the ripped pieces in the kitchen waste disposal; his illegal betting slips, most likely, in case he got searched. Or money he could not explain being in possession of? Cannon was always up to something.

Chef would not want his own staff locker searched, either. He probably had a range of hotel optics set up in there for his own consumption; his own, free bar. A bloody good chef he might be but he was well known for being an out-and-out alcoholic who spent many a night keeled over a table in the Bald Pheasant Inn.

Then, where had Betty Jessop gone, once again? She seemed to have done a disappearing act, again. There was absolutely nothing in her room but an empty gin bottle and her employment detail forms in the waste paper bin. Mrs. Fairbrother had followed Gareth about in all his investigations. "Ross should have realised that the woman is entirely unreliable." Then with her eyes on the empty gin bottle, "A drunk!"

Gareth said. "She must have realised that she was unemployable. Taken her case, bag, clothes, everything. She has done exactly the same thing before."

"Maybe she should be put on the missing person list, also." She had a sick expression on her face because it was all heading one way only, to the closure of the Fairview County Club Hotel. And financial ruin!

Gareth shook his head. He had more critical things to do than to check up on a strange, older lady who had the Jubb genetics in her make-up. Sometimes…though he dare not say it loud and especially to Gloria …he saw something of Hannah and Lizzie in Leonie. She had a similar figure with a tendency to thinness. And tiny, too. If her facial looks were very similar to Ross Fairbrother, Gareth refused to dwell on it. He was her dad, not him. He had held her in his arms as a newborn baby and walked the floor with her when she had cried. He had fed her and changed her nappy. He had watched her first steps and taught her how to ride a two wheeler bike. She might have the same blue eyes and natural fairness that Ross had, also a way of looking at people sometimes as if, temporarily, she had been unaware that they were there, but, as far as he was concerned, a physical similarity was the end of Ross Fairbrother's paternal offering. He refused to acknowledge that nature could allow anything that nurture could not. If Leonie had always been better at practical tasks and activities than academic things, unlike him and Gloria, he put it down to a lack of ambition. Not that that mattered. She was a girl with high, moral values and they were proud of her. He regarded her personal integrity as something learnt from her home background and not inherent from either the Jubbs' or the Fairbrothers'. Strong minded, too, unlike her birth mother.

He could not bear to think of her lost to himself and Gloria. What he must do now was to avoid becoming narrow-minded, but leave his investigation open to encompass all those people who had recently impinged on his daughter's life, not just Lovick Johnson, though he still suspected him first and foremost.

He had already started with those present. People who lived-in at hotels, particularly the itinerant workers, were sometimes people who were running away from something they did not wish to face in their lives; divorce, loneliness, a fear of their own obsessions or proclivities, guilt. If they had not come here to hide, they had past lives outside of the community that would need looking into for no more justifiable reason than to eliminate them from his enquiries. He had been allotted a massive budget to locate Bluithe Harcourt because, as far as his superiors were concerned, this was a showcase event for the right kind of police publicity. What he did first was to ask for a forensic team to be flown in by chopper. He'd throw his own meagre pot of money in as well; every penny, if it became necessary. Come to that he'd throw himself in, head first, at any risk personal or professional even if it meant losing the job he loved doing. She, his little Leonie, was his light and his salvation; his future and his destiny. That he was sure of as his paternal love for her drove a stake through the tender, hidden emotions of his fearful soul when he thought that she was in danger or no longer living. God help them all. More than anything, God help his daughter.

Some thirty minutes after the search party left the hotel, the message came through that Blue Harcourt had been found. But not so, his Leonie!

***

Mrs. Fairbrother saw nothing other than a face forged and beaten from cold, grey iron as she stood outside the cubicles, watching Gareth Jones bring the tools on his belt to bear on breaking into her expensive lockers, with no concern for the damage he was doing as he prised them open. Ross was the only one to hold the master locker key but Gareth had refused to wait for her son's return in his impatience. The hotel accounts had yet to recover financially from the expense of fitting out the basement, staff quarters, some six years after the work had been completed. She saw no reason to put up with his vandalism except that as long as he was following different trains of thought to her own, she had a chance to consider what she should do for the better. She, therefore, followed him about as he went between the cubicles of those who seemed to be causing a serious disruption to profit being made, both at the hotel and within the other strands of her business; that of smuggling contraband.

She was further worried because she had been informed by the security man, who had started work only that morning to oversee the Christmas trade, that there was blood, also, inside the dog's kennel. The prospect of physical harm having come to an employee never boded well for any business. Not to mention the lawsuits that could be made if someone injured themselves through careless practice at her hotel. The dog had disappeared, too. Its tether had been cut. There were marks in the snow to indicate that it had been dragged, forming a pink stain on the snow, the guard had said, and that something else had slid over the snow to where a very deep, open shaft had been left unguarded.

Mrs Fairbrother had felt her stomach do a complete somersault, then, because if the shaft was exposed so was the merchandise which Bluithe had been packaging and crating for a removal that had been unable to take place because of the snow.

It was within her natural ability to cope with challenge head-on which brought her back to her sharp senses again. She listened very, very intently, with that look on her face which others had learnt to fear, as the security guard complained that there was a bottomless pit open to the public. Anyone could drop down there and disappear for ever more, he had informed her. Shouldn't the health and safety of the hotel guests and employees come first? Someone was down there, too. Footprints indicated that activity had taken place there only recently. It had been the guard's assumptions that the daft pot-holers were at it again; down there in frog suits and wearing helmets with waterproof torches, swimming through the underground lakes and splashing through torrents, between climbing down through the rock chimneys and tunnels as if it was natural to mankind to behave like weasels and stoats. Daft buggers! "Can't cover it over, either, if there are people still down there."

Mrs. Fairbrother had no idea how the shaft had come to be left open other than that Bluithe might have come up that way and, for some thoughtless reason, had left the board off the shaft entrance.

Confusion was reigning, all round. She did not like it one bit. First the weather turning against them, and then Gareth was suspecting things, then this! Her first inclination was not to pass this information on to Gareth but to make some comment in agreement, perhaps saying, as a hint for the security guard to mind what he was saying in the near future, that her son was a pot-holer of some repute and when all was said and done, the adventure sports brought a lot of tourists to the region. She would ensure that it did not happen again.

Yet she knew that she had to say something to Gareth because if she did not then the security man would. She might get away with covering it over and then saying that any significance towards Leonie had escaped her, but lives and livelihoods were at stake in more ways than one.

She was, also, genuinely worried about Leonie Jones whom she had known since babyhood and whom she had decided to favour by showering her family with one of the superb Christmas hams which Chef had stored in his cool larder, for no other reason than that her son seemed to hold her in great affection. After an initial reluctance to agree to the special attention Ross was placing upon the object of his fancy, it had occurred to her that any wife would be better than none in his situation.

She had not been blind to the attraction between Leonie and Lick Johnson, whose nickname she found utterly disgusting, but what she saw was a danger that Leonie might be snapped up by someone else. In fact her despoilment may already have taken place but what did that matter in this day and age? She was a sensible girl who would have protected herself. Even Mrs. Fairbrother had had to concede as much to Ross that she was a sensible girl. She would soon tire of a man who went about with bells on his shoes. Better Leonie to be the woman to usurp her own position than one who would refuse to work and expect the cosseted life.

Also, she had always harboured doubts concerning Ross's sexuality; a matter of great shame to a mother who had grown up with old fashioned values concerning sexual morality. Leonie Jones, even if young enough to be his daughter, would stop the tongues from wagging. Besides which, she would like nothing better than to look upon the face of a grandchild before she went to her grave. Why else had she kept the Fairview Hotel going through thick and through thin? Risking everything. Ross was quite wrong when he thought her determination to be solely driven by a dogmatic personality. A lifetime's work and duty had to amount to something, had it not? Other than the Bankruptcy Courts. Why else had she done what she had done if not to see what she had worked so hard to achieve go on into the future, her name added to posterity as someone who had built up an empire to be proud of.

Lovick Johnson was a different matter. He seemed to be missing, too, according to Gareth. The crude young man could go to the dogs for all she cared. Though, of course, she had to be careful that she represented her position of an employer as that of a surrogate mother to all in her employ, irrespective of their social position.

Humanitarianism was what the public always judged on, so the right noises had to be made and the odd word of praise sung here and there especially if he had family to worry over him. One's reputation was all and her own the most important. She would deny, forever, even if evidence was forthcoming, that she was head of a smuggling gang, when it had been an activity which she had engaged in solely for the benefit of the hotel.

This reminded her that what she must do with some urgency was burn her little black book. It was far too incriminating. She had seen Cannon putting something out of his pocket into the kitchen waste disposal system with a look of urgency on his face as if it should be got rid of as soon as possible. If it was something he did not wish to be found in his possession, there were far better ways to get rid of it and especially now that the furnace in the basement had been relit. Her incriminating evidence would be burnt beyond any reconstitution as soon as she could assure herself that no one was watching. In fact she would do it even before approaching Gareth concerning the open shaft and the blood in the dog kennel and the dog itself missing. The man had lost any wish to respect anyone's privacy. He would be ordering a complete search of the hotel; every cupboard, every drawer, every nook and cranny. He was ruining her business!

The task of burning the evidence was quickly accomplished. That problem dealt with, she could turn her attention to whom was causing such problems for her, in the first place. Whoever had opened the entrance, and left it exposed, could have only mischief against the Fairview Hotel, and in particular herself, at the root of it. Someone wanting the ring exposed and its members caught, perhaps. Someone who planned that the goods hidden within the chamber at Barnston Bridge would be found and little to be done about it as matters stood at present. Bluithe Harcourt? She would never be able to fully trust the man again. Or anyone else for that matter! She would have to guard herself from all directions and all comers, but was confident that she was a match for any challenge. Duplicity was one of her better skills, as well as an ability to think matters through using a knowledge of all people involved.

Then, no sooner had the search begun, but Bluithe was 'found' just as she intended. That changed things, only as much as he need not now be linked with black market racketeering. However, astuteness to the inevitable was telling her to be open with the facts. There was nothing to be gained, now, by trying to intimidate in order to keep people quiet, which was usually one of her more successful ways of manipulating and guiding the behaviour of her staff. Gareth Jones was not corruptible even if his wife was. She would have to tell Gareth Jones what the security man had told her before he learnt the same from a circuitous route and suspected that she had been withholding information.

Trouble was, the contraband was still in the chamber at Barnston Bridge and no one dare go anywhere near Barnston Bridge to move it. Or to discover why Bluithe had not gone home following his reinstatement to the ring, after he had completed his task to narrow-box the last of the goods for shifting.

Had everything gone to plan, the goods would have been moved this very night, snow permitting, in a van she had arranged to borrow from a local farm. If the contraband was discovered, the loss would be expensive but, at least, no one would be incriminated as long as Bluithe was not still there. It was a troublesome thought that he could have become trapped in there and one that had nagged continually since he had been reported missing. When Marty would have gone to take a look, she had prevented it. "Too dangerous. We'll have to hope that the specials will be involved in looking for him. They can do what needs to be done without casting suspicion."

"With Ross and that Lovick Johnson with them?"

"I'll find some way to distract Ross. I can do nothing about the other. Maybe he has harmed Leonie in some way."

Marty had scoffed. "More like got her in his clutches for no more nefarious a reason than getting her out of her knickers."

"Well! Really! Do you have to be vulgar?"

Marty enjoyed nothing better than seeing the queen discomforted. "One thing's for sure, Mrs. Fairbrother...you won't have been wearing yours when your Ross was conceived, same as my wife wasn't when our twins were. In some things we're all equal!"

She was not amused, and let him know it by disconnecting her call with suddenness.

So, she told Gareth what she had been told by the security man. Adding that maybe the dog had fallen down the shaft, cut itself, scrambled out and then gone somewhere to lick its wounds other than back into its kennel. This in a vain hope that he would not go down there. It looked, she reiterated while enlarging on what she had been told, as if the shaft had been covered over for years with a board and the vegetation grown over it. No one ever went that way through the woods because the bird hide and the old well, as attractions to guests, lay the other way. She had certainly had no prior knowledge that another shaft was open to the surface within the hotel grounds; otherwise they would have had it sealed off for the sake of health and safety. Ross was very keen on that. They had gone to inordinate lengths, she reminded Gareth, to have the other underground entrance, via the old well, permanently closed off to the public for the same reason, after Bernard Jubb had lost his life there. "Of course, we all know that the ridge is riddled with potholes."

Gareth nodded. Then he looked at her coldly. All he did was nod, scowl, and cock his head at her, keeping his thoughts private.

Mrs. Fairbrother felt concerned about that look because usually he was friendly and helpful. That had been before his daughter's whereabouts was unknown, though. Now, he trusted no one and was assessing everything, where normally he would have smiled and thanked her.

Then he dropped his bombshell. "I'm about to arrange a warrant to shut this hotel. The only people to come in here will be forensics and other members of the police force who I'm flying in. That helipad of yours will come in very useful. Cancel your guests. Close the gates and put the security man on it. No one to come in. Got it? Tell Ross to cancel that airlift he's been planning. No one leaves and no one comes in from this very moment."

The veins on her cheeks engorged and her eyeballs bulged so that they stood out as green as the leaves in the Christmas flower display on the desk in reception.

"You can't do that! What about Christmas?"

"Christmas is cancelled until my daughter is found, Mrs. Fairbrother."

He even made it official. He phoned Quinton Constabulary and told his commanding officer that that's what would happen. Not, please, could it happen? He told him he had already done it. It would happen. This time it was the Fairview Hotel, not the Bald Pheasant Inn that had a lock-in.

Twenty-five

Ross was in his element as he expertly guided his snowboard over virgin snow, down between the rough bark of closely growing trees, the birds rising from their branches as he glided silently past; the smell of winter vegetation in his nose and a broad smile on his face as a weak sun began to pour gold over the ermine cape that had been thrown over the valley below.

The rooftops of Barnston Farm were quite clearly visible, as was, below that, the squat, village buildings after the tree-lined lane; the spired church, the community centre, the square with its obelisk and rows of terraces to mark its shape, the Bald Pheasant Inn and then the sloping fields down to the motorway which seemed to have disappeared except for the tall crochet hooks he knew to be road lights when darkness came; the only sign that there was a motorway under the blanket of snow when not a single vehicle could be seen upon its hidden lanes.

Ross knew this place like the back of his hand and yet had never thought himself to be a part of it. He had gone away to school and had not been a part of that, either. Then joined the army from Sandhurst where he had reinvented himself as someone else; that man being a man of action who could make decisions, lead from the front, be trusted with the lives of others, this in spite of never having been able to protect those who mattered to him most.

When he had returned to help his mother run the hotel, it had been because he had come to know the value of what he had thrown away, too late. Leonie, after Bern had died, had been the only reason he had stayed through the long, boring years. Now, he wondered, perhaps, if it would have been better, for all, to have done what he might otherwise have done and gone off adventuring around the world. Lived life instead of tolerated it with his obsessive need to claim back what he had willingly given away to Gareth and Gloria. Been his own man instead of his mother's lackey. Let sleeping dogs lie. Life's regrets! But then who did not have those?

There was no going back now, either. It was far too late. He had started the fall of the row of carefully laid dominoes, set up in his mind twenty-five long years ago, the last one laid, simply by leaving the letter on Leonie's desk for her to find, as he had no doubt that she had done already, been shocked by it, perhaps, because he had added a few last sentences as a post script, before finally determining, without a change of mind, to leave the blunt truth for her to find, "…you will find that after today you will be a very different person. You are my daughter, a Fairbrother. From this day on, your twenty-fifth birthday, you will have every advantage that I can provide." Shocking! Why had he done that? Writing it down had been as blurted and clumsy as all that he had tried to tell her in spoken words. Was it any wonder that she had taken herself off to think? Required time to herself. Maybe telephoned his solicitor when he had given her the number and had given his solicitor a directive to speak on his behalf.

He had chickened out when it had come to telling his mother, as he had intended to do. Instead he had sat in her company the evening before, nursing his brandy, brooding while his mother made phone calls. What did she want the use of a transit van for? He found himself unable to say anything but make grunts, agree with her, let his mind be somewhere else.

His mind had not wandered from his mission, however, as he deliberately kept behind the men he could see through the trees. The three special policemen would not know quite how closely they were being watched. They seemed to have forgotten, already, their implicit instructions and skied closer and closer together. Ross stopped repeatedly to watch them through binoculars, his breath rising in steam, when finally they made no pretence of following orders and gathered in a huddle close to the bird hide where the ground was flat. There, with breath rising, they stood on skis and talked with relatively little effort, though Ross could not hear what they were saying.

Where Lovick Johnson had got to, God alone knew. If the lad could ski, Ross would have been extremely surprised when it had taken him all his time just to keep up with them on flat ground, and stay upright. He would probably be finding this terrain exceedingly difficult which was why he was lagging behind. But he had to give the lad credit. He was trying. Ross had had a lot of bone-head, raw recruits pass through his army training programmes who, like Slick Lick Johnson, at first seemed hopeless cases. The way to sort the wheat from the chaff, he had found, was not to look as much at their skills upon entry but at the degree of dedication and enthusiasm they brought to succeeding where others expected them to fail. That was what he had seen in Lovick as well as a desperate wish to impress Gareth who seemed to have already developed a huge dislike of Leonie's chosen one.

What did it matter, anyway? They were on top of the Christmas preparations. The rest of the staff would be on their way in. His mother could manage which was why, after Gareth had asked him to take over because he had to stay at the hotel to make sure that his daughter was alright, Ross had switched off his phone and put himself into the mindset he had always been able to access with great relief, from being a child. He could leave reality behind him. Become Davy Crockett, fight bears and keep an eye out for Apache. Be the kind of man who other men could respect. There had been no one since Bern and never would be. As long as he could be out in fresh air, challenging the elements, he could cope. Especially when he had a mission. He had a mission to accomplish, now.

The three special policemen were already behaving suspiciously when they skied off, one behind the other, in a direct line down through the trees. Ross followed them with his binoculars. They were going somewhere specific; not searching, not looking carefully about, not making random pathways, not stopping to listen out for a man who might be lost, injured and calling for help; dead even. They were skiing as fast as the trees would let them as if they knew something upon which Ross had not been informed and would not be privy to. Maybe, Gareth had been right!

All Ross had to do was to follow their tracks, down to and left along the part of the river bank where the water roiled against exposed tree roots and there was no proper path. It was the side of the river which was difficult to walk on as it had no proper bank until it came to a large stone from where boys fished in summer. This stone was achievable from the road by using the steps built into this side of the bridge. This set of steps was symmetrical to those on the other side; the ones used to attain the river bank from the main road which led up to the Fairview Hotel.

Time for Ross to follow when they passed from his sight. It was a simple matter of following their tracks to know what they were up to; all the time ensuring that they would have nothing to suspect that he was following them. They would think that he and Lick would be weaving a slower journey through the trees, taking care to be observant of what was close by their skis.

When he came to Barnston Bridge, he hid within the saplings from where he had a good view of the bridge structure and the men, themselves. They had gained the slab of stone and were taking the steps up to the road. They had abandoned skis and poles by leaning them against the stanchion of the bridge for the third man to pick up as a whole and carry them up. He caught sight of two of them again coming down the other side, while the other man waited, arms full of skis and poles, on the road. When Ross used his binoculars to check, the third man, whom he recognised as the butcher from the village, Mr. Greaves, still stood on watch on the bridge but looking only towards the rise as if waiting for someone he was expecting to come from that direction.

Ross almost missed what happened next within the sweep of his field glasses and an indecision of who to watch now that their group was split. The appearance of a black car's roof, as it stopped by the butcher, was enough to have Ross draw a sharp breath. His mother's car he was sure. Then his suspicion was verified. She got out, spoke to the butcher, her face full of anger, her finger pointing down to the river bank, or the bridge stanchion to be exact, in a stance of giving an order as opposed to making an enquiry, and then got back into her car again with some abruptness. Why would she do that? Mr. Greaves was nodding as if he was in full agreement with her instruction and then waved down to his friends who were at full attention to what was being communicated via their colleague and related by his mother. Ross knew all of the men distantly and was aware that none of them should have a degree of familiarity with his mother that their meeting conveyed to him was really the case. He also knew that they were involved in the smuggling because the butcher had been involved when he and Bern had been running contraband.

Was his mother involved, too? Was that why he was often surprised at how long the goods he brought back from France lasted, in the stock cupboards of the hotel? Was it more than her stated good management and a tight control of pilfering staff that allowed the hotel to be viable still?

Things were making sense, even if they were things he did not wish to acknowledge! Suspicions were surfacing, or was it fact; facts that he had witnessed for himself.

Scanning back down under the bridge; Ross, watching still, through binoculars, was to be surprised by something else. The other two men were there one moment and then the next had disappeared. Where? They could not have gone elsewhere in the time he had watched their third member talk with his mother. But where had they hidden themselves? The mystery deepened as he watched Mr. Greaves follow the other two down the same steps, lay the skis and poles against the brick stanchion on that side of the bridge; the far side to Ross but clearly visible, and set them to balance. What he did then was to look about carefully, before going behind some shrubbery and the stout trunk of an oak tree growing by the side of the bridge. Ross was making his own interpretations of their behaviour and it had nothing to do with the men needing to go behind a bush to relieve themselves.

What surprised him next was that the first two appeared from behind the same bushes carrying another human form between them, each man with an arm under the middle man's shoulders as he was suspended between them. They were dragging the figure dressed in a black rain coat, over white overalls, with one strap trailing against the muddy path. The figure looked to be in pain, crying out while responding to their request to be quiet, face stretched, and holding a leg high once he was able to find space, his mouth barred about discoloured teeth, but groggy, very groggy.

Bluithe Harcourt! Hurt but alive from the look of him!

Once out, the specials hauled him up between them into a chair-lift hold and consulted each other, firstly, before supporting Bluithe more securely. Mr. Greaves quickly followed them out with the same tool bag which Ross had been familiar with for the past twenty-six years.

It was a moment not to be missed. The exact moment when their mission should have been celebrating their success. Whoops and cries should have been heard. His phone, had he had it switched on, should be ringing or their whistles marking the moment. And Ross having an unmistakeable sense that they had known where Bluithe Harcourt had been lost, all along. They had gone there directly but then had had to be further directed by his mother.

Ross did the best thing he could think of; he found his mobile phone, switched it on, and made use of its camera function on zoom to record the successful rescue which seemed to be occurring in the wrong place, if his suspicions were correct. Bluithe being found within a hidden chamber surrounded by contraband, most probably, would need some very careful explaining away.

They made off with Bluithe, thereafter, with as much haste as the snow would allow them, not up to the main road where they might await an ambulance, if one could get through with the fall so deep, but under the road bridge and along the river bank. Where the hell were they taking him? The third man, the butcher, who carried Bluithe's tool bag, collected all their skies and poles and then ran after the others, the skis and poles banging together as he struggled to keep up.

One thing was obvious to Ross; they had found the very man they were all looking for, yet wanted it to look as if he had been found elsewhere. Further along the river bank, perhaps? Well out of the way of Barnston Bridge? Ross suspected somewhere in the area of the open Weir House, which had been recently built to provide an overflow system to divert the river water, when needed, away from the village. It was regularly visited and checked to ensure that the sluice gates were operating, but not with any regularity so that someone might be there and their presence not noted for several days.

How clever his mother was, for this was exactly her way of dealing with things! The rarely visited building would be an excellent shelter in a blizzard and give an excuse for Bluithe's clothing being dry and his having managed to remain alive after a night out in the open, when even a penguin might find it hard to survive.

Ross was quite sure that they would collude to obscure the exact place where they had located Bluithe Harcourt after he had suffered some form of accident and then been overcome by the coma when he would be in need of an injection of insulin as quickly as possible. Ross's face darkened further, when he wondered again if he might have misconstrued the reason for his mother stopping her car to talk to them in that imperious way of hers. She might simply have been making an enquiry as to how the search was going. Not like her! Not the usual inconsiderate behaviour of a woman who had great difficulty thinking of anyone but herself. A woman who would not have given Bluithe Harcourt the time of day when his rank was no more than that of a lowly painter and decorator.

Not unless she had involvement with them all, of a more personal kind. One that entailed profit! Ross was convinced. He could see his own army training having guided her in the way she managed them also…management by objective…knowledge afforded on a need to know basis only…orders to be obeyed without question. The same style he would have brought to a covert operation himself.

Ross let them go then, making his own way to the red brick bridge and to the spot where he had seen them mysteriously disappear and then come out with Bluithe Harcourt and his tool bag. He was carrying his snow board under his arm, and sauntering, looking about for anyone watching, as he moved from his hiding place, specifically Lovick Johnson who had, most probably given up the quest and gone back to the hotel.

By the time he reached the bridge to make the crossing, the men were well on their way, just distant figures, moving quickly, against the bright snow. He switched his phone to the call register. It quickly let him know that he had unanswered calls. Thinking, as he walked, of the men's actions and the sheer irresponsibility in not getting immediate medical attention for Bluithe; a man so obviously ill and injured that he had had to be carried away like a sack of flour. Not a young man either, for whom shock, combined with the need for an injection and the extreme cold, could be a serious issue.

The calls were all from his mother. Ross's face darkened. Had what he had just witnessed, come about from her orders? He could see no other explanation for the whole scenario he had just seen unfold with his own disbelieving eyes.

He suddenly realised, too, that since his father's death, she had been battling like a tigress to save the hotel. If she had to cheat the government of its taxes to do so, she would not feel guilt. They paid exorbitantly as it was. But how much air needs to be pumped into a cadaver before one realises that the person is dead? No matter how this ended, maybe it was time to sell out to a chain, cut and run, accept the inevitable.

He returned her missed calls. "Hello, Mother. You've been trying to get in touch?"

"Ross, at last! You must call Gareth and get him to call off his search. I'm absolutely sure that Bluithe will be found soon and this silly little girl will turn up. The man's become demented. Power mad! He's closing the hotel, Ross. Done it, in fact. Closed the road and set our security guard on the gate to ensure that no one goes in or out. No one is to have admittance and no one is to leave."

His eyes narrowed. She could not have time enough to get back to the hotel. "Where are you, mother?" He had just seen her on the bridge with his own eyes.

"Trying to remain sane, that's where I am. Where else but in my private quarters, hoping and praying that you will come back soon and put a stop to Gareth Jones ruining us. He's asked us to stop the airlift, Ross. He's searching all the rooms. No one is to come in and no one is to leave. The staff are up in arms but what can I do? The place will soon be swarming with police. He's even preventing the live-out staff from arriving. Unless this ends quickly...!"

Ross interrupted her ranting. "So Bluithe is found, is he?"

"I've just had a phone call to suggest that that is the case, yes. I can't say that it's right until Gareth has been informed. My source is usually reliable though. Down by the Weir House, I believe. Broken leg. I gather he was simply out walking without his mobile phone when it happened yesterday. He seems to have a broken leg and been in a light coma due to needing his injection. The Fell Rescue will get him down to the hospital in Quinton. There is absolutely no need for this dreadful situation to continue. You must do something quickly, Ross, or we will be ruined."

"Has Leonie turned up, yet?"

"No. But we all know that she has a reputation for being dreadfully late for her work."

"She was sleeping in the hotel, mother."

"Leonie will be somewhere perfectly safe without the slightest idea that anyone is looking for her. You must worry, now, about that young man who seems to have claimed her affection, temporarily, if you are so smitten with her. Gareth seems to be of the opinion that he's done something to her and managed to get away. He isn't with you, is he?"

"No." Then he frowned with a cunning light in his eye. "That's not to say that he isn't with the specials. They seem to have disappeared as well. Maybe it's them who have found Bluithe if your source of information is correct."

Silence, on that one. His mother was far too clever for verbal traps.

"So Gareth's still worried about Leonie?" Ross asked, consulting his watch but still inclined to think that she had read the letter and become so excited that she had forgotten that she should be working.

"Needlessly so. It's the opinion of others that she's with Lick Johnson. Or on her way to see her mother. Or out shopping. Most probably with this new boyfriend of hers. He's not helping in the search, at all, according to Gareth who, unlike others, seems to think that he's done a runner. He's used the skis he was given to get away after harming Leonie. Utter nonsense! The chap can't ski well enough from what I observed earlier to go anywhere but head over heels. There are people here who are saying that they've made a tryst and have simply been detained. Cannon and Chef are laying bets on it."

She mentioned nothing of the bloodied knife found in Lovick's locker, her excuse to herself being that Gareth had asked her not to mention it to anyone though others had been paying sly witness to his search of the staff cubicles. That fact was already circulating the frightened staff within the hotel.

What was more likely was that Lovick Johnson was responsible for the blood in the dog kennel and Max being missing. Or so she hoped now that her main worry, Bluithe Harcourt, had been successfully dealt with. He was well away from the stash-point.

Ross was keeping his own counsel also. He hoped that the specials, on his mother's instructions, had not prevented Lovick Johnson from accompanying them on their desperate mission to rescue Bluithe if the whole operation had been directed by his mother. He had an impression from memory of having seen his mother put her head through the window to talk to one of the specials as they had made their way round the side of the hotel to start their search. She had been looking scathingly at Lick, even while shouting, "Good luck. He'll be safe and well, somewhere," or words to that effect.

He recalled that she had had a private word also in the ear of the butcher and the solicitor earlier in the foyer of the hotel while they had been making preparation. Ross asked her again. "Where are you, Mother?"

"At the hotel. Where else?"

"In your room?"

"Where else?"

"It was just that I thought I saw your car, just now, on the road. In your room? Doing what?"

"Are you questioning me, Ross Fairbrother? Well!" She disconnected.

His mother was lying through her loose false teeth without a shadow of a doubt.

As far as Ross was concerned, there was only one thing to do; take a look behind the oak tree and screening bushes to see what lay behind. He had come well equipped. He had a torch in his pocket with working batteries from a stock he had bought in Quinton the day before last after the staff had been complaining that there were none at the Star in the village. One had to be properly prepared with snow on the way!

As soon as he went behind the oak tree bare of leaf, he saw the narrow slit in the brickwork of the bridge, maybe some fifteen inches wide. What lay beyond was a piece of exterior grade plywood to act as a door. The specials had even brought it closed behind them when they had brought Bluithe out. All he had to do was to slide it over to see a dark space within. The smell that came to his nose was immediately recognisable; like disused air raid shelter, underground train stations, and an earthy dampness which pinched at his nostrils.

His torch assured his footing as he stepped within through the narrow space. What he found was not surprising. As expected; a cold, damp, dark chamber stockpiled with goods, dripping with soak water and filled with that familiar sound of fast running, underground rivers. His worst fear that his mother was involved with the smuggling ring was confirmed when he saw that an attempt had been made, probably by Bluithe, to package wine into festive crates. Something no man would do, but typical of his mother.

A wheelbarrow lay on its side with its sludgy contents spilled into a mound, a spade abandoned on top of it. A cardboard crate had, upon it, Bluithe's red woolly hat. A crumpled blanket lay close by. Some kind of mining had been going on because the wheelbarrow had been full of soft, gritty silt. Someone, most probably Bluithe, had been excavating an opening which looked to have become silted up long ago, probably by river flooding. A corridor had been newly opened up. His light was not strong enough to see where it led. What its roaming light exposed also, was an excavated staircase up, just as there had been up from the chamber where he and Bern used to meet, so very long ago. He could guess that it would lead up to the grounds of the hotel, connecting chamber to chamber as it climbed its way, and perhaps connecting with other passages gouged out by millions of years of underground rivers, coursing through the rock, eroding potholes, then changing its pathway. Under the ground, this ridge was like a sieve.

He listened intently. The noise of the fast flowing underground rivers was intense. The sluice gates must have been opened to take the overflow to the river in preparation for the snow beginning to melt. What he thought he was hearing other than that, was consumed in the gushing. Was he imagining the sound of whelping? Someone crying? Someone shouting?

Any quest to investigate further, over to a dark side of the chamber where the strange sounds were coming from, was cut short by a warning bleep on his phone that the signal was failing while someone was attempting to contact him. He had to go outside again to read the text message from his mother expecting her to merely confirm what she had told him earlier...Bluithe Harcourt being, by now, officially found down at the Weir House, with a broken leg. What he read had him tucking his board under his arm and high tailing it back to the Fairview Hotel as quickly as he could make it.

Smuggling was no longer his worst fear; Leonie was in danger. "Ross, get here, quickly. Leonie kidnapped. Evidence in the palm of my hand. Gareth gone to investigate open shaft by gun room. Not answering his phone. Meet me at the bird hide. Be careful not to be seen."

***

Mrs. Fairbrother hoped that Gareth had not been informed of the fact that she had slipped away from the hotel for what had been no more than a sleigh ride, on skidding wheels, in bright sunshine, through the thick layer of powdery snow, which the snow ploughs would not now be moving, down to Barnston Bridge and back again. She had simply told the guard that Gareth's instructions would not apply to herself. There was an urgent errand she had to make which should take no longer than a few minutes. She did not tell the guard that this errand had been made necessary because the chamber at Barnston Bridge was not common knowledge amongst the smuggling ring members. Only herself, Marty and Bluithe were aware of the exact location of the secondary, short-term storage facility, due to it having been thought wise, and agreed amongst them, that such information need only to be afforded on a need-to-know basis.

She had not dared to use her mobile phone to contact Mr. Greaves or any of the other specials who worked for her. They had been very well paid for providing information concerning their local policemen's whereabouts and providing occasional distractions. Also, to move merchandise when a stash needed emptying quickly.

She had had no choice in the need to inform the specials that they would have to be the ones to find Bluithe, if, indeed, he was still in the chamber, and get him away to another location where they would find him safe and well. She had had to take whatever contact opportunity presented itself as natural, which came about by grabbing opportunity as presented, out of anyone's hearing, of course. She had had no choice but to get to Barnston Bridge to advise them further when she trusted no one to make wise decisions, but herself.

It had all been so hit and miss that all she could do now was be thankful for small blessings. After parking her black B.M.W. with all the aplomb of having simply been checking that the outside entrances of the hotel were now shut to all trespass, Mrs. Fairbrother stepped a booted foot covered in snow, through the front door of the Fairview Hotel.

She was assailed no sooner had she closed the door behind her and began the business of stamping the snow off her boots by a very nervous Cannon waiting specifically to talk to her. With worry on his face, though why was unfathomable, when he had often expressed a dislike of Leonie with accusations which proved to be unfounded.

He informed her that Gareth had gone off to look at the open shaft, close to the gun room and the blood stained, empty dog kennel close by. "Said you'd said. He's been talking to the security guard. Is it true about the knife?"

Gareth had asked her not to mention it to anyone because it would cause the staff who had been refused permission to go home, or anywhere, for that matter, to become hysterical. But the walls of an establishment such as this had eyes and ears as she had long since discovered. However, she considered it impertinent of him to ask. She deigned not to reply. She would have coffee, please, Cannon, served in Mr. Ross's office, a command imparted with one of her frowning, bile-green stares and much sucking of dentures. "Someone needs to remember that we are running a hotel, around here. That stupid, silly girl!" The last phrase saw Cannon covered in flying spittle.

As she stamped her way to the rear of the reception desk, banging down the counter flap as she went, she considered the damage that was being done to her business. All this, just because Leonie had failed to tell someone where she was going. The knife, along with a pair of boots, both with blood traces, had led people to denote that murder had taken place when all it probably was, was one of Chef's which Lick Johnson had borrowed to whittle something or some such other innocent act. It was definitely a hotel butchering knife, probably not cleaned of animal blood when the stupid boy had taken it. It quite amazed her what preposterously stupid things people did with mindlessness. Sorry, Mrs. Fairbrother, but I never realised that a damp plug can blow all the fuses and plunge the whole hotel into darkness!

Inside she was raging with anger. The financial implications of the hotel shut-down hardly bore thinking about and especially after Gareth had so dramatically put the knife inside a freezer bag and then into the hotel safe with instructions that it was not to be opened for any reason. The same safe in Ross's office; the very place she was heading. And what now? No other than Chef stood before her, swaying like a tree in a hurricane, any work he might invent for a day without guests to feed obviously put on hold until he had his own questions answered. His finger pointed upwards. His sallow face looked upset; his hands were shaking. "Listen! Choppers coming in loaded with policemen."

Her staff were as children. "A waste of public money if you ask me," replied Mrs. Fairbrother, stamping her boots to get off the rest of the clingy snow and not much caring, for once, that she was soaking the carpets. "Why aren't you at work?"

Chef looked beside himself with worry. Had he a police record? Was he likely to be arrested for some crime committed while under the influence of the drink which emanated from his pores as a pungent vapour? "A forensic team with portable kits, I heard him say on the phone. That knife. Cannon thinks it's one of mine. It's got the hotel name on the blade."

Mrs. Fairbrother sighed and, in part, sympathised with his worry. He was accountable for every knife in the kitchen along with every other piece of kitchen equipment. "I admit to having recognised it as such, myself."

"I didn't do nothing to Leonie. All my knives are accounted for. It will be one that went missing years ago. That Betty Jessop will be behind this. She stole one then and caused all kinds of mischief. She's a Grim Reaper is that one. I saw her no more than an hour ago, going down to her room dressed to kill. "

"Don't be foolish. The woman has absconded because we now require proper references and she will have none. Ross should never have employed her again after the last time. Some innocent reason will be identified shortly for the knife being covered with blood. Leonie will walk in here without the slightest knowledge that her father has gone totally overboard in trying to locate her whereabouts. Bluithe Harcourt has been found alive and reasonably well by all accounts."

Chef scowled. What did he care if he hadn't? Then asked the

question that was really bothering him. "Will we be paid while all this is going on, Mrs. Fairbrother?" He was considering doing a bunk over the fence to the Bald Pheasant because the bars and cellars were all locked up by order of Gareth Jones. No way was he staying without money coming in. Not when he needed a drink.

Mrs. Fairbrother's eyes narrowed at him with wicked intent. Chef believed in fairies and mythical people. Her eyes reminded him of those of the green goblins which he often saw within the bushes when on his way back to the Fairview from the Bald Pheasant Inn. They were unpleasant little creatures that jumped on his back and kept pushing him over and making him stumble.

Her sigh was heartfelt. "Foolish man! Get back to the kitchen. Do you think that I don't know what's in your locker? Whether you are paid, or not, depends on this business doing the necessary trade to afford to pay you your wages. Prepare for the guest meals as if nothing has happened. I am quite sure that we will soon find that both Leonie and Bluithe are safe and that the guests will arrive as planned."

She was glad to shut the office door on him with a slam which was not in keeping with her usual creeping practice. It was worse than being a parent to a brood of immature children. Unless Leonie Jones turned up quickly, they would lose all their Christmas trade, even the casual trade from the villagers who would, in ordinary circumstances, be filling the public bar and using the restaurant to launch their Christmas in a style only on offer at the Fairview Country Club Hotel.

She should have been wallowing in satisfaction and have the police off her back with Blue Harcourt having been found. It would not be too late, either, to move the contents of the store at Barnston Bridge if the van she had hired for tonight, with chains on its wheels, could make it out of the village to the motorway which was presently being heavily salted and gritted. Now what was the prospect? Income: zilch! Expenditure: excessive! Bankruptcy would beckon and be at their door within a month. Where would she and Ross be then? She knew where Ross would be; most probably scaling Mount Everest.

The phone on Ross's desk rang. She expected it to be Gareth informing her that he had lifted the ban on the hotel and it could now be open for trade as planned. It was Mr. Greaves, the butcher, talking cryptically in case others were listening. He would, perhaps, have had time to have a word with Bluithe.

"Just to let you know that the gift wrapped Christmas hampers in the storeroom have been tampered with. A trespasser, I gather, who likes to wear a wedding dress. A lot taken and quite a lot of disruption. Also, I was told by the same man, who has a very bad cold and a croaky voice, by the way, but is otherwise okay, that some work has gone on with extending the premises to join with another. Better to cancel the order, I think."

"Thank you for informing me, Mr. Greaves. Are people to be trusted, these days?"

"I don't think so. It seems someone pointed her gun at him."

Hannah Jubb!

She put the phone down wondering what else could befall her. What was this about Hannah Jubb trying to break through from the old cavern workings to pilfer the stock?

She was surrounded with fools, idiots, mad people, was she not? Ross was no help because he had become soft and would have nothing to do with her quest to keep the hotel solvent at any cost. All he was interested in these days was mooning over Leonie Jones. The sooner he married the girl, the better! As she made her way into the office in the foyer, after Cannon had told her that Gareth had gone to take a look at the shaft, she thought of Lizzie Jubb, with a shudder. For a time, before common sense had arrived, she had thought that Ross might give in to her blackmail and marry her for the sake of the child. What a disaster for them all that would have been, with the baby born dead, and Lizzie's mental state getting worse and worse over the course of twenty-five years.

Things could have been worse! Mrs. Fairbrother decided to be positive as she opened some of the mail that Leonie would have dealt with if she had turned up for work that morning. It was the same small bundle of internal memos, reports and staff requests, because there had still to be a Royal Mail delivery, with one large brown envelope which she had gripped so tightly, earlier, in fear for Leonie and thoughts of an axe murderer within the hotel

She had placed the large brown envelope to the top of the pile. It was the one which she recognised as having been the same given to Betty Jessop for her to give all her employment details, even while recalling that she had seen the forms, themselves, deposited in Betty Jessop's waste bin. She promised herself that she would have the woman blacklisted through The Hotelier's Association International. Nothing would give her greater satisfaction.

Mrs. Fairbrother's mouth was set into the self righteous, letter box shape most known to her staff, as she finally got round to slitting open Betty Jessop's brown envelope wondering what it could possibly contain when there was something quite bulky within.

What came out as she withdrew her hand were photographs. Small photographs which had been taken by an old fashioned Polaroid camera;

the type which a few minutes after being taken, came out of the camera, already processed and printed, in colour. The thick photographic paper felt sticky in her hand as she wondered what in heaven's name Betty Jessop was up to now. She had still to get over the last time she had been in the hotel and caused such horrendous mischief.

There were about a half dozen of them; small, roughly four inches by three, in size. With the photographs came a set of invitations. She had seen exactly the same white card, printed with silver lettering and decorated with hyacinth blue and purple bows once before, long ago. Her heart leapt in her breast. Her breathing stopped. Dear God in Heaven! She looked at the Polaroid photos again. What Mrs. Fairbrother saw filled her with horror.

Twenty-six

Marty had to abandon his car on the lane in front of Barnston Farm. The snow had blown so deep into the dips that the van was like a plough as it nose-dived down, skidding perilously, the engine juddering as his foot made confusing clutch and gear manoeuvres. He had not a clue which way to turn the steering wheel because the tyres had lost all grip and he could not see where he was going. It was a bit like waltzing on a frozen, snow covered lake, blindfolded. The tide of gathered snow was rising over the bonnet of his van and creeping higher and higher up his window as he ploughed down the rise. He could see nothing ahead as he slid downwards. He might have ploughed on through, regardless, thinking that an insurance claim was no bad thing if he could manage a collision with a hard object sufficient to get a new bumper to replace the rusty, dented thing that was half hanging off, anyway, have his leaking radiator replaced and a broken light fitted with a new glass, without spending a penny more than his fifty pound excess, even if he did lose his no claims bonus, and not do any damage to himself. Gloria came wrapped in her own bubble wrap. But neither his car nor Gloria was having any of it.

As the engine died from cold and a lack of petrol, he heard Gloria growl from her undignified position flat on the rear floor of his van, looking more like a decommissioned Zeppelin than a woman. "We're close enough. We'll walk from here."

As Marty got out of his van, he knew that he had a mammoth job ahead of him; a reversal, in fact, of the process of getting Gloria Jones into his van. What a pantomime that had been!

As for Gloria, she would make any spectacle of herself, experience any ridicule; undergo any discomfort, in order to be where her determination intended they should be.

Not at Barnston Bridge, as Marty seemed to think as being the only way up to the Fairview Country Club Hotel, but at Barnston Farm.

A small crowd had, in fact, gathered at the windows about the square to watch and wonder. Would she make it or not? She had not travelled in the passenger seat same as everyone else but been relegated as cargo, to the rear. Gloria had been unable to get up into the passenger seat of Marty's transit van; her leg would simply not bypass the hanging apron of her belly sufficiently to rise high enough to the step, never mind for her then to haul up her massive weight. Instead, with eyes closed and ears deaf to the titters, she had had to lie her top half on the cold metal floor to the rear of the driver and passenger seats, with the double doors to the back of the van open. The floor was stained with all kinds of pub swill but nothing could resume her previous delicacy now that she had the bit between her teeth.

She had had to agree to Marty upending her and pushing her in like a plump, old sofa, while she humped herself along in the fashion of a caterpillar, until sufficiently within so that he could slam shut the doors. What she had not seen was his furling bow to a much amused audience before he had made it up into the driver's seat, calling over his shoulder. "They'll be thinking I'm taking you out to lunch, maybe. You always did like to travel in style, Gloria."

She had been sweating buckets and was wringing wet by the time they got underway, cold as the metal floor might be. But Gloria was managing; panicking but managing not to give in to the waves of fear that kept coming over her. Somewhere in her core, deep inside the blubber which was insulating her from the cold, was an iron bar of premonition that that place where her daughter had been born was now the place where Gloria should go to set her free.

It was hard to explain. Like she was being guided by some unseen radar. No telephone calls from Gareth either. Or what she wanted to hear most; her daughter telling her that it was okay. She was safe. It was as if she was being lured back down twenty-five years to account for herself.

Why she felt this unfathomable pull towards Barnston Farm had something to do with Bluithe Harcourt and the smuggling gang and the events of the past twenty four hours and, in particular, Lizzie Jubb all mixed up together like sick until the separate components of the objects of her dread where indistinguishable, one from the other.

It was the vision of Lizzie viciously throwing snowballs at Leonie only yesterday morning, chasing her, intending that the missiles hit hard home and hurt, that had floated to the top like an oily slick, then slid her back through the years, recalling Lizzie peering into Leonie's pram with her hands outstretched. That memory was what had haunted her for years. The guilt had been truly unbearable.

What had she and Gareth done to the woman? How can one steal so valuable a thing as a child and think nothing of it? Why had they joined in the ridicule of a sick and chastised woman who had become unable to function properly because of the damage done unto her, more than that which she had sought for herself in her deluded mental state? Was she, herself, any better? Were her own malfunctions more to be empathised with, when they had been brought on entirely by her own underlying disgust with herself? No! For they were greater, more wicked, more despicable for the gain. Such precious gain!

All she could think as she approached her own infernal hell and all its demons, had been; "Take me, not Leonie. Please, God, let my daughter stay safe."

Gareth had not phoned her back which he would have done in jubilation had their daughter been found alive. Or, if the worst had happened, with pleading hands outstretched for comfort in his grief. Some things had not been transcended within their relationship, even though she had done her best to push him away, because Gareth's eyes had always reflected the same bitter guilt. She could not bear to be reminded.

Marty had taken several calls upon their journey. What he had said over his shoulder to Gloria had been, "That was a near call." Shaking his head over and over again. "Bluithe's turned up. I don't know what the fuss is about. What's a bit of clap and a broken leg when all's said and done?"

As they came to a juddering, silent halt in front of Barnston Farm, Gloria had a moment's distraction, thinking of her poor, dead, deformed, little baby who was still buried under the tree in the Jubb's orchard where Lizzie had grieved. She spent a moment recalling how she and Gareth had sat in their car, Leonie in arms, fast asleep, while some sort of funeral service had been conducted on the other side of the stone orchard wall by Hannah and Lizzie. Lizzie's cries and shuddering grief had followed her as an echo down all the years, growing louder and resonating more, the closer they all came to Leonie's twenty-fifth birthday.

Marty cut into her revelry. "We'll have to walk from here. The snow's too deep and the lane's become impassable. I'm warning you, Gloria. You'll never slip through the slit in the brickwork at Barnston Bridge."

Marty knew because Mrs. Fairbrother couldn't either which had been why he had had to work with Blue Harcourt to open up the chimney to the land in the ground of the Fairview Hotel, cover it with a board, soil, sods and moss and hide a ladder on the far side of the gun room for her to get up and down to make her inspections. The old bird trusted no one!

They had had to join two tunnels by excavating the rock and cut in steps, cemented to make them safe, to get her up and down. The dog had gone crazy, but the work had been done when Ross had been over to France bringing back legitimate supplies for the hotel which got mixed in with the ones he or Bluithe brought over. Ross was off with the fairies most of the time and never seemed to realise that they got a hell of a lot out of the litre bottles he brought back from France, himself. Chef and Cannon knew better than to investigate anything that went on in dark places, even had they heard something, if it involved their senior management. While Cannon told tales on some folk, he was canny in the choice of his victims, though his choice of Blue Harcourt as the last to suffer from his vindictive mischief, had been a trigger to all the fuss of Blue's disappearance, if not Leonie's, who Marty thought would have taken a day off for her birthday and gone shopping.

Mrs. Fairbrother had had to sack Bluithe entirely because Cannon had been watching and listening outside the door to Eagle Suite. Reasons for not doing so might have been asked by the staff who detested favouritism when they all knew Blue to be a lazy sod, forever skiving and nipping off to do foreigners in Fairview time. To have done, otherwise, would urge people to start looking deep, a bit too close to the truth of the matter. That being that Blue Harcourt had always been her main contact with the pyramid ring, all men, because she would not brook another woman involved in all that needed to be kept secret. Blue had been sacrificed to the cause and just had to put up with it; not something Blue Harcourt was good at! He had also taken one of her little black books in revenge. Stolen into her bedroom and taken damming evidence out of her private drawers to try to influence her into giving him his job back. He had shown it to Marty who had advised him to give it back. "She won't be blackmailed, Blue."

Blue Harcourt had thought different. Somehow, though, it had all got smoothed over.

More to the point, he was convinced that Ross was not in the know because if he did he'd put a stop to it. Since Bern Jubb's death, Ross Fairbrother had reformed himself. Not that there weren't still rumours circulating.

In terms of his astuteness for business, Marty, being a business man himself, could not think of a single person less suited to running a hotel business than Ross Fairbrother. The only thing he was good at was playing at Action Man but still not clever enough for the specials and the double games they played. Ian Garstang had been unable to stop bragging, and especially in his new light of knowledge of who 'The Boss' actually was, that they had lost him easily. They had got to the chamber at Barnston Bridge by following Mrs. Fairbrother's hastily given instructions without her son in attendance to get Blue away to a place where he might be found without giving any games away. They had pulled the wool over everyone's eyes, it seemed. Got away with it.

This thought caused him to give forth a great sigh of relief as he opened the battered rear doors to his van and surveyed the vastness of his problem. How to get Gloria out?

One phrase came to mind from a Ladybird book he used to read to his twins…

"… he pulled and pulled with all his might …!"

The enormous turnip in the story had taken a whole line of heavers. Where to grab was the problem because Gloria seemed to be securely wedged. He managed it in the end by taking hold of the black tent coat she was wearing and heaving with all his might. Out she came with her skirts over her backside and what a backside at that! She would hardly walk let alone climb up through the narrow steps they had put in the rock for Mrs. Fairbrother: This other 'much-much-too-fat-lady', was tripled in size, and would soon have to give up the ghost of her idea of reaching the Fairview Hotel by the subterranean way Marty had in mind, when she eventually saw that her mission was impossible.

Get up through the potholes and chambers to the Fairview? She would not even get in through the slit! Marty would have bet on it. The entrance was so narrow that they could hardly squeeze themselves and the merchandise through the gap in the brickwork at Barnston Bridge. There was no telling her, though. Gloria had a reputation for not listening to the advice of others. She would have to see that for herself.

And things were becoming serious. Marty wasn't daft. Policemen were crawling all over the place. They were not weathermen manning the helicopter now circling the top of the ridge. These were the big guys coming in from Manchester or Leeds in a police helicopter, probably because a young girl was missing and there was evidence, perhaps, that she had been harmed and was not just absent from duty, if what her mother had told him was correct. He had also taken a forbidden call from Cannon, just as Gareth was collecting all mobiles and laptops in, so taking steps to control Fairview staff communication with the outside world, with sensitive information that a bloody knife had been found in Lovick Johnson's locker, which was the basis for Gareth starting a murder investigation. Both Marty and Cannon had rolled their eyes at that one as if they were sharing a face-to-face. As far as they were concerned it would have more to do with black magic and the winter solstice than a strolling minstrel who wore bells on his boots. Strange things went on in those woods at night! They were quite happy to abet the theory, anyway.

He sighed heavily when, finally, Gloria made the last stage of unpacking the vast trunk of her enormous body from the back of his van. He smiled at her with what he hoped was a helpful attitude before he ferreted about to find a rope, a torch and two bars of chocolate from his emergency kit which he always kept handy.

He locked up his vehicle with care and attention because people would pinch anything round here even when in the middle of nowhere and there seemed to be nothing within worth pinching. Then he set off in big strides with the rope over his shoulder, carried like a true mountaineer, wading through the wind piled snow towards the fast running, roaring river and the path that would lead to the red brick bridge. He was aware of her not following only when he offered her a bar of chocolate over his shoulder and his hand was not ripped off as if being mauled by a hungry bear. When he turned, he saw that Gloria had not even begun following him and was facing the wrong direction. She had her hand to the farm gate and was in the process of opening it up while looking over the virgin snow to the cowsheds. He had to retrace his steps.

"Where you going? It's this way."

"Not me. You go that way, Marty. I'll see you inside."

"It's all bricked up that way, Gloria."

Gloria shook her head. "Bluithe Harcourt doesn't know everything and neither do you. There is another way in. Lizzie showed me once."

"Showed you what?"

"Another way into the caverns that leads up to the Fairview Hotel. It's how they get the water into the byres from the river."

"What?" Marty was stunned. How could a girl know all this?

"Men!" Gloria scoffed. "Think you know everything there is to know about Barns just because you spent the whole of your childhood up a tree or in a dug-out, whittling sticks. Well, you don't know everything. I know things about the caverns that you don't know. There's another entrance and that's where I'm heading."

She had that snout face on; the bad tempered pig in her glowering eyes. She was big enough to fell him just by falling on him if her mood got nasty. Anything to keep Gloria distracted and happy. He had heard, if not seen, some of her hysterics in the past, shoes flying at Gareth's head, mostly missing and thwacking against walls and doors as he beat a hasty retreat to his police station across the square, the man having to keep his head under the parapet or be seriously maimed, only ever venturing in these days when Gloria had been pacified by the troughs of feast from the neighbours who felt sorry for him. The snorting beast was only ever tranquil when eating. Besides, he was curious.

Not that he much liked the look of the place as Gloria put her considerable weight to opening a five barred gate wedged with snow. The thaw had begun. Soon, the cloth which made the farm look almost attractive in the encroaching sunlight would be gone, and what was underneath his feet exposed. Yuk! "Bags not knocking."

"I've no intention of knocking. If Hannah or Lizzie are about to ask what we think we're up to, I'll have to remind them that I am Gareth Jones's wife. She would have been out by now, anyway, waving that shotgun of hers about. Maybe she's having a nap."

"There's no smoke from the chimney. It'll be like a fridge in there?"

"Maybe they're both where I think my Leonie might be. If not, I need to be up there, anyway. At the Fairview, knowing what's going on."

As she intrepidly led the way across the yard like a galleon in full sail, towards the sheds, wading a new, dry, diagonal cutting through the snow which had only, otherwise, been churned up from the direction of the house itself, Marty could smell and hear the farm animals even if, thankfully, none were to be seen; pigs grunting happily in their sties, hens fluttering and clucking in the barn, the cock disturbed to a warning crow and the cows lowing to each other, the latter being the direction in which Gloria was heading. He could hear the donkey's hee-haw from the far side of the house, thankfully at a distance and, hopefully, contained by that sheet of corrugated metal across the space between the gable wall and the lane. As if in objection to their presence, a battering noise hit the silent air as if it was bucking them strong, back hooves inside its shelter and they were clattering against a wooden door.

"Snow's the only time it's ever stabled. Lizzie told me when we were children at play." Gloria was whispering over her shoulder, though why they were both whispering in reverent tones, was put down more to fear of seeing Hannah with a shotgun pointed at their head, than any fuss the donkey was making.

Marty kept his own counsel over his wonder of why she was coming this way. Blue Harcourt had been privately bragging for some months about his mid-night escapades at Barnston Farm when he considered Hannah and Lizzie to be fast asleep. He had been looking, he said, for another opening to the big caverns used by Bernard Jubb, after seeing Hannah going into the sheds one night with a lantern in hand, looking a bit like a ghost of Florence Nightingale, and not coming out again. He had been night fishing down at the river because he hadn't had a licence on a very warm August night. The big, flat stone by the bridge had always been a deep pool where carp and pike liked to escape the rush of the river when daft women like Lizzie Jubb weren't trying to drown themselves.

He had been passing the gates on his way back home, in the pitch night dark and dressed all in black himself, when he had seen her. He had stopped walking and waited only because he didn't want her telling Gareth Jones that she'd seen him with a fishing rod, even if his pail was empty. Gareth would be duty bound to inform the Fisheries Police and before he knew it, he'd be fined heftily. He'd needed a fag, anyway, so he'd found himself a place in the trees waiting for her to reappear when all she could possibly have been doing was checking on her cows for the night, maybe a calf due to be born, but they usually managed okay for themselves. When after a half hour she hadn't come back through the door, Blue had gone to look for himself. Her lantern was on the shelf to the back of the sheds; a candle stub in a jam jar with a string about its neck, but Hannah wasn't present.

Emboldened with curiosity, and wondering if Hannah had been hiding money, he had ventured within. There had been no sign of her. All he could hear other than the cows moving in their cages was the fast, gushing flow of the river on the other side of the shed which had a strange echo within the metal walls and rafters despite the straw underfoot and the silage.

Blue had been convinced that Hannah was making for competition with their own black market ring. So he had begun watching the farm on a regular basis. No one came and went when he had been vigilant and still he had been unable to detect where Hannah had gone to when all in the byres seemed fixed and there were no doors to the back wall, the one that had been open before Bern had died, having been very securely bricked up. There had been a way into the caves, they all knew that, which Ross Fairbrother had had bricked up at his own expense as well as the exit through the maintenance door inside his well. It had been a supposition of Blue's that old wounds had been healed, rifts mended, because there was only ever one reason for hiding a way into a cavern or underground passage…black market merchandise! Hannah Jubb and Ross Fairbrother had to be in it together!

"Curiouser and curiouser!" Marty wanted to know what Gloria had in mind. "Where we going?"

"The cowsheds."

"There's nought in the byre but cows. There is no entrance to the caverns from the sheds. The only way in, still left open, these days, is Barnston Bridge and the council controlled one for the sightseers and trained pot-holers on the other side of the ridge. Even then it's not deep, though it would probably join with Barnston Gill somewhere along its rise."

"Says you! Follow me!" eyes rolling back at him, her breath short with the kind of exertion she had not made for years.

Marty thought this was a better way, anyway. Better that Gloria did not see the stash. Mrs. Fairbrother would go ape-shit if she knew that he was giving away their secrets. She would never believe that Gloria had known about it anyway.

He did not believe her; anyway, even as she slid back the huge, rolling wooden door to the byre on its cast iron, rumbling wheel and he went forward to help her.

The smell that met them was warm and very stinky. The place was dark except for the white patches on the animals and the reflection of the outside sunlight on their big, glinting eyes. The disturbance had them all mooing in their separate spaces, hemmed in by bars and facing each other along each side of the byre. Their udders were full as if they hadn't been milked for some time. Certainly not that morning, when some of them were dripping milk and in obvious discomfort.

All they could see besides the penned in animals and the huge cattle feed silo, was cowpat on concrete, stone troughs filled with water and feed which ran down either side of the outside walls and, to the rear of the big shed, great slabs of dressed granite in huge flags, which had long formed a stout wall behind which passed the banks of the river itself, some few metres beyond where they were standing, on the other side of a narrow band of trees.

They could hear the river in full spate, roiling and roaring, though there were overflow channels and machinery in the Weir House which would divert the water into the reservoir, to prevent it from overflowing its banks, once the river water came above a certain level. Now that the sun was shining, the melt water would amass and, unless redirected, combine to send the river thundering down to Quinton with a massive danger of flooding the towns along its banks when the channels were insufficient. It was, despite there being a huge manually operated wheel to make the sluice gates open and close, a computerised system that had them open and close. Too little water in the river was as bad as too much. A lot of the local farms had banking right down to the river itself so that their cattle could drink with ease. The volume of water flowing in the river was monitored as it cascaded over the weir on the other side of the pump house giving the information the computers needed to open and close the sluices when no one was in attendance.

Yet as the melt water collected, the sound of its spate might cause some people to worry about flooding despite the storm drains. Marty could remember back to being a boy when this side of the river would flood until Bern had developed a system whereby he had channelled the overflow and used it to quench the thirst of the animals in his shed before any excess was diverted back into the river, further on, away from his farm buildings.

As soon as Marty could adjust his eyes he looked for the old bricked up cavern entrance. He found it unbreached, to the left hand side of the large byre where the cows responded to their disturbance by raising their tails and lowering their heads, cow eyes watching. Beyond the cows, on the back wall, was a two metre wide patch of rough brickwork which went from the concrete floor to a jutting rock outcrop close to the roof, as if the byre had been built off it and the only thing holding the ramshackle erection up was the peg it provided. This was where the old entrance to the caverns had been, where Bern Jubb had taken his taper and then lost his life in the old well at the hotel which had been gained some fifty or so metres up the steep rise of the ground, through the tree roots and under the first layers of subterraneous rock. A hidden world, kept hidden. Council land? Private land? Anybody's land under the surface as long as the natural tunnels could be accessed and those trespassing had the courage to wander in pitch black dark without even a twinkle of natural light. Dangerous places, gouged out by the passage of water needing to find its way off high land by eroding a way through soft rock when, over millions of years, heavy rainfalls eroded a way through to the valley below. Much of it still unknown, some of it plotted by enthusiasts, but most of it prevented from ordinary access in order to protect the lives of local children.

Marty, with deep curiosity, let his eyes travel from the rough brickwork and along to the huge, granite flags which made a flat, unbroken wall right to the other side of the byre. The flagstones were all in line except for the last one which jutted out over the stone water troughs running a metre up off the concrete floor, large, iron water pipes taking it all round three sides of the shed in a system of jointed elbows where the pressure of the water alone, as well as the superior height of the river, allowed it to rise and then fall again over the big, rolling doors. This was the way that Bernard Jubb had diverted the river water to prevent his farm being flooded, an ingenious watering system which was a back-up to his domestic supply when the ground froze.

"So where's this entrance then? I can't see nothing."

Gloria's face was a picture of triumph. She pointed over to the jutting flag. "See over there where them big stone flags have been set to make a wall. Look at the last one where the water's piped through."

Marty bent his head down to hers to listen all the more intently, he'd know things that Blue didn't if what she was saying was true, while he cocked it to look where she was pointing, his hands in his pockets because he was freezing, but intrigued enough to start believing.

"The stone troughs have got water that comes from an underground stream, fed by the river. Finds its own level so doesn't need pumping unless the river's very low or its drought or something. Lizzie showed me when we used to play together as children. That last big flag on the other side to the old cavern entrance ..." a fat finger pointing, "...it overlaps the others as if it's too big to fit into the space left for it. See how it sits on an oak runner and that runner extends all the way along the wall …looks no more than a shelf when it's full of old paint tins and rags and that candle in a jar which they've left burning, all at one end…that's to take the wheels the flag runs on."

Marty looked to see another baton of hardwood at the top running along the beam which supported the corrugated iron roof. Still, it all looked fixed and well fastened in to him.

"Behind there is a wide stair going down through the rock and under the river itself. You come eventually to a corridor which goes off in two directions. One tunnel is very low and goes to meet the chamber at Barnston Bridge. Only there was a pile of loose silt and stones to block it off when Lizzie took me that way when we were children. Ahead is the most amazing place I've ever been in. Not a cavern as much as an excavated room…"

He was beginning to see and to believe because Gloria was making sense of it through her explanation. It all tied in with what Blue had told him, too. There was even a candle burning inside a jam jar just as Blue had described Hannah's homemade lantern. He interrupted her in order to give him more time to absorb the information, making a map in his head and matching it to memory. "Let me think for a minute."

There always had been a silted up passageway from the chamber at Barnston Bridge along this way, on this same side of the river, under the built up pathway. The soft rubble and clay had formed the obstruction to a passage, probably, either washed down there from above or brought in when the river had risen and left behind as deposit when it had receded again when the river had slowly changed its bed. One only had to look at old maps of the area to see that. He had one framed on the wall of his pub, in fact, put there by the interior designer at the brewery who had said that local maps draw in trade. They helped ramblers orienteer themselves and saved the landlord constantly being asked directions when busy. They had not been much good to Lick Johnson, though, because the lad hadn't consulted them, not that Marty cast him a second thought. "Bern did all this? Is it connected to the hotel?"

Gloria nodded in answer to his last question. "Think so. Lizzie told me that there's a natural bath of warmish water up inside the passageways where the rock takes heat from the ground in summer." She didn't tell Marty that she had been told by Lizzie that there was where Bern Jubb and Ross Fairbrother had used to bathe together, naked, in lamplight. Hannah had seen it, too, and got very angry about it. That had been the first time that Lizzie had seen Ross naked. She had become fixated on him, after that, constantly trying to attract his attention when Ross would come to the farm to commune with her dad, jealous of their relationship, wanting to have them both and not each other.

Then Gloria, sly-eyed, "It's Mrs. Fairbrother whose fund manager, isn't she?"

Marty gasped. "How do you know…?" Then realised he'd allowed her in on the biggest secret in Barns.

"I didn't, till now. I wondered why she brought the ham that made me so ill. She either wanted me out of it, serving revenge, or needed to compromise Gareth if the shit hit the fan. One thing's for sure, she wouldn't give Leonie a Christmas present. She doesn't know…" Gloria's lips clamped tightly shut and her eyeballs danced from side to side. It was her turn to nearly give away secrets.

"Know what? I tell you, you tell me!"

"Not this one, Marty. If you find out about this one, it won't be me doing the telling."

Marty scowled. Women always managed to manage men in the end. "But it was Bern who dug out this chamber you're telling me about?"

Gloria shook her head. "Been here for as long as the farm's been here, so Lizzie said. It was Bern who excavated it bigger for his own reasons."

"How you get in then?"

Gloria's head wagged over to the back wall of the byre. "The flag that sticks out slides if you set your fingers right into them little crevasses and remove some wooden pegs set into the granite."

"Why go to all this trouble?"

"Lizzie said it was the stair, the passage and the cavern which were excavated to allow her dad to put his pipe work in from the river for the cows to have water flowing constantly through the troughs in here. Look, see, it's constantly moving like a little brook and goes out through the iron pipes after filling the troughs on the other side of the sheds. Saved them lugging water in here or having to pay for a stand pipe in the yard which would be metered."

"But what's this cavern used for? A stash?"

"No idea. Bern used to go mad if me and Lizzie got into them. The caverns always were good hiding places. Better, too, than Barnston Bridge."

Marty refused to take up the hint and develop it. The less Gloria knew the better, though he knew she'd seen enough from that window of hers in the middle of the night when the rest of the village was sleeping to make good guesses. What he did was scratch his head "Well, I'll be damned! It's linked to the chamber at Barnston Bridge, is it? How did you know?"

Gloria shook her head at him as if he was some kind of idiot. "I used to follow you and Bluithe, sometimes. Never with Lizzie, though. I don't think she knew about the chamber at Barnston Bridge...at least, I don't think so. I followed you two, there, to the chamber at Barnston Bridge, one day, and then came back later. I had my Jack-Jack-Shine-a-Light with me. I got through a gap no wider than a foot or two at the top of this heap of soft sludge. Into another tunnel on the other side, only it was wet with water dripping into it and I didn't know how deep it might be. I gave up, then. I was on my own. If there'd been a cave-in, I'd never have been found."

Marty nodded. He and Bluithe had discussed going through that very same way time and again. The water, on investigating by throwing pebbles, had been only an inch or so deep. They had heard the rats, too. Marty hated the things. Also, Mrs. Fairbrother had insisted on her orders being followed to the letter and no time wasted by getting diverted when there had been a short stairway to make, straight up an easily accessible chimney, which took them directly up to the shaft at the Fairview Hotel.

So Gloria, clever Gloria, was not as pig-brained as she looked! She had a degree, someone said, from Manchester University, in Occupational Therapy. Totally wasted on any woman, Marty considered.

"Go on," he said. He wanted to hear it all.

"There's nothing more to tell other than I heard noises that could only have been the cows in Bern's sheds. And voices. Sounds carry through the tunnels even over the noise of the river."

"You tell anyone?" Marty was mesmerised.

Gloria nodded. "I went home and told my mum. She gave me a clout for admitting to having gone somewhere that was forbidden. She said that if the Bogeymen found out, I'd be in for more of a whipping than I'd got from her already. I was to keep my mouth shut and never go near again."

"We'd better get in there then."

They had to bring a reluctant cow from her pen to make the space they needed to get at the flag; more for Gloria than Marty's sake. The animal objected by raising its tail and making a deposit on Marty's shoe. It had to be wiped off with a handful of cattle feed. Then Marty moved some of the old rags, the candle in the jam jar and paint pots and putting his fingers into the notches in the flag, feeling carefully until he located the first round peg. A swift, hard tug and out it came. Slightly higher up was another. You had to be in the know about this. Little wonder that despite all Bluithe's prowling and searching he had not been able to find this secret way in. As soon as the second peg was released the flag began to slide open.

"Spooky, ain't it?" he whispered.

"This place shouldn't have any daylight. I can see a light. I can smell something burning, too."

There was a smell of paraffin and burning rag.

Gloria said, "Someone's in there." She tugged at Marty's sleeve when he hesitated.

He'd had enough women in his life telling him he was a weakling. He'd be buggered if he'd have Gloria talking ill about him, too. So forward he went feeling cowed by a place that had such an eerie feel about it; he was forty eight, not eight any more, when all was said and done. He'd never whittled sticks, either! Blue had done that.

Their way was dimly lit but they could see a parade of steps just wide enough for Gloria to follow behind him. Flames flickered from burning sconces on the roughly hewn wall in a draught of disturbed air and fanned the burning wicks from the paraffin lamps which sat upon the cobwebbed steps leading downwards; a long, low parade, one after the other, down into deep, unknown shadow. The smell was familiar as was the noise of the river.

Twenty-seven

A cool draught of air drifted over them. Gloria, for some strange reason, felt sure that she could smell food. Her nose twitched. The cavern was well ventilated so maybe cooking smells could travel inside the spaces from houses round about. Strangely, it was not as cold as it had felt outside. She could hear the flow of a raging, underground river as she and Marty crossed over the low stone wall; she rolled over on her stomach in order to get her legs astride; Marty making a scissor movement, though he looked far from happy about it. Once they began to descend there would be no going back. Gloria started the descent. Marty followed with great reluctance.

Then something quite unexpected; a dog barked three times as if sensing their coming. They reacted together, jumping towards each other and holding on tightly to each other's clothing. It sounded as if the barking was coming through a megaphone when the dog barked again; the strong, deep bark of a healthy dog guarding its territory from strangers.

How had a dog got in here? Then before them, a shadow came to stand against the dim, yellow light at the bottom of the steps they walked down. Gloria felt as if every nerve ending was clamouring; get out of here, get out. But not without her Leonie, that was prompt enough to stand her ground even if the weakened muscles in her legs told her that they would not bear her weight much longer.

A wandering light made overlapping circles and flower patterns over the chiselled stone surfaces of the tunnel as it grew in brightness. Marty had to be dragged along in his reluctance to go further. "Someone there! Run for it!"

"No! My daughter…! We're not going anywhere!"

The shadow was elongated; long and thin and had a long thinner shape projecting out from its shoulder. It was pointing something towards them; a shotgun!

Gloria gasped and had to steady herself, galvanising herself not to panic.

When Marty would have turned to run, she grabbed hold of the waistband on his trousers. "Oh no you don't!" He was abruptly brought to a halt.

The shadow moved; a thin, slight, tiny figure in a long, grey-white dress with a veil over its head, hands covered in the same white gloves. The give-away because she always wore white gloves, no matter her other clothing, when out in the village stirring up trouble. Lizzie Jubb! Who else?

Though when she spoke, Gloria experienced an uncertainty. Lizzie or Hannah? It was the way she had the shotgun held firmly to her shoulder. There was something different in her speech tone and manner to the one Lizzie used.

The laugh was a cackle of pure joy, just as the creak of the safety catch on the shotgun being removed could be heard. "Come through, come through. Guests already! The more the merrier. You're the first to arrive other than Leonie. Your Leonie's been chosen to be my Maid of Honour. No need to worry as long as Ross turns up. The dress fits as well as if it was made for her. My cousin Betty should have worn it but she's long since dead. We'll find you something smart, too, in a minute. There's sherry and champagne on the table, inside. Help yourself."

Gloria's hands clutched themselves together over her breasts to stop her heart from thumping its way out of her chest. Leonie was alive, thank God! She gasped, blinked back tears, but stalwartly refused to give in to the overwhelming relief beating like bird wings deep inside her somersaulting belly. She was feeling sick again but it won't have to matter. Leonie was here, safe even yet. That's all that mattered.

They were waved forward by that menacing gun pointing their way across a corridor lit by a flaming torch and up some gouged out steps to where Gloria hoped that Leonie would be waiting.

Marty was flabbergasted. "What are you playing at, Lizzie Jubb?"

"Who says I'm playing?"

"Does that mother of yours know…?"

Gloria dug her elbow deep into his ribs. The worst thing that could happen now was not to take her seriously because this wasn't Lizzie's usual style of naughty behaviour.

The words came through the veil in serious tone, even while as yet incomprehensible to those made to listen. "I didn't send either of you an invite. Gate crashers, are you? Coming in the back way. Only Ross and the vicar to come that way."

"Just humour her, please," Gloria whispered to Marty deeply under her breath.

"I could have that…"

"Since when did a Jubb point a gun and not mean it? My Leonie, Marty! You heard her. I have to see her."

The gun waved them onwards. "Quite right! Think I've got enough cups and saucers. If I'd 'a' thought you were coming, too, Marty, I'd have ordered a barrel or two. Bit of a celebration here, later, see. Only got wine and good French brandy as well as a sweet sherry, of course, until the champagne toast. Table's spread already. Get in. Bluithe Harcourt helped me. He came just at the right time, he did, when I was wondering how I was going to get it all done in time. Saw they'd found him and carted off quick."

Marty was still under the impression that he was in charge. "Now, Lizzie…If Leonie's alright there's no harm done, is there. Just put the…"

"There will be unless you shut up. That way, ahead of you. Should have been done this way the last time, if we'd had any sense." The gun was waved in their direction; she meant to labour her point.

If Marty wanted to get himself shot that was his business. Gloria moved ahead.

Gloria could not believe what she was seeing as she forced herself not to stumble while she looked about frantically for Leonie. The chamber was huge, cathedral like in its dark outer reaches and where a set of roughly hewn steps seemed to have been formed by human hand to provide a means up through the ridge. The excavated walls were lined with burning torches, paraffin lamps, battery torches, to cast yellow light through what otherwise would have been pitch blackness. She felt warmth, not chill. She had a feeling of unreality similar to that which she had experienced earlier as if this was all just part of a bad dream. This can't be happening, her mind said. Food…wine…a celebration! A wedding! Where was Leonie?

Then her eyes saw the bizarre sight of a dining table in the centre of a vast space of rough, excavated stone, around which was set six Chippendale chairs and a love seat for two with a heart shaped back at the head of the table. The table sat on carpet as did the chairs. Her head was swimming. She was looking through disbelieving eyes at a room set for a feast. A white tablecloth of the best quality Irish linen had been spread and laid with tarnished silver cutlery. Pretty china plates, with cups and saucers, with an old fashioned 'Ming Rose' pattern, stacked in a pile ready to be used. Threaded between these items, artificial posies of white silk orange blossoms and bright purple violets were dotted here and there, tied together in bunches with hyacinth blue ribbons; all a bit sad and crumpled looking as if they were as old as the hills.

Cloth serviettes of hyacinth blue linen had been folded into little silver rings. Silver dishes had been filled with small, purple, flower-shaped sweets and candies; one of Gloria's and Lizzie's old favourites, 'Love Hearts', with their future predictions of romantic fate inscribed on their surface; recalling two little girls sitting on a fence in a buffeting, summer wind and reading into a single word on the sweet their own interpretation of what was to become of them ten years hence. None of them had said 'jilted'.

Dear God! She deserved whatever punishment Lizzie metered out, but Leonie didn't. What had she done with her? Gloria could see the table through the glaze of fear which was making her eyes flit instead of search for her beautiful daughter. She knew that this was meant to represent the meal that Hannah would have had the whole village sit down to in the tent, in the orchard, to celebrate the wedding of Mister Rossiter Fairbrother to Miss Elizabeth Jubb; their child already conceived and growing strong and healthy in Lizzie's belly.

Meanwhile, Marty's eyes were taking in the table. He was not accepting this nonsense as seriously as Gloria. It was just another of Lizzie Jubb's attempts to make mischief. Gone a bit overboard, this time, though, from the look of it if judged by the way the table had been spread. The candelabra, tarnished but still proud, held proper tallow candles, even if they had lost their straightness. They were still to be lit.

In the centre of the table was a three tiered wedding cake which looked to a very peckish Marty as if each section had lain in a sealed tin for over twenty-five years; the icing gone yellow and probably too hard to sink one's teeth into. He had used to see the like before, in his boyhood, made by Hannah Jubb, winning prizes at the summer fair for her baking. She had used to ice cakes for weddings, just like this one, with lattice work and iced roses and little silver balls for stamens. The tiny, toy bride and groom to the top stood crookedly to attention on a small, black plastic disk, arms linked, their painted bodies worn as if much handled.

And food! So much food! Sliced ham and cheeses, fancy bits out of packets, baguettes and herby dips, sliced garlic sausages, olives and so many different sauces. Far more than the three of them could eat. Marty expected that at any moment Gloria would make a bee-line for the table, take a seat, and begin to stuff like only Gloria could.

In fact, the smell held no attraction at all for Gloria, especially when she had sight of the ham which looked to be decorated the same as the one she suspected of making her so very ill. She swallowed down hard on a wave of nausea and clenched hard on her buttocks as memory kicked in.

Marty, who was just as conditioned as Gloria was to appreciate the stimulus of the sight before him, could be heard smacking his lips as if unable, even with a shotgun trained on him, to resist the sight of a feast fit for a king. Enough drink, too, to splice the main brace on a battleship. Even champagne with proper, wide-rimmed glasses; not those little fluty things that stop the bubbles bursting all over one's face, thirty quid a bottle. He was looking at sherry bottles and golden, French brandy and recognising the labels. Where had she got the trays of wine, brandy and sherry glasses, all twinkling as if someone had polished them with a bit of hot breath?

Even a box of fat cigars lay open. Marty recognised the paper bands around each one. There were schooners full of cigarettes and no sign of Blue Harcourt who would have been going round pocketing as many as he could. Marty, was partial to a fat, mellow cigar after a good dinner with a glass of French brandy cupped in his other hand, head back in a comfortable chair and blowing smoke rings, feet up on a pouf in his parlour at the Bald Pheasant Inn.

At this particular moment in time, what he felt he needed more than anything else was a stiff drink. Champagne beckoned. For something to do with his jittery fingers, and to look anywhere than at Lizzie Jubb with her shotgun trained upon them, he went forward and began to untwist the wire on the ice cold champagne bottle in a silver bucket, snow in the bottom, noting as he did so that he had settled on a Brut 2006. They had already flooded the village with it. All the other brands of food and drink were the same, too, as they had brought back for illicit sale. Only one place she could have got this lot. It all linked in with what she had said earlier.

Gloria chastised him as if she could not believe her eyes. "What do you think you're doing? We've come here to look for my daughter not for you to drink yourself silly."

Marty took no notice, at first. He carried on the process he did so many times in the course of his work that he could open a champagne bottle with just a trail of cold vapour before the bubbles started rising, not a drop wasted down the sides of the bottle, in fact. He stopped unwinding the wire only when he heard a loud panting and a lot of little whining whelps.

Over in the corner, a large brown, long haired dog sat propped on its two front legs, wagging its tail, tongue lolling, excited no doubt by all the begging for food to be done despite there being a bowl of water and an empty food dish close to where it sat. The dog had been fed it seemed. It was tethered with a length of wire through its collar to a ring in the wall. It had a bandage round its leg.

"That's Ross Fairbrother's dog. It ate my pub cat, last year. Ross bought me the tabby I have now. Max isn't it?"

Lizzie didn't seem to be too pleased by his reference. "Licked my hand it did. Jumped up on the knife. Dogs don't ignore you. Always liked dogs, me. I told her not to kill it. That's bad, Lizzie. Bad!"

Then, Gloria froze to the spot where she stood close by the table, after watching Marty's incomprehensible desire to open a bottle of champagne with her own hands shaking.

Leonie's voice rose over the din of the rushing water and her own rapidly beating heart. It came from the right hand side of the chamber and behind them. The corner was where the sound of the roaring water was coming from. A thin, echoing voice came to hers which shivered with both relief and fear. "Mum! Over here! I'm here. I'm here!"

Marty groaned under his breath. Things were going from bad to worse. Bluithe, Ross's dog and now it looked as if Lizzie was really getting vicious. This wasn't an innocent game of snowballs. Or a session smashing empty bottles. Or putting dog dirt through letter boxes. Lizzie's eccentricity would seem to have tipped over into real madness. What had she done to the girl?

Gloria looked, gasping, her head swimming again. Trying to take it all in at once was impossible. Her eyes would have to adjust as well as her brain to make organization of the mass of confused and confusing images. Her ears and her head would have to clear. All she could whimper for the moment was, "Mum's here, darlin'."

More faint whispering from her petrified daughter who was standing looking every bit like a fairy balanced on the end of a stick while spume glistened in a light that had been placed like a spotlight so that she could be clearly seen. "Do as she says, Mum. Do as she says. She's put me out on this projection of stone over the water. It's very wild and very deep. I'm not held on. I can't balance much longer. My hands are tied together with wire. Oh Mum!"

Gloria wanted to collapse but fought the urges to scream and start throwing the crockery and cutlery at Lizzie Jubb. "I can see, Leonie. I can see. We have to keep calm. Remember dancing class. Don't panic, darlin'."

Leonie's whispered words were accompanied by a very satisfied rumble of laughter.

"You don't understand, Mum. We're all about to die unless Mr. Ross comes and marries her."

"Best listen to Ross's ex-girlfriend. Listen good to your daughter, Gloria," the gun toting bride said abruptly, her manner warning. "You too, Marty. Go on, have some of that champagne. Finish opening the bottle if you like. I'm partial to a bit myself. Always did like Babycham."

Leonie took the opportunity to tell the tale, her voice a-tremble while looking upwards, as if she dare not look down. "She had a knife but she's since put it in Lovick's locker with the dog's blood on it so that he'll be blamed. She tied my hands with the wire and threw the dog down the shaft. Then she made me climb down a ladder into a hole, near the gun room. This room was all set as you see it now. I had to put this dress on in that horrible house before she brought me here. She went back to put the knife in Lovick's locker when the coast was clear. Then she came back to the house, and found that wedding dress from some boxes. I didn't see Hannah. She was out somewhere. I hurt my knees when I fell. Oh, Mum! She's got a gun."

Lizzie's temperament changed. She went from placid to annoyed in the space of a moment. Her voice spat with contempt at Leonie who she waved the barrel of the gun at.

"Spoilt brat! Ne'er done a day's proper work in yer life. Standing behind a desk, flirting with men. Flirting with my Ross. Saw the way he looks at you. It's me, he'll marry! Not you!"

Gloria whispered to Marty. "Humour her, please."

Lizzie spoke sharply again, as if reminded of her mission, leaving no doubt that her words were to be obeyed. "S'up to you lot, not me, what happens to that brat of yours. All I did was to give a helping hand along the ledge, then turned her about, where you can see the trouble she's in. Leonie's right. River's below her and running high. Sluice gates are open. Nobody would live if they fell down there. They'd just get sucked under. Water fights with itself to come out lower down the banks unless someone closes the sluices and redirects it a different way. Fall in there and you're a dead 'un."

Gloria found a shaking tongue to speak. "Why, Lizzie? What's she done to you?"

"Stolen my Ross, that's what."

"I don't think you understand. Nobody knows but ..."

"Quiet. Shut yer gob! She's there just to make sure that Ross comes to the wedding this time. As long as no one tries to get her off the rock, she'll be alright. He should be here with the vicar, shortly. That mother of his as well."

Gloria was fighting the desire to faint as she concentrated only on Leonie and the dangerous place she was in. What she saw broke the dizziness into sharp shards of panic which plunged like knives into her maternal soul. Leonie was standing high on the very end of a narrow piece of rock that jutted out horizontally over a deep, spume filled hole; something that looked like a natural well with the river roaring under her. Her daughter was as light as thistledown; a tiny little bit of a fairy, if she was given a wand the illusion would be complete. She was standing as tall as she could, and as straight, as a vapour-like mist rose all around her which glittered like diamonds in a bright white light from a single spotlight beam. Gloria did not have to see to know that the roiling, thundering river was directly below her. One slip; one moment of weakness, was all it would take for her to fall to her death because not even an Olympian swimmer could survive such threshing waters.

Stunned, all Gloria could do was to look with fear upon the dangerous placement of her daughter. It was like she'd been made to walk a pirate's plank. She was entirely dependent on maintaining her balance, hands strung together invisibly while holding a posy of violets. "Leonie, darlin'. What's she done to you?" A silly question when she could see it all so clearly now, it had all been explained.

Gloria noted the bridesmaid dress which had been of the same style worn by her sister, Pauline, at her own wedding to Gareth. It was flounced, Little-Bo-Peep style, over a lilac net underskirt. At the curve of her tiny waistline was a huge bow of purple velvet which matched the colour of the posy wedged between her caught wrists; a style of dress that might have been thought fashionable for a bridesmaid at the time that Lizzie had made her plans to marry Ross. She had been made up to look as beautiful as her potential allowed with full make-up and her fair hair piled high in purple velvet ribbons and stuck with so much lacquer that it looked like gold mesh in the light from the spotlight. The make-up suited her, too. Her feet were clad in purple slippers.

Gloria instinctively knew the dress to be the one that Hannah would have sewn for her daughter because she would not have known what else to do but follow Lizzie's irrational desires. Part of Lizzie's trouble that! Her parents had placed Lizzie at the epicentre of their lives in order to ignore the trials of a failed marriage. Pulled her this way and that, they had, between them. Is that what she and Gareth had done with Leonie?

Gloria thought, no! That was not what they had done. She had grown up with a balanced personality that appreciated others as well as herself. Leonie had found herself; was her own person. She was old enough to know. Blame and guilt would be apportioned when the truth would come too late but there could never be a right time for pulling the rug from under someone's feet. The metaphor was too much. Gloria bit back bitter tears. The foundation which Lizzie had given her looked about to fracture and fall away.

"Looks a picture, don't she?"

Gloria opened her mouth to speak. It had become so dry that her top lip stuck to her teeth. She started to prepare her daughter for what had to be said. "Darlin', I'm going to tell Lizzie something about you that's perfectly true. It will be a shock but you must not let it…"

Lizzie was becoming more agitated. "Quiet! Don't want anything happening to Leonie, do we? Mustn't distract her from standing nicely like a bridesmaid should. Her's alright there for the mo as long as no one makes her wobbly. I remember dancing class, too. Yous and me used to go together. Ballet class. Feet together, girls. Chin up. Shoulders back. Eyes fixed on a spot in the distance. Now, stand still, girls, hands by your sides."

This was about using Leonie as the lamb to the slaughter, if Ross Fairbrother did not do what he was told. No cancelling anything now.

And who was there to stop her? Where was her mother? Where was Hannah who, previously, had always managed to talk her daughter down, back to some contact with sanity, lock her in her room where she might sing lullabies, her voice drifting so sorrowfully through the round, stained glass window in the attic of the farmhouse as she sang to her dead child? Where was Hannah?

"All's well as long as you all do as you're told. More to come, as well as my Ross. He'll come this time. No choice in the matter. Should have got the message, good and proper."

"Oh Mum! My knees have gone wobbly."

"Think of something else, darlin'. Just don't look down. It should soon all be over."

Lizzie agreed. "You stay where you is, minx. One move, I'll shoot the rock out from under you. Thought you could snatch him from me, did you?"

Gloria dare not scream in case it caused Leonie to lose her balance. Marty was looking at the champagne bottle. He seemed to be trying to come to terms with the gravity of the situation.

Calmly, quietly, with dignity, Gloria took the only tack she could think of after that threat had been given. "There's something important that you should know, Lizzie. Take a good look at Leonie. Her colouring … the shape of her face…her figure…"

"Know all I need to."

"No you don't. All I ask is that you take a good look at her. Who does she…?"

Lizzie began to shout with a petulant voice. "Not listening. Quiet. Other things to listen for. Guests on their way who don't know we're holding the wedding in this chamber yet. Vicar's late, too. I have to listen out for them. Her won't fall as long as she stands real still."

Gloria felt the panic overwhelm her muscles. Tears flowed. Her legs turned to jelly. Her weight dragged her downwards into a shivering heap. She almost fell.

Marty moved closer. He had listened and was looking at Leonie closely. Something dawned clearly upon his reflection on Gloria's words "Well. I'll be buggered…!"

Lizzie carried on talking. "No need to fear the water. It should have taken me away to a better life. Promised me it would until others stopped it. My friend, Old Man Green Beard's down there. Not yet, he says. That's all he says…not yet!"

Gloria felt Marty's hand under her arm as he lowered her to sit. He had dispensed with opening champagne. The heavy bottle stood with its wire partly twisted.

When he would have obeyed her request to carry on opening the bottle, Lizzie was giving him contrary orders he dare not disobey, her shotgun waving his way and then over to the hewn wall, under the tapers.

"Cardboard boxes, yonder. While your getting a nice hat and a sprig of holly for Gloria, Marty, find yourself a topper and a scarf as well. There's a nice white scarf with tassels; used to belong to a toff. Ross's been told no less than top hat and tails for our wedding. Only the best for my wedding. Everything bought and paid for. Won't go to waste this time."

Marty did as he was bid, his face pulled into an unusual shape, his eyes looking constantly to Leonie, his head shaking whenever he looked at the bride in her full veil and a wedding dress that had seen better days. He found the scarf and the hat. Put them on.

It was when Marty was rummaging in the boxes for something to fit Gloria that another shocked voice could be heard.

Gareth's tones, deep and carrying, his boots clipping as they struck against the rocky staircase. He had come with a torch which he switched off and pocketed. "What the…? Gloria? How've you got here? Marty? What the hell is all this?" Then, more quietly; "Leonie! Thank God!" Then, more quietly, "What are you doing standing there?"

Gloria spoke desperately. "I'll explain quietly, Gareth. She's been made to by Lizzie who's got that gun pointing at us all. Whatever you do don't make a dash or she'll fall. There's nothing holding her on. Her hands are wired so that she can't balance to walk."

Leonie saw her father's face spread in anger. She, too, made an attempt at preventing her father from attacking Lizzie Jubb which his face suggested might be the only course of action his anger might allow. Her voice shook with fear while attempting to be light hearted. "It's a party, Dad. Stop being a killjoy. Just sit next to Mum. Marty was opening champagne. Have some."

Gareth's face was fraught with amazement. Her bizarre words, pleaded from such a dangerous situation, caused him to take more heed than the hot anger in his head suggested. Then he thought to treat Lizzie Jubb as he always did; cool things down, smooth things over. "Now, Lizzie! Does your mother know about this?"

Lizzie sneered behind her veil. "Course she knows. Hannah knows everything. Just asleep, that's all. Tired after a night of it. Up in her chair. Cup o' tea with a splash of gin in it. Where else?"

"She won't be pleased, Lizzie. This is bad."

"It's you lot's bad. Not me. When Ross comes I'll be Mrs. Fairbrother as I should be."

Marty made a stupid comment, "You can't get married without a vicar or a registrar. Who's to marry you?"

Lizzie put her tongue out at him under her veil. "The vicar. Who else? Threw me out of his church yesterday, he did. He never was a nice man." The bride brought her shotgun round to point at his chest. "You'll stand for Ross, Gareth. Best man."

"I've called for a major police investigation…" He was about to close in.

Gloria went into overdrive. "Gareth, sit down, shut up and think! Until Ross marries Lizzie our daughter is in danger."

Only then did he seem to realise the predicament they were all in. "I'll take a seat. Don't mind if I do," nodding in the direction of a whisky bottle.

"Good advice." Lizzie had the gun pointed now at his daughter. "Gun's primed. The shock will reach her quicker than you can or a bullet. I don't want her falling into the water any more than you. Your fault if she does. Gloria always did have a good head on her for giving other folk good advice while ignoring it herself. Better still, do what Marty's doing. Go rummage for something nice to put on. Not polite to attend a wedding in a padded anorak. There's a bowler will suit you. Nice jacket, too. Not many weddings where you get dressed up for free."

Gareth looked stunned, white-faced and impotent.

Gloria spoke to him sharply. She knew Lizzie of old. She needed to be humoured. She reiterated what he had already been told. "Do as she says, Gareth. Please. There's only one thing to do. It's time to come clean, I think."

Gareth's face keened with alarm. "No! Be quiet. That'll only make things worse."

Leonie heard the start of an argument. As ever, she, figuratively speaking, stepped between them knowing that it would be up to her to uphold the peace. "I'm alright, Dad. Mum's right. Get a hat and take a seat. Have a glass of champagne or a sherry. Whiskey makes you drunk."

"I'll have to make a phone call, Lizzie. Mind if I use my phone."

"Don't work inside the ridge. Them men as came for Bluithe tried it this morning. They didn't see me here listening to all they had to say."

"Blue Harcourt will be dealt with."

"I like that." Her mood was settling again to one of satisfaction. "Broke his leg doing a bit of a job for me as it happened. It saved me shooting him in the kneecaps and that's a fact." She laughed sharply. "Clever me, when I gets to thinking things out. Knew you'd come down here once your daughter was reported missing and the door over the shaft was left open."

"People know I'm down here, Lizzie. The police from Manchester will be following on down."

"Them lot? Not without some expert help. Told Mrs. Fairbrother in my letter not to tell anyone until it's all over. No one with you? Ross and his mother not with you? Left her the invitations they couldn't refuse. Pictures and a place, time and date. An invitation that Ross can't refuse, this time…or else!"

Gareth was thinking out loud. He looked worried now that he had come to realise that Gloria was right. Lizzie must be humoured. They must all show willing to play her game of a fairytale wedding if Leonie was to be brought off the rock. He spoke earnestly. "When I left the hotel, Ross was out looking for Bluithe. His mother wasn't around as far as I could tell. They may not understand what you want them to do."

"She will have found the brown envelope though? She will have opened it by now."

Then suddenly someone else came into their midst, torch in hand, as if her path was one she trod regularly in silver heels with gold toecaps. Mrs. Fairbrother was dressed for a wedding. She wore a green silk dress and matching coat, a large feathered hat and black gloves. Over her arm she carried a black patent leather handbag. She had a carnation pinned onto her clothing. Her sneer told that she was not here of her own volition. She did not even look surprised to see the rest of the assembled company.

"Well! If it isn't Mrs. Big Belly!" the bride jeered.

As Marty put a hat on Gloria's head that might have done Gloria Swanson proud, she let her expression tell him that his taste in ladies' fashion required refinement. She spoke to Lizzie in a manner that told her that she was less than a human being and no better than a rat in her cellars. "Ross will be here shortly. I managed to contact him in the end. Why's Leonie standing out on a plinth dressed like that?"

No one answered. She was left to work it out for herself.

"He's gone to get the vicar."

For a moment the shotgun shook with Lizzie's excitement. Her voice was deeply satisfied. "I knew he'd see where his duty lay in the end. Now, while we wait. Let's have a bit o' music, shall we?"

On the table, ready and waiting, was an old fashioned, portable, battery operated tape player. Lizzie pressed a button. The large spools turned and the wide brown tape ran between them; Handel's Messiah.

Betty Jessop had paid a small fortune for the batteries in the Star but worth every penny! "Now Marty's here, he can give me away. Mrs. Fairbrother, you can pour us all a sherry."

Mrs. Fairbrother took a seat just as Marty and Gareth joined Gloria around the table. She brought the tray of schooner glasses before her and the sherry bottle. One strong pull and the cork was out. The golden brown liquid, aromatic of concentrated grape, glugged into bright glasses.

The hat on Gloria's head looked ludicrous. It was shortly joined by a feather boa and a pearl necklace. They were each aware of their own, idiotic appearance as eyes met and unspoken messages passed between them. The top hat was too big for Marty and the bowler too small for Gareth's large head. They were dressed up like children making pretence, even Mrs. Fairbrother whose feathered hat and black gloves had come from her own wardrobe.

In Mrs. Fairbrother's hand she held the photographs that had been contained within the brown envelope. The ones she had shown to Ross when eventually he had met her secretly in the bird hide, after her instruction that he was to come immediately because something had happened to Leonie. These, she passed onto Gareth under the table cloth. He must make no mistake of the threat they contained. He, too, looked upon them with horror while Lizzie allowed it with a rumble of laughter as she stood guard over them all, gun on her hip. Then at his daughter. Then back at the photographs.

Gareth took his time examining them, lifting them when Lizzie looked to be proud of her amateur photography. The pictures accompanied a green ink, scrawled order to come down through the potholes and follow the notices which announced the way to the wedding ceremony, followed by the signing of the register at the church, and a reception. The photographs were of gravestones; Bernard Jubb's recognised as the unattended oblong of sanctified earth in the village cemetery, with weeds growing to obscure the inscription. Another; a picture of a tiny cross under an apple tree in an orchard with the donkey looking down upon the words, "Lizzie's babby. Rossiter Bernard Jubb, Died 22nd. December 1984." One grave, an ornate sepulchre which they might all know later to be that of a Fairbrother ancestor, had been included perhaps for its gothic architecture and its preoccupation with angels of death. There was another of an upwards shot of some rafters, perhaps, and a set of four casters on a square shape with ropes hanging down; meaningful to Lizzie Jubb, if nobody else.

It was the last that was truly gruesome; obviously a grave with a headstone that had been draped with a sheet of white upon which bore the symbol of a heart with a knife drawn through it and the words, 'Kill, Lizzie, kill'. Under which was the name of her target: 'Leonie Jones. Rest in Peace'.

"She must be told," was all Mrs. Fairbrother said.

It was obvious to Gareth and Gloria that she had become a holder of their secret, at last. Ross had had to tell his mother that he was Leonie's father. He had had to. All she had said was; "Well at least you aren't the raving puff I'd always imagined."

Twenty-eight

Ross came a different way to his mother and Gareth. She had taken his tail coat and striped trousers, his high collared shirt and silk cravat along with a top hat that had once been his father's to the bird hide. This was because she had warned him that the police, who were now in attendance, would not allow him to leave the hotel once he had entered.

There, while he had changed quickly, they made sense of what was happening. There would be plenty of time for discussion and fingers of blame to be pointed, later. Alicia had received the news that Leonie was her granddaughter with an ironic smile, making just the one scathing comment. Otherwise, she had listened to every word he said with intense concentration...the fact that Lizzie's child had been a healthy, baby girl...how she had been passed off as the daughter of the local policemen...and their deformed infant buried as a Jubb, instead.

She accepted no blame when he brought her own dishonesty to book. "Sometimes, one has to do what one does, because one feels compelled to do it," was her only defence.

She had brought a carnation taken from the counter flower display on Leonie's reception desk and threaded it into the button hole of his lapel before making her way in a different direction. Ross had taken to his snowboard again, only abandoning it when he came up the side of the bridge and saw that the snowploughs had been at work to clear the village streets from the bridge downwards. After the bridge he could see a police cordon, fully manned to stop anyone going up the hill as the deeply drifted road was searched. Knots of people stood about talking, watching, excited by it all. Barns had never had a possible murder before. It was now public knowledge that Leonie Jones was missing.

His jog down the rest of the hill to the village square was that of a man who kept himself fit. After turning right, he kept on running until he passed the community centre and turned down a path which would take him to the Rectory, next to the church. If people had looked out of their windows to see a man dressed for a wedding, and seemingly late, he was at least going in the right direction.

With no time for a polite ring on the bell, Ross had simply made a very abrupt, silent invasion of the manse when his housekeeper would have shooed him out again.

He found the fat goose in black skirts within his study. He rose from writing a particularly impressive sermon, stirred and cheeks red, and looked at Ross with complete surprise when Ross found his Book of

Common Prayer from his desk, slapped it into his hands, shoved the vicar's jacket at him and said, gruffly. "Your presence is necessary at a wedding."

All objections were stemmed by physical management of the vicar's person as, when in the hallway, he forced him into a mackintosh, wrapped a scarf around his neck, shoved a felt trilby on his head and then frogmarched him past the stupefied housekeeper. Outside, he then bundled him into his own unlocked vehicle, the keys in the ignition, ready and waiting. "Drive to Barnston Bridge and quick about it."

"This is an appalling affront to ..."

"Shut up you pompous idiot! Just drive."

The vicar had an offended light in his eyes but his memory on his collection plates which these days only the Fairbrothers contributed to in any satisfactory amount.

At Barnston Bridge, Ross instructed the vicar to stop driving. They abandoned a vehicle not properly parked and with the keys still in the ignition. Panting now with the rush, the vicar found himself bundled down the steps and then urged to run, pushed and prodded from behind, by Ross Fairbrother. Close to the river bank, the snow was thinning quickly. Where the lane parted the trees, Ross gave him the instruction to bear left. Almost near to collapse, it was a relief to find that their destination was Barnston Farm where the gate stood open and the snow disturbed in a diagonal line to the cowsheds, another to the house.

"Am I to find the funeral service? Has Hannah's soul been reaped at last?"

"Find the marriage bits and be prepared to marry me to Lizzie Jubb."

Entirely bemused, the vicar's response had been an incredible, "To whom? Oh, I think not, Mr. Fairbrother! The bans have not been read. A marriage has to be approached with wise counselling from those of us who seek to ..."

Ross lost his temper. "Why are fucking vicars so much like little boys with attitude? Do you really want Gareth to know where the communion wine comes from?"

"What language! No need to become nasty, is there?"

They went into the caves the way Lizzie had directed Ross to do. Ross was putting on his top hat, pulling on his cuffs and straightening his cravat even as he took to the hewn steps.

"Hurry up," leather gloves put on quickly. Always a vain man, he wondered if his hair was straight.

When Ross and the disbelieving vicar entered the excavated chamber, Lizzie cried out with joy. "At last! Knew it. My love! You won't regret this." Then to the rest of the press-ganged company. "Everybody stand. I've got the ring. Same as I had all them years ago."

Ross tried not to react too noticeably when he saw where Leonie was so perilously placed. The vicar seemed not to notice at all.

From somewhere down her bosom she produced a shiny, gold band. "Afterwards, we can get down to the church to sign the register. It's for the babby, you see. So as he's not a bastard even if he is dead and buried." This was for the benefit of the astounded vicar. "Then back here for the feast. Don't mind who comes. The more the merrier once the deed's done."

The vicar was put forward by Ross and made to turn as Lizzie came to stand by his side, her eyes gleaming with every particle of her madness showing, as the unwilling congregation stood as directed. His goosy eyes grew as large as ostrich eggs as he looked at what Lizzie was waving about, under his nose. Where was her mother? He had always had a fear of Hannah Jubb because he had deliberately cut her off from the church after Lizzie had caused so much trouble. Despite having some sympathy with her plight, he knew which side his bread was buttered.

Then what he saw was the shotgun placed at ease. Lizzie didn't put it down and her white-gloved finger did not leave the trigger. She merely rested it away from her assembled wedding guests, pointing upwards. However, leaving it both primed and cocked, with her finger on the trigger. He knew her to be a crack shot like her mother. He had hidden away in his vestry for three whole weeks the first time he had failed to read the nuptials at her wedding. He dare not refuse her again and hope to remain alive, of that he was certain. A look of panic spread over his face. His teeth splayed and his chin buckled. His hands shook. He was incapable of saying anything other than, "I now pronounce you man and wife."

Lizzie scowled. "That was quick!" She raised her veil, throwing it back angrily from Betty Jessop's and Miss Carnage's rat tails and smudged make-up. All of the assembled company, other than the vicar, recognised them immediately. Gloria had noted Betty Jessop in the village the previous afternoon when watching out for Gareth. She had seen the dark-eyed make-upon Lizzie's face before, when she had spates of coming down to the village to cause mischief late at night, though such had not happened for quite some time. To observe Lizzie in dark clothes and black make-up had always been the most chilling.

"No troths plighted! Now, do it again but this time, proper." She handed the ring to Ross who took it into his palm and looked at it as if it were a cyanide capsule.

Ross saw just how deranged she had become in that instant. Her once pretty face had been scraped of every vestige of youthful plumpness until each hollow feature was drawn and sharp and vastly tired. She wore no teeth so that her crescent moon chin and nose were almost meeting. Her blackened eyes looked wild as they glittered at everyone like rhinestone bling, the gun perched, Lizzie on the very edges of herself.

What was the point in compounding their misery further? If he went through a wedding ceremony he could henceforth cast her aside and bring Leonie from the edge of disaster. He could see her, knees shivering; blue lipped and hands clutched in front of her. She was in that dangerous predicament only because of his actions. He had paid her too much, ill construed attention and Lizzie had found out. He did not need to see more to understand that she was perched over raging waters and the peril they presented. He was aware, too, that Lizzie was Leonie's mother as surely as he was her father. His own mother had been right in the only advice she had given him since he had told her the news which had shocked her to the core. He recalled her words even as he faced an insane woman he detested. Those words echoed in his ears: "The greatest natural, human force is that of a mother's love for her child. Believe it or not, Ross, I would do anything to save you even if it meant sacrificing my own life. Lizzie did not deserve the lies told to her no matter good intention. It is time now to tell her the truth. Nothing else to be done."

And so he knew it. So, too, did Gareth and Gloria know it. He could see the guilt in their eyes. He translated their nods as assent, despite their foolish garb.

His face spread with weakness and trepidation. He found contact with Lizzie's desperate pale and glittering eyes which pleaded for him not to let her down as badly again. He even placed a hand on her own bony hand through the white glove and squeezed it. Lizzie's eyes filled with tears and shone up at him. Softly now, he said slowly so that she had time to digest his meaning. "There's something you need to know, Lizzie. Something that was kept from you because Hannah wanted it to happen as much as we did."

"And what's that now? Other than that the bans haven't been read out for people to object to." Lizzie's voice was like a timid creature poking out to see the lie of the land. "It's the babby, see…"

"Let's bring Leonie from the rock so that we know that she's safe."

"No! All you'll do is have him marry you to her!"

Ross knew the futility of trying to persuade her further. His arm crept about her shoulder and he turned her peculiarity towards his own softened features. "It's the baby I'm going to tell you about, Lizzie. Before

I say anything more I have to tell Leonie something. It will be a shock to her, too, Lizzie." He called over to her. "You must be prepared to be shocked, Leonie, by what I have to say now."

Leonie called, shivering dreadfully, "Be quick, Mr. Ross. Mum said, too. I just want to get off this rock."

Ross took a deep breath. "Your parents are here to support what I say. It's the truth but you must be prepared to be shocked by it. Please don't lose your balance. Keep concentrating."

Leonie's voice came with angry desperation, now. "Be quick, please. I can't stand here much longer. My legs are tired and icy cold. I'm going to fall."

Gloria pleaded. "Please, Lizzie, please..."

Gareth found voice. "Let her off there. My daughter's going to..."

Lizzie wasn't having it; too easy to be tricked by them. "No! She'll have to stay there until we're properly married. I won't have it rushed. Waited too long."

Ross squeezed her shoulder and kept his hand against its bony surface. "We can't wait. Not if you want our child to live, Lizzie. Leonie is our daughter not Gloria's and Gareth's. Our child did not die at birth. It was not a malformed boy but a healthy girl. That baby girl is Leonie."

Her face stilled. Her eyes narrowed. She looked at Leonie then back at Ross. "What? What you say?" The gun toppled with a clatter. Her eyes grew as big as saucers and turned to look at Leonie again as Ross continued his shameful confession. Her freed hand fluttered in the air like a disturbed bird. She had dragged at her breath and already tears were flowing; tears of anger, of blame, of hate?

"The child you buried was not our child, Lizzie ..."

Gloria cried out, her voice deep and breathless. "It was mine! That poor baby boy was mine. Born dead. Hannah gave away your daughter because you ... in your illness ...you couldn't cope. She became ours."

Lizzie was stunned, reeling back, shaking but bedazzled as she looked at Leonie who was looking down with her head cocked; hard to know just what the child was thinking but enough to see - to know - that she had no physical likeness to either Gareth or Gloria. Her words were slow murmurs. "I see now...Ross's face...my figure before I became so thin and tired...look of Bern, too, in the way she..." Then distrust, sudden and sharpening. Her voice became hard, disbelieving. "Leonie? My babby! She's the child I gave birth to? That were a babby boy. So much pain and blood. It cried. Then it died. Hannah took it from me afore the afterbirth came. Said it better not to look. But I saw it after...later...later that same day...fingers fused together and its head caved in."

Gloria was weeping. "That baby was mine! It was dead at birth. I delivered it alone just as Gareth came home with Leonie because Hannah said that Ross should be the one to look after his own flesh and blood."

Gareth spoke, his hand gripping Gloria's as if asking for forgiveness. "It wasn't planned. It just happened with us all in agreement. We all knew the truth except for Leonie…and you, Lizzie. The malformed boy was my son, not Ross's. I had a brother born the same." Then he raised his head to Gloria. "I…I'm sorry. I should have told you that all the blame was mine. There's always someone to be blamed. It's human nature to avoid it. I felt demeaned."

Gloria's mouth quivered. Her chin dimpled like orange peel. She'd have plenty blame to lay later; if a 'later' there was to be.

Lizzie quickened, frowned, her whole being drenched now with confusion. Her eyes glittered as she looked at Leonie, moving forward, slowly forward, her arms stretching out.

Gareth had to be prevented from jumping on her by Gloria's restraining hand and Mrs. Fairbrother's glowered warning. She was going to bring Leonie off the rock.

Only Ross went forward with her. The vicar held back; not church business!

After a deeply indrawn breath, Ross said. "I'll marry you, Lizzie. Leonie, will you be our maid of honour?"

Leonie looked beyond understanding anything other than her trembling knees. "I can't move. My knees are going to give in at any second."

"Not till it's done, Ross. You sure? Leonie's…?"

That was when the cork exploded from the champagne bottle with a sound so loud and sudden that for a moment they all thought that the shotgun had gone off. It reverberated and then echoed all about the chamber. They all screamed out. Leonie included. Unfortunately, the terrifying sound was sufficient to interfere with her balance. Without arms to extend, she was entirely a victim of her own fight against gravity.

What happened, happened in slow motion. She began a slow tilt to her right which no amount of knee and torso movement seemed able to stem. Her head went back and left to try to right herself, her elbow jerked so that the posy fell before her. She followed it with a shocked look on her face. Otherwise silence. They did not even hear a splash as she parted the roaring waters and vanished within. Leonie was gone from them.

Lizzie was on the plank of stone before any of them, looking down. "He'll not have my daughter that Old Man Green Beard. Me, yes, not her. Hand her back. I won't let you have any child of mine. Take me.

Take me instead as you should have done all them years ago." Her leap was that of an angel soaring into dark, wet space where water vapour shone like the bursting bubbles from a glass of champagne, lit by spotlight, as her white dress and veil floated about her spread limbs, down and down to the crashing waters after her daughter. As she fell, came her last cry. "I'm coming, Bernadette."

No one had tried to stop her even as they all ran forward to look down onto the threshing darkness with spume beginning to coat their faces and a desperate wish in all their hearts for a miracle to occur. Fear sprouting its furry, unfurling, icy fronds as they stood mute and staring. There was nothing to see over the parapet but blackness and the roaring splashing of a roiling river on its way through narrow tunnels to the sea.

***

In another part of the underground tunnels, Lovick Johnson had a major problem. He was not only wet through, limping, bleeding from a head wound, freezing cold and frightened of the terrible darkness as he felt his way like a blind man, he was, also, totally lost of any sense of direction, once again. His petrol lighter had given up even the weak flame it had afforded as he had abandoned the clumping ski boots and made his way bare footed save for a thin pair of very wet socks, along a rocky surface which had initially seemed to lead him in the direction of cows.

Alas, Lovick was wandering without direction, feeling with fingers that felt as if they would never again pluck a guitar string. The Death March played over and over in his head. There was no focus of hope because the dark was complete and all about him. No opportunity to give way to the panic he felt either because the blackness wrapped him in its own mute swaddling where his own breathing sounded like an organ tuning up. He had tried shouting. He had tried whistling. Now his mouth was so dry that he could not make voice at all. Since leaving the chamber where he had found himself in a bath of cold water, all about him was dry and very cold. His lighter had given up lighting almost as soon as he had struck it.

He had thought he knew the way back up but then as soon as he had struggled to get off the ski boots and slop his way out of the water, he had lost any sense of direction he might otherwise have retained. Not only had he had to crawl and slither and shuffle over cold, hard stone, a balance wheel in his brain told him that he was going down, not up. He was also thirsty, hungry and desperate to get out of this place. After what seemed like several hours when only two or three had passed, he had not a shred of optimism left. He was entombed as surely as the servants of a pharaoh.

The situation was this time far worse than the last time he had been lost and wandering. There was no choice but to go on. He doubted that anyone had seen his decent from terra firma into this place of eternal darkness; it felt like he was halfway to hell. Even his scout master couldn't help. Life was paying him back for rubbing his hands together gleefully when he had found out that his old headmaster had died under the wheels of a bus: Not being a loving enough grandson: Causing his parents to run off: Landing up in jail.

Landing up here! What would his own epitaph be, he wondered, if anybody registered him as missing, presumed dead? As far as Quincey would be concerned, it would be just another excuse for a booze-up, only this time crying into his beer, instead of laughing. Would Leonie come looking for him? Not if her dad could help it!

Devoid of choices, all he could do was feel his way onwards, stumble about if he could stand which he had to, where possible, because his jeans were scuffed and ripped so badly that his knees were now starting to bleed. So he alternated; walk and feel, bang head, down on hands and knees, a bit of bottom shuffling thrown in. The only thing he could do was follow a vague draught of cold air. Sometimes, he had to sit still and wait for it to find him but it was his only hope. The one thing he could not risk doing was staying put because he was wet through and the cold was beginning to get to him. How long would it be before hypothermia set in and he began to ramble and hallucinate? Apparently, all that happened after that was that you lay down and went to sleep in the cold. It seemed like heaven to Lovick. Anything was preferable to the black nothingness in which he found himself. Sensory deprivation not being his thing.

The sounds of the cows had deserted him but, suddenly, he became aware of them again while the draught of cold, fresh air on his face became stronger, almost like a breeze. A smell, too. Food, of all things. Could he hear voices? Not only cows, but human voices, too! He was perhaps hallucinating already; the process towards death had already begun. Then he could hear that sound of thrashing water, again, but much, much more clearly. Like hearing a piece of music which expressed itself in thunderous swirls and lappings and fizzings upon the hollow spaces and hard, echoing surfaces about him.

As he inched forward, hands outstretched to the cold rock to his right side, the sound of the rushing river was getting louder and louder. His foot hit the straight edge first. It was right under his left foot. He could feel it through the bottom of his ragged sock. His toes curled against it. He ran them along a sharp edge that was right-angle straight; a cement step.

Cautiously, he crouched until he had the straight edge under his fingers. More cautious still, he stayed where he was, secured his left hand to hold him and started reaching further. A step or steps? Hands outstretched, he waved them about. Nothing but air. The breeze had now become a wind that was flapping his hair.

Then he felt something that could be nothing else but manmade if he recalled correctly the sensory stimulus of weeks spent chucking cement and sharp sand and other stuff into mixers from the pan of an Irish navvy's shovel and then watering it to the texture of Greek yoghurt using a plastic hose pipe. The soft, squidgy feel of an inch diameter, cylinder of plastic was within his feeling finger tips. He pulled it. It was attached to something, rock solid safe, as if put there as a handrail.

Lovick changed his position to sit on his bottom, his hand never for a moment leaving the life line should he suddenly plunge into the utter blackness ahead. Slowly, he inched his way onto the step, feeling more steps under the soles of his feet. The hose pipe was a guide and hand rail to show him the way.

Joy leapt inside him. He was on his way. He was going down with guidance. Somewhere before him began to dance a pinpoint of light. The wind was turning into a gale as if the rock in that place was acting like a wind funnel. The powerful music of thrashing water was growing louder and louder. It was playing loud and merciful in his head. Light began to wash over his feet. He could see what was left of his torn jeans as he inched down and down, step after step, on his bottom, like a baby. From somewhere above him was the spirit-soaring source of light as, at last, he came upon the underground river. Lovick did not question where it was coming from just as he never questioned daylight.

Then disappointment dawned as savage as any that he had felt in his previous life. He was still trapped. He was on a rocky ledge with an underground river before him. A raging, roiling torment of black silted water drummed against his ears. The air was alive with particles of moisture which wet his face and clothing no sooner had he come upon the ledge. The thrashing waters were swilling over the edge, rising, he thought, and threatening to force him back up the steps. There was no going forward. He would have no other choice than to turn back; to return to the darkness to try to locate his way to salvation, by a different path.

Not until he'd had a drink, though. His thirst at least might be satisfied if nothing else. He wished now that he hadn't discarded the ski boots, or at least one of them to use as a vessel. He had nothing but the cups of his hands. The only safe way to use them would be to lie himself down flat on his belly and reach in with his face close to the roiling stuff which was a bit like looking inside a washing machine filled with dirty clothing, mid cycle. This he did by getting down painfully on hands and knees and then reaching into the murky depths.

He had taken a few mouthfuls when he wondered about the source of light. It was coming from above, from a car headlight he thought stuck into a cleft of the rock, beaming down at him. A car headlight, of all things? Voices, too, more than just one set. Were people out looking for him? What could he see? He strained his head to look upward. He doubted that what he saw and heard was anything more than an illusion caused by his exhausted state. Something that looked like a girl's skirts and golden hair? Nah! The process of death through exposure had started. Hypothermia was playing tricks with his brain. How long would it be before the numbness in his extremities spread to his brain and started the other sensory failures which would send him to sleep and then shut down his organs with an ever-slowing pulse?

Would he look like his granddad at his last breath? Face grey, hollow and full of whiskers, nose beaked and mouth open, head right back in the quest for air! Too many fags! Would his life linger without closure in this cold, godless place where he might never be found? Wandering still about the tunnels and chambers, to become a tale in folklore; the wandering ghost of Barnston Gill! Would anyone seek to discover what had happened to Lovick Johnson? Would anyone care?

The mighty bang nearly caused him to bang his chin on the hard rock as he delved for another handful of icy cold drink. What the hell was that din? If he had possessed a single nerve ending that was not frozen with cold, he might have jumped out of his skin.

He heard human cries and looked back up again to see the head of the figure encircling her own standing position. A bit like some of the girls he dated who drank too much and then had a job walking straight. As her head came down towards him, he saw who it was. He cried out, "Oh, my God!" He watched her descent and felt the wash of the river water as Leonie's body displaced some of the thrashing icy liquid as into the river she went.

He reached out his hand to follow her but Leonie was gone.

***

She had landed in the water directly below where he lay on the rock. She was tumbling with the boulders and stones, going under and round and upside down before being brought full cycle with the swirling water while it fought to pour itself through a narrowing spout of rock and thus to the open river.

She came up spluttering and gasping, a hand, now free of its binding, was raised, imploring, though she did not seem to be looking at anything. It was like she was looking within herself and saw nothing but surprise at the unexpected turn of events; death by drowning. Her face was one of stunned disbelief as she was whipped again around and around with the stones and boulders being carried by the water as if no more than mere grains of sand. Her small hands sought to find the umbilical cord that might save her from the pull of the sucking funnel beneath her. She could feel it dragging her down even as she fought to remain on the surface of a raging flood that would soon be flung with great force through the metal sluice gates and into the river to join a less violent flow.

Lovick reached his hand out to touch upon hers just as the river would have taken her under again. His fingers clamped her wrist, though the power of the water was more than he understood. A giant belch of the water pushed her closer. He had her firmly held.

He was holding onto her wrist with all his strength as a white sack with a human face plunged down past the hand he was holding. The second wash of icy water seemed to stop Leonie being dragged away from him but pushed her closer still before she could be tugged away again and dragged under. The water was fighting to have her, so hard did it pull while Lovick closed his mind for once to the possibility of failure. Not this time, not this time!

Whatever else had fallen in had gone under and away, disappeared from sight save for a froth of white lace; the veil which swirled round and around until it formed what looked like the face of an old man with a long white beard before catching in the vortex and being sucked away.

Lovick could hear her name being called. "Leonie! Leonie!"

His determination grew to mammoth proportions. He found a strength he thought he would never possess. Nothing would make him let his Leonie go; nothing. Yet the river seemed to be more determined than him. His fingers had begun to slip. She was passing out of his grip as her small hand began to pass through his clutch. Leonie was as near as a heartbeat to following Lizzie.

Then an incomprehensible thing happened. The water suddenly slowed, lowered its tide-line dramatically, stopped fighting and calmly gave her up. He had her reeled in and into his arms before it stopped flowing altogether. The only time in the whole of his life when Lovick Johnson had been at the right time, at the right place, with the right things happening to do something that was life changing. The only time in the whole of his life when he had gone fishing and found himself going home with the catch he most desired.

His arms closed about her as her arms came round his neck and she clung to the white knight of her girlish dreams. This one had proved to be the one not to disappoint her.

By the time the rope descended with Ross Fairbrother on the end of it, he was standing with Leonie lying against the length of him, his heart thumping wildly in his chest, she too shocked from the glaze on her face to do anything more than weep with her face buried into his wet, ripped clothing.

"I saved her," Lovick said with the bemused tone of a chance hero. "She's shocked but okay. Whatever else fell in didn't make it. Got swept on under the rock before the water stopped."

Ross could only be thankful. Leonie was alive. Not so Lizzie. The computers at the Weir House must have closed the sluice gate which fed this particular overflow channel in time for Leonie to be saved with Lovick's intervention, but not in time for Lizzie.

He raised his head and shouted up through his tears to the faces hanging over the parapet of jagged rock. "Lovick saved Leonie. No sign of Lizzie. She will have been washed through to the river by now."

Only gasps and cries of joy could be heard. Lizzie was already forgotten. Lizzie had got what Lizzie deserved. "Thank God! Thank the Lord!" shouted the vicar joyfully. "Leonie is saved."

Then, all except the vicar, hung their heads and cried.

Twenty-nine

The snow building competition had to be cancelled, not because someone from their community was missing but because there was no longer any snow. There was a pot of money to be used in the coffers of the competition organisers but they would find another way of spending it for the public good. Things move on. Coming events break the sorrow over the sad things that happen to others, but which are passed. Christmas did just that.

It seemed as if few people were bothered about all that had happened at Barnston Farm, and the fact that Hannah Jubb was still unaccounted for, once the initial searches had been made and the incoming police had taken statements, the latter having moved into Gareth's police station and taken it over. Gareth was on extended leave and intended to stay so until what the public now knew had passed into folklore.

The butcher's wife, now being the only key holder to the upstairs room, other than Gareth, had opened the station and the upstairs rooms to the itinerant policemen who were wondering just whose name, and what crime, should be put before the police prosecution service. After all, it would be necessary, somehow, to justify the vast amount of ratepayers' money that had been spent on a murder enquiry which turned out to be a dog with a cut paw and three missing person searches when all that had occurred, so far, was people being cut off in the snow, and the supposed kidnapping of others. Who, as it turned out, had simply been invited to a birthday party and lavish reception in an unusual location.

There was a body recovered from the river, but it turned out to be the suicide of a woman with a history of mental illness who had tried to end her own life before in exactly the same fashion.

Then there were the bones of a deformed baby, under the tree in the orchard at Barnston Farm, which would have to be sent for examination before burial in Gareth Jones's family grave. There was nothing suspicious about this, however, as the home burial of the baby of the woman who had committed suicide was common knowledge, with a proper death certificate issued by a doctor, at the time, to say that the newborn baby had been grossly deformed and dead on arrival. See all, hear all, say nought! The villagers gossiped amongst themselves but said nothing to anyone else.

The only matter yet to be cleared up was the disappearance of the suicide woman's mother who seemed to have vanished off the face of the earth. An old woman with a reputation for being reclusive and as difficult and unstable as her daughter had been, if the reported behaviour was anything to go by.

Where was Hannah Jubb?

No amount of calling brought her forth from house, or byre or sty or barn. No amount of looking showed her to be hiding away her cringing grief in that ramshackle house of hers. If, indeed, she had seen the cars come into her yard, and knew the contents of the body-bag carried from the riverbank on a stretcher to the waiting hearse.

Was she ashamed of what her daughter had done? Of what Lizzie had done to Leonie? Her own daughter! Hannah's granddaughter! Though that snippet of information had not been spread beyond the village. Leonie, a lovely, young woman, too, who had been crowded about by so many that loved her and assisted to the ambulance; carried in the arms of her handsome, attentive lover, then driven away in the care of her parents and Ross Fairbrother, who snapped at his mother when she said that he should stay behind.

"She's my daughter, remember?"

It was out!

Was old Hannah Jubb hiding in the hay? Curled up in a cupboard? Gone wandering in the caverns, through corridors and potholes and chambers, which only she would know? The old, flat-tyred bike was still present as was the rusting, red tractor. The animals kept their secrets even when put into lorries and carted away; their premises thoroughly searched and nothing come of it.

It had been left to Marty to drive the vicar back to his manse where his sermon would be awaiting completion, not a single prayer or blessing said as far as those involved were concerned. He had, however, told Marty that his church would be full the coming Sunday as his congregation consulted him concerning this day's events. He might refer to the wickedness of the human condition, with vague reference to Lizzie Jubb, confident in the knowledge that there would be plenty, meaty Old Testament stuff to back him up. And New Testament, come to that!

"Which one was it had someone's head on a platter?" asked Marty. The vicar did not answer. Marty would have to be in church come Sunday morning to find that one out or start reading the Bible for the first time in his life.

Marty knew that he would have a full house, too, in the other place of village worship; the Bald Pheasant Inn. Yet another tale at the bar from which he might earn 'one for yourself, landlord' though not until his statement had been taken by an incoming police officer. What he'd do was what he always did when made such an offer; he would add the cost of a very large, expensive, double brandy, at retail price, to the customer's bill, and then pocket the cash.

When he got back to the village the buggers had already got wind that something had gone on. "Had to happen sooner or later," was the opinion most commonly spoken.

And in the days that followed, still no sight or sound of Hannah, even when the sightseers came and stood at the gates on the other side of the orange and blue tape and the sign that read: 'Barnston Farm. Keep out'.

Lizzie's body had been brought from the river on the very same day upon which she died; maybe no more than an hour or so later. The search and rescue teams were now on the lookout for a missing, old woman of over seventy years of age whose daughter was lying in the mortuary down in Quinton, pending a post mortem, and whose livestock had had to be moved out to neighbouring farms, save for a donkey.

It was Christmas Eve and Hannah had been absent from the farm for over two whole days when, feeling concerned, Lovick had looked about for a bag of oats but found that all the animal feed had been removed from the farm along with the other animals. He could not leave it to starve; not a donkey at Christmas! What he did was to find the food from Lizzie's wedding table, which otherwise would have been wasted, and put it in a bin to carry to the orchard for the donkey to eat, as well as ensuring that it had fresh water in the old stone trough. He wouldn't go anywhere near those nipping teeth for love nor money; nobody else would either, or those kicking rear hooves. Then the donkey began to look decidedly sick. Its haws brought up puddles of sick and its back end dripped.

It was Gareth that twigged. "I think we'd better send the word out for the French food and wines to be binned. The donkey's suffering from E Coli or I'm a Dutchman!" The symptoms were exactly those that he and Gloria had had to clean up before he could get a wink of sleep, in the same bed, snuggling up despite her refusal, as yet, to accept his apology. They had no one else to turn to in this time of emotional need. Auntie Pauline had gone off to Turkey with her new boyfriend and wasn't coming back early for love nor money. The weather was good.

It was the day before New Year; the day they had marked as the last time they would go out on extended searches and again check over the farm in case she'd crept back in the night and was hiding somewhere. The weather was still cold but there was no more sign of snow. Even the wind had abated. There was almost a feeling of peace in the still air. It had become more likely that Hannah Jubb had taken herself off somewhere where she might never be found again. There was even a sense of resignation to the fact that what had happened to Hannah might remain a mystery never to be solved.

One thing now seemed sure; that there was no other soul living at Barnston Farm other than the donkey, which no one had been able to get near enough to catch once it had kicked the hinges off the stable door and took itself back to the orchard where it refused to be caught. The bad tempered beast showed its teeth to anyone who went anywhere near it. It turned its back and kicked out its hind legs. It squared up its strong shoulders and then went to hide itself in shrubbery where no one could see it, but it could see everyone else, big ears twitching, hawing and coughing. It soon became clear the donkey would starve to death unless the meagre grass in the orchard was enriched with a bag of feed.

Lovick, Gareth and Ross had gone out on foot, this time, to make yet another search party though little hope was left in solving Hannah's disappearance. The volunteers had slowly dwindled when it all seemed to be leading to nothing. People had had other things to do anyway. Then there had been the Christmas entertainment at the Fairview Hotel to savour. Lovick had been shaking his bells, beckoning a hand, and proving his worth. Scandal had reeled the fans in, now the world knew about Leonie Jones being the real daughter of Lizzie Jubb and Ross Fairbrother. 'Let's go and do a bit of gongoozaling'; a local phrase for looking where one shouldn't and gathering gossip. They had ended up boogying the night away after the best entertainment they had ever known. It had been rumoured that Slick Lick Johnson had been temporarily upgraded to Entertainment Manager, interim only, by Mr. Ross, out of gratitude for saving Leonie from the underground river; fair recompense, most thought. He had kept rehearsals for the panto going, too. It was a case of everyone wanting to go to see a hero and his heroine and so the panto, still to come, was on everyone's lips.

Apparently, if the tale that was being passed around from mouth to ear was right; all those involved in her birth had agreed that on her twenty-fifth birthday, the truth would be told. In that, those named, all stood together. There was even a friendliness noted between Mr. Ross and Gareth, though it was said that Gloria was looking askance at Mrs. Fairbrother, something about not trusting the woman. Something to do with the gift of a ham and it having been the crossroads to Gloria going on a diet, donning an apron and doing her own cooking and housework again. Others were of the opinion that Gloria should be grateful.

Time was moving on. A new year was soon to dawn. Even though Ross was keeping the search going for Bern's sake, he knew that time had come to leave the mystery unsolved save for one last try.

And so, the three of them; Ross, Gareth and Lovick, met at

Barnston Farm after the animals had been taken away, the house had been searched several times over and still neither hide nor hair seen of Hannah. Even the Manchester policemen had stated that they could do little else in finding her. Ross, Lovick and Gareth were on their own in the course of yet another random search for Hannah Jubb. There were, in fact, just a couple of days to go to Lizzie's funeral which everyone dreaded as an awkward affair to be got over with, with as little fuss as possible.

When the policemen in white overalls went to the orchard to the rear of the farmhouse to dig up and take away the remains of Gareth and Gloria's son from under the apple tree, they found that what should have been an easy task was being made impossible. They had a major problem on their hands in the form of one very cross donkey.

Ross, Gareth and Lovick had just returned to the farm after another fruitless search of the fields. They had agreed for one last, unlikely search of the potholes, too. Nothing! The house had been declared out of bounds because the investigation of Hannah's whereabouts was still in progress. They had seen the marked car parked on the yard so guessed that the house was being visited.

It was as they crossed the empty yard, where they had to imagine what it had been like when Hannah and Lizzie had been living there, when they heard a commotion coming from the orchard. That it was to do with the donkey was obvious from the brays and haws they could hear as complaints from a still sick and aggravated ass with a headache, probably, and the rustlings of undergrowth, rent the morning quiet. They went to see what was going on when they could hear raised male voices coming from the same direction.

The corrugated metal sheeting had been removed so that they could walk over the stubbly clods of earth round to the winter-bared orchard, to the rear of the house, without its usual barrier. There they found two, very irritated Manchester police officers, as the logo on their headgear declared, in white suits, rubber gloves and Wellingtons, with very red faces and breathing hard, because if there's one thing that a maladjusted donkey knows how to do, besides biting and kicking and barging, it's how to give the run-around. The disobedient offender against law and order was seen to be hiding in the centre of a clump of very prickly holly and looking out at them with intent to cause further damage. The two officers were about to give up on trying to complete their objective which was to exhume the remains under the tree, marked by the cross which Lizzie had made for it.

Lizzie's donkey was double trouble. It would not let them near the apple tree where Gareth had told them was where the remains of his dead son lay. He found himself reminded of the very thing the donkey was protecting. The grave of the child that was really his son. Nothing but bones in a butter barrel, now. Like Gloria, he had wanted them to be left where they had originally been buried with the little cross which Lizzie had made for marking the spot, though he knew that would no longer be possible, because genetic tests were called for.

The disturbance was why he and Gloria, with Leonie lingering behind, not really participating, had previously gone with the vicar to lean over the wall and make a kind of declaration of 'belonging', by them, his birth parents, at this place where he had rested for twenty-five years before his tiny coffin was removed from the soil. They had stood on the lane for no reason other than that the donkey was inside the orchard going crazy. There was no way it would have let them in just as it was now objecting so strongly to the invasion of the two policemen.

Though no one but themselves had been watching, Gareth and Gloria had harvested the soul of Rossiter Bernard Jubb Jones into their minds and hearts, before the policemen would come to remove the tiny bones for examination.

These were the men come to do that very thing. While they had managed to remove the sheet of corrugated tin, any approach to the grave was marked by a braying, battle charge which had driven them back again.

"We'll have to get the vet to fire one of them tranquilising darts," one of them said.

Lovick could tell he was an animal lover because it was said with such regret.

"Just look at them teeth!"

"It will have to be caught," Ross agreed. "It can't stay here, that's a fact. It needs a vet's attention and it will eventually starve to death without the trees being in fruit. There's a sanctuary, I know, should take it. If we can manage to catch it, that is."

Gareth felt superior. As far as a bad tempered donkey was concerned, he knew that Manchester policemen were no match for a local bobby when it came to getting it where they wanted it to be, which was out of the way. "We'll have to lasso it. We'll need a rope."

The policemen had come prepared with spades, tree saws, forks…everything needed for an exhumation, bar a rope.

Lovick raised a finger. "I know where there's some rope. In Hannah's kitchen, sort of hanging down from the rafters."

"We'll get it together," Ross said. "Let's go in together." Then to the policeman whose patience wasn't with bad tempered donkeys, "Come with us so that we aren't accused of tampering or pilfering. The house still has a lot of things of value, within."

Gareth's eyes rolled. He'd never tampered with or pilfered anything, other than a baby daughter, in the whole of his life.

Lovick still had a few bits and pieces of costume to supply for the pantomime and bore that in mind. He wasn't shy of taking things when he couldn't see Lizzie's old dressing up clothes being of value to anyone else.

Ross wouldn't have minded a pair of overalls to protect his clothing, either, as they ignored the ban of entry on the glass porch and went inside. His face was spread with disgust even as he trailed his way in, behind the others. Ross was even fussier than Lovick when it came to foul places.

The place stank. His nose wrinkled further as they saw that the house was still heaving with the dust and dirt and ruin of a whole generation, holes in the floorboards where the rats and mice had chewed their way in to get at the feed bags which had once been stored in the hallway, leaving their droppings behind. All that was left, now, were odd trails of litter, here and there, and a spillage of paraffin. The animal feed sacks and paraffin carboys which Lovick had had to squeeze through with a sense of personal danger from avalanche had been removed with the animals but no one had done a clean up.

The house had been thoroughly searched time and time again, from top to bottom, but until the premises was released as a site of possible evidence to support a missing person enquiry, no one was entitled to enter, without accompaniment by a police officer, Gareth not included because he was now regarded as a witness to something that had gone on, only no one knew quite what!

Despite the fact that Gareth had called at the house many times in the pursuit of warning Hannah about Lizzie, he was still appalled by the conditions they had been living in. He found himself touched by sadness also. Lizzie's blue woollen coat and red hat with the false, brown plaits attached to it, were still hanging on the pegs in the hallway. Leonie's own clothes had been removed from the floor where she had dropped them when asked to dress in the bridesmaid clothing. Gloria had burnt them.

The clutter everywhere was extreme and made worse by the search. The house had been finger printed. Lovick had cringed when he had been asked to voluntarily provide his own for elimination purposes when Gareth told the Manchester police that he had stayed there. They had been sent off to Manchester where he knew a match would be made. He thought that Gareth was unaware of his prison sentence but once the report was returned, it being classed as non urgent, he could see his chances of courting his daughter, drifting away. She had been remote from him, also. He couldn't say that he blamed her. What would she want with an impoverished, gnat brain like Lovick Johnson?

Clever at some things, though. It was Lovick who led the way into the kitchen because he was the only one of the four men who entered to know the whereabouts of this rope they were seeking. It was in much the same state as he had seen it when Hannah had gone to see to her cows that night when the first snow had fallen and he had been able to take a good look about her rancid, unwholesome, filthy kitchen space. Just moved around a bit.

"In here," Lovick said. "It's looped over the rafters. I saw it and wondered why anyone would want to keep a rope up there."

"How could anyone live in this heap!" and that from a policeman who thought he had seen everything, "It really stinks."

Gareth felt guilty, though why he should was beyond others. Maybe he could have done more.

Lovick was pleased to see that the cardboard boxes filled with clothing were still where he had put them, himself, after bringing the boxes back to the house from the caverns, along with the bin of food for the donkey, with a waste-not, want-not intention of coming back to find what he wanted. Only to find that when he did so, the house was locked and a police notice had been pinned to the door because Hannah Jubb was nowhere to be found. The missing person searches were not yet over.

He pointed out the rope while seeing that the dead pig was still on the draining board and the bucket of congealing blood still on the floor beneath it. Both now looked maggot ridden and the flesh was moving. The stench was nauseating. He would let the men get the rope while he had the chance to find what he was looking for; some brightly coloured cloth to make a few gnome hats. Any belts and false wigs and beards also welcome. He thought that Hannah wouldn't mind him having some of Lizzie's dressing up clothes now that she herself no longer had a use for them. Now that there was no one here, it was his last chance to find the bits and pieces he needed when he had willingly taken over Leonie's job of providing the costumes for the panto. Leonie was on sick leave and this Belinda woman was back. International hotelling had not worked out it seemed because they had expected her to be polite to people! He would not let Leonie down, not when he was trying his best to get her to still be Snow White to his Prince. The alternative would have to be to give Cannon a kiss!

He had put them back where he had first seen them, against the same wall where Hannah had kept them. They were tumbled about a bit by a lot of untidy rummaging and a lot of the hats and scarves had disappeared but there was still plenty to choose from, along with the box of white gloves which would no longer be needed. Lovick couldn't bring himself to touch those.

While he began to rummage, he directed his colleagues to where he thought they might find rope. "Over the table. See it dangling down from above. Maybe at one time they hung the meat up there to cure. Should be long enough and strong enough to make a lasso."

"It's more than likely a drying frame for drying clothes up there," Gareth disagreed. "What my mother used to call a maiden and others a clothes horse. Hauled it up and down on a rope." Everything had been moved off the table in the course of all the searching and onto the floor. "I'll climb up, take a look."

Ross was looking around as if mesmerised by all the mess. "God in heaven! How can anyone have lived like this? The smell's enough to be a health risk. They should have been compulsorily moved out years ago. She looked after her animals better than she looked after herself and Lizzie."

Gareth was trying to make sense of what he was looking at while standing on the table and peering upwards into the gloom of a roof space with open rafters. He could see something that had been hauled aloft on the same rope that would be useful for catching the donkey. Though he had a fervent wish that someone else would be on the other end of it when finally the donkey was caught.

An armchair! That's what it was; an armchair! It swung slightly when he reached a hand to touch one of the four corners and he saw that the square base had casters. There was a fetid smell up here, too; one he had smelt before, in fact, in the course of his duties. His suspicions were aroused. "It's not a clothes horse. It's an armchair, I think. An armchair, same as the other one in front of the fireplace. Make space for it and I'll lower it down."

The accompanying policeman was impatient, standing with arms folded, not helping at all. "Queer place to sit! Hurry up. It's New Year's Eve. I'd like to be home, back in Manchester, before midnight, if possible." Then to Lovick, "You Quincey's friend, then?" Eyes curious and accusing, looking down at the bells and ribbons on his very clean and polished boots with a quizzical eye.

How did he know that? The finger prints results weren't supposed to have been returned yet. Lovick smiled vacuously and deigned not to answer; not with Gareth Jones listening.

He was busy, anyway, finding treasure which no one could object to him having; the sequined fabric that would make an Elvis cape being first into his pocket, some faux-fur which would always come in handy. A pink silk frock he rolled up into a ball and rammed into his pants' pocket, thinking as he did so of Dolly and a new string to his guitar when he started playing Country. Lovick was beginning to realise that a charity shop could be an Aladdin's cave for an all round entertainer.

That suitcase might be useful, too, as a means of carrying stuff back to the hotel once they'd caught the donkey and had it carted off to the animal sanctuary. The small, cardboard suitcase with the string handle was right down at the bottom of a box as if it had been hidden. He might have had it but for the catches being rusty and when he opened it up it had a stink which reminded him of damp cupboards. The one under his gran's kitchen sink had smelt much like that when she'd forgotten to rinse, wring and dry her floor cloths. It emanated from the dull coloured clothes within. Seen them before, somewhere, and the big, plastic handbag with zips and different pockets only he couldn't think where. When he opened it up there was a set of Allen keys within and one that looked like his own locker key from the staff cubicles at the Fairview Hotel. Useful tools were Allen keys. A spare locker key wouldn't come amiss, either, though he'd like to know which bright spark had placed a bloody knife in his locker as a joke to prompt a murder enquiry. Cannon, perhaps, who had mysteriously noticed the dog's blood on his boots? Or Chef, who couldn't remember what he got up to half of the time? They had both denied it and pointed the finger at that Betty Jessop who had upped and done a runner again, but who didn't know Lovick from Adam so why would she do such a thing? And who would wear stuff like this? A black shroud and velvet, hooded nightgown? The box of face paints and make-up would come in handy though. Enough to frighten the kids at a Halloween Party if you were the type that got a thrill out of frightening children. Lovick had never seen the point of practical jokes because there was always someone who believed them. Just to prove his own point, he picked up the bottle-bottom glasses and tried them on but they distorted his vision so much that he dropped them back into the suitcase again and snapped it shut.

Lizzie's character clothes, of course! Poor Lizzie who he felt sorry for when they all said that she had tried to save Leonie after Leonie had got a bit tipsy and decided to act daft by 'walking the plank' and lost her own life in the process. Leonie had said that Lizzie had plunged after her to save her once she knew who Leonie was. Lovick believed it because he had done dafter things himself in the days when he had been stuffing his nose with the white stuff instead of trying to face his own fears of the dark. Got that one sorted! He had managed to buy a watch with a luminous Mickey Mouse face and numbers which glowed in the dark.

Some things had puzzled him for days after he had found himself a most unlikely hero. Why did Leonie have some thin wire wound round her wrists which she said had come undone when she had fallen into the water? Lovick had thought that to be sinister, at first, until he heard that the wire was the same sort as the dog had been tied up with after its cut paw had been bandaged. When you have nothing else, you improvise!

It was not as much a wedding party as a birthday party, anyway. People celebrate in the strangest of places and he had to admit that the underground caverns had atmosphere, even if, no thank you, he wasn't after going inside another one, ever again, for life or money. He had stayed at the top manning the guide rope and doing look-out when Ross and Gareth had been down there looking for Hannah. Everyone knew that Lizzie had this daft illusion about Ross one day marrying her and there had been no other ploy to get her to listen to them with a respectable vicar present to give some credence to Leonie having been swapped at birth with Gloria's poor, dead, deformed baby. There were even papers to prove that nothing shifty was afoot, even if it had all been conducted in private. These papers having been lodged with Ross's solicitor at the time the swap took place and everyone having signed them, except for Lizzie whose mother had used her right to act for her when Lizzie had never been considered able to act for herself. It had all been done for everyone's best interest.

Of course it was a shock to the whole community and not just to Leonie. It would be a shock to anyone to know that on your twenty-fifth birthday you were going to turn from a poor, little match girl into a rich princess, like one of Grimm's fairy tale characters. Lovick wouldn't have minded a shock like that, though. Instead of no one, he'd have someone to care where he was and how he was faring. Leonie now had three people fussing after her. All she could do was sulk! She was staying in, her mother said, when Lovick had tried to have a quiet word about her still being his girl. Fat chance now!

What did it matter, anyway, that her mother had been a bit strange, he wanted to tell her. There were a lot of strange folk masquerading as 'normal' and getting away with it. Though Lizzie had been naughty he had to admit. He'd seen what she'd done with his telephone after Gareth had handed it over to him from the lost property box on the wall of his station after someone had found it in the exact spot where Lizzie had left his guitar after taking it. He had spent ages wondering who Lovely Jubbly was before he twigged and simply deleted it.

Then, treasure! Hah, hah! A wig with a pirate scarf attached to it. He'd always fancied playing Captain Hook in Peter Pan. Not Peter himself, mind! You could keep the soppy, lost boy stuff!

He looked at the filthy, tatty scarf with the white rat's tails of human hair with a growing curiosity because this he had seen before. He was certain sure! It did look like human hair, too, so very, very fine and white, like the real hair of an old person. Hannah's face grew before him as he had first seen her, looking at him through the porch glass, fear in her eyes, but little wonder as it turned out, wearing exactly the same scarf as this.

Dare he suggest to the others what he was thinking? Gnat Brain jumping to conclusions again. Now, Johnson! Imagination running away from you, lad! Always did read more into things than the evidence warranted.

Maybe Hannah had been bald as a coot and the hair and the scarf in his hand was her way of keeping her head warm. His granddad had never removed his cap, even slept in it, rather than let his gran poke fun of a bald head.

Something else, though, about the physical likenesses between Hannah, Lizzie and Betty Jessup…like they were, most probably, the same person? Come off it, lad!

He looked deeper into the same box and came out with Hannah Jubb's filthy, shit-smeared, brown gabardine coat. That he could definitely be sure was the one he had seen her wearing; brown gabardine, big buttons. It was covered with reasonably fresh muck from the cows and dried pale coloured hen crap, too; both soft centred as his thumb soon discovered. The hen crap had been encrusted on the white and brown eggs Hannah had had in her bucket when he had added the one he had found on the tractor seat. He could see her worn hands in his mind's eye. Was that why Lizzie always wore gloves so as not to give the game away? Lizzie was reported never to have lifted a finger to help on the farm; hands as soft as a newborn baby's.

He dug deeper into the same box and came out with a pair of stout boots that had never seen a polishing cloth in years of tramping the filthy farmyard, tongues bulging, laces frayed, recently dried dung on the soles of these, too. Also several pairs of thick, stinky, army socks with holes in the toes and heels and a few, smock-type frocks like those his gran had done her housework in. All in one of Lizzie's boxes like they made up a set for dressing up in.

He started explaining what was only a developing theory while Gareth stood on the table, head back and peering up into the dark void above the open rafters, Ross looked up at him and the accompanying policeman continued an impatient wait. "Thirst beckons, lads, get on with it".

"Look at this. I think I know why we can't find her. It's because she hasn't been in existence, here, for a very long time. Lizzie was Hannah or Hannah was Lizzie, don't know which."

Gareth frowned down at his hands. He was undoing a slip knot on the rope. "What are you talking about, lad? I came here often enough. I spoke to Hannah, myself. Then the post mortem has confirmed that the body is that of an emaciated woman of no more than fifty years. Lizzie was slightly younger than that."

Lovick nodded. For once, though, he thought he was right. "She must have been good at playacting, though."

Ross saw what Lovick had in his hand then. "All her life. She had these imaginary friends who seemed to coexist the one with the other without ever overlapping."

The policeman, who had only ever been given a description of Hannah Jubb, had known a lot of queer folk in his time. "I read the daughter's medical reports. She had what was called Multiple Personality Syndrome. Some kind of brain dysfunction caused at birth."

Lovick would have liked to be able to say that his own brain dysfunction was probably caused by his birth and not his lifestyle. He understood that when one was on one's own it could be so pleasant to populate your mind with imaginary friends who did what they were told, instead of what they wanted. It was a fine line between sanity and insanity. Poor Lizzie!

"Maybe Lizzie needed her mother, still, if she wasn't to be carted away. It doesn't strike me that Lizzie Jubb was stupid, even if her perceptions were sometimes distorted and confused. So she dressed herself up to look like her mother while keeping the farm going. All she had to do was to wear the right clothes."

Time for Lovick to show them all what he had found in the dressing-up boxes. He drew their attention by lining each item in his hands up on the edge of the table for them all to see. "I just found these in the boxes, over there. Hannah's scarf and hair...her coat...her boots...her socks...her baggy frocks."

Ross and the policeman came to look. The policeman claimed the scarf and hair.

Then they heard Gareth's voice over and above the creak of the rope running over the pulley wheel.

"Something queer going on, here."

He heard Gareth's intake of breath as Ross guided the armchair down from below. The policeman had already ceased indifference and was as intent, as they all were, upon seeing what they found as the armchair settled on the wide table top of a once proud farm house.

"Good God!"

For there, within a filthy tarred-up chair, sat all that remained of Hannah Jubb. A complete skeleton, its bones arranged in order though the ligaments seemed to have disappeared. It had become stuck to the chair fabric, clothing collapsed and black with noxious substance but not as offensive as the smell of the pig, as if the decomposition had occurred many years before. Where its leg bones lay on the seat cushion was also a pair of army-style boots inside which still resided, one in each boot; a pair of woollen socks.

"I think we've found her," Gareth said unnecessarily.

The skull of Hannah Elizabeth Jubb seemed to smile back despite all her teeth seeming to be missing. The bleached, white head was balanced on an unstained, embroidered cushion, one that had been very finely stitched with the words Barnston Farm and the date 1994 in cross stitch. The cloth was green linen.

Ross seemed to make something of this. "Hannah would have embroidered the cushion under the skull. I think that we can assume that it's her. She looks sort of peaceful as if she'd just sat down to partake of a bit of rest and relaxation. She's even got a cup of freshly made tea to drink."

The policeman was careful not to touch the cup. What he did was lean over the table to sniff it. "With gin in it. Must be fresh. Strange way to take your gin if that's your tipple."

Gareth was stunned. "If this is Hannah….then who let the cows out of the barn and spilled the milk and the feed? I saw her in the flesh less than a week ago. She was fighting fit."

Lovick said, "Lizzie. It was Lizzie. I never saw them together, did you?"

Gareth frowned as he thought back through the long years on so many times that he had come here remonstrating. No, he had to admit, it was many a long year since he had seen Hannah and Lizzie together.

Ross agreed. "Clever lad, Lovick Johnson. There's more to you than meets the eye."

The policeman was assessing the mechanism for hauling the armchair up and down. "I have a feeling that this has been up and down on the rope on a daily basis for a good many years. Look at the frays on the rope where it's worn against the pulley."

Ross said, "Lizzie probably only ever wound her up there when there was a chance of this being seen. Even made her comfortable with a cup of tea. A splash of gin in it. Maybe that's what her panic was about on the night you came and interrupted the police search. She was frightened that people would discover this truth, not the other about the secret chamber gained from inside the byre…but this!"

Gareth nodded.

Ross shook his head sadly. "Shall we ever know the full truth? They both suffered because of me." They could not know of Hannah's hurt and her shame for Bern's infidelity with him. But Ross felt it deepen his own guilt.

Gareth disagreed. "We all let them down. All of us. Both of them done badly by. Everyone in the village should be feeling bad about Hannah and Lizzie, not just you and me."

The policeman got out his phone and punched in a few numbers before ordering yet another body bag. "While you're at it get a local farmer to bring a horse box. We've a donkey still to catch."

The rope had to be abandoned because it was now evidence. The policeman made a lot of other calls, 'yes-sirring' and 'no-sirring', to most with the odd 'thank you, Sir', his face glowing because he'd probably get a pat on the back out of using his observation skills and ability as a lateral thinker to solve what others couldn't. Was Hannah actually enjoying this? Lovick thought that her absent eyes were twinkling!

When they went out again into the clean, fresh air, breathing deeply, without a rope, they saw the other policeman standing in the yard with the donkey calmly standing behind him, truly tamed.

"I just took a call to say what's in there. Lucky you. There'll be a commendation going. I hope you realise that I've done my bit. Box is on its way. It just gave up the fight and decided to come with me."

Then he laughed and showed them the bag of apples he had bought in the village, from the Star, for his lunch, eyes twinkling brightly. The donkey lightly nipped his fingers with big teeth as it accepted another one, then hawed, looking at the house, looking at the barn, looking at the shed.

Lovick gave it a friendly pat. That's when it stood on his foot, crushing the bells.

When he raised his left foot and shook it, the bells had been silenced. Soft lad thought that maybe it was time to start taking life more seriously.

***

They had all gone but him, when he did what he had been planning ever since he'd caught sight of it hanging on the wall, over the boxes in Hannah's kitchen. It was an easy matter not to release the catch on the lock when he was last out of the house, ready to nip back later.

What he stole was a family photograph; a family grouping on a picnic in the ripe, full fields of harvest corn, on a day bright with sunshine. Hannah and Bern sitting with Lizzie between them. He could see the likeness to Leonie when he looked at her hair and her petite figure. Her parents were dressed nicely, looking well fed and affluent. That she had been a problem child was not apparent.

He then hobbled to the village and knocked on Leonie's door. Gloria answered, taking his offering off him. She listened to what he had to say and then slowly nodded. What a brilliant idea!

Thirty

Leonie felt as if she had been removed from the scene of her own life after the events of the day of her twenty-fifth birthday. She had not returned to work and doubted that she ever would because Belinda had returned and had taken her desk over. Back to the kitchens she supposed until she remembered that that old life had gone, passed, never to be reclaimed. She had no wish to be Lizzie Jubb's daughter and certainly not Ross Fairbrother's. Time did not run backwards.

For more than a week she had stayed in her room and sulked, cried and refused most callers, even those bearing flowers and a birthday card, even her Auntie Pauline who returned to Barns without a clue what had happened. For the first time in twenty-five years her birthday went unrecorded by a special cake and French champagne. Always a very special treat of some kind. While her parents were trying to carry on as if nothing had happened, Leonie was getting more and more annoyed. Then they'd had that stupid ceremony over the wall at Barnston Farm with the vicar in attendance and a donkey honking at them all the time. If it had not been so distressing, she might have howled with laughter.

Then, people were getting on her nerves. Why was she being treated as if she had undergone a tragic bereavement? Lizzie Jubb had tried to kill her even if she had repented when she realised that Leonie was her birth child and been the one to lose her life. They had never known each other, though, even as the pile of unopened condolence cards on her dressing table grew ever bigger. Then, of course, news had spread that they had found Hannah. Probably murdered by her demented daughter.

Finally, at Mrs. Fairbrother's insistence, she forced herself to go back to work on the reception desk at the Fairview Hotel because Belinda told Ross where he could stuff it one day and had simply walked out after a guest had complained about her attitude problem.

It was almost New Year when she resumed rehearsal for her role as Snow White. Lovick looked mightily relieved. Cannon was throwing daggers at her again.

Yet, now, there was no denying who her genetic father was. If she was to earn enough money to live, she was forced into daily contact with him. Rich she might be one day, but she had about forty three pounds and ten pence in her savings account.

Thankfully, Mr. Ross kept their relationship the same as it had ever been, though he did once enquire if she had opened a letter from himself, to which the answer was no.

"Where the devil did it go to, then?"

They had both blushed in exactly the same way, at the same time, with the same effect, before looking the other way. There was an awkwardness between them that was ten times worse than anything before. But for the therapy of her work which kept her busy, she doubted she could have coped.

The first of January dawned, the guests departed, she got the show over with. It went down well. She tried not to notice the cheers and claps that came her way because what was probably amusing the audience was the awful degradation she was feeling. If she had had any money available to her when it was all still on paper only, she would have packed her bags and gone away, somewhere. As it was she had had to grin and bear it. Even Mrs. Fairbrother who had apologised for giving her mother an infected ham had to be tolerated without snapping. Though she seemed to be teeth gritted, herself, to accepting a fully grown, new born granddaughter. Leonie scowled at her. "Chef should lock his larders, in future."

"That's not a bad idea, Leonie. Put it in the staff suggestion box, will you."

She kept Lovick at arm's length even though she saw him constantly trying to reach out to her. There was this kindness in him that made her want to cry. The way he looked at her and understood in some ways. It was weakening at a time when she wanted to stay hard.

Maybe, the funeral might change things. This closure thing that Mr. Ross kept harking on about. It did not help to think that in any other circumstance, she would never have even dreamt of attending a Jubb funeral. The village idiots. The mentally unbalanced. The laughing stocks and butt of all jokes from the likes of Bluithe Harcourt who was hobbling about on sticks but remarkably quiet.

And she was one of them, genetically proven through physical characteristics which could not be denied and the testimony of others; her father's the most pertinent. All she could think of were the slights and insults and accusations made against them. A whole lifetime of them. The way she had been lied to.

The day of the funeral came with rain and wind and odd flashes of thunder and lightning more associated with the storms of summer. Leonie was expecting that only herself, Gareth, Gloria and Mr. Ross…who she could not bring herself to refer to differently…would attend the church to provide some form of service prior to Lizzie's interment in her father's grave, where Hannah's bones would go following their release from some forensic place in Manchester.

Lovick might come and sit to the back, because he wasn't 'village', but she would rather he not include himself in the service when he had no relationship with Lizzie.

He had nothing better to do, he had said. Once the pantomime was over, his contract of employment ended, he had nothing more to do than pack his kit bag and make a return journey, adding with a smile, that he hoped not to get too lost, this time. He would stay on long enough for the funeral and then go on his way. There was an evening bus which would take him to the nearest station and from there back again, from whence he had come. Back to Manchester and his own ramshackle life with Quincey dragging him out to places he would be better to avoid, strumming his guitar and hyping it like crazy in grubby pubs and seedy clubs, just to earn a living, a Chinese on Saturday and a different take-away all other nights of the week. Sorry Quincey! His heart wasn't in it! He had already deleted the names and numbers of his old girlfriends from his phone. Not that he had told Leonie any of this. All he did was to say that he wished for things to go well for the coming funeral. If she needed anything...!

Leonie, for her part, watched him become distracted in last minute preparations for the pantomime. He had seemed to have gone off her, good and proper, all their passion swamped by a cold bucket of river water and the Jubb's reputation. She didn't blame him. He'd said before that he was insulted when the villagers had assumed that he was related to Hannah and Lizzie Jubb. She so wished that she could think of herself as wholly the daughter of the local bobby and the talkative, chubby Gloria, like she had before.

The church was cold when Leonie, Gloria, Gareth and the Fairbrothers met together in the vestibule, next to the piles of dog-eared prayer and hymn books, wiping feet on the worn coir matting, though Mrs. Fairbrother had arranged for the ladies of the church to deck it with flowers. Not lilies. Leonie saw that the stephanotis, chrysanthemums and forced hyacinths must have cost a small fortune. No expense spared. They had even been adorned with swags of purple ribbons.

But then it was all a big cover up, wasn't it? A con, a hype, call it what you will. Like a Fairview Country Club Hotel publicity campaign. She had been advised by Mrs. Fairbrother, who wanted as little as possible broadcast of what really went on that day, in order to save the reputation of her hotel, to say that she had simply gone home to sleep when she had been unable to settle in a hotel cubicle and no one had been aware of it. She must keep the details of an abduction to herself. Had they supported the fact that an abduction had taken place at knife point, it would have caused the hotel to remain closed instead of the order being lifted immediately once they all knew that Leonie was safe and had been in no danger in the first place.

Who would gain from that? Instead of which, two missing person searches with successful outcomes, in the midst of snows, such as they had never seen in their lifetimes, with the plights of the lost and abandoned broadcast nationwide, was the most positive publicity the hotel could have had. Once the snows went, additional guests had come in droves, the hotel had been bursting at the seams, with the health and beauty and leisure centres, not to forget the pool, all doing great business. Ross took guests out on orienteering courses, horse riding and clay pigeon shoots and enjoyed every minute of it because sport always took his mind off everything else.

It was a time of hard work. Leonie should know because it had been a very overworked Belinda who had walked out, unable to cope. If the staff did not get a Christmas bonus after all the extra work, then the Fairbrothers' would get lynched.

Besides which, she should respect the fact that she would from now on have to remember that she was as much a Fairbrother, as she was a Jubb, genetically speaking. The sad thing being the disinterest in Lizzie Jubb, as a tragic human being, due to her mental history and troublesome, eccentric behaviour, which only served to corroborate Leonie's feelings that if her birth mother was of no consequence then she was of no consequence, herself.

Even their enquiries over Hannah's unreported demise had relegated her to not being worth police time when there was no one to prosecute and no crime would appear to have been committed there, either, once they had a time of death set at roughly fifteen years previously, and the skeleton giving no evidence of foul play.

It all added to Leonie's loss of self esteem which no amount of inheritance could override. But where else could she go? What else could she do? But cling to the loving support of her adoptive parents who tried to make her understand that above and beyond all else, the pretence in the long run, was, and always had been, for her sake, even if they had failed to tell her the truth. If anything, a huge weight had been lifted from them because they might now acknowledge that the bones in the butter barrel under the apple tree in Hannah's orchard, was the son they had never known, but whose tragedy need no longer be kept secret.

Somehow, the turbulent weather seemed appropriate for the day ahead. Leonie was glad that she had chosen to wear the frogged jacket, a pencil skirt and a new pair of boots because of the cold inside the church. The vestibule was like an igloo.

Everyone else in attendance seemed to have gone to the trouble of looking smart. The fact that Mrs. Fairbrother wore the same green silk outfit and large feathered hat that she had on the day that Lizzie had died, seemed to be insensitive but then she had never been a woman to be considerate of others. And who was to say what kind of clothing was suitable for a funeral, these days? Some people came with the intention of celebrating life rather than mourning death. Widows didn't dress in black anymore or leave their curtains closed for a required six month period.

Mr. Ross, too, had on the same dapper clothes as the ones he had been wearing that fateful afternoon when the 'accident' had occurred. Top hat and tails, a silk shirt and a fancy cravat with a diamond stud in it and those nice quality gloves which made his hands look very big. Leonie couldn't abide looking at them or him. If he touched her, she'd slap him.

But her mother looked nicer with every passing day. Gloria's dark blue suit and white silk blouse hung off her because she had started to lose weight dramatically with all her walks and Tai Chi and sensible eating.

Her dad's suit was brand new because he was still temporarily out of uniform. He wore it with a pink silk tie and a rose in his lapel, identical to the one in the spray on her mother's jacket. Her dad had never had any idea about appropriate dress outside a policeman's uniform. Her mother had even suggested that he might be colour blind. Was it usual to wear button holes at a funeral?

It was Mr. Ross who remarked, looking on Leonie, but remembering back through time. "Your grandfather, Bern, was a kind man. I was extremely fond of him."

"A good farmer, too." said Mrs. Fairbrother, with unusual charity. "One should not be persuaded to think that your birth family, on Lizzie's side, was always as it became. They were respectable citizens and good parents to a very difficult child. They loved her, dearly, despite her strange little ways. Hannah fell down the stairs which started a premature birth. Lizzie started having fits as a baby."

The vicar was one of the people whom Leonie despised the most. Her mother had let drop that Mrs. Fairbrother had offered to pay for the church communion wines, in future, in exchange for him not saying just why Ross had frog marched him out of the manse.

The villagers were the worst for making up their own version of events because Marty had never split, just as the vicar hadn't, about what had truly happened. The wrath of Mrs. Fairbrother was something to avoid at all costs. He had received his warning even before he had got back to the Bald Pheasant Inn, on his mobile phone. As well as being aware that now that he was on the right side of Gareth Jones he might as well stay there.

The specials were not that lucky. They each got a letter of

dismissal in the first post after Christmas and not a leg to stand on when they might have some awkward explaining to do. Gareth would be taking his community policemen on, as and when, on a temporary contract in future and vetting them carefully, when he eventually went back to work. They owed him a lot of back holiday time and overtime and he was bent on taking it.

Leonie had, of course, to accept the vicar's clammy, outstretched hand when he came to greet them in his usual flowing robes and waddling like an arrogant goose. In his hand he held a scrap of paper which bore a kind of clumsy script most definitely not his own. He seemed rushed and a bit bothered, his cheeks afire, and avoided eye contact with their small group of mourners. Leonie wondered if it was because he was under the pressure of blackmail not to speak of what had happened at Barnston Farm, though he hadn't seemed to take in the situation fully because he had been so very frightened for himself.

But Gareth had got the measure of Mrs. Fairbrother and was not frightened to let her know it. All her little black books might have been burnt by herself in the hotel incinerator. It was with a respectful grimace that she opened the envelope, left under the wipers, on her car windscreen, with a note that said. "Make sure this stops. I have copies. Signed Gareth."

They were all at stalemate. Time for a truce. Time for the village of Barns to begin another year in a better state and frame of mind, honest, too. It had been Lovick's idea because he had always had to turn the negative things in his life round to make them a positive or go under. Only one thing had led to another and suddenly the whole village was riding the same hobbyhorse, with those that could, doing all they could, to repair the damage.

This was why Lovick Johnson lagged behind and didn't follow Leonie, her parents and the Fairbrothers into the vestibule, but hung back at the gate. He had taken all the bells off his boots, along with the pink, orange, yellow and blue ribbons, and relegated them, from this day forth, solely to his stage wardrobe.

The village folk were saying that his appearance had definitely taken a turn for the better as they had watched him stroll down the hill, kit bag over his shoulder, hair newly styled, and guitar in hand. They approved of a new beige shirt with long cuffs to hide his Mickey Mouse watch, worn with a brown, wool tie and a smart pair of black, multi-purpose pants under a new warm, padded jacket; a sign that things were changing. Some might have thought that he was imitating some of the style of Leonie's dad. But that's what happens when a lad knows want he wants…and comes into money. His wages plus a nice, fat, welcome bonus. He had most of his pay packet in his back pocket, still unspent, and with good intentions to start saving some if he was ever going to get that semi-detached with a Porsche 911 in the garage, second hand, of course. He would buy himself a proper suitcase, too, he thought, as he stashed the kitbag in the bushes and stood outside the church and waited, guitar in hand, for the local florist who came with a large, flat cardboard tray and handed him a carnation button hole which he fastened on with a pin.

When the long, black, single hearse rolled up, there was the sorrowful sight of a real oak coffin, with brass handles, not as cheap as might be expected, and mounded up with a bouquet of the same flowers that adorned the church.

Standing in the vestibule with the large doors opened so that the coffin and its crown might be brought in, Leonie was surprised to see seven men get out of the double row of seats in the front of the hearse. Besides the driver, Marty, the three specials, Bluithe Harcourt in a plaster cast, Chef and Cannon all got out wearing Sunday best, smart and dapper and waving to a growing number of people collecting on the pavement as if this was a happy, not a sad, occasion. She was amazed to see them each collect a buttonhole and pin it onto a lapel.

As they waited for the funeral director to organise the transfer of Lizzie's coffin to their shoulders, Bluithe Harcourt came forward to Leonie, a cautious smile hovering. He was limping on a leg bound in a plaster cast and looking ashamed of himself. For once, no cigarette. "Given them up," he explained. "I've got something here for you, Leonie."

What he brought from his pocket was a badly damaged doll. Its eyes had been lost long ago. Its plastic was stained and marled and most of its dress had rotted. "I stole it off her because she was always top in the spelling bee. Sorry, Leonie." He had tears in his eyes as he said it. "I am, too. Just open my bloody gob and the brain gets by-passed. Don't mean the half of what I say. Sorry."

Leonie realised that he was apologising directly to her. Not Mrs. Fairbrother. Not Ross. Not her parents. Not knowing how else to respond, she nodded and looked over to the altar steps where other items had been donated; a photograph of the Jubb family taken long ago, in a fancy frame. An array of certificates and other official looking family papers. Bits of jewellery in an open, inlaid box and other small items of no particular value but interesting to look at. What Lovick had started, Gareth had finished.

They parted for the coffin to precede them into the chancel area of the church. The mourners followed, solemnly. Leonie had thought that there would only be their small group and maybe the ghoulish lot who preferred funerals to weddings and came to watch, invited or not. Even they wouldn't turn out, on a day such as this, to pay their respects to a Jubb.

Then they started coming down the middle aisle of the church. All the people she knew from the village who would once have known the proud family from Barnston Farm when it had been a thriving concern. Each and every one of them wore a button hole and was smartly dressed. Each and every one of them dressed more for a wedding than a funeral. Someone nodded over to Leonie, "A bit late but we're here. Looks lovely, doesn't she, Gloria? You've all done a good job."

Strange and even stranger when Leonie looked over to the coffin. The undertaker was removing the coffin lid. Leonie blinked and blinked again. Her mother and father put their arms about her as they came to stand either side and held her there.

"She does look lovely, doesn't she? Scrubbed up real good. They dressed her up real lovely at the undertakers. Charity shop made the contribution of the wedding dress. Said it was the least they could do because Lizzie kept them going."

Leonie had to look at the wax-still face to see the closed, lifeless eyes and set lips to know that she was, indeed, dead and not about to spring out to play one of her naughty tricks. For some reason she looked more beautiful than Leonie could ever recall seeing Lizzie Jubb looking, with her faces full of absurdly applied make-up, usually made more grotesque by a pout. What she wore today had been properly applied.

But a wedding dress? Virginal white, a sweetheart neck, a bow about her tiny waist, flowing skirts and tiny white silk pumps. The lady from the florist shop brought forth a posy of fresh violets and placed them where Lizzie's hands had been crossed. "Hannah used to be good at flower arranging, you know. Won prizes. Strange what you forget about people until your memory's jogged."

When Leonie looked about the church, the pew ends had been decorated with stephanotis and violets in swags of silver ribbon. More like a wedding than a funeral. The vicar stood before the coffin with his bit of paper not at the lectern where he usually conducted the funeral service from.

People took their seats, some bringing odd bits and pieces to go next to the doll and other personal memorabilia on the altar steps, next to a framed photograph of the Jubb family in happy times. Leonie's eyes settled on a framed portrait of Hannah as a young woman, another of Lizzie as a plump, naked baby lying on a hand knitted shawl spread out before the fireplace at Barnston Farm, so much like her own taken as a baby by her mum and dad.

Something cold was pressed into her palm; a pound coin. The baker's wife looked on at Lizzie with a whimsical smile on her face. "Hannah gave me that once when I had no money for my kids to go on a school outing...pound note, not a coin, back then. She said I needn't pay it back. I should have done but I didn't. It's never too late, is it? You're her granddaughter. Take it."

Someone else brought a head of Savoy cabbage and placed that on the step. "Tell you later. Hannah and the cabbage. You'll laugh fit to burst."

Someone else produced a school group photograph taken when Lizzie had been a troublesome milk monitor. She had been smashing milk bottles even back then. Leonie had only ever known cartons. "That's her. Front row, second from the right. Hannah made all the pinafores we're wearing. Green check cotton. She gave a lot of her time to others when Lizzie was growing up. It was only later that things turned sour."

Someone else brought a baby's bonnet and placed it on a step. Leonie could only guess at that one.

Someone else an old cup and saucer. "Always liked a good drop of strong tea, did Hannah. With a drop of gin in it. When's she coming to join her daughter? I'll be bringing the gin to that one."

A recipe for carrot cake...a set of dolls house furniture fashioned from old pill boxes...a photograph of a wedding cake...a child's knitted jumper. All kinds of bits and pieces went onto the altar steps.

"What's all this about, Mum?"

Gloria squeezed her hand tightly. Leonie could feel that she was fighting tears because her hand was shaking. "Lovick said that we should try our best to think of all the good things that Hannah and Lizzie did for others. We got talking in the village. We thought instead of making donations of flowers or money, we'd contribute an object to a memory box and write a bit about it. All them things will mean something to the person who brought it in relation to Hannah or Lizzie. Mine's the packet of Love Hearts. See that white leather bound book that's leaning against the altar?"

Leonie nodded.

"It's filled with all the cards and written messages people have sent."

Leonie nodded, somewhat awestruck.

"Now, look behind you. What do you see?"

Leonie saw a church full of people. People still coming. Then the church bells were peeling, not a funeral march but the triple bells to call folk to a wedding.

When the vicar called order, silence fell, bells stopped ringing. It was only then that Leonie realised that Lovick had taken a seat to the front and was picking out the tune of Handel's Messiah, as best he could on a guitar. His playing wasn't perfect.

Leonie and her parents took their seats with Ross's mother, the rest of the mourners behind them. Only Ross stayed standing by the coffin. He had something in the palm of his hand.

The vicar began to read from the crumpled piece of paper. "We are gathered here today for the solemn purpose of interring the body of Elizabeth Bernadette Jubb into sanctified ground. Firstly, however, we will bear witness to the marriage of all our hearts and minds in one common purpose…the joining of hands about the body of this woman to assist her journey from life. Let's bow our heads for a moment's silence, when we may each remember Elizabeth Jubb with kindness."

Leonie felt her eyes flood with tears but not before she saw Ross Fairbrother slip something onto Lizzie's lifeless left, ring finger; the wedding band. For a moment, her birth parents were united while her real parents did what they had always done; supported her, loved her, did their best to make the bad things better.

Leonie raised her head high.

"I've been so very lucky to have you. Thank you."

Now the funeral could proceed.

***

It was late afternoon. The party in the village square was still buzzing when Lovick picked up his kit bag and guitar and made for the bus stop. It looked as if the whole village had turned out. But, then, why wouldn't they for a free do?

The talk about Hannah and Lizzie Jubb was now open. Hannah's bones would be interred within the same grave as her husband and daughter once released for burial. Instead of backbiting, people were being kind. They would be talking long into the night with the beer flowing and the food provided from the Snow Building Competition Fund.

Some were already tipsy but everyone was polite and behaving themselves. There would be no fights outside the Bald Pheasant Inn, in the square, this night. Though Lovick was feeling downcast because Leonie had spent the day talking with anyone and everyone but himself. Now he was leaving and he had not had chance to have a word. Not even to pass on a phone number, written down on a slip of paper. It would be up to her.

At seven in the evening the party was still going strong with outside butane heaters blasting to keep everyone warm. Lovick had sat alone throughout on the fringe of Gareth and Gloria's acquaintance. He had spent the whole afternoon looking at the assembled company and thinking, between occasional conversations, that he liked this place. He had totally revised his opinion. The vibes were good. If the villagers had to be reminded, occasionally, to be nice about each other at least they showed that they could be.

Not that it was possible for everyone to be as happy as Leonie seemed to be. Marty stood in his pub doorway with a lugubrious face because the free booze was still flowing and dampening his trade. He had the look of a man who was being subjected to a public mugging.

Chef and Cannon were on their way to spending yet another night in the village cell but if they didn't watch out there would be a caution for public drunkenness going along with it and a summons if they misbehaved in future. The locum bobby had been a new broom with stiff bristles, sweeping clean. Gareth wasn't sure but he was considering a change. He might apply for a transfer. Gloria was dead against it.

Leonie had circulated, speaking to anyone and everyone but Lovick, himself. The humorous tale of Hannah Jubb, though the time scale would suggest that the preposterous event had really been designed by Lizzie, had seen a head of Savoy, adorned with plastic eyes and a nose and a mouth from a Mr. Potato Head, with a wig and a plaid head scarf tied about its roundness, placed on a pike to watch over the wall to keep strangers at bay. Or it had until the donkey had eaten it. People laughed; there was an outpouring of affection, caused by the drink that turned the funeral of Lizzie Jubb into a joyful occasion.

It seemed that there was no reason for him to stay now that the Fairview was closed, though Leonie would be supervising some of the renovation work which was a never ending round of repairs and decoration.

Ross ...who Leonie still referred to quite formally as Mr. Ross... and his mother had left for their holiday in the Scottish highlands, so to check up on the opposition. Ross had suggested that Lovick might consider returning at Easter as Entertainment Manager. Lovick quite fancied playing kids games all day and then strumming and singing in the evenings.

Trouble was that without Leonie as his girl, the prospect seemed dismal. What was the point of having the best dinner he could think of in front of him and then not being able to eat it? Worse still, watching some other man smack his lips and then enjoy the fare while he sat at a different table, watching, and miserable. Such an analogy was the only way he could describe his unrequited feelings for Leonie; a sort of empty, yearning hunger and a massive reluctance to pick up that kit bag and go on his way. First time ever he'd missed someone before he'd even left their company. He wanted her so much that he had this block of concrete inside him, called unhappiness. But you can't make other people love you, can you, as much as you love them?

Lovick sank the dregs of his beer, with a heavy heart. He had stuffed himself full of buffet food and consumed no more than a couple of pints of beer; the same home brew stuff as he had had in the Bald Pheasant but delivered free out of a barrel, propped up on a saw horse, and served in a plastic cup.

He had a journey ahead of him which he would rather not make at all. But go, he must! Leonie had been ignoring him all through the helter-skelter day when she had frowned, smiled, wept, laughed and was now finding herself a centre of attention as people came for a chat, gave her a hug, made her feel valued again.

The village lads hung about her still, making her blush as they shared their heaped plates of food and flirted. He didn't blame them. Leonie looked so nice in her frogged jacket with a Russian style fur hat to keep her ears warm. Happy, too, now. The result of positive thinking. He'd been doing it all his life to make the best out of bad situations. Time to go.

He was at the bus stop waiting in the dark shelter, the bus just turning in, when a tap came on his shoulder.

"Where you off to?"

He turned to see Leonie, arms folded, head cocked, and her nose red with cold.

"Back to Manchester."

The door of the bus opened and the driver gave him a funny look when Lovick hesitated. He wanted to be off. "I ain't got all day, lad!"

Leonie caught at his new jacket, her fingers examining the cloth. "Oh, no, you're not!"

Bossy! But Lovick found himself not minding that. "Where do you suggest I go, then?"

Leonie drew him close to put her arms about his neck. "What about this flight to the stars on that spaceship of yours?"

For a moment Lovick was speechless. All he could do was stare as her face spread into an amused grin.

"You getting on or not?" It was the same bad tempered bus driver as the one who had brought him in. He looked upon the young lovers as if seeing the first rash of a developing disease which would ultimately lead to a blighted wellbeing.

Lovick shook his head.

"I'm your last hope, son," advised the driver with a shrug and a sad shake of his head.

The door of the bus folded closed without him on it.

Lovick felt a flood of relief wash over him. Then she kissed him in a way that suggested that she had already booked her own ticket on their flight to the stars, which he so much wanted.

Lovick was panicking. "I've nowhere to stay. Not unless Marty has a..."

Leonie's eyes glinted up at him as she unbuttoned his padded jacket and snuggled herself in tight against him, her arms falling about his waist. "I know a place with lots of empty rooms where we can be private. Got a key to the front door, too."

"You sure?"

"Of course I'm sure."

Lovick couldn't believe the joy which leapt in his breast. Of course he had to make fun of it. "You won't think I'm fast and cheap if I say yes, then?"

Leonie giggled. "If I thought you were fast and cheap, Lovick Johnson, I wouldn't be standing here. What you are is special and kind and I've chosen you. Besides, Eagle Suite needs finishing. Mr. Ross asked me to ask you if you fancy a job doing a bit of painting and papering until the season starts in April. Bluithe's decided to retire early so the Fairview will need a decorator. Up to it?"

Lovick nodded, a huge, warm smile growing, his eyes shining like lanterns. He knew where the Christmas magic had gone this year; it felt like he was receiving a lifetime's worth all at once, that ball of golden glow warming him to the core.

When they turned to walk on and her arm came through his, he knew that he would never be the same again. He could hear bells ringing where there were none.

***

They remained blithely unaware as both Chef and Cannon tottered after them, all the way home to the Fairview Country Club Hotel, loitering behind, only sufficiently for Lovick and Leonie to be unaware that they were being followed. Cannon had the distinct impression that he was soon to win the sweepstake because the lad had yet to leave the village and the finishing post was clearly in sight. They had a tenner riding on it. Chef opened his wallet and handed over a note, unsmiling, even before getting

Sacher Torte

there, but knowing the inevitable: Lost again!

Lightning Source UK Ltd.
Milton Keynes UK
22 February 2010

150441UK00004B/15/P